THROUGH THE FOREST, DARKLY

RANJAN KAUL lives in Delhi and works with a publishing house. An MA in English literature from the University of Delhi, he completed his B.Tech. from IIT Kanpur and subsequently did a postgraduate stint in industrial design from IIT Bombay. He has written short stories, a few of which have been published. *Through the Forest, Darkly* is his first novel.

THROUGH THE FOREST, DARKLY

RANJAN KAUL

hachette INDIA

First published in 2010 by Hachette India
An Hachette UK company

www.hachetteindia.com

SRD

ISBN 978-93-5009-080-0

Hachette India
612/614 (6th Floor), Time Tower,
MG Road, Sector 28, Gurgaon - 122001, India

Typeset in Minion 10.6/14
by Eleven Arts, New Delhi

Printed and bound in India by
Manipal Technologies Limited, Manipal

FSC www.fsc.org
MIX
Paper from responsible sources
FSC™ C104740

In memory of my father

Victor Kaul

Prologue

THE PALL-BEARERS CARRYING the makeshift bier made of bamboo cross-beams walk up the steps leading to the open door of the crematorium, followed by a handful of mourners. A man carrying a black, dappled snake coiled around his neck blocks their path. Pushing forward the head of the snake, its forked tongue flicking menacingly, he tries to terrorize the pall-bearer nearest him to give alms—the mournful-looking, tall, young man recoils in anger and pushes the alms-seeker away.

The bier is carried solemnly into the electric crematorium, dingy and dusty, smelling of rotting flowers. There is the sound of pigeons cooing and thrashing their wings, punctuated with the rat-a-tat of their beaks hitting the glass panes of the dust-laden ventilators. A priest, shaped like a buffalo, meets the pall-bearers and instructs the bier to be lowered to the floor. The corpse has been trussed up tightly with thick strings and covered completely with a shawl bedecked with flowers. Without much ado, the priest proceeds with the rituals, asking the young man—the son of the deceased—to place small bamboo pieces dipped in ghee at specific points on the dead body and scatter wood shavings and crumbled dried leaves over it.

The priest encourages the mourners to also participate in the ritual. An attractive middle-aged woman, wearing a string of pearls and an embroidered white sari tied low on her waist does so eagerly, dusting off the remnants of dried leaves from her hands. The priest glances at her covertly; she moves away. Suddenly, her face turns ashen as she notices a young, dark-skinned woman with short hair, wearing a salwar-kameez ensemble and a silver nose ring. Giving the young woman a cold stare, the older woman shifts her gaze back to the lifeless body.

As the priest chants holy words, the young man circumambulates his father's corpse a number of times, allowing water to flow out steadily from a water-filled terracotta pot that he carries on his shoulders. On the last round, the young man, at the priest's instruction, lets go of the pot, which breaks into shards on the floor. The priest uncovers the face of the dead man and dribbles holy water into the corpse's mouth. Then, standing aside, he invites the mourners to pay their customary last respects. One by one, everyone but the dark young woman—who remains standing, with bowed head and hands clasped in front of her—walk around the body seeking blessings with folded hands. The corpse seems to be imbued with godliness, the body of an iconoclast whose dream of becoming a revolutionary had been shattered early in his youth.

Brushing aside the flowers and untying the strings that bind the corpse to the bier, the priest removes the shawl. Some mourners pick up the bier and place it on a pair of rails at the furnace door.

The hatch door of the red-hot furnace opens like the jaws of a dragon. The rails slide in, throwing the corpse into the flaming furnace and, with the clang of the closing hatch, the body is transformed forever into ash.

An uneasy silence echoes through the dark forest as the slender sal trees momentarily cease their incessant murmuring. Scores of adivasis stand quietly in a wide circle on the expanse of green cleared for the memorial ground in the pale shadow of the trees. With tear-laden eyes, they watch their village elders plant a red flag on the stone cenotaph erected for their departed leader. A short woman with buck teeth and a red bandana around her head steps forward and places a garland of light yellow flowers from the amaltas tree at the base of the monument. The other adivasis walk on to the ground in groups, carrying wooden posts or slabs of stone with delicate carvings or stylized drawings, which they've constructed in memory of their loved ones who died that tragic day, many of them barely out of their teens. As they erect the memorials, some of them light a ban—an earthen oil lamp—at the site; some leave behind the favourite belongings of the departed: a glass bangle, a bead necklace, a peacock feather from the traditional head-dress, a spear.

This is a ritual for the dead, but there are no bodies—no one could have gone to the blood-soaked maidan to retrieve them.

Twenty months earlier

1

MENAKA STOOD IN FRONT of the bathroom mirror applying the last touches of copper-coloured dye to her hair, humming an old Bollywood melody. She was excited. She'd finally be meeting her nephew Aseem for dinner. She'd noticed a considerable change in him over the two years he'd been away, pursuing a postgraduate diploma at a business management institute in Pune. The added muscle, the arms and shoulders sinewy and strong, was much like many of the Bollywood hunks with their smooth-shaven chests. But the change was not just physical: it seemed to her that he had undergone a near-complete transformation from a diffident, callow youth to a mature, confident man.

What had piqued her was that he'd spent no time with her since his return to Delhi: just a fleeting visit the day after he'd arrived. He had not been not like that earlier. During his schooldays he was at her house every other day, reading, watching television, gorging on his favourite foods. Through college, too, he'd been a frequent visitor; in fact, he'd often stayed the night at her place if he attended a late-night party in her part of town. It was a house where all his needs were met and, more, a house where he could ask for anything and was never denied.

She remembered waiting anxiously on a wintry December morning in the corridors of a government hospital while her sister Ritika underwent a Caesarean. The infant was entrusted to her care in the first few weeks after his birth while Ritika recovered from the surgery. She'd taken up the responsibility with ardour and devotion.

Over the years, her involvement in Aseem's life had grown into an obsession. Menaka rued the day she'd hustled Ritika into letting her fund Aseem's business school education after he'd graduated with miserable scores. 'You don't want him to be a failure, stuck in a lousy job all his life like his father, do you?' she'd said to her sister. Truth is, she'd missed Aseem horribly during his seemingly endless absence.

While she was elated that Aseem was back and they'd be meeting for dinner, what irked her was that Ritika's husband, Avinash, would also be there. Menaka cursed aloud at the thought, even as she spotted a distinct mark left by the dye on her manicured left hand. Pulling the plastic gloves off hastily, she examined the tiny hole in the glove that had allowed the viscous dye to seep in and stain her hand. She cast the offending pieces of thin plastic into the refuse bin.

Relieved at having accomplished the delicate task of converting her tell-tale strands of grey into a fashionable copper colour, Menaka stepped out of the bathroom in her bathrobe. Sitting in front of her dressing table, facing a large mirror framed with polished mahogany, she parted her hair with her fingers, looking for the perfidious signs of white at the roots. As she peered closely in the mirror, she noticed crow's feet around her eyes. Oh, oh! Time to go to Dr Nawalkar for another round of Botox.

She moved her gaze to Ritika's reflection in the mirror. Her sister was sitting cross-legged on the bed, surrounded by school notebooks, which she was checking with a red pencil stub. Menaka strode across the room and plonked herself on the bed, with her back to her sister. Taking the hint, Ritika rose on her knees and peered at her sister's coloured hair to check for white strands.

'It looks fine,' Ritika said, completing her examination, moving away from the foul odour of the dye, and back to her work.

'When did Aseem say he'd come?' Menaka drawled after a while. She'd been trying to cultivate an American accent for some years now.

Too engrossed in work, Ritika didn't answer.

'When did Aseem say he'd come?' Menaka repeated irritably. 'You *did* ask him to come early, didn't you?'

'Yes, I did,' said Ritika, looking up.

'Let me call him,' Menaka said, whisking out her new swank cellphone and clicking on Aseem's contact number. 'Hi! You remember, don't you, that we've a dinner date?'

'Oh damn! I clean forgot,' Aseem spoke from the other end. 'Actually, one of my buddies is celebrating his birthday and is taking all of us out. I'm really sorry.'

Menaka was careful not to allow her voice to betray her disappointment. 'Of cour-rse, dar-rling, no pr-roblem. Have a good time.' Switching off the cellphone, she turned to Ritika: 'Aseem *always* does this.'

Aseem was taking a shower before leaving home to meet his friends from college. He wasn't enthused at the prospect. The only reason he'd agreed to go out with them was to avoid meeting Menaka and her husband Aroon. He quite knew how the evening with his pals would unfold: after gathering in the Central Park at Connaught Place, they would all go exploring its basement market, Palika Bazaar, which boasted of the best bargains in the city. The market was a veritable labyrinth in which any first-time visitor could easily get lost, with subways leading to it from all directions. This was perhaps also what made it alluring to its inveterate shoppers: they'd discover new shops with every visit, from jewellery and trinkets to iPods and pirated porn.

Palika Bazaar had been Aseem's favourite haunt as a college student. He'd visit the market almost every week with his pals, mostly to pick up x-rated pirated CDs, which they'd later watch in the confines of a hostel room. Of course, a lot of their time would also be spent in the pursuit of pretty college girls.

Some experiences while he was at the business school had transformed his thinking. Pursuits of the amorous kind or scouring Palika Bazaar for low-resolution visuals of crude lovemaking were no longer activities that interested him. His main aim now was to set his life on an even keel, confronted as he was with the choppy waves of unemployment and indecision. It'd been more than four months that he'd been looking for a job, sitting long hours on the Net, scouring newspapers for vacancies, contacting placement agencies, sending résumés. The business school hadn't provided any help. 'Times are bad,' the placement in-charge had said, shrugging his shoulders.

The shower didn't help to sort out his mind. What he felt frustrated about was that he was no longer sure about pursuing a career in business management; he'd begun to get the gnawing feeling that going to business school might've been a mistake. He'd explored the possibility of working for a development agency but the only job that had come his way had offered a mere five thousand rupees. He couldn't possibly live on that. He didn't wish to remain a burden on his parents any longer and he was equally desperate to break free from the cords of his dependence on Menaka and her husband Aroon. But presently there was nowhere for him to go, no map to navigate by. He felt helpless, like a novice visitor lost in the bewildering passages of Palika Bazaar.

The only decisive thing he'd done so far was to consciously avoid meeting his uncle and aunt, who would've liked to see him join Aroon's advertising firm. He saw this as a plot to ensnare him and control his life. As it was, Uncle Aroon had paid a hefty donation for his admission to the Pune business school when he couldn't make it on his own because of his low college marks and poor CAT scores. He didn't want to begin his professional life with another falsehood: getting a job because of avuncular contacts.

Aseem had been thoroughly spoilt by Menaka as a child. Uncle Aroon had contributed no less, forever buying him toys and gifts to win his affection and keep Menaka in high spirits. During the summer breaks, Aseem would spend weeks together at the Kumar home. Doting Menaka would lavish love on him, measured in huge helpings of culinary delights, and give him unrestrained access to the giant television in her bedroom and an endless supply of comics. Aseem would lose himself as in the fantasy world of the picture books, imagining himself as a superhero rescuing the planet from crimes heaped upon it by creatures from an alien world. Accustomed as he became to wallowing in the luxurious splendour of Menaka's home during his schooldays, he was disinclined to go out to play. Naturally, when his mother Ritika would come to fetch him in the evenings, he'd refuse to budge. So it came to pass that the Kumar household became a second—and preferred—home for Aseem, much to the chagrin of his father.

Menaka's home was also a place that offered him other exciting experiences. Once, when he was barely twelve years old and indulging in his favourite pastime of watching Walt Disney cartoons and munching oven-fresh cookies, Menaka came out of the bath wearing only a petticoat and a towel barely covering her upper body. Aseem made to get up, but only just: the scene on the television was reaching a climax. She asked him to stay on. Holding one end of the towel loosely with her hand against the curves of her ample bosom, she went across to her cupboard and pulled out a lacy pink brassiere. Sitting with her back to him, she let the towel fall and began wearing her bra. Pulling the straps behind together, she asked Aseem to hook them on. As he reached for the hook, he caught a glimpse of her generous breasts from the side, loosely confined within the cups of the brassiere. The sight excited him terribly, and for the first time in his life he felt the stirrings of manhood. It required a monumental effort on his part to turn his gaze away.

During the summer break at the end of his first year at business school, Aseem went as part of his project work to Prabhas village in the Western Ghats, which his institution had adopted with the aim of transforming it into a model village. The students were sent there every year to hone their management skills by carrying out various development activities.

It so happened that the year Aseem visited Prabhas a severe famine had affected the entire district. The fields were dry and barren, caked and criss-crossed with fissures. Along with a couple of his batchmates, he visited a farmer's hut. The farmer's two starving children had just been served their evening meal of rationed-out portions of a thin gruel of millet. The elder child quickly finished his meagre meal, and before his younger sibling could eat hers, he reached out and scooped up the leftover portion from her plate and put it in his mouth. The younger girl screamed and attacked her brother, running her little head into his body like a torpedo and biting his arm. Before anyone could intervene, the two children were fighting like wild cats; they only stopped when their mother lashed out at both of them.

The sight of the two hungry children had a profound impact on Aseem's young and impressionable mind. He realized that there was a world out there that was different from his own; it set him dreaming of doing something that would alleviate the misery of the poor.

But now, dispirited with the way life had treated him so far, Aseem frigged away his frustration under the shower. Life was bloody hard.

There was a bark accompanied by a scratching sound at the bedroom door. 'It's Rambo, my shweetums,' said Menaka, easily recognizing the sounds made by her pet and getting up to let it into the room. The dog bounded in gleefully, rubbing its wide muzzle between her legs.

Rambo was a hyperactive spaniel with long ears, a round head and a silky, light brown coat. Its tail, which had been docked to two-fifths its length, was wagging with joy, in constant motion like a fast-moving pendulum. Acquired from an American diplomat, Rambo had become Menaka's passion. She dressed him in designer clothes and shampooed his buff coat with Isle of Dogs in her bath tub.

Hearing the ringing tone of the landline, Menaka went across to pick up the receiver. It was her father on the line.

'Hello, Dad,' said Menaka. 'No, Aseem won't be joining us for dinner . . . What? . . . Aseem said he was going out with his friends . . . No, Dad, we'll not go out for dinner now. But why don't you come. We can have early dinner. Ritu is already here and Aroon said he'll come on time. Shall I send you the car?'

'No, beta,' said Girdhari Lal. 'I'll make it on my own.'

'I don't know what his problem is,' said Menaka irritatedly, as she put down the phone and turned to Ritika. 'He *never* allows me to send the car for him. As for Aseem, the less said the better. He conveniently forgets a date even after confirming it.'

Ritika didn't reply. Menaka bent down to fondle Rambo, holding his ears and rubbing his back.

2

GIRDHARI LAL WAS GETTING ready to go for dinner to Menaka's. He took out a starched blue-and-white checked Arrow shirt and a pair of grey Arrow trousers from his old wooden almirah. He was particular about what he wore whenever he went to meet Menaka, knowing how particular she was about brand names. He normally got his clothes stitched by an old bespectacled tailor in the neighbourhood, whose long black beard had slowly turned grey and then completely white over the years.

How time had flown. Girdhari remembered how, when he was barely twelve years old, he had to flee the land of his birth when the country was partitioned. He lived with his parents in the old city of Rawalpindi, where people of all ages and religious hues gathered to hear Baba Rode sing Sufi verses in the blue-domed mosque and Pandit Pukhraj sing bhajans inside the Hanuman temple. Every evening he'd pester his mother to allow him to go to the halwai to drink hot milk laced with a thick layer of malai and crushed almonds.

On the day the news came that the country was being partitioned, he was at the halwai's. Suddenly, he heard sounds of a commotion and saw dozens of men pounding down the street. Brandishing knives and daggers, the men rent the air with spine-chilling screams, 'Maro! Sab ko maro! Ek bhi haramzade ko zinda nahin chhodo!'

Now, as he buttoned his shirt, the ear-splitting screams of death echoed in Girdhari's mind and a shiver ran down his spine. He'd managed to escape with his parents and cross the newly demarcated border, sitting on the metal floor of a train toilet secured from inside and packed with other terror-struck passengers like shrink-wrapped frozen peas. The smell of human excreta and perspiration was overwhelming, the only whiff of fresh air entering from the hole of the toilet seat. And when the marauding men had barged into the train, it was this strategic hiding place that had saved his life. The nauseating stench of that horrifying night drifted back to him.

Girdhari picked up the bottle of the Armani cologne that Menaka had presented him on his last birthday and liberally sprinkled it all over his clothes. He then moved to the mirror on the dressing table in the room to check on his appearance one last time. His eyes went to the dresser next to the mirror, to the photograph of his wife Champa holding baby Menaka in a white frilly frock in her arms with Ritika by her side. He fondly wiped the glass of the frame.

Girdhari's parents had married him off to Champa when he was barely twenty-one. By then, he'd begun to sit in the grocery store with his father, which his father had opened near their home in Patel Nagar in west Delhi soon after they'd crossed the border. Champa was petite and shy, with large eyes and skin the colour of freshly brewed tea. Girdhari loved his young wife from the day he set his eyes on her on the wedding day, all of her, including her dark complexion. Ritika was born within a year of their marriage, a spitting image of her mother, and he had now not one but two people to love.

Menaka arrived two years later. She was chubby and beautiful and fair-skinned like her father. Girdhari's joy at Menaka's birth, however, had been overshadowed by his grief at Champa's death during childbirth. With two small girls to take care of, Girdhari had little time to mourn. His father had died of tuberculosis soon after Girdhari's marriage and he had to manage the grocery store. With the help of his widowed mother, Girdhari raised his daughters with great love and care.

Ritika grew to be a small-built pretty girl, with large eyes like her mother's. Though Menaka was younger by two years, she began looking the older of the two once she turned thirteen, because of her fuller figure and larger frame. Girdhari wanted to marry off Ritika once she completed her BA and got a job as a schoolteacher, but her dark complexion came in the way of attracting a suitable match. Finally, after six months of futile search, he received a proposal from one Inder Bahal, a college teacher of English literature residing in the neighbourhood, for his son Avinash.

Avinash had had a fairly tumultuous time in college, but had nevertheless managed to complete his MA. A studious boy right through his years in a missionary school, he'd been made to read Dickens and Shakespeare and Tennyson at a very young age by his father. His father had told Avinash, 'You can recall what you read when you grow up and understand it then.'

Avinash had performed brilliantly in his school-leaving examination and gained admission in one of the most elite colleges in the city. But in his final year of BA, his studies took a back seat, and he developed a revolutionary fervour, influenced by his reading of the works of Marx, Lenin and Mao.

But fate had willed that Avinash would not become a revolutionary. One dark night, when the only sound that could be heard was the barking of stray dogs, Avinash had rung the doorbell of his home. Trembling and barely able to stand, his right arm crudely bandaged with a piece of cloth caked in congealed blood, he'd stood there, dazed and disoriented. A distraught Inder Bahal had brought in his son and sat him down and removed the makeshift bandage. On Avinash's arm was a deep gash that reached almost to the bone. A shocked Inder had dressed the wound without uttering a word, while

Avinash's mother watched the two of them with tears streaming down her cheeks.

No one in his family could ever get him to disclose what had happened that night. After the incident, he became a different person altogether, as if the stab had touched him deep inside. He became a recluse and lost interest in life and together with it his self-esteem and confidence.

At his father's behest, Avinash had registered for an MA and after two uneventful years scraped through the final examination. Two years of postgraduate studies didn't shake off his despondency or restore his self-confidence. So, it devolved upon Inder Bahal to find a job for his son, which he managed successfully with the help of a close friend who had connections with the bigwigs in the bureaucracy. It was not a high post, but it was a permanent job in a semi-autonomous, obscure government organization involved with some kind of research and statistics. Inder Bahal had hoped that the office routine would help to get his son out of his depression. But this didn't happen, and Avinash remained a recluse. Relatives and friends then suggested marriage as a possible solution, with the expectation that the responsibilities of a householder would draw Avinash out of his shell.

It was under these circumstances that Inder Bahal, who lived in an adjoining lane and knew Girdhari, came to visit him. After exchanging pleasantries, Inder Bahal came straight to the point. 'I've come to ask if you've found a suitable boy for your elder daughter. Her name is Ritika, isn't it?'

'No, Inderji, we haven't found someone for Ritika yet. Do you have someone in mind?'

'Well, as a matter of fact, I was thinking of my son.'

Girdhari hadn't taken long to agree. He'd known Avinash since he was a child, and knew him to be a responsible and bright boy, though he was unaware of his revolutionary leanings. Moreover, Avinash had a permanent job and the family didn't want any dowry. What more could a father ask for?

Aseem had been born within a year of Avinash and Ritika's marriage and, when he turned two, Girdhari decided it was time to get Menaka married. When word got around that Girdhari was looking for a match for his attractive second daughter, there was a queue of suitors. But Menaka didn't like the young men who came to see her, dismissing them all with petulant waves of her hand. She set down her terms to her father: 'I want him to be like you, Dad.'

'Like me? I'm old.'

'But still handsome,' Menaka had said, smiling.

She also put the additional condition that her suitor should be fabulously rich and yet not be in business, or at least not someone sitting in a grocer's shop: 'Not like you, Dad.'

Girdhari was most worried that at the rate she was going she'd be left on the shelf like an unsold item in his store. So it came as a welcome relief when Menaka finally accepted the proposal from a certain Aroon Kumar, a young management professional working as a client service executive with an advertising firm. His father was a wealthy man and owned several properties in Delhi.

With both his daughters married off, Girdhari found more time to attend to his store. He was a good businessman and courteous with his customers, and within a space of five years his business grew enormously. He lived a parsimonious life, and put all his savings into buying a largish plot on the main road and constructed a three-storey shopping complex with a basement. He let out the first floor to shopkeepers and retained the remaining part of the building for himself. He converted the basement and ground floor into a general store, while the second floor became his residence. He named the complex MeRi Plaza, an acronym derived from the first two letters of the names of his daughters: 'Me' and 'Ri'. 'I have two Lakshmis,' he'd say, referring to his daughters. The name was a masterstroke and his sales quadrupled—it appealed to customers who wanted all things Western and to those with a newfound nationalistic fervour, it read 'mine' in Hindustani.

Menaka was pleased with Girdhari's achievements. 'Very good,' she said patronizingly. 'I can now proudly say that my father owns a shopping mall.'

Girdhari left his flat on the second floor of the MeRi Plaza complex and slowly climbed down the four flights of stairs to the ground floor, trailing his fingers along the cement banister. He walked out of the complex and stepped on to the pavement. A hot May wind was blowing, unsettling the dust and litter on the street. Even though it was late in the evening, the dusty haze of a lengthened summer day lingered like an illness. He waited for a while for the traffic to pass before crossing the main road to hail an autorickshaw. He didn't own a car though he could very well have afforded it. Sitting in the autorickshaw he looked around at the changing vistas of the city. Roads had been dug up and resembled the excavation site of an old ruin. There were traffic snarls every day. Concrete constructions abounded and there were half-completed flyovers and the floating slabs of the metro rail under construction. Even the footpaths had not been spared: they had been broken down and were being given a facelift—streetscaping they called it—in preparation for an international games event.

There were new shopping malls with brightly painted billboards juxtaposed with the older small retail outlets, all vying with each other to sell the same branded goods. To attract more footfalls, the billboards had become more alluring, with flashing signs and darting lights to entice the budget-conscious customers during the economic downturn. The shopping landscape had really changed since the time he started sitting in his father's grocery shop.

Girdhari asked the autorickshaw to stop near a taxi stand a short distance away from Menaka's home in the posh colony of Vasant Vihar. He disembarked and got into a cab. Menaka would be incensed if she saw him driving up to her house in an autorickshaw.

3

AVINASH WAS SITTING ALONE, sunk into one of the sofa chairs in the massive living room of the Kumar household, switching channels intermittently on their large LCD television. The room was chock-a-block with curios and artefacts of cut glass, brass and silver placed on all possible surfaces—on glass shelves, on side cabinets, on the glass centre table with elephant-shaped legs. Looking obtrusive in one corner was a horse-shoe bar with a projecting hood like a cobra's, holding upturned wine glasses hanging from grooves on its inside.

Avinash wore a cream shirt over brown trousers, with a worn-out leather belt fastened below his bulging stomach. One of the buttons of his shirt had come undone owing to his wide girth. At fifity-five years of age, his hair had greyed prematurely and almost all of it was white. His face was round and there were dark circles around his puffy eyes. He looked uncomfortable in the chair, and Rambo, growling near his feet, didn't make it easier for him. He abhorred visiting the Kumar home. Given a choice, he'd have stayed at his own flat, but he'd always relented because this was one of the few things that the usually undemanding Ritika had asked of him.

As footsteps shuffled at the entrance, Rambo barked and ran to the door, leaving Avinash much relieved. Escorted by the excited dog, Girdhari entered the living room. Avinash rose from his chair to greet his father-in-law. Hearing Rambo's gleeful barks, Menaka came to the living room, with Ritika in tow. Seeing his daughters, Girdhari Lal's face immediately lit up.

'Hi Dad, you're looking very smart,' said Menaka effusively.

'Hello Papa,' said Ritika.

Girdhari placed his hands in blessing on his daughters' heads and sat down opposite Avinash, at one end of a three-seater. 'So, why's Aseem not joining us for dinner?' he asked.

'He said he was going out with friends. He's *useless*,' grumbled Menaka, sitting down in a sulk at the other end of the three-seater.

'Children are like that, they have no time for the family,' said Ritika.

'You go on defending him and he'll end up doing nothing worthwhile,' said Menaka, with a pointed glance in Avinash's direction.

Girdhari noticed the glance but didn't say anything, while Avinash remained expressionless. There was palpable tension in the room and for some time no one spoke. Girdhari shifted his gaze from Menaka to Ritika and back, and seeing that no one was going to make an attempt at having a conversation, turned his attention to the television screen. Avinash moved forward to hand the remote to his father-in-law.

Just then, Aroon made a musical entrance, walking in excitedly with his arms outstretched:

'Pee Kay peekay fresh ho jao,
Garmi bhagao, khush ho jao!'

'Hi folks. Sorry for being late. How do you like my new jingle?'

'It's nice. Very nice, Aroon-ji,' said Girdhari, always encouraging. 'I like it very much.'

'Thanks. It's for a soft drink to be launched next month,' Aroon explained, swaggering to the bar. Still looking for more accolades for his musical composition, he fixed his eyes on Menaka. 'What do you think, dear?'

'I don't like the tune,' Menaka said. 'And why choose a name like Pee Kay? It sounds so . . . so horribly pedestrian, like a drink for dogs.'

'The name's all in the mind, dear,' said Aroon. 'But the dog idea is brilliant. I must tell my client about it. "Pee Kay for Dogs!" Sounds jolly good! Ha, Ha!'

'Why not something more majestic like "Regal"?' asked Menaka.

'Simply because our client wanted Pee Kay, after his name—P.K. Malhotra. Ingenious isn't it?' He fixed his drink at the bar and began walking to the three-seater but then stopped in his tracks. 'Sorry, I'm such a poor host. The usual, everyone? Or will it be Pee Kay? Ha, Ha!'

'Yes, whisky and water, please,' said Girdhari.

'Avinash?' asked Aroon.

'I'll help myself,' said Avinash rising from his chair to join Aroon at the bar. He was more comfortable with Aroon than he was with Menaka. Not that there was any commonality between them—they'd always been on the opposite sides of the lens through which they viewed the world.

Aroon fixed the drinks and handed them to the two sisters and Girdhari, before returning to the bar to pour an extra large whisky for Avinash.

'So, what's the latest on Aseem?' asked Girdhari of no one in particular. 'I've not even spoken with him since he returned. Has he got a job?'

'Not yet, Dad, he's trying,' said Ritika. 'You'd be among the first to know.'

'I can easily help, if he'd let me. It's no big deal for me, you know,' said Aroon, expansively. 'When you're in advertising, you get to know a lot of important people. Aseem just has to say the word.'

'He insists he'll get a job on his own,' said Ritika. 'He doesn't want one with anyone's influence.'

'Why is Aseem so reluctant?' asked Aroon.

'You should make him understand, Ritu,' said Girdhari. 'Well, that's how it happened in our days. No campus placements, no advertisements, no interviews. It wasn't easy. Yet, people landed jobs because someone knew someone who knew someone. Using contacts was nothing to be ashamed of. Children of this generation are so self-willed.'

'I don't know what happens,' Ritika said. 'He makes it to the last round, but then something seems to go wrong.'

'Don't worry. This is not the best of times, you know . . . we're still recovering from the recession and all that. But something will surely materialize. He's a bright kid, after all,' said Aroon. 'Otherwise, you know very well, he has a standing offer to join me.'

'That's the problem,' said Ritika. 'He's adamant about not wanting to use your influence or joining you. He has another final interview with a company called MCG next week. I'm praying he gets the job.'

'MCG, did you say?' Menaka asked.

'Hmmm,' said Ritika with a nod.

There was a sudden gleam in Menaka's eyes. Excusing herself, she went out to the corridor and into her bedroom. Closing the door behind her, she quickly called her friend Gitanjali who was married to the CEO of MCG Ltd.

'Remember Aseem, my nephew?' Menaka spoke softly into her cellphone. 'Poor boy, he's been running from pillar to post looking for a job without taking anyone's help. And now guess what, darling? Of all places, he's applied for a job at MCG. Do you think you could put in a word?'

'Consider it done,' Gitanjali replied without a moment's hesitation. 'Of course, I'll make sure he gets the job.'

'Thanks, dear. Aseem mustn't get to know. Otherwise he'll be cut up. You know how these youngsters are.'

'You don't need to say more. Now tell me. When are we meeting?'

'Very soon. I'll give you a call.'

'Don't forget. It's been a long time.'

'I certainly won't. Bye-ee,' said Menaka, switching off the cellphone. She stood in front of the mirror for a while, smiling at her reflection. Life was so simple. Why did people have to make it so complicated? With the smile still on her lips, she walked back to the living room.

The rest of the family was watching the popular Kal Ka Aaj channel, which claimed to have access to the next day's news. Menaka, too, began to watch the news channel, which she found more engrossing than the entertainment channels.

A bleary-eyed reporter was giving a minute-by-minute commentary on the saga of a two-day-long rescue operation of a ten-year-old boy who'd fallen into a bore well. The next news item had the camera panning to the inside of a temple. Menaka instantly recognized the Bollywood superstar offering puja in the temple to appease the gods and set right her stars which were in the wrong astrological house and were obstructing her betrothal. Immediately following the puja footage were repeated shots of a wannabe singer kissing an 'item girl' at his birthday bash. The news was particularly exciting today.

Then a 'Breaking News' item caught everyone's attention. Over thirty Maoists in the forested regions of the state of Chhattisgarh had ambushed a police patrol with rifles and heavy artillery, shooting dead six policemen and severing the head of another. 'This is where they ambushed the policemen,' shrieked the emotion-charged reporter, while the camera zoomed to a bloodstained trench. 'The policemen had no idea that they were walking into a trap.'

'So much violence! Aroon-ji, this is even worse than the 26/11 Mumbai attacks. What's the world coming to? These Maoists are such a menace! And they say they're helping the adivasis,' said Girdhari. 'Self-styled Robin Hoods.'

'Robin Hood, my foot,' said Aroon. 'They're terrorists, plain and simple. Mass murderers and killers. We had terrorists coming from outside the country and walking into our hotels, but these bastards are home-grown in our own backyard. Hardly a week goes by without some horrible news or the other about them. Last month a van carrying fourteen armed CRPF men was blown up when it ran over a mine planted by these Maoists. There were no survivors.'

'What about the Rajdhani train they derailed, Aroon-ji? So many passengers would have died had it not been for the alert engine driver. Why don't they want to follow the law of the land?' said Girdhari, spreading his hands in despair.

'Don't ask me,' said Aroon. 'These bloody commies won't allow the country to function. They won't allow roads to be built, mines to operate, industries to be set up, elections to be held. Even travelling in this country has become so unsafe. Where does one go from here? How do you expect anyone to invest in this country if we cannot ensure their security?'

'The government's doing something about this, Aroon-ji,' said Girdhari. 'They've even set up a special anti-Maoist force.'

'Nothing's going to come of it,' said Aroon. 'What we need is proper security. We should draw a lesson from what the US did after 9/11. Not a single terror attack has happened there after that. We need a combing operation by the regular army. The Maoists are holding the country to ransom and all the government will respond with is empty talk.'

'I believe they are even involved in drug trafficking and crime,' said Girdhari.

'Not surprising, is it?' said Aroon. 'After all, they are goons.'

'Why can't they catch them? Why don't they call in the army?' Menaka interjected, not wanting to be left out of the discussion.

'Because we're a soft state, dear. We've no security worth the name, no proper mechanism or technology or training to deal with terror,' said Aroon, sounding agitated. 'All we have are a bunch of lousy politicians and a lousy government that just wants to sit on its backside and do nothing but gobble up our taxes.'

'Why don't they ask America for help?' suggested Menaka, trying to sound wise.

Avinash chose to remain quiet, suppressing the ire that the discussion provoked in him, and took a gulp of his whisky. The rest of the family, including Ritika, had little idea of his past, when he'd been in the grip of a revolutionary fervour.

The television channel was now the 'human interest' angle: a reporter was interviewing the wife of the policeman whose head had been chopped off. The wife was hysterical, tears were streaming down her cheeks and she was beating her chest. The interviewwas supplemented with repeated visuals of the severed head, the reality show captured on the camera of a cellphone by an enterprising bystander.

'It's so barbaric,' said Ritika.

'I'll switch off the TV,' said Menaka and reached for the remote lying on the centre table near Avinash, who averted his eyes from her by looking into his whisky glass, as he finished the dregs.

4

GOPAL SUBBARAO STOOD ALONE, like a military general, on a mound deep in the interiors of the Bastar district of Chhattisgarh. The ground on which he stood sloped down to an enchanting green expanse beyond which was a range of hillocks. About half a kilometre behind him was a dense forest, predominantly of sal trees, many of them grown to their full height of thirty-odd feet, the canopy formed by their broad, leathery leaves buzzing with light-winged insects and chirping birds. In the forest lived the animals of the wild: the panther and the wild cat, the spotted cheetal and the barking deer, the wild pig and the yowling jackal. This was Dandakaranya, an ancient land of forested highlands and gushing waters, where the mythological Dandak made his abode. From ancient times, migrants from nearby places had swarmed the land and made it their home, enchanted by the landscape. Because of its inaccessible terrain, the region had proved to be a formidable barrier against external interference for many centuries, allowing diverse cultures to flourish. Today, self-styled Maoist groups like the one led by Gopal had infiltrated large tracts of the forested land and were providing parallel governance—or Janatan Sarkar (people's government) as they referred to it—to the adivasi communities.

About thirty years old, Gopal was of a medium build, with bushy eyebrows that met over the bridge of his nose. He wore a uniform of fatigues and a cap with a red star pinned on its front. A pistol was pushed casually underneath a broad belt at his waist. It was late afternoon in the month of May and the sun was blazing, but there was a soft breeze that brought relief from the heat.

A few metres below him to his left stood Moesa, also dressed in fatigues, with a red bandana around her head. She was the Maoist commander of the dalam—a guerrilla squad—which had taken upon itself the onerous task of protecting five adjoining villages. An adivasi with buckteeth, she was short-statured, with small, steely eyes and high cheekbones. An AK-47 was strapped to her back, while a sheathed knife hung from her belt.

A short distance away was a group of over three hundred men and women, mostly adivasis. Many of them sat on their haunches in a double arc, while a few were standing. Most of the men were wearing lungis and were bare-chested or wore loose shirts or vests. Some of them carried gamchhas on their shoulders. The women were dressed in short saris and necklaces of metal, stone or cowrie. Some of them had their chests covered with their saris or wore short blouses; a few of the older women had nothing on their upper bodies. About a hundred of them—the majority of them women and some barely out of their teens—were wearing military fatigues. All hundred were armed. Some AK-47s, .303 guns or self-loading rifles; the others carried sickles, scythes, bows and arrows. In the centre, three village elders were seated on a crude wooden takht facing the double arc, constituting the self-styled praja court, or the people's court of justice.

Gopal nodded his head to give the signal. Taking the cue, Moesa ordered the proceedings to begin. From somewhere behind the group, two scrawny adivasi men with bound wrists were dragged out in front of the gathering by two uniformed dalam members, a man and a woman.

Moesa stood alongside the elders, facing the group. 'It was Telam here who saw them,' she shouted, pointing to a young adivasi with stringy hair sitting on his haunches. 'He saw these two pigs with his own eyes exchanging tendu leaves for just a packet of rice with the filthy thekedar, Dugga. That same Dugga who has refused to pay the agreed rates. We'd all decided to boycott him. These thekedars deceive us with paltry rates and false weights, and exploit us. We've been fighting for proper rates and yet there are those, like these two, who barter our tendu leaves for measly portions of foodgrains. They're renegades and must be punished. It is now for the honourable praja court to pronounce the final verdict.'

'Do you have anything to say in your defence?' asked one of the elders of the taller of the two offenders.

'Forgive me,' said the offender, trembling, his hands on his ears.

The elders conferred with the each other and then delivered the verdict summarily, 'He has no defence.' They then summoned Moesa to convey their decision and execute the punishment.

With a gesture of her hand, Moesa indicated that the taller offender be brought to the centre. The woman guard thrust him forward, prodding him viciously with her foot and rifle butt.

Lurching and stumbling, he landed on his hands and knees at Moesa's feet and pleaded for mercy. Moesa walked up to him and spat on him venomously. Taking out the knife from her belt, she cut the rope binding his hands together. Then, lifting his right hand, she held it high above his head for everyone to see. She gestured to a woman sitting in the front arc to hand her a sickle. With her left hand still holding the accused's right hand aloft, Moesa sliced off his thumb in one deft stroke of the sharp, curved blade of the sickle. The man howled like a wounded animal as blood flowed out of the stub of his thumb, as though from an open tap. The gathering was stunned into silence. The second offender was similarly questioned, adjudged guilty and meted out the same punishment. His agonized cries rent the air, coalescing with the howls of the first offender and travelling deep into the forest.

Gopal Subbarao now addressed the gathering in the local Gondi dialect, 'This is only a warning for anyone who dares barter away tendu leaf pickings. Next time, the punishments will be more severe, much more than you can imagine.' Softening his tone, he continued, 'You must understand, fellow comrades, the thekedars are our enemy. They want our movement to fail. Don't get taken in by their measly offers. Their only interest is to plunder and exploit our land. You must not allow that to happen. This jal, jangal and jameen are *ours*. Only *we* have the right to use them. We'll develop our land ourselves and there'll be plenty for everyone. We'll grow our food, dig ponds for drinking water, build schools for children, have health centres for the sick. You must be patient. It will be a long and arduous struggle. But victory will be ours in the end.' He paused and looked fiercely at the gathering. 'Now, tell me. What should we do with this dog Dugga?'

For some time, no one spoke. Then one of the elders on the takht burst out in Gondi, 'Kill!' As though at a signal, the crowd erupted in a loud chorus, 'Kill! Cut off the enemy's head!'

'If that's what you want,' said Gopal. 'It shall be done. Lal salaam!'

He turned around and nodded his head to indicate that the third offender be brought centre stage. A woman guard dragged out the offender with a rope tied to his hand—a short, thin barefoot adivasi called Koramu, naked above the waist, the ridges of his ribs clearly visible. Moesa narrated the charge: while pretending to be a Maoist supporter, Koramu had been spying for their main enemy, the Shanti Kadam, and had been instigating the villagers to defect to the other side. 'Koramu has committed a heinous crime,' Moesa said, her voice shrill and strident. 'He has betrayed us. He's a traitor.'

Moesa looked at the three wise men behind the table; she knew the verdict already. Even as the village elders articulated it, she prepared to take action, reaching for the AK-47 on her back and gesturing to the woman guard to step back. She had a personal stake here and no one dared stop her. Her brother had been kidnapped by the Shanti Kadam forces while he was working in the fields and was murdered in broad daylight. She had been howling for revenge and vengeance since then.

As soon as the guard cut the ropes around his wrists, Koramu made to run. In a flash, Moesa took careful aim. Rat-a-tat-tat-tat went her automatic AK-47, pumping bullets into his body frenziedly. The bullets stopped him in his futile bid to escape and he dropped on his face like a dead duck, blood spouting from his bare back like water from a sprinkler. Moesa walked up to the spot where Koramu had fallen and, giving him a vicious kick to turn him over, she shot another round of bullets straight into his chest. A deathly silence pervaded the air. The dead body was dragged away by its legs, leaving a red trail on the sloping glade.

5

ASEEM OPENED HIS DRAWER and looked at the interview letter from MCG Ltd. He'd already been through a group discussion and two rounds of interviews. The following day was the final interview and he was sceptical about getting through since his experience till now hadn't been encouraging. He'd already interviewed with three other companies in the course of the last three weeks, but none of them had worked out. He was tired and frustrated by it all; his patience was running thin, slowly being replaced by a tide of angst against the world at large. Whoever he met would tell him that to swing a job one needed contacts, and yet he hoped that on this occasion he'd make it. MCG was a large multinational company; surely their recruitment practices were more professional.

Aseem remembered the last time he'd attended a final interview. His sixth sense had told him that he would not get the job even as he was walking into the plush, carpeted room with leather upholstery and big French windows. A stern-looking man with greying side-whiskers and a receding hairline was sitting behind a large table at the far end of the room along with two other men. The balding man had done all the talking, the other two nodding in agreement even before he'd completed a sentence. When the inquisition was over, the three of them had smiled in well-rehearsed unison and had wished him better luck for his next interview. As he'd left the room, he'd felt a sudden urge to grab them by their throats and knock their heads together, or, better still, to shove a fist up their rear orifices and twist their guts out.

Menaka was furious. At such times, she was not an attractive sight: her eyebrows were knitted together and a deep furrow had formed between them, her nostrils had widened, her breathing had quickened and the tip of her nose had turned red. In fact, she was red all over. Her longing to see Aseem was becoming agonizing. Since the past many weeks she'd been trying desperately to get him to come over, but he'd remained elusive. There was a time he'd come running to her house to gorge on the goodies she'd made just for him. And now, wretched boy, in spite of all she'd done, he didn't have time for her, *for her?*

She felt lonely and depressed. She was weary of watching American soaps and the local fare of scheming sisters-in-law sowing seeds of discord. She was tired of crude reality shows with belligerent participants and rude music competitions where judges staged walkouts. She was even getting exasperated with Rambo and his slobbering. She couldn't sleep: the airconditioner in the room had given her a cold and a splitting headache, and turned her nose redder.

She decided to call up Ishita, an old friend of hers from school. Ishita and her husband had recently returned to the country after spending many years in the US. Ishita's husband, Yogender, ran a successful business exporting manufactured metal items. Both Yogender and Ishita were devoted disciples of Swami Sri Shivaramakrishnaji. On one of his earlier trips, Yogender had been taken to the swami by an acquaintance because his business in America had been going through troubled times. One look at his face and the swami had declared: 'Return to the country of your birth and all will be well.' Yogender had done just that. Today, even with the world markets floundering, his business was flourishing and he and Ishita had become eternal devotees of the swami. Recently, they'd acquired a huge farm in the outskirts of Delhi to set up an ashram for the swami.

'You'll have a long life,' said Ishita. 'I was just about to call you.'

'Really?'

'I was going to the ashram and thought you might want to come along.'

'Ashram?' quizzed Menaka.

'You see, there's a friend of ours who's come all the way from Texas and he wanted to visit the ashram and meet Swamiji.'

'An American?'

'His name's Christopher. He's enamoured of yoga and Eastern spiritualism. So, I thought I'd take him to meet Swamiji.'

'What does Christopher do?' asked Menaka.

'Christopher used to run a successful law practice in the US before he decided one fine day to give it all up and find meaning in life. He began reading about Eastern philosophy and spiritualism. One of our friends in the US told him about our spiritual quest and we got talking. We invited him to over to India. He's staying with us.'

'Has he become a yogi or something?'

'Not really. Why don't you come along and meet him? It'll be a good change for you,' Ishita said. 'I'll pick you up at five.'

Menaka didn't really have any great interest in yoga or spirituality, but a meeting with the American Christopher held an altogether different appeal. 'I'll be ready at five sharp,' she told Ishita.

Ishita rode to Menaka's in a chauffer-driven BMW. She stepped out of the car, a plump figure in a white salwar-kameez with short dark brown hair, and hugged Menaka warmly. Looking over her friend's shoulder, Menaka took a peek at Christopher sitting in the back seat of the car. He had a broad frame like that of a rugby player and was blond. He wore twinkling diamond studs in his ear lobes. Meeting her eye, Christopher greeted her with a namaste. The chauffer jumped out to open the doors for the two ladies. Ishita took the front seat, while Menaka sat beside Christopher in the back.

It was late evening by the time they had negotiated the heavy city traffic to reach the ashram in Chhattarpur Farms on the city's outskirts, but the May heat was palpable as they alighted from the cool confines of the car at the ashram gates. The three of them walked down a curving red brick path lined with conical ashoka trees. Menaka walked briskly in the long shadows of the trees. They reached a gathering of fifty-odd people sitting cross-legged on mats facing Swami Sri Shivaramakrishnaji, who was wearing a saffron robe. The swami had an unkempt beard and long hair, which he had left untied. Alternating smears of orange and white glistened on his forehead. The visitors sat on adjoining mats right in front of the group. The swami was demonstrating pranayama exercises against the backdrop of an orange-streaked sky.

Christopher immediately began doing the exercises, blocking one nostril with his middle finger while breathing through the other, and then switching fingers dexterously to alternate his breathing. Seeing him, Menaka tried to follow suit, but found her nose blocked. She went through the motions nevertheless, cheating a wee bit by breathing through a slightly open mouth. The sharp-eyed swami was quick to notice this; he took out a handkerchief and blew hard on it like a trumpet. Conscious that the swami had noticed her predicament, Menaka scowled and her eyebrows knitted together.

'We need to be true to ourselves,' the swami said, in a soft, lilting voice, after the breathing exercises were over. 'We need to cleanse our atman, we need to seek God within us. We need to find peace within ourselves. We should not let anger take over. Anger leads to violence and misunderstanding. It creates enemies. We should learn how to rein in anger and not allow it to get the better of us.'

The swami took a few steps forward. 'I will now demonstrate to you the shashank asana, which is the pose of the moon. Because of the posture, it is also known as the hare pose. If you practise this pose, you can eliminate anger,' said the swami, using his hands to indicate the supine body of a hare.

'Sit as you do in the vajrasana, the thunderbolt pose, and place your palms on the thighs just above the knees, like here, and close your eyes. Relax, relax, keep your spine and head straight. Now, while inhaling . . .' He went on for a while describing the asana. '. . . Hold your breath for five seconds. Now, simultaneously inhale and slowly raise your arms and trunk to the vertical position.' Here he took an audible deep breath. 'Breathe out while lowering the arms to the knees, like this. Repeat this three times. Everyone done it? Good. If you practise this regularly, it'll give you multiple benefits. It will stretch your back muscles, tone your pelvic muscles, relieve constipation. And, most importantly, eliminate anger and calm your mind.'

'We'll now end your session today with the shavasana, the corpse pose,' continued the swami. 'Lie on your back, your arms by your sides, close your eyes, and relax. Allow all your muscles to relax, one by one, starting from your toes. Relax. Good, very good. Repeat after me: Om Shanti, Shanti, Shanti.'

The swami blessed his devotees and walked gracefully away to his house in the ashram premises. Ishita led Menaka on a guided tour of the farm, past a large expanse of green, a swimming pool and fountains with coloured lights, to an opulent farmhouse. A white-liveried butler saluted them as they entered the sprawling house, and served them tea in gold-lined teapots together with cakes and muffins. Then the two of them drove back, leaving Christopher behind to spend time with the swami, much to Menaka's dismay.

There was a call from Ritika on Menaka's cellphone soon after they left for home. 'Aseem's been hired by MCG and the posting is in Delhi itself,' Ritika said over the phone excitedly. 'God is great. He's answered my prayers.'

'Fantastic,' said Menaka. 'I knew it.'

'How did you know?'

'I mean . . . I mean, I just knew Aseem would get the job,' said Menaka quickly. 'He's such a bright boy. It was only a matter of time.'

'What he's most pleased about is that he got the job on his own.'

'I'm so thrilled. We must celebrate. I'll throw a grand party at my house. And Aseem *better* be there.'

6

MENAKA WAS AT HER favourite spot in her bedroom, facing the large mirror above her dressing table arrayed with curious-shaped bottles and vials of cosmetics and perfumes, readying herself for the party. She applied her make-up with care and wore an exotic perfume that smelt of crushed lilacs. It was an important day for her: the party, after all, was in Aseem's honour.

She turned around, her gaze resting on the three silk saris she'd shortlisted for the evening—a tussar, a Kanjeevaram and a Banarasi tanchoi, now laid out on the double bed. She wished she could've worn a Western dress for the occasion, but owing to the flab around her midriff she'd decided that a sari was the best cover-up. She chewed her lower lip in avid concentration till it hurt as she made her choice, but the biting pain didn't resolve her dilemma. And Rambo flitting around her with his tongue hanging out didn't help either.

Facing the mirror, she held each of the saris against herself by turns, her mind whirring like the drum of a washing machine as she imagined herself dressed in each of them. It didn't take her long to decide. She'd wear the cheaper tussar—a turquoise sari with a dark orange paisley border—because it had a matching backless blouse with a plunging neckline. She fondly recalled that when she had last worn the ensemble, the men couldn't take their eyes off her.

Her choice made, she called up Aseem to remind him about the party.

'I haven't forgotten,' said Aseem.

'You'd *better* come,' said Menaka.

'Yes, yes, I will.'

'You don't sound too eager. Aren't you happy that you've got a job now?'

'Of course, I am,' said Aseem, though a job as a sales executive in MCG was not a career he really wanted to pursue. But did he have a choice? This was the only way to get the financial independence he craved for and needed to plan his future.

The party had warmed up. Swirling blue-grey smoke of tobacco and hashish, French cologne and perfume, single malt whisky and Campari and wine, raucous laughter and house music, all intermingled to make a heady cocktail. Standing tall in her high heels, Menaka's eyes darted from one end of the living room to the other to see how the party was faring. On the far side, a group of dancers were swaying wildly. Nearer her were the glitterati: a fashion czar surrounded by models wearing his outrageous creations in animated conversation with a celebrated hairstylist who'd recently undergone a sex change operation in Bangkok and was now proudly displaying her well-shaped implants in a tight-fitting frilly shirt. A photo-journalist was flashing neon bulbs at the celebrity group. Menaka dashed across to the group so she would be seen in the frame.

The guests at the party stood around in amorphous groups, in changing sizes and shapes, forming and breaking up like clouds. White-liveried waiters serving drinks and snacks weaved between the clouds of people. Menaka directed them towards the celebrity guests, who spoke in loud voices to make themselves audible above the music and din but ended up hearing only themselves, which they didn't seem to mind greatly.

She spotted Aseem sitting in one corner of the room in serious conversation with Swati—the daughter of Menaka's former collegemate Divya Carot-Reddy, who till recently was an active member of the National Communist Party. Swati was dressed casually in a pair of jeans and a white shirt and was wearing silver jewellery—silver bangles, a silver nose ring and dangling silver earrings. Menaka got to meet the mother and daughter only occasionally now, mostly at parties. She knew little about Swati, except that she'd studied in an engineering college somewhere in Andhra Pradesh before shifting back to Delhi.

Perhaps Aseem needs rescuing from this woman, Menaka told herself, and went towards him. Aseem rose from his chair and looked her up and down, 'You're looking gorgeous.'

'Thank you, dear,' said Menaka, pleased with the compliment. Ignoring Swati, she took hold of Aseem's upper arm firmly. 'Come, I'll introduce you to some important people.'

I'll . . . I'll just join you,' Aseem mumbled, trying to extricate his arm.

Just then, Menaka heard the unmistakable laughter of Aroon's client P.K. Malhotra, the liquor baron, emanating from a distance behind her. 'Har-har-har-har,' P.K. was guffawing along with Aroon in the midst of a bevy of fawning young women. Realizing that it was more important to meet Aroon's patron, she reluctantly let go of Aseem's arm. Casting a derisive glance at Swati, Menaka walked towards P.K., a large man with an ample posterior, and hugged him tight to her chest and kissed him on the cheek. P.K. was visibly drunk and was taking turns with Aroon to crack lewd jokes. Menaka laughed at the jokes wantonly, punctuated by wicked winks at the baron.

From the corner of her eye, Menaka noticed a fashionably turned out Gitanjali chatting with Ishita and a young man with blond hair pulled back tightly into a ponytail. The man had his arm around the waist of a young woman in a black dress with a low-cut back revealing a dragon tattoo. Excusing herself from P.K.'s ribaldry, Menaka moved to the group and whispered in Gitanjali's ear, 'Thank you for fixing Aseem's job.' Gitanjali smiled in reply, but before she could say anything Ishita had veered the conversation to her current obsession: the swami.

'He's truly our saviour,' Ishita was saying. 'I don't know where we'd be if not for him.'

'Really?' said the young woman with the tattoo.

Just then, Ishita was interrupted by a call on her cellphone. Excusing herself with a smile, she moved away to the corridor outside the party hall. 'What? WHAT? Not possible!' she exclaimed, nearly screaming. 'NO, it *can't* be! I can't believe it! Are you sure? . . . What do they want? How much? Oh God! What'll I do? All right, all right, tell them we'll get back. Don't lose contact with them. I'll call you right back.'

Hearing Ishita's frantic voice, Menaka went up to her. Ishita had collapsed on her haunches and was breathing hard; her face looked drained, as if she'd seen a ghost.

'What happened?' enquired Menaka, touching Ishita on her shoulder.

'It's unbelievable,' said Ishita with tears in her eyes. 'Yogender has been kidnapped by Maoists. I don't believe it.'

'Why? Where did this happen?'

'In Bastar.'

'Bastar? Never heard of it. Where the hell is it?'

'Somewhere in interior Chhattisgarh. Apparently, armed Maoists entered the house of the managing director of an iron ore mine whom Yogender had gone to visit.'

'How were they allowed to enter? Wasn't there any security?'

'There were four armed security men who were guarding the house. The Maoists shot all four of them.'

'Oh God!' exclaimed Menaka. 'When did this happen? Is Yogender all right?'

'I hope so. But no one knows what happened exactly,' said Ishita. 'This afternoon the finance officer of the mine received a call from the Maoists demanding a heavy ransom.'

Seeing the two distressed ladies, Aroon walked across to them quickly. Menaka told him about the kidnapping. 'Bloody commie swines,' said Aroon. 'What do we do now?'

'I don't know,' said Ishita, snivelling. 'I don't even even know if Yogender is alive.'

'Don't worry, dear. He'll be all right,' said Menaka, trying to look brave. 'Aroon, we've got to do something.'

'Of course. We'll do something,' said Aroon. 'What's the ransom amount?'

'It's huge,' said Ishita. 'Five crore.'

'A million dollars!' exclaimed Aroon, doing a quick mental calculation, and let out a double whistle in disbelief. 'That's a whole lot of money, man.'

'And I don't have that kind of money in the bank,' continued Ishita. 'They've given us only three days to pay the ransom amount.'

'Not to worry,' said Aroon. 'We'll rustle it up somehow. First we have to ensure Yogender's safety.'

'Let's ask Tiger,' said Menaka.

'Who's Tiger?' asked Ishita, standing up and straightening her dress.

'Tejender. You know him. He's here at the party. Come, let's go talk to him,' said Menaka.

'No, wait. He's a cop. I don't want the matter to go to the cops,' said Ishita, beginning to weep bitterly. 'I don't want anything to happen to Yogender. Oh God, what should I do?'

'Tiger's not a cop any longer, sweetie. He's retired,' said Aroon. 'And he's the best person to give us advice. We've got to take him into confidence.'

'Motherfuckers,' said Tejender Sekhon, known to the public at large as Tiger, who till recently had worked with the country's security forces and acquired a great reputation for containing terrorists notwithstanding his penchant for feeling up ladies' bottoms. 'The Maoists are dangerous. They can go to any extent.'

'No!' screamed Ishita. 'Poor, poor Yogender. Please, save him.'

'Don't worry. He'll be all right. They won't act in haste,' said Tiger. 'But I'm afraid you may have to pay out the ransom. Have you spoken about this to anyone yet?'

'No, not yet,' said Menaka. 'As of now, only Aroon and I know.'

'Good,' said Tiger. 'Keep it that way. You arrange for the ransom amount and, meanwhile, I'll find out more on this.'

'Surely you'll be able to do something?' said Aroon. 'You have such a reputation. You've got to help us.'

'I'll try,' said Tiger, his fingers twirling the ends of his waxed handlebar moustache. 'But you must understand . . . they're plain and simple crooks after money. Unfortunately, the government has been too soft on them and allowed them to flourish.'

'Why, what should the government be doing?' enquired Aroon.

'Deal with them as they would with terrorists, what else,' said Tiger.

'Couldn't you have done it when you were in service?' asked Aroon.

'Of course. But they never asked me,' said Tiger sardonically. 'Even today I say give me a free hand and I'll clean them out within thirty days flat. That's a promise from Tiger.' The fingers of his hand, which had come down to his side, began to twitch as he found Menaka's posterior attractively positioned by his side.

Ishita had begun to weep again. 'I don't know what to do. Where will I get the money from?'

'Shhh! Let's keep quiet about this now,' said Menaka, noticing the guests looking in their general direction. Not wanting to let others know of the crisis and terminate the party prematurely, she walked to them to get on with dinner. 'Har-har-har-har,' P.K.'s laughter overpowered the rest of the sounds in the hall, as she went past him to the dining area.

Menaka noticed Avinash swaying a bit as he made his way back to the far corner carrying the dinner plate in his hand. All of a sudden, a woman in a tight skirt, holding a wine glass, inadvertently hit his elbow. The food on Avinash's plate splattered onto the ground. People turned around. The decibel level in the room fell dramatically. Even P.K. stopped laughing.

'Stupid oaf,' hissed Menaka, in a spontaneous reaction to the unfortunate turn of events. She quickly walked up to the place where the mishap had occurred, even as a waiter ran across to clean the floor. Rolling her eyes, she admonished Avinash under her breath, 'Can't you watch your step? You shouldn't be drinking if you don't know how to hold your liquor.'

The party was over.

7

YOGENDER WAS WALKING THROUGH the hazardous terrain of the harsh interiors of the district. Beside him was Rahul Bhasin, the managing director of the mine in Bastar. Their wrists had been tightly bound by a thick rope held at the other end by a young adivasi lad, barely seventeen years old, with a shadow of soft hair growing around his chin and upper lip, an AK-47 strapped to his back. Moesa led the group with five other adivasi Maoist comrades, all armed with rifles and revolvers. The eight of them had been walking more or less continuously for a day and a half, avoiding the frequented roads, from the time Moesa and her dalam members had kidnapped Rahul and Yogender. It was June, and even though the dense forest of dappled green protected them from the sun's rays, the heat was intense. The two captives, both of them middle-aged, pot-bellied and clearly unused to walking long distances, were exhausted. Their clothes were wet with perspiration and their bodies—where thorny bushes and bramble had penetrated their clothing—were scratched; their feet had developed blisters. Yet the two of them dragged their weary feet somehow, stumbling and tottering as if they were drunk. They'd learned the hard way that protesting didn't help; rather, it made matters considerably worse. The previous day an exhausted Rahul had sat down, refusing to move on. He'd been prodded in the cleft between his buttocks with a rifle butt by the adivasi lad. Since that time, there had been no groans or moans, and they'd allowed themselves to be herded forward like cattle.

The only respite they'd got till now was on the previous night, when they'd stopped to rest in a small clearing in the forest near a rippling brook. There their captors had lit a fire and allowed them to quench their thirst from the flowing waters. Their wrists had mercifully been untied and they'd been thrown a loaf of bread to share between them. Fatigued, they'd lain down on their backs, side by side in the light of a half moon, their heads pillowed on their folded arms, their legs now firmly tied at the ankles. While the adivasis guarded them by turns, the two of them gazed up at the constellations in the clear night sky and sent up prayers, amidst the wind whistling through the leaves and the night calls of birds and wild animals. Anxious and terrified, they slept fitfully. They were roused with the first rays of the sun filtering into the dark forest and instructed to take a quick wash in the cool waters of the brook.

As Yogender and Rahul trudged now for the second successive day with the morning sun in their eyes, they were more reconciled to their predicament. The soreness in their limbs had dulled their senses; they were almost unafraid, mentally prepared for the most horrific of fates.

Menaka was woken up at eight-thirty in the morning by her maid, with a barking Rambo in tow for moral support. There was a crisis at hand. There'd been no water supply since the previous evening and the underground tank had run dry. Would Menaka call for the water tanker, the maid wanted to know. Groggy and half asleep, her mascara messed up, Menaka looked a horrible sight. She'd been up late into the night with Ishita, trying to find ways to raise the huge five-crore ransom.

'Did you have to wake me for this?' screamed Menaka. 'Couldn't you've asked saab?'

'Saab golfing gaye hain,' replied the maid.

'Oh hell!' said Menaka, suddenly remembering she'd wanted to speak with Aroon about asking P.K. for a loan. She called Aroon immediately.

'You must understand, dearie,' Aroon explained. 'I can't possibly. P.K. is a client whom we're still trying to cultivate.'

'You can't ever help,' said Menaka switching off her cordless, even as she was distracted by Rambo jumping on the bed and running over the bedclothes. 'Take him away,' she shouted at the maid.

The maid called out to Rambo, but remained standing in the room wearing a long face, 'Pani tanker.'

Menaka finally relented and called for the water tanker. Just as she'd switched off the phone, Menaka received a call from an excited Ishita. 'I've been able to get together the ransom amount.'

'Wow! How did you manage it?' enquired Menaka.

'Christopher.'

'What about him?'

'He'll be lending the money.'

'Really? When did he offer it?'

'This morning when he called to enquire about Yogender. I told him what we'd discussed last night, that I was thinking of mortgaging the farm and borrowing the ransom amount from the bank against it. He said I needn't do that and I could borrow from him instead.'

'That's sweet of him.'

'Now we need to arrange for the ransom to be sent to those Maoist bastards,' said Ishita. 'I'm so worried, Menaka. I hope they've not harmed Yogender.'

'Don't worry, dear. I'm sure Tiger will be able to help us. Everything will be all right,' said Menaka, trying not to allow her voice to betray her own anxiety.

It was early in the morning in Satwal village, a couple of kilometres from the white, sandy banks of the Indravati River in Bastar, but there were already several adivasis hard at work, constructing an artificial pond. Gopal had taken personal interest in the project and galvanized the villagers to volunteer to work on the pond. The task had not been easy; the digging itself had taken more than two months, with pickaxes and shovels and spades. There had been huge rocks embedded in the earth that had taken a lot of effort to dig up. Once the pond had been dug about six feet deep, the bed had been levelled carefully with large flat stones. Stolen cement, carried in open jute bags slung on bamboo poles and carried across the shoulders of two young villagers at either end, had been used to cover the crevices between the stones and rocks.

The pond was nearing completion. Gopal looked pleased as yet another flat stone was placed at the edge of the pond to make the side embankment. Soon the monsoon rains would come pouring down to fill the pond. No longer would the villagers have to walk to the river for an hour each way to fetch water. There'd be reason to rejoice and imbibe the intoxicating mahua liquor and chew on small fish from the pond. But there was time for that yet. And while Gopal had reason to feel satisfied with his achievements since he'd first made his way to Bastar some years ago, he knew the challenges ahead were far greater.

Gopal had been part of a Maoist group since he was a student in an engineering college in Warangal in Andhra Pradesh. The only son of a small farmer in drought-prone Telangana district, he'd seen starvation and exploitation of the poor villagers by moneylenders and patels, the landlords. Among the brightest in the village school, he'd won scholarships through sheer hard work and gained admission to the engineering college. But, unknown to him, his father had borrowed heavily from the village moneylender, pledging his small patch of land to be able to afford the fees for Gopal's college education. In college, owing to his impressive academic record, the handful of Maoists in the hostel had sought him out, and it was a matter of a time before the young student became Comrade Gopal.

Gopal began devouring Marxist and Maoist literature and within a few months he'd become an ideologue of the college unit of the Maoist group. During the winter break in his final year, he went to attend a secret conclave of the Maoist Commmunist Party as a special invitee. There, for the first time, he learned about the underground dalams that the party had established to systematically eliminate and target-kill their 'class enemies'. The targets had been carefully chosen—patels and moneylenders, state officials and politicians, senior police officers and suspected informers colluding with the state.

In the last semester of college, news came that his father had committed suicide. When Gopal rushed home, his sobbing mother revealed the cause of the tragedy to him: his father's inability to return the heavy debt he'd incurred to pay for Gopal's education. Filled with guilt and anger, Gopal resolved to become a full-time revolutionary and avenge his father's death. After his final examinations, he joined a dalam that was running the most violent of operations under the highest conditions of risk, and soon acquired a reputation as someone who could not only strategize but also kill with impunity. Because of his proven record, he was appointed the leader of a dalam of a dozen members. In consort with his party leader, he devised an audacious plot to kill a key minister in the state.

One afternoon, when the minister was returning from an election rally in a rural belt, Gopal along with his dalam members waylaid the minister's white Ambassador and shot the minister dead, as also the driver and his bodyguards. From that day, Gopal acquired a heroic stature in the party and he began to regard himself as some kind of a revolutionary hero.

Meanwhile, the state police of Andhra Pradesh was of course not taking things lying down. They had formed a highly trained special security force called the Hyenahounds that had been assigned the formidable task of quelling the increasing Maoist insurgency and capturing their key leaders, like Gopal. Seeing the onslaught from the Hyenahounds, the Maoists had decided to move northwards to Dantewada, the southern part of Bastar, where they already had a small base. The local population in Bastar, comprising a majority of adivasis, had been living in conditions of abysmal poverty and had been victims of police atrocities ranging from their poultry being taken away to their women being raped. The Maoists, who'd taken up cudgels on behalf of the adivasis, had found it easy to influence them. Realizing that they were now highly vulnerable to attacks from the south by the Hyenahounds, the Maoists strategized to buttress their base in Bastar and see if they could expand from there. The Maoist Communist Party placed upon Gopal the onerous responsibility of going to Bastar to implement this plan. The leadership of the party saw this decision as a double whammy: Gopal would not only be shielded from the Hyenahounds who were targeting him but the party would also be able to exploit his expertise to strengthen their base in Bastar and make further inroads into the forested region.

Gopal had been given rigorous guerrilla training and familiarized with the treacherous Bastar terrain and then given charge of two well-armed dalams. He and his group of twenty trained Maoist cadres entered south Bastar from Andhra Pradesh across the sandy lowlands of the Godavari. They wound their way past the iron ore mines near the Bailadilla hills—so named because of their resemblance to the hump of a bull—to Dantewada. They had lain low for some time, picking up the local cultural nuances and a smattering of the local Gondi language, and then slowly ventured to win over the confidence of the adivasi villagers.

Gopal and his comrades started by holding meetings with the villagers, asking them to discuss their problems freely. Initially, they took up small causes of the adivasis. For years, the adivasis had been demanding higher rates for picking tendu leaves, to no avail. One day, acting on a complaint from one of the villagers, four of them barged into the home of the thekedar and, putting a gun to his head, negotiated a settlement: the minimum wages for collecting tendu leaves was raised from a meagre twenty paise a bundle to ninety paise. On another occasion, when a local tehsildar was found to be demanding bribes to regularize encroached land, strong-arm tactics were employed to teach him a lesson. In yet another instance, they encouraged the villagers to loot the house of a sarpanch who was cornering funds that had been earmarked for development schemes. Having slowly gained the confidence of the local villagers, Gopal and his band were emboldened to now take on the might of a big paper mill. They persuaded the villagers to carry out a protracted strike against the mill, demanding rates higher than the paltry ten paise per bundle of bamboo culms. Hard negotiations followed and the rates were trebled.

Gopal and his comrades thus won the sympathy and support of the local population and began enlisting some of them to join their movement. Soon, they formed their own sanghams consisting of ten to twelve elders in every village, overthrowing the local panch leadership, and began to govern the villages through them. One by the one, much like the way crystals grow, more and more villagers came forward to join their movement. Some of them were trained in the use of firearms and were enlisted in the dalam cadres; others were asked to form cultural troupes and travel from village to village to spread the Maoist revolutionary message through song-and-dance and pantomimes. Once they'd built a sizeable cadre, Gopal and his original dalam members spread out into adjoining districts to gather more support for the movement.

Meanwhile, the horribly outnumbered and poorly equipped police slowly withdrew to distant areas, fortifying themselves so as not to get attacked by the dadalog, as Gopal and his fellow

Maoists began to be referred to by the villagers. But those at the helm at the police headquarters did not take this humiliation lying down. They stationed a new set of trained armed police to man the thanas and then launched a witch hunt for the Maoists by combing the villages where they'd been attacked. Relying on information from the local thekedars, zamindars and panch members, they began wreaking their vengeance by singling out local adivasis on the slightest of suspicions and rounding them up to question them on the wherabouts of the Maoists.

Among the people whom they had picked up was Moesa, then a young girl barely fourteen years old. She'd gone to the forest to collect firewood along with a few other girls from her village when two armed policemen picked them up and locked them in the thana. No one in the village got to know where they'd disappeared till one of the villagers who'd visited the police station to register a complaint saw and recognized the girls. The villagers approached Gopal for help. The following night, Gopal led his dalam members to attack the thana, killed all four policemen on duty and rescued the girls, as also many other adivasis who'd been languishing behind bars on various charges. Gopal had become a hero and the surrounding villages his bastion.

Gopal went round the pond and peered into the forest, squinting his eyes to focus on a narrow trampled path at the far edge of the forest across a small clearing of green sparsely speckled with bushes. After a short time, he spotted what he was looking for. First it was just a flash of red, but then he saw it distinctly. Surely, that was Commander Moesa waving the red flag. There was jubilation in his eyes; the mission had been successful. Moesa and her companions were distinctly visible now. They shouted greetings to each other as Moesa quickened her stride while the other dalam members accompanying her began to sing and dance, holding their rifles high in the air. Then everyone at the pond site also broke into song.

While Moesa and her comrades tied the two abducted men to a pole, Gopal's mind was already racing ahead. He'd received a message confirming that the ransom money was being arranged for. In a week or so, he'd go to the town of Jagdalpur to pick up the ransom amount and with some of that pay for a cache of arms stolen by a couple of helpful security personnel from the police armoury. Yogender's capture had been a bonus that had allowed him to double the ransom. They'd initially planned to kidnap only the mine owner Rahul Bhasin.

8

IT WAS THE MONDAY after Menaka's party. As he returned from work, Avinash Bahal sat perspiring in the oppressive June heat on a window seat of a chartered bus. The passenger beside him was asleep with his head lolling on Avinash's shoulder. For nearly thirty years Avinash had worked in the same office, though he had little idea what use was made of the work he did there and recorded in piles of dust-laden, moth-eaten files.

At the moment, however, his mind was not in the office. Since the party at the Kumars, he'd had trouble sleeping and had remained awake most nights, tossing and turning and sweating profusely. Disturbing images of the disastrous scene at the party kept flashing back—the humiliation of Menaka's rebuke and her calling him 'stupid oaf' tormented him. He was indeed a stupid oaf, a fool, to let her get away with her insults all the time. He hadn't always been like this, given to accepting any situation without reacting. In college he'd been different: an angry young man, reckless with romantic ideas, wanting to fight for equality and justice through a communist revolution.

The passengers in the bus were suddenly thrown forward as the driver braked sharply at the red light of a busy, smoke-filled intersection. This jolted Avinash's neighbour a wake. He pushed himself upright and glared accusingly at Avinash, as though he was responsible. Soon, the man had slid down on the seat, his head lolling on Avinash's shoulder yet again.

Avinash peered out of the bus window, beyond its round metal cage-like bars. As the bus waited for the traffic lights to turn green, a variety of people looked up at his window: an adolescent boy selling cases for cellphones; a man hobbling on crutches, thrusting the evening paper into his face; a girl cradling an infant on her hip holding a hand out for alms. He fished for coins in his pocket and handed them down to each of them, pulling in the paper through the window just as the bus began to move.

There had been a time when he'd steadfastly refused to give alms to beggars. They were part of the system that he abhorred, that he wished to change. Handing out coins instead of compelling the alms seekers to take the battle to the streets only perpetuated the system. Today, he disliked beggars, disliked poverty, disliked the face of misery in the slums that he could not escape seeing as the bus crossed the Yamuna towards Patparganj, where he resided. He wanted to get away from it all, all these grim reminders of reality.

He turned his head away from the window and looked at the copy of *Mid-Day* lying in his lap. The paper had screaming black headlines: a Swedish woman had been raped in a park; the son of a prominent businessman had been kidnapped for a huge ransom; an ageing politician had been caught on camera during a sleazy encounter with a fashion model; a group of Maoists had blown up a bus carrying security personnel and a few civilians, killing fifteen of them and injuring another twenty. It was only a few days earlier that he'd heard of Yogender's kidnapping. The Maoists were resorting to gross violence and cruelty and extortion these days, and losing public sympathy. It had been different earlier.

Avinash's mind went back over thirty-five years to his own college days. About a dozen of them squeezed in a tiny hostel room, listening to their leader, Upamanyu Chakraborty (or U.C., which besides being an acronym of his name also reflected his penchant for using 'you see'). He remembered U.C. distinctly—a short fellow with thick-framed spectacles, delivering lectures on Marx and Lenin and Mao, vociferously discussing strategies to bring about a revolution in the country. He spoke of the glorious deeds of his comrades led by Charu Majumdar and their espousal of the cause of the poor peasantry and how they'd seized power through an uprising in Naxalbari, a small district in West Bengal. U.C. told them of the beginnings of the movement, of the tribal youth who had a judicial order to allow him to plough his land but had been brutally attacked by a bunch of goons hired by the local zamindars, and how the comrades had galvanized the poor peasants to retaliate with violence and wrest back the land.

'Many of the region's oppressed poor in the countryside, you see,' U.C. would say, his eyes turning a fiery red behind the spectacle frame, 'the peasants and sharecroppers exploited by landlords and trapped in the clutches of moneylenders have joined us. The movement has spread like wildfire. So, you see, this act of rebellion fully implemented Comrade Majumdar's declared strategy of a revolution that called for unarmed peasants turning viciously on their armed oppressors, killing them mercilessly and snatching their weapons to found an army that would liberate the whole country.'

No one would've imagined then, Avinash thought, that all these comrades subscribing to Comrade Majumdar's ideology would be loosely termed as Naxalites after Naxalbari, the district where the uprising took place.

Sitting in the hostel room, Avinash would write pamphlets and paint posters, even as in an adjoining room long-haired followers of the hippie culture and flower power would be listening to the Doors and Led Zeppelin and Jethro Tull and the Beatles on self-assembled sound systems, and talking of love and peace and Mahesh Yogi.

Their meetings would carry on late into the night, after which they'd all spill out into the college lawns to be joined by stray dogs gambolling and sniffing the grass, till the dew seeped through their trousers and wet their behinds. Before daybreak, they'd go around the university campus on bicycles, pasting the posters they'd prepared and scrawling slogans in thick black paint on empty walls and toilets: 'Long live peasants' and workers' unity,' 'Proletariat zindabad', 'Workers of the world unite', 'Death to feudal landlords', 'Down with revisionists'. Classes would be bunked the next day to recover from the early morning excursion. They'd wake up for lunch and in the afternoons distribute pamphlets in colleges and later sit in their hostel rooms to study serious Maoist literature for discussions later in the evening with U.C. Once, they organized the mess workers in their hostels to demand winter uniforms and better wages and living quarters. The strike ended up as a damp squib: other students protested, the police was summoned, three workers were sacked, and the strike was contained within a week.

In the last year of college, matters turned serious for Avinash, when a secret plan was unfolded to him and his college comrades. The high command, U.C. told them, had decided that the situation in the countryside was now ripe for a people's revolution. 'All that's required, you see, is a chingari, a spark, to trigger the revolution, to rouse the exploited masses from their slumber, their passive acceptance of their fate. And the rest will follow, you see, like night follows day.'

The plan was hush-hush and U.C. gave out only a fraction of the details. Around the time Mission Chingari was planned, the police had begun to crack down on the Naxalites, especially in the states of Bihar and West Bengal, where they had the largest presence. They rounded up the revolutionaries, or anyone suspected of being one, at the smallest pretext. The police would throw the alleged Naxalites behind bars, torturing them till they spilled out the details of the actions they'd planned or revealed the names of fellow comrades, or often simply shot them in false encounters.

The only information U.C. gave out to Avinash and his comrades was that they'd be taken to a village in the countryside on the banks of the Punpun River near Patna in Bihar to carry out Mission Chingari. It would take them about sixteen hours by train from Delhi to a small town called Danapur, where they would have to board a bus and then walk the final kilometre or so to the village—their final destination. Besides a few handkerchief-like landholdings where the small farmers barely eked out a living, most of the large doublespread fields surrounding the village were owned by rich zamindars, tilled by agricultural labourers who were allowed only a measly share of the grain they cultivated. If the farmhands needed a loan to marry off their daughters or cremate a family member, they borrowed it from the benevolent lord of the land they tilled for a price—that they'd continue to work on the lands till the loan was paid back with interest through their sweat and toil. Most of them had been tilling the land for generations, because their meagre earnings never gave them enough to eat, leave alone return the ill-fated borrowed money. The objective of Mission Chingari was to forcibly take away the land from the zamindars and hand it to the tillers. It was a romantic ideal that had readily appealed to Avinash and his fellow comrades, appealed to their sense of right and wrong, to their notions of equality and justice.

U.C. told them that four of them, including Avinash, were to go to a remote region in Bihar, dressed as simple village folk, and they'd receive instructions from time to time. They had only a week to make the preparations. They fished out their old pyjamas and shirts and chappals. One of them, Sachchida, who was from Bihar and spoke the local Magahi dialect well, became the official trainer to teach it with proper grammar and intonation. It was like in a play, only here they were not actors but players in real life, with an invisible director—the high command. No complete script was handed to them; it'd be given to them at the end of a scene, or so they were told, or perhaps there was no script at all and they were required to play by the ear. The wide countryside would be an open-air stage and the toiling masses the expected participants.

Two days prior to their departure they were taken to the outskirts of Delhi, where, at a makeshift range, they practised shooting with a 9 mm pistol. It was all surreal and soul-stirring as they shot at the targets; it didn't register with them then that they were being trained to shoot at real people.

Before they knew it, the final bell for the curtain call had been rung, and they were sitting as inconspicuously as they could, as U.C. had advised them, in an unreserved train compartment of the Janata Express. They gazed out through the iron bars of the windows as the train sped past green fields dotted with thatched huts, beyond which lay large tracts of dry and barren land. They dozed off intermittently till deep sleep overcame them in the comforting darkness of the night.

They were met late in the morning at the railway station by a well-built youth with a bulbous nose in a white kurta-pyjama who introduced himself as Comrade Satish. He had a no-nonsense demeanour and he led Avinash and his fellow comrades from Delhi to a small eatery for tea and biscuits before pushing them into a crowded, ramshackle state transport bus. There were deep pits on the road and the bus took its time to take them to their destination, halting whenever and wherever someone hailed it to stop or wished to disembark. At one of the halts, a young man in striped pyjamas and a blue vest handed over a cloth bag to Satish.

The road ended at a canal crossing, across which there was a narrow culvert that led to a mud path with a few shops on either side. It was in the pale shadows of the evening that they crossed the culvert and walked down the path, past a few shops—a grocery shop with a few goods on its shelves covered by dust, a cobbler bent over a broken shoe in a tiny shack, a kiosk selling cigarettes and bidis and paan, a couple of tea shops with rusks and biscuits in dirty glass jars.

It was another ten-minute walk through wheat fields till they reached Satish's house, where a wooden plough and a long bamboo stick rested against its outer wall. The house was a modest two-room brick-and-mortar dwelling with a corrugated aluminium roof and a floor made of mud and cow dung. Inside the house, some pots and pans stood on a shelf on the wall and on the floor near a small fireplace lay two trunks. A few clothes were strung across a string in the far corner. This would remain their abode till Mission Chingari was accomplished.

They washed themselves at a hand pump under a mango tree, watched by a weary ox tied to a stump chewing the cud. Satish's wife, her face behind a low ghunghat, cooked them a modest meal of boiled rice and watery dal, which she served with mashed onion and whole green chillies. After the meal, exhausted as they were, they retired for the night.

Next morning, as soon as they'd woken, Satish took them to one corner of the house. Here, from inside a shallow pit below a trunk he pulled out a large cloth bag and opened its contents to reveal a collection of weapons—a .303 rifle, two crudely made pipe guns, a pistol, a couple of choppers that had belonged to the village butcher, two daggers, and some bullets in a plastic pouch. Satish displayed the weapons like someone who'd returned from a visit overseas and was proudly showing off his purchases from duty-free shops. A couple of axes and sickles standing against the wall beside the cloth bag completed the armoury.

All they needed now was to wait for the signal and the next set of instructions. A courier would come, they'd been told, and instruct them on exactly what they were supposed to do. They would be given a list of the zamindars they were to attack. It was to be a well-orchestrated exercise with simultaneous strikes across the country.

Satish and his wife then left with their ox and plough. Avinash and his three comrades were under strict instructions not to stir from the house, so they gave some money to Satish to purchase rations and provisions from the village stores. During the day, they remained confined to the house, huddled together in the heat, watching the door with furtive eyes, waiting for the courier to arrive.

Three days passed, but no one came. They became restless and miserable, their bodies bitten by crawling insects that surfaced in the night and their stomachs shrivelled with the meagre morsels that Satish and his wife doled out to them. They felt abandoned and lost. Satish just shrugged his shoulders when asked when the courier would come; he knew as much as they did. On the fourth day, Sachchida developed a high fever that was accompanied by an uncontrollable shivering. At last, there was something for Avinash and his other comrades to do—take care of the patient. A few days later, Sachchida broke into a sweat, and the fever subsided.

It was in the wee hours of that very morning that it happened. A group of men—could have been a dozen or even more—armed with lathis and knives crept up stealthily to the house. Before they could say U.C., Satish and his wife had been pulled out and tied to the mango tree while the rest of them were attacked with lathis and beaten mercilessly. Caught completely unawares, they didn't get a chance to reach for their guns and the ammunition bag in the pit. Untrained in armed combat and hopelessly outnumbered, there was little they could do. Avinash tried to resist, reaching out for the throat of one of the attackers, who whipped out a knife from a belt tied around his dhoti and stabbed Avinash in the arm. He cried out in agony, while the others, seeing the knife and Avinash's bleeding arm, gave up all forms of resistance.

After beating them black and blue and leaving them incapacitated, the attackers departed, but not before giving the comrades a warning to leave the village before the break of dawn. Mortified and disenchanted, the four of them somehow pulled themselves together. One of the comrades tied Avinash's bleeding arm with a torn piece of cloth. Then they packed their belongings and fled the village. The Chingari had failed to ignite.

The bus lurched again and the newspaper dropped into his lap. Somewhere, somehow, something had gone horribly wrong. Was it a seditious mole who had squealed on them? Where had the other comrades disappeared? Why didn't the high command send the courier with the promised set of instructions? He'd never know the answers. It didn't matter now, anyhow.

With the trauma of Mission Chingari behind him like a distant nightmare, Avinash tried to analyse the reasons for the failure of the Naxalite movement of the sixties and seventies and why it'd practically withered away into oblivion just when it had fired the imagination of so many youth like him in the country. Was it owing to the ruthless state repression? Was it a fault in the Naxalite leadership? Had they misread the situation? Or was it because they'd become so secretive that they'd stopped trusting each other, which had ultimately led to internal dissensions and a fratricidal war among the cadres? Perhaps there were other factors as well: lack of formal training or experience among the cadres; shortage of weapons and ammunition; and, most importantly, their inability to mobilize the masses at the ground level. The final body blow had come, of course, with the arrest and death of Charu Majumdar, and those who followed had probably neither the passion nor the charisma to take on the mantle and drive the movement forward.

Though he hadn't abandoned his revolutionary beliefs, his family was more central to him now. Putting aside the humiliation at the party, he worried about Aseem. A job with MCG selling consumer goods was certainly not the path he'd have liked his son to take; multinational firms such as MCG were the new colonizers, taking over the world with their weapons of mass consumption. He only hoped that the job would somehow free him from Menaka's enticing clutches. So it was the MCG job or the Aroon–Menaka duo. It was hardly a choice. Feeling helpless, he reached out unconsciously for the evening paper in his lap, clutching it tightly as if for support, but soon leaving it in a crumpled state.

The bus crossed the bridge over the drying river bed, passing a flyover under construction for a Games Village and then the Akshardham temple with its expansive grounds and sprawling car park illuminated by blazing lights. The bus swerved to the left after ducking under a flyover, turned right at a red light near the Mother Dairy factory, and came to a halt. Avinash followed some passengers down the aisle and stepped down. The evening sky had turned a smouldering grey, as the streetlights cast confusing shadows on the pitted phosphorescent road. He was in no hurry since he'd be going into an empty flat—Ritika would still be at Menaka's and Aseem too wouldn't have returned. He decided to go to the park nearby. He walked in and sat on a green wooden bench, watching a couple of children play. After some time, he got up to go home.

He stopped at a small tin shack selling cigarettes, paan and confectionery in large glass jars, and bought a packet of candy. Entering the premises of the cooperative society where he lived, he stopped by the open window of a flat on the ground floor, where a little girl was studying under a tubelight. He gently knocked on the window to draw her attention and handed her the candy; she rewarded him with a joyous smile. The image of her smile accompanied him as he climbed the stairs and entered his first-floor flat.

9

IT WAS THE MONTH of July but the monsoons were playing truant and it had become unbearably hot and humid. Aseem sat at Girdhari Lal's air-conditioned, glass-enclosed cabin in MeRi Plaza discussing his work at MCG. Girdhari Lal was at his expansive best, imparting knowledge of his trade drawn from decades of experience to his grandson. Two screens mounted in front of him captured the live action—with the help of hidden cameras—of the portions of the store he couldn't see through the cabin. Spread across two floors, MeRi Plaza sold all kinds of groceries and consumer goods. The ground floor stocked grains and pulses, sugar and spices, snacks and biscuits and chocolates, bread and eggs, tea and coffee, soaps and shampoos, all arranged neatly in shelves amid dangling, red-and-yellow pop-ups. Down in a sprawling basement were the big boys—washing machines, refrigerators, microwave ovens, television sets, sound systems.

It'd been nearly two months since Aseem had taken up the sales executive's job with MCG Ltd—*The Company that Thinks BIG*—which claimed to produce and market BIG-sized products for BIG-hearted people. After two weeks of training, Aseem had been sent to the field to hone his set of skills by a BIG ordeal by fire: a BIG territory with a BIG target when a BIG recession was on. 'If you achieve your targets,' his BIG boss had told him, 'you can make it BIG in MCG and earn BIG bonuses. Otherwise, you'll be a BIG goner.'

Initially, Aseem didn't quite take to MCG. Spoilt at Menaka's where he had been given everything at the hint of a whisper, he didn't find cajoling and pleading with retailers an entirely pleasant experience. He had wanted to call it quits on the very first day he was sent out to collect orders. The first customer asked him to return another day, another asked for more discount, a third narrated a string of complaints, the fourth launched into a discourse on the sorry state of retail stores. But knowing that he had no other recourse, Aseem persisted gamely.

Luck favours the brave, they say, and so it came to be in Aseem's case. The sales territory he was assigned to happened to include Girdhari's MeRi Plaza. Once Girdhari Lal learned of this, he promptly arranged to become a dealer for MCG and began taking an active interest in selling the company's products. Soon, he was helping Aseem book orders from other shops in the vicinity using his clout as the president of the shopkeepers' association of the area. The shopkeepers were only too happy to oblige him and place orders for MCG products—their BIG packets of wafers, their BIG boxes of chocolates, their BIG bottles of shampoos and conditioners.

Life at MCG thereafter became more comfortable for Aseem and he began to meet his weekly sales targets regularly. His superiors were delighted and within a month they'd assigned him an even bigger territory and a far more challenging target. His fellow sales executives envied and admired him and sought him out for tips on how to boost their sales.

Aseem was now visiting his grandfather to inform him about the new larger territory he'd been assigned. Sitting across Aseem, Girdhari Lal was overjoyed with his grandson's progress at MCG. Looking at him with pride, he dreamt of the day when Aseem would take over MeRi Plaza and expand it into a massive shopping mall. There was really no one else in the family who could develop the business after him.

Aseem opened his briefcase and fished out a list of dealers and retail outlets in his new territory and placed it on Girdhari's glass-topped desk. Girdhari pored over the sheet of paper, ticked the names he knew personally, and then picked up the phone on his table. 'Hello Chaturvedi-ji,' he said. 'How are you, ji? . . . And how is your Mrs? . . . And your son is in college already? . . . How time flies. With your blessings, ji, I'm very well thank you. I've good news. My grandson Aseem has joined MCG. Yes, yes, how they grow . . . I need a favour from you, ji. Can you help the boy by giving him some business, ji? . . . No, no, he will come and meet you personally. I myself have been buying MCG products for the last two months. They've also been putting out ads on the TV, ji . . . You've seen them? Very good. When should he visit you? Ji? . . . Thank you, thank you, ji. I will send him tomorrow morning. We must meet soon one day, Chaturvedi-ji.'

And so it went on, phone call after phone call, and Aseem's programme for the next week had been chalked out. What Girdhari Lal achieved over the phone would've taken Aseem weeks to accomplish.

But Aseem was unhappy. The fact that he had to rely on his grandfather to achieve his sales targets rankled him. From wanting to get away from his dependence on Menaka and Aroon, almost all of his success was in fact now attributable to his grandfather. Wearing a mask of obsequiousness and politeness to achieve sales targets, managing supplies or listening to customer complaints didn't rouse the kind of passion in him as it appeared to do amongst his colleagues. The job had become painful and mind-numbing. He wanted to do something more meaningful, but he had no idea what that might be. So he went from shop to shop with a plastic smile on his face, booking orders, arranging supplies, collecting dues. Life for him was wearisome, tedious.

Menaka called up Ishita to enquire about Yogender.

'He's fine now,' said Ishita, sounding more relaxed. 'Till a couple of weeks back it seemed he'd never get over the trauma of the kidnapping. He just wouldn't speak. There was a terrified look in his eyes and he was barely eating. But then sessions with Swamiji have brought him round. He's now much, much better, back to his normal self almost.'

'I'm so glad to hear that,' said Menaka.

'Menaka dear, now that you've called, there's something else I'd like to talk to you about. But not over the phone,' said Ishita. 'When can we meet?'

'How about lunch at Yellow Brick Road tomorrow?' suggested Menaka. 'One o'clock sharp?'

'Done,' confirmed Ishita.

Because of the stress of the past few weeks Menaka had allowed herself the luxury of unrestrained eating. She struggled to pull a tight pair of Lycra jeans over her hips. For Yellow Brick Road, it was the most appropriate wear. In any case, there was nothing to hide from Ishita, certainly not Menaka's posterior. Taking a deep breath to tuck her stomach in, she pulled up the zip of the jeans successfully and smiled.

Carrying two big shopping bags, Menaka walked into the restaurant, her high-heeled shoes clicking loudly. The restaurant was a throwback to the West, with lemon yellow painted furniture and photographs and posters of American yore. The paint on the tables and chairs appeared to have been deliberately sandpapered to give them an antiquated look, but it was contemporary rock music that played in the background. Ishita was already there, sitting at a corner table, near a bunch of blue-uniformed schoolboys chomping on hotdogs lathered with tomato ketchup.

'Sorr-rr-y. I came a little ear-rly for some shopping and didn't r-realize that I'd got late,' said Menaka, rolling her Rs, harmonizing with the atmosphere. She dropped the bags to her side and sat across from Ishita. 'Have you order-rr-ed?'

'No, I was waiting for you.'

'I'm sor-ry. I feel so guilty.'

'Don't be silly. I'm really not hungry,' said Ishita, examining the menu card. 'Maybe I'll just have a sandwhich.'

'It'll be a footlong and Diet Coke for me,' said Menaka. 'Why don't you also tr-ry the footlong? They're fabulous her-re.'

'I've turned vegetarian, dear.'

'Oh! Of course! Swamiji's influence, isn't it? So, has Yogender given you any details about the kidnapping? Where those horrible terr-ror-rists took him? What they did with him?'

'Hasn't said a word. But he's back to working with a vengeance.'

A waiter came to take their order.

'I'm relieved that Yogender's all right,' said Menaka after they'd ordered. 'Now Ritika's got me wor-rried about Aseem.'

'Why, what happened?'

'She feels he doesn't like his job.'

'Ask him to attend Swamiji's discourses.'

'I'm not sur-rre he'd like to do that.'

'Why don't you all visit the ashram next Sunday? Bring Aroon along at least, if you can't persuade Aseem,' said Ishita. 'We've invited a lot of people. Swamiji thinks Yogender's bad patch is because of a misalignment of his stars. He says we need to hold a satsang and feed at least two hundred people to alleviate Yogender's troubles.'

'Aroon and I'll certainly try to come, but I can't speak for Aseem,' said Menaka.

The waiter came back with their orders and placed the dishes on the table. 'Enjoy your meal,' he said with a practised smile.

'Menaka, dear, there's something important I wanted to talk about,' Ishita said as soon as the waiter had left, dropping her voice and bending forward on her elbows. 'You know, Yogender and I have made it our mission to spread Swamiji's word across the globe. We're both convinced that he's really the answer to the world's infinite problems.'

'How do you want me to help?' Menaka asked, looking to attack the footlong with her fork and knife.

'I was just thinking, dear,' Ishita said, 'it'd be wonderful if Aroon were to take it up as a project to . . . well . . . er . . . how should I put it? . . . to market Swami Shivaramakrishnaji so that people across the world can benefit from his spiritual wisdom.'

'To mar-rket Swamji?' Menaka rolled her eyes, trying to slice her footlong with a knife and fork. A piece of sausage scurried out from inside it like a mouse from a hole and rolled to the side of the plate.

'Aroon can charge his full fee, you know,' Ishita said, pretending not to notice the truant piece of meat. 'Christopher has promised to fund the entire project. In fact, this is what I wanted to tell you. You know the ransom money Christopher gave? We've yet to return it. Yogender's export business has been dull, and we've not wanted to break our investments. Christopher has suggested a way out. To adjust the ransom amount, he'd buy off the farm from us and build a proper ashram for Swamiji. The amount we borrowed could be adjusted against it. What do you think?'

'Why not?' remarked Menaka, dropping her cutlery and using her fingers to eat. 'Christopher seems to have a lot of money. Is he still staying with you?'

'No. Christopher has now become Swamiji's disciple. He sometimes helps him with the yoga classes. Of course he's not a patch on Swamiji. Swamiji is *so-o-o* good,' said Ishita.

'Really?' said Menaka, licking her fingers.

'So would you bring Aroon along to the ashram next Sunday?'

'Let me check with him.'

Aseem decided to call it a day as soon as he left MeRi Plaza, and went home early. He trudged slowly down the footpath in the busy shopping area to the parking lot half a kilometre away where he'd parked his new motorbike. The bike was an essential condition for the job, so he had bought one recently on a loan. Pedlars lined the footpath selling a variety of wares. A woman in colourful attire was selling patchwork cushion covers in a riot of colours. A young boy carrying pirated shrunk-wrapped bestsellers drove a hard bargain with a bunch of college girls. A man with a stump was aggressively selling spurious perfume bottles. An urchin carrying plastic toy motorcycles thrust one before his eyes, 'Two for ten, two for ten.' These were the real sales people, Aseem thought.

As he neared the parking lot, lost in thought, a young woman in a hurry passed him by. At first, he didn't notice her, but soon a mental image of the woman formed in his mind, and he realized quickly who she was: Swati. He picked up speed to follow her, consciously lengthening his strides. As he neared her, he called out, 'Swati! Swatee-ee!'

Swati stopped and turned around, 'Hi, Aseem. Fancy meeting you here.' She was wearing a beige salwar-kameez and a maroon printed chunni. A large, open bag slung from her shoulder from which exercise books peeped out like baby birds in a nest.

'I'm here on work,' said Aseem. 'How about you?'

'I too work down the lane, in the slums. I teach the children there.'

'Yes, I remember you mentioning that at the party. Must be very satisfying. Wish I could do something like that.' Then, on a sudden impulse, he asked, 'How about coffee?'

'Not today, Aseem,' Swati said, smiling. 'The children will be waiting. But definitely some other time. Give me your number and I'll call.'

Swati left soon after they'd exchanged their cell numbers, walking quickly away without looking back. Aseem, rooted at the spot where Swati had left him, followed her with his eyes. It would've been good to have coffee with her. He really didn't want to go home so early. It'd been a couple of months since he'd met Swati but he remembered their meeting vividly—her unaffected charm when she spoke animatedly about her work with slum children. He was sorely disappointed that he was unable to spend time with her.

Ritika rushed from the kitchen to answer the doorbell. Her eyes crinkled with joy at the sight of Aseem at the door. Her hands and nose were dusted white with flour.

'What happened?' asked Aseem.

'What happened where?' asked Ritika before she noticed the flour dust on her hands. 'Oh, this? I was making rotis. It's good to see you early, beta.'

Aseem wiped a speck of flour off his mother's nose and followed her to the kitchen, which was pokey and crammed with a marble counter on three sides and open shelves on the walls. But it'd been done up tidily, one row of neatly arranged jars with lentils and spices and other cooking ingredients on a narrow shelf, metal pots and pans on another, and steel bins for grain and sugar below the marble counter.

'Where's Baba?' Aseem enquired after his father.

'He must be in the bath,' said Ritika, getting back to making the rotis. Aseem watched her for some time without saying anything. His mother was able to imbue so much devotion in the simple act of making rotis, he thought. He wished he could get half as involved in his work.

'You're looking distracted, beta,' Ritika said, turning a roti over on the heated tawa sitting on the gas burner. 'Anything wrong?'

'No, Ma. I'm all right.'

'Something surely is the matter,' said Ritika, lifting the tawa away from the flame and placing the roti over it directly. 'Is it a girl?'

'C'mon, Ma. Don't be silly,' said Aseem. 'I'll go and have a wash now.'

'Fine, beta,' said Ritika, using her fingers to pick up the fluffy cooked roti from the flame and putting it in a round steel container.

As he went to his room down a short corridor, Aseem came face to face with his father coming from his bedroom carrying a whisky glass in his hand.

'How was the day?' Avinash asked.

'The usual,' said Aseem, looking at his father deprecatingly, and walking past him.

Avinash nodded and walked back to his bedroom, closing the door behind him.

'Dinner's ready,' called out Ritika. 'We'll eat as soon as both of you are ready.'

'I'll be out soon,' Aseem called back from his room.

The family of three ate a simple meal of dal and roti and a vegetable dish of peas and potato but made little conversation. Aseem went to bed after reading for a while, but could not sleep for a long time.

The chiming temple bells in the vicinity pierced the early morning quiet of the Bahal household. Ritika was already awake; she'd not slept well, worrying about Aseem. Her maternal instinct told her that something was troubling him. She drew the curtains of the open window in the bedroom, letting in fresh fragrant air and sunbeams feebly through the morning haze. She was greeted with the enthusiastic twittering of birds on a nearby tree, the gurgling pigeons on the window sill of the flat opposite, cawing crows wheeling above. She stood at the window for some time and was rewarded with a glimspse of a lone, now rare, sparrow that hopped on the window ledge for a while before flying away.

Ritika turned back to see Avinash still asleep, flat on his back, his half football of a belly moving up and down with rhythmic purrs of snoring. She picked up and folded the clothes he'd dumped on a chair. Then she sat at the edge of her bed and opened a wooden almirah set into the bedroom wall. The second shelf housed her miniature temple, where pictures of Hindu gods were lined up: at the back, festooned with tiny silver paper flowers, stood a hand-painted framed picture of Rama and Sita with a larger-than-life Hanuman standing guard over them with his mace on his shoulder. In front of the picture was a small brass idol of Lakshmi; alongside the goddess was a marble carving of Ganesha and pictures of some other gods and goddesses.

Ritika closed her eyes tightly and brought her palms together in front of her chest. She mouthed her prayers silently, fervently invoking each god and goddess in her mind's eye in slow succession. She didn't wish to take chances and leave any of the divinity out, lest they get annoyed. She needed all the help she could get to tide over her sea of troubles. She worried about her husband Avinash, who she feared was slowly turning into an alcoholic; she worried about her son Aseem, who looked unsettled in his job; she worried about meeting her monthly expenses against the rising inflation. She prayed for domestic bliss for her dearest Aseem; may he find a good wife and settle down—someone who'll love him and take care of him.

Ritika finished her prayers. Looking over her shoulder at her husband, who'd stopped snoring. She knew he was awake, but would feign sleep till she'd completed her prayers. This was the arrangement she'd worked out with her non-believing iconoclast husband—she was free to worship when she pleased, but the gods could not be displayed.

In the beginning, she was shocked at Avinash's unrelenting stance when it came to her religious beliefs. It was so unlike him because he was accommodating in almost all other matters, even when it came to visiting Menaka. She'd pleaded with him to allow her a small ledge for her gods in a corner of the flat, but seeing his unyielding stand, she'd resigned herself to the almirah arrangement. They hadn't quarrelled after that; he on his part had remained extremely supportive and caring, which made up for everything else.

Ritika bowed her head one last time, opened her eyes and shut the almirah door. She was ready for another day.

Aseem nearly jumped with excitement when he saw Swati's name on his cellphone display just as he was about to leave for work.

'I'm sorry, Aseem,' Swati said. 'I must've sounded rude when we met the other day. But I was running late, and those children in the slums are so restless. If I'm delayed by even five minutes, they run off to play and never return. Can I take you out for coffee this Friday?'

Aseem was elated, jubilant, on top of the world. Life was worth living after all.

10

AVINASH SAT AT HIS new desk the next day, contemplating a glass paperweight. The desk was not new really; in fact, it was rather old and made of solid teak. It was only new for him; after working for over a decade in one part of the office premises, he had been shifted to another area and assigned this desk, which even by generous reckoning was not less than four decades old. The teak surface looked coarse and rough. And the ritual of cleaning its top with a wet rag performed ardently by the old office peon Ramdass had only made it lose whatever little sheen or colour it might have had. The legs of the desk were not level. In the morning when Avinash had come to office and leaned on its left side, the leg diagonally opposite had risen perceptibly, reminding him with considerable mortification of the frisky Rambo with his hind leg cocked up. The handle of one of the drawers dangled precariously like a man hanging at the edge of a precipice.

Avinash took out a handkerchief and wiped his neck. It was hot and sticky and the noisy desert cooler mounted on a window a distance away only added to the humidity. He looked worried. A few weeks earlier, he had received a stiffly worded note on his old desk: the government was pleased to inform him that it had redesignated him and he'd be assigned a new job profile in due course; till then he was to make the necessary arrangements to shift to his new location and await further instructions.

Avinash stared at the changing shapes and colours encased in the glass mould of the paperweight, which he gently rolled over the roughened tabletop with the tips of his fingers. He observed the plastic world of green and red shapes of ferns and plants that served no purpose save of ornamentation. The glass mould enclosed a world like his own: trapped, purposeless, frozen in time like a fossil. The changing colours were only an illusion, viewed as they were from different angles, different perceptions, but in reality static. However, the world had changed, and he had not been a part of the change. He could now only wait for things to happen, as they inexorably would, without expectation. He'd long stopped being a participant; he was now merely an inconsequent spectator.

Avinash looked around at the office: the building had over the years become dreary and decrepit, the glass of the broken window panes hadn't been repaired, the fans squeaked like newborn mice and water seeped through the walls when it rained. The office had no back-up generator, so when the power went off (which happened quite frequently), most of the office trooped out to the public park to sit under the cool shade of neem and jamun trees.

He turned his head towards the wall lined with old steel almirahs with peeling cream paint containing old records in moth-eaten registers. An old clock with a brass frame that had lost its lustre hung on the lime-plastered wall gradually, unhurriedly measured time with a thin seconds hand. He waited for a minute to pass, and then another. The two thicker hands moved close to each other; in a short while they'd merge. It was still an hour to lunch break. Probably nothing would happen. Was something meant to happen? Was he expecting anything to happen? He didn't know; he didn't really care.

Avinash rummaged through the papers in the in-tray lying in the left corner of his desk. Nothing new had arrived; only a few official circulars, which he'd already gone over several times that morning. He reached for his briefcase lying by his chair and placed it on the table. Opening it, he brought out a plastic folder and the

'Situations Vacant' supplement of the morning newspaper. He scanned each page of the supplement scrupulously. He marked some advertisements—all asked for business school graduates. He gently tried to pull out the bottom drawer of the desk, not wishing to disturb the top drawer because of the delicate support of its loose handle. It was stuck, and after a few futile attempts it opened slowly, grumbling and groaning like an old man. He scrutinized its contents. There were some paper clips, the inner plastic ring of a scotch tape, a twelve-inch scale, broken bits of an eraser, two empty ballpoint refills, some rubber bands, a pencil stub, a pair of small scissors, some wood shavings, lots of dust. He took out the pair of scissors and tried to push the drawer back in, but his effort was in vain, and he left it jutting out a couple of inches. He then neatly cut out each marked advertisement and placed the clippings carefully in the plastic folder—which carried a label, 'ASEEM'—before putting it back into the briefcase.

Avinash gazed at his surroundings. The section in front of him to the left had seen a complete changeover. What had been separate individual desks had made way for a modern office with chest-high Bhutan board partitions containing over a dozen computer-equipped, L-shaped tables. There were some new young workers he didn't know. Hired on contract to convert the masses of data in the registers stored in the metal almirahs into digital files, they worked on the computers with unwavering attention, their eyes glued to the blinking monitors, their nimble fingers hitting the keyboards with great agility. Avinash turned to the other side of the office farther down to the right, where renovation was going on at a brisk pace. Planks of partition boards and chairs had already been moved in. Big cardboard cartons, presumably containing computer equipment, lay in one corner. A couple of electricians were laying new cables and wiring.

New technology didn't interest him, it never had; he'd been unable to understand the fascination that drew so many young people to cyber cafés like rats to the Pied Piper; he'd never felt the urge to learn the ways of the blinking new machines—he'd found them impersonal and daunting.

He sat back and looked up at the slowly rotating fan and the ceiling covered with cobwebs. An overwhelming feeling of ennui welled up inside him, clutching him like a giant serpent. Feeling claustrophobic, he walked up from his chair and moved across to a broken window next to the one with the mounted cooler. He looked out; there were dark clouds in the sky, but it was not raining.

Avinash stood there for a long time. Not wanting to go back to his desk, he sauntered up to a younger colleague, Prakash, seated in the renovated section. Prakash had been with the organization for over a decade and was among the few people in the office Avinash talked to. He was an unassuming man with small eyes and hair coming out of his large ears, but, unlike Avinash, he had quickly adapted himself to the world of computers.

'Hello,' Avinash said.

'Hi,' said Prakash, looking over his shoulder but continuing to work on the keyboard. 'Anything new happening?'

'Nothing really. Things are much the same.'

'How're things with you?'

'The usual,' replied Avinash.

'Hmmm,' said Prakash.

Neither of them spoke for some time. Avinash continued standing, looking at Prakash's computer screen.

'How about you?' asked Avinash after a while.

'Much the same,' said Prakash. 'Anything new in your section?'

'Nothing much.'

Silence ensued.

'You carry on,' said Avinash, after a while, and walked slowly back. Ramdass, the peon, came to his desk and delivered an envelope. Avinash waited for Ramdass to leave before opening it. He drew out a sheet of paper and looked at it. It was another routine circular.

Disappointed, Avinash went back to gazing at the glass-enclosed mould of plastic ferns.

11

SWATI CAROT-REDDY LIVED alone in a small bylane off Flagstaff Road in Civil Lines on the second floor of a rented barsati flat with a cemented terrace, which she'd lined with potted plants. The barsati was close to where her mother Divya lived near the university campus, although it was a longer distance from her workplace. The only child of her parents, Swati was close to her mother, but chose not to live with her. Her parents had separated two years ago and Divya now lived with a professor of history at the university, Professor Rabindra Gupta, a self-styled communist who smoked bidis and wore long khadi kurtas and Kolhapuri chappals. But it was not for this reason that Swati stayed separately—she was in fact quite fond of the professor—it was more to do with her own fiercely independent nature. She was quite content with the privacy of her barsati room and the open sky above.

Divya and her husband Moorli Reddy (Mooli, for short, which means radish) were both members of the National Communist

Party. They'd joined the youth wing of the party as students, and had participated in gentle acts of student unionism such as marches to Parliament to protest against the visit of the then American President Nixon. But the radical pair had become better known for the torrid romance that had blossomed between them, which came to be known as the Gaajar–Mooli affair. Divya Carot was nicknamed Gaajar (a translation of her surname after disregarding the single 'r') for her fiery revolutionary ideas.

The Gaajar–Mooli romance had an interesting history. Mooli came from a family of rich peasants in Andhra Pradesh and had inherited a sizeable wealth at the age of thirty when his father had died. By then his inclinations had already moved leftward through his association with the National Communist Party as also the ravishingly beautiful Gaajar, who'd been attracting a host of admirers in the party with her trademark large red bindi and lustrous dark brown eyes.

Mooli invested his wealth wisely. But in a fit of romantic benevolence inspired by communist ideals, he divided and distributed his father's private lands among the farm workers who tilled it, on the condition that they run it as a cooperative. While this act invited scorn from the two big farmers in the village, it drew the admiration of the farmhands. It also sent his esteem soaring among his comrades and his status in the party quickly climbed up by several notches. More importantly, the act struck a chord in the heart of the lady with the red bindi and shifted her affections towards him in a more permanent manner. So, when it came to the time that he asked for her hand, she was already so enamoured of him that she gladly accepted his proposal.

All in all, what Mooli lost in terms of landed property he more than gained by his betrothal to Gaajar. Swati was born within a year of the Gaajar–Mooli marriage, and grew up listening to discussions that revolved around Lenin and Marx and the organization of industrial workers and poor peasants. She was a bright child with a natural inclination for numerics and, so, when she completed school, it came as little surprise to those who knew her that she chose to study engineering at a leading engineering college in Warangal in her father's state of Andhra Pradesh.

Just about the time Swati joined college, her parents began to drift apart, Gaajar being unable to reconcile herself to the fact that Mooli had reached the higher echelons in the party—a member of the Politburo, the party's think-tank—while she'd been left behind in the hierarchy. National elections were a year away, and the party decided that Mooli should contest the parliamentary seat from his district, given the influence he already wielded there. Till the elections, he was to go and stay in his village and work with the poor peasants in the district. Piqued by the fact that she'd not been given a higher position, Gaajar chose not to accompany him. In fact, she vehemently protested against his candidature: a deep-seated gender bias had created a glass ceiling in the party in relation to its women members.

There was another reason. Even as Mooli was making his plans to journey to his village in Andhra Pradesh, she was already receiving amorous overtures from Professor Rabindra Gupta, a party sympathizer and a generous contributor to its coffers. Professor Gupta had begun to woo her by helping her to organize morchas and dharnas to protest against atrocities committed against women. Determined to remain in the public gaze to make a point with the party bosses, she always led these protests from the front, drawing strong media attention.

Given the charged atmosphere at home, Swati was indeed happy to live in her college hostel at Warangal. Through the first six months of college, she remained an exemplary student, but in the latter part of the year, she came under the influence of Gopal Subbarao, who was in his final year in the same college.

One evening, at a meeting held in one of the hostel rooms, she was strongly attracted to his arguments about bringing about a violent revolution by treading Chairman Mao's red path.

Owing to her exposure to revolutionary ideas since she had perched on her father's knee as a child, it was not difficult for Swati to comprehend what Gopal was speaking about. These views were reinforced by what she witnessed during the following summer break when she visited her father's village. The small farmers' cooperative formed at the behest of her father had planted cottonseeds in the small strips of land they owned. The decision to grow cotton rather than the regular wheat crop was taken owing to the higher price that cotton fetched. They'd borrowed heavily from the village moneylender, a middle-aged farmer called Rajaram, for special seeds and fertilizers to grow cotton. But while the farmers were slowly learning how to run a cooperative farm, the rain gods were in no mood to accord them the necessary cooperation and decided to give the districts a miss that year. As a consequence, the soil became parched and dry. There was no cotton. And no grain. To add to their woes, along came Rajaram with his henchmen, hounding them for the money with threats and vile abuses. The poor indebted farmers, frustrated because of their inability to feed the hungry mouths of their families, began committing suicide, hanging themselves from the leafless branches of drying, dying trees.

Seeing the pathetic situation of the starving widows and their children, Swati felt helpless and angry. She became convinced that the democratic path to revolution through elections that her politician father had chosen, or the protests that her socialite mother organized, could not alleviate the misery of the poor. Not for her was the Gaajar–Mooli kind of revolution that was slow and uncertain like the gait of a pregnant woman carrying a dead foetus in her womb.

By the time she'd returned to college after the summer break Swati had developed a profound conviction about the Maoist path. By then, Gopal had already left to work for the party in the rural belts of Andhra Pradesh. She remained in touch with him and became an active member of the core Maoist group in college. And when she completed her graduation, there were a handful in college who like Gopal had also joined Maoist groupings in separate pockets elsewhere in the country. There were others like her who remained sympathetic to the cause but took up jobs and went their separate ways. Swati did not join any revolutionary grouping—although convinced of its ideological content, she could not reconcile herself to a life of bloodshed and violence.

Returning to Delhi, the initial task she set out for herself was to find a means for a livelihood. She took up the first job she could lay her hands on—as a technical support executive in a knowledge outsourcing firm in Noida on the eastern outskirts of the city. Within a short time, she shifted to a more challenging assignment in an engineering consultancy firm located in Rajendra Place in Delhi. But her heart and mind were elsewhere, among the poor and the underprivileged. Her mother would sometimes work among women living in slums, and it was on one of these visits with her that she decided that she'd volunteer to teach slum children.

She continued to remain in touch with Gopal and he'd contact her on those rare occasions he'd visit the city and would inundate her with Maoist literature. 'Who knows,' Gopal told her on one of his visits. 'One day you'll help us to mobilize slum dwellers to join the revolution.'

'Oh, come on,' Swati said. 'Let them be. They barely know where they'll get their next meal from and you're talking of a revolution.'

'The day's not far when we'll reach Delhi,' Gopal said. 'Just you wait.'

12

GOPAL WAS BENT OVER a short-wave battery-powered radio placed on a bamboo table in one corner of his hut. A walkie-talkie and a pistol holster lay beside it. The hut was a small, two-room dwelling with mud walls and a sloping corrugated tin roof in Satwal village. The first room as one entered the hut was his working area, containing a wooden shelf stacked with paper beside a table; an AK-47 rested against the wall nearby. His uniform of fatigues and the olive green cap with a red star hung on a nail behind the bamboo entrance door. The other room was equally modest with an unmade bed, a metal trunk, a ramshackle wooden almirah, a grass broom, a bamboo drum that stored grain, and a wooden stool on which was placed a terracotta pitcher and a metal tumbler. A small window let in the late-afternoon sun.

The radio hummed and crackled as he adjusted the knob to tune into BBC News, which he listened to every day to keep abreast of happenings around the world. After a while, he switched off the radio and went and lay down on the bed in the other room. The fading rays of the sun from the window hit him directly in the eyes.

He closed his eyes and looked back on his years in the Bastar region. He hadn't done too badly for himself. Yes, his comrades had certainly done the groundwork, but the actual task of liberating the villages one by one had been accomplished under his command. From learning the local Gondi language, to winning the confidence of the adivasis, to training them in guerrilla warfare, and finally organizing attacks on the sahukars, mukhias, thekedars and patels had called for considerable strategic thinking.

The real turnaround had come when he'd rescued Moesa and other adivasis from her village who'd been languishing in jail.

Since then, Moesa had become a fanatic follower. He'd taught her how to shoot a rifle, the intricacies of guerrilla warfare and the secret sign language they used. She'd been an enthusiastic learner and soon she was recruiting and building her own dreaded dalam, trained to shoot and kill without giving any quarter. Like Moesa there were other adivasis who became his loyal supporters and who'd die for the cause. Among them was Prakrit, a key sangham member. He recalled how difficult it'd been in the beginning to organize the sanghams—the Maoist peasants' and workers' organizations—to help overthrow the traditional village leadership of the panch and set up gram rajya committees in their place to settle disputes and run development projects. Prakrit had been one of the first sangham members he'd appointed.

But the anti-Maoist movement called Shanti Kadam had severely stymied his plans. Perhaps it'd been a strategic error in the way they'd handled the incident in Latru village. When a handful of the village leadership in Latru had shown signs of dissent and were goading the villagers not to cooperate, it'd been a mistake to try to scare the villagers into submission by firing at them. They should've made an attempt to talk things out instead. The firing had inflamed the villagers and started the rumour that the Maoists were out to invade their villages for the sole purpose of looting and killing.

Fearing the attack, several villagers had evacuated their homes at the behest of the Shanti Kadam and had been summarily bundled into makeshift camps prepared by the state government. With the backing of the patels, mukhias, miners and tendu leaf thekedars, the Shanti Kadam had then exploited the vulnerability of the adivasis living in these roadside camps to shore up support for their own movement. Politicians and state officials had also lent their support in luring the adivasis with government jobs as Special Police Officers—SPOs—and the machismo of guns.

Gopal was apprehensive that sangham members like Prakrit would be targeted by Shanti Kadam activists. If he was unable to provide protection to loyal members like Prakrit, he feared he'd lose more supporters.

Medhak stopped his bicycle outside the bamboo gate of his sister Nirali's thatch-roofed hut. Corncobs hanging on wooden rafters supported on crude bamboo poles lined the entrance to her home. On one side of the hut, in an area cordoned off by a bamboo fence, a few hens and roosters shuffled about aimlessly. A motorcycle rested on the fencing.

Medhak called out aloud to his sister, 'Nano, are you ready? Let's go.'

Inside the hut, Nirali's husband, Prakrit, was playing with his one-year-old daughter when he heard his brother-in-law's voice. 'Medhak is already here,' Prakrit told Nirali. 'How much more time are you going to take?'

Nirali didn't respond, but quickly put on some bright red lipstick, adjusted her short red sari and slung a patchwork cloth bag over her shoulder. Giving her daughter a parting hug, she left the hut, with Prakrit following close behind, holding their daughter in the crook of his arm.

Medhak, standing akimbo across the bicycle, greeted them by raising a fist to his temple, 'The village looks deserted.'

'I know,' said Prakrit, returning the salute. 'The SPO was here last week exhorting the villagers to attend the Shanti Kadam sabha meeting today. He was threatening that if they didn't go the village would be razed to the ground. Many of the villagers have gone to attend the meeting out of fear.'

'They're making our lives very difficult,' said Medhak.

'I wish you didn't have to go,' said Prakrit.

'We don't have a choice, do we, brother,' said Medhak. 'There's not an ounce of grain in our house.'

'Do you want to take the motorbike?' asked Prakrit.

'I'd rather not,' said Medhak. 'It'll make unnecessary noise and attract attention. The cycle is fine.'

'You're perhaps right,' said Prakrit, holding his daughter tightly in one arm, and closing the bamboo gate with his free hand. 'Be careful.'

'Don't worry, brother,' Medhak said, as Nirali sat sideways on to the bicycle. He then gave the cycle a gentle push with his leg to get it moving.

Medhak rode his bicycle on the mud path, keeping it on one side under the shade of the sal trees. After cycling for half an hour, they reached a patch of uneven ground where rocks glinted in the rays of the sun. Medhak stopped, and waited for Nirali to dismount. After walking a short distance, Medhak wheeling his bicycle beside him, they came across some memorials made of stone and wood with banderoles atop them. Medhak looked around, and ensuring that no one was watching him, bowed his head. Nirali joined her hands.

They continued trudging for some time, negotiating the rocky terrain on foot. Just as they'd crossed the clearing and were about to reach the edge of a forested area, a group of six young men armed with sticks and spears and knives suddenly appeared from behind the trees.

'You're Prakrit's brother-in-law, aren't you?' said one of the men, holding a bamboo stick.

'And who is this wench, you Maovadi dog?' said a second man, pointing a knife at Nirali's chest.

'My nano. Please don't . . . don't touch her,' said Medhak in a terrified voice.

'So, why aren't you at the sabha meeting?' said the first man, grabbing the bicycle and throwing it to the ground.

'We're going there now. We got delayed. Please, please, let us go,' said Medhak, bending down to pick up his bicycle.

'Delayed, uhh? What were you doing? Fucking your nano? I'll show you, you Maoist runt!' said the first man as he began raining blows on Medhak's bent back with his stick.

Nirali began to run, but two men gave her chase and pulled at her sari. She fell on the rocky ground. The second man slapped Medhak hard on his face, once, twice, even as the first man hit him on his knees with a thick stick and brought him down, raining more blows. The second man raised his knife and poised it between Medhak's eyes.

The cacophony of the forest birds drowned the agonizing, helpless screams of the brother and sister.

Gopal was training some new Maoist cadres from the neighbouring villages on how to hold the .303, when he saw a crowd of villagers in the distance half running, half walking towards them. As they neared, he recognized Prakrit's thin form leading them, his daughter in his arms. Dismissing the trainees, Gopal walked swiftly towards them.

'What happened?' Gopal enquired as he neared them, looking at Prakrit, who was standing still, not saying a word, his eyes red, blazing.

'Why don't you say something?' said Gopal.

'It's all over, dada,' Prakrit said, tears in his eyes.

'What's all over?' Gopal asked. 'Why don't you people tell me?'

The villagers began to narrate how they'd found Medhak with

knife slashes all over his body and his eyes gouged out. Nirali's body had been found a short distance away, bruised and battered, her clothes ripped apart.

'Sisterfucking sons of bitches,' said Gopal.

'It's all your fault, dada,' said a villager, emboldened by the tragedy, looking at Gopal straight in the eye.

Gopal turned his head away and was silent for a while. Then he asked, 'Do you know who's behind this?'

'Dugga,' said a villager.

'The motherfucker,' said Gopal. 'By the last drop of my blood, we'll avenge this, brothers. Justice will be done. We'll strike once and for all. Don't lose heart.'

Early next morning, Moesa was many kilometres away in Tumar village, having walked through a path in the dense sal forest. Leading a team of eight of her most trusted dalam members, five women and three men, armed with guns and knives and sickles, she stealthily approached a mud-plastered house with a slate-tiled, sloping roof gleaming in the moonlight. The group slowed down as they neared the dwelling.

Moesa gave her comrades instructions through gestures to take strategic positions around the house, and then pushed open the front door with the back of her fist. Four of them charged in, while the other four remained outside, on guard. One of them took out a torch and flashed it around the room. A sleeping boy, barely ten years old, and his mother, who'd been woken up by the light and the noise, looked up, terrified at the sight of four armed people.

'Where's Dugga, you bitch?' Moesa said roughly through her buckteeth. The woman didn't answer, cringing with fear, pulling her son towards her. Moesa pulled the boy away from her, and pointed her knife at his chest.

'Quick, tell me where Dugga is,' said Moesa, 'or I'll kill this bastard pup of yours.'

'I . . . I . . . I don't know,' said the terrified woman. 'He hasn't been home for the last three days.'

'You lie, you whore,' said Moesa, digging the knife point into the boy's chest.

The boy howled in pain; the woman screamed, 'I really, really don't know. Take whatever you want but please spare the boy.'

Moesa pushed the boy away and went up to the mother. Holding the tip of her knife between her breasts she pierced the woman's blouse, letting out a streak of blood. As the woman let out an agonized scream, Moesa took out a 9 mm pistol from her belt and shot her dead. The boy cried out helplessly. Moesa showed her pistol to the boy, who whimpered and cowered in a corner. Then she turned around to one of her comrades who was carrying a sickle and gave a command with a slight movement of her head. In a matter of minutes the mother's head had been severed and blood gushed out of her in a torrent. Moesa turned her back on the slain body and left with her comrades.

Dugga's turn would come for sure; it was only a matter of time.

13

SWATI WENT TO TEACH the slum children every Tuesday, Wednesday and Friday. South India Coffee house, where she'd invited Aseem, was close to the slum. She was already there waiting for him outside the coffee house when he came reeking of a mixture of cologne and after-shave.

She led him into the cafe, holding open the door for him. He followed her awkwardly, meandering his way clumsily between the metal chairs and laminated tables. The two of them found a table in a corner and sat opposite each other. Swati called for a waiter to give them menu cards.

Once they had placed their orders, they settled back in their chairs. Swati had a charming smile on her face; Aseem smiled back sheepishly. He found her to be beautiful: doe-eyed, with a small, straight nose, her smile moderating the effect of a firm jawline. In fact, he found everything about her attractive: her dusky complexion, the delicate silver jewellery she wore, her long black hair.

'Are those the school books you use for the children?' Aseem asked after a while, pointing to her bag.

'Yes, let me show them to you,' Swati said, taking out a notebook from her bag and opening it on the laminated tabletop. 'See, we prepare these books for the slum children ourselves with lots and lots of colour pictures.'

'Very nice,' he said, looking through the book. 'You must be enjoying it.'

'Very much,' said Swati, closing the notebook and putting it back in her bag. 'What do you do in your spare time?'

'Oh, nothing really. Read, watch TV. Nothing creative or meaningful. Most of the time goes in the job.'

'What's it like?'

'You mean my job?'

The waiter came with their order of coffee, which he served in small steel tumblers.

'Yes, tell me about your job,' said Swati, stirring sugar in her coffee.

'What's there to tell?' said Aseem, hesitant and embarrassed to talk about his work. 'Booking orders, visiting dealers and retail shops, cajoling them to order my company's products. It's so . . . so hollow and meaningless.' He looked down and paused to take a sip of his coffee.

'But it gives you a livelihood,' Swati remarked.

'True, that it does,' said Aseem, surprised by her remark. 'But I'd like to do something that can give greater meaning to my life.'

'Nothing in this world is black and white, you know. I too work with a consultancy firm, don't I? Everyone has to search to find what they want in life.'

Aseem didn't respond immediately. Then, looking down into his tumbler of coffee, he asked, 'Do you think I could work with you in the slums?'

'Sure, why not?' said Swati. 'Why don't you come down one evening and take a look at what it's really like to work in the slums?'

'I'll happily do that,' said Aseem, smiling.

'Are you busy?' asked Ritika over the cellphone.

'I was just going out to meet Ishita,' Menaka responded. 'Anything important?'

'It's about Aseem.'

'If it's about him, let's talk now.'

'I'm worried. Aseem's just not himself of late. He looks lost and troubled.'

'Are you sure you're not imagining things?' Menaka asked. 'If there was something really bothering him, surely he would've told me.'

'I can see it in his face,' said Ritika. 'I've a feeling that he doesn't like his job.'

'Did *he* say it?' questioned Menaka.

'He doesn't have to say it. I'm his mother,' said Ritika matter-of-factly. 'I just know.'

'All right, if you say so,' Menaka said, not really convinced. 'But give him time. It's just been a couple of months since he joined MCG. And, you know, it could as well have something to do with a girl.'

'It's not that. I've already asked him.'

'All right. I'll check about his job. But, you know, it would've been so much better if Aseem had joined ImpaKt.'

'You know very well he wants to make it on his own.'

'Yes dear, I know.' Menaka paused before continuing. 'But what if I were to tell you that I got him the job with MCG?'

'Oh God!' exclaimed Ritika, aghast. 'Is that true? He'd be shattered if he got to know.'

'Don't worry,' said Menaka triumphantly. 'I won't tell anyone.'

Menaka was exhilarated. If Aseem really disliked his job at MCG, he was sure to feel frustrated sooner or later. Then she'd get to work on him to join ImpaKt.

14

MENAKA WAS DREAMING. CHRISTOPHER was all over her, with his tousled blond hair and white skin. He kissed her gently on her face and neck. He moved lower and buried his face between her breasts. She held him there, moaning. Then all of sudden he vanished from her arms; in his place was a dissolving image of a man in flowing white attire, disappearing into a forest veiled in mist.

A succession of alarm bells woke Menaka from her bizarre dream. Soon, the maid was at the door carrying tea on a tray. Menaka looked beside her; Aroon was not there. She heard the sound of water and surmised that Aroon was in the bath. It was a Sunday but they were to visit the ashram to explore the Swamiji project. Aroon had readily warmed to the idea: it was a godsend at a time when his clients had become stingy about loosening their purse strings for advertising. Menaka pulled herself up to the bedrest to drink her tea. She took a sip and looked at her watch. It was seven-thirty already; she'd have to hurry and get dressed. The always-punctual Ishita would be at their doorstep at eight-thirty sharp, for sure.

Christopher was waiting at the entrance to the ashram to greet Ishita, Menaka and Aroon. His attire had undergone a transformation—he wore an orange kurta-pyjama and wooden khadaun on his feet—and was beaming from ear to ear. His forehead was smeared with a crimson tilak and his head was shaved except for a clump of hair at the back, which was tied into a knot.

'Namaskar, Namaskar!' Christopher said cheerfully, his hands folded in front of his chest. 'Welcome! Welcome!'

'Hi, Chris. You look handsome in a kurta-pyjama,' said Menaka and then waved her hand in Aroon's direction. 'Meet Aroon.'

'Namaskar, Christopher,' said Aroon, who'd taken out his camera from its case and had begun clicking photographs.

'Kripananda,' said Christopher, continuing to keep his hands folded.

'Kripananda?' asked Ishita with a quizzical expression.

'Swamiji has given me a new name—Sri Kripananda,' said Christopher.

'Nice name,' said Menaka. 'But I prefer Christopher.'

'I've also taken a vow of celibacy,' said Sri Kripananda.

'Celibacy?' mumbled Menaka, and frowned.

'Please follow me,' said Sri Kripananda, without responding, leading the three of them into the ashram, which had undergone a visible change. Freshly planted saplings lined the newly laid red gravel path, bisecting the lush lawns. Four people with crimson tilaks on their foreheads and wearing orange dhotis and turbans were tending to the lawns. A couple of them moved on their haunches, slashing at the overgrown grass mercilessly with long scythes like soldiers on horseback beheading their enemies. The other two were crouched intently over a bed of flowers, working on the soil with garden tools. Rotating sprinklers placed strategically in the lawns spurted water jets.

'This is all Christopher's . . . err . . . Sri Kripananda's doing,' said Ishita. 'The ashram's changed so much under his charge. It's unbelievable.'

'Thank you, but it's all because of Swamiji's blessings,' said Sri Kripananda, pointing to a few wicker chairs placed on the veranda of a low-roofed farmhouse, which was now the swami's chamber. 'We'll wait here. Swamiji will give us darshan after a while.'

'Swamiji is a very simple man,' Ishita said. 'He comes from humble beginnings.'

'His is a fascinating story,' said Sri Kripananda. 'Swamiji, who was named Anand at birth, was born in a village near the town of Narayanpur in Chhattisgarh. Owing to a disability in one of his knees, he began walking very late and that too with a pronounced limp. His father sought the help of a renowned yoga guru, Swami Niranjan. The guru assured him that Anand would be cured, but he laid out a condition: if his knee became all right, he'd keep the boy with him; however, if the guru failed to cure him, Anand would be returned to his parents.'

'Rather a difficult condition,' commented Aroon.

'I know,' continued Sri Kripananda. 'The poor parents were heartbroken but agreed for the sake of their only son. The young Anand turned out to be an ardent disciple, and within a year his disability had vanished. And so he remained in the custody of Swami Niranjan. By the age of twelve, Anand had mastered many yoga asanas that even experienced yogis are unable to perform. Swami Niranjan gave his young disciple the name of Shivaramakrishna, the all-knowing, all-gods-rolled-into-one.

'For the next six years Shivaramakrishna learned all that Swami Niranjan could teach him. His teacher then told him, "Son, there's nothing more that I can teach you. It's now your duty to share your learning with others." Since then, Swami Shivaramakrishna has been spreading all that he learned at the feet of Swami Niranjan.'

As Sri Kripananda completed the swami's story, a sevak emerged from the inner sanctum to say that Swamiji was now ready to receive the visitors. The sevak led them to an inner chamber, where the swami was sitting cross-legged on a large divan in the centre of the room. Behind him was a framed photograph of his guru, Swami Niranjan, wearing a long white beard and sitting bare-bodied on a tiger skin. Aroon quickly took some photographs as they entered.

Sri Kripananda first introduced Aroon as the country's leading advertising guru and then Menaka. The swami blessed them both with long life.

'We've heard a lot about you, Swamiji,' Aroon said, clicking at the same time. 'It'll be our privilege to help you spread your message.'

'Not mine, my guru's message,' said the swami, turning his head around to the framed image behind him. 'All that I've learned is because of his blessings, my child. Sri Kripananda has also told me about you. You're also a guru, he tells me, a marketing guru.'

'You embarrass me. But we'll do the best we can,' said Aroon. 'Swamiji, if it's all right with you, could you teach us one or two typical yoga poses?'

'Typical?' asked the swami.

'Swamiji, something which you've . . . how should I say it . . . something we can say is your copyright.'

'I don't know about copyrights, beta, but I'll show you the shashank pose,' said the swami, going down on his knees. 'You know why it's called the shashank pose? "Shash" means moon, and "ank" is lap. The next time there's a full moon, observe the dark patches carefully. You'll notice that the patches resemble the shape of a hare with the moon in its lap. The moon emits soothing and calming vibrations and sends out peace waves that are not visible. The shashank asana also has a similar cooling effect. Cool, calm, shanti.' Closing his eyes, the swami continued, 'Hares adopt this pose. Don't they? No? White moon . . . white hare . . . Shanti! Shanti! Shanti.'

Aroon quickly clicked some photographs of the swami resting in the shashank pose.

'You'll also work on this project, beti?' enquired the swami, looking at Menaka as he resumed his cross-leggged position on the divan and opened his eyes.

'Yes, Swamiji,' Menaka said. 'If that is your wish.'

Later, while driving back, Ishita asked Aroon what he had thought of the swami. 'He's okay,' said Aroon. 'But he needs some sophistication before we can launch him in the corporate world, you know. But I think we can swing it.'

'You're free to do whatever you think needs to be done,' Ishita said. 'Sri Kripananda has explained everything to Swamiji. He's quite game. And, as I've said earlier, Sri Kripananda will freely give whatever finances are needed.'

15

A WOUND HAD BEEN festering on Gopal Subbarao's left shin. At first, he'd barely noticed it; it was a small reddish scar a quarter-inch in width, which he'd dismissed as an insect bite. But soon it had begun to itch, and when he touched it, it felt tender. A week later the wound had become larger and there was a numbing pain as well. Finally, he'd agreed to show it to the wadde, the village doctor Kamu, who came to Gopal's hut carrying some herbs and a lit ban to ward off evil spirits. Kamu heated the dried leaves of the herbs on the lamp and crushed them in his palm. As he applied the herbs to the wound, he simultaneously chanted under his breath. 'Stop it!' Gopal shouted. 'You just apply the herbs. I don't want to hear this mumbo-jumbo.'

'As you wish, dada,' the well-meaning Kamu had said meekly and fallen silent. For some time the wound had subsided, but soon it had resurfaced again, assuming a more virulent form, increasing in size, and becoming angrier and angrier. Kamu, when he saw it again, mumbled that had he been allowed to recite the verses the wound would have healed by now. An enraged Gopal had then pointed to his AK-47 and said, 'Go away before I shoot you.'

Looking at the wound now, red and beginning to ooze a pale yellowish fluid, Gopal debated if he should take the risk of going into town to show it to an allopathic doctor. Not now, he finally decided; he had more serious worries. Following Moesa's attack on Dugga's family, the Shanti Kadam activists had retaliated and set fire to many of the villages under their control. With their villages smouldering, those who'd escaped had had no recourse but to seek shelter in the roadside camps set up by the state. Grains and provisions had become difficult to procure for those who'd stayed back—there was fear of the Shanti Kadam activists attacking them if they tried visiting the weekly haats.

He worried that the villagers were becoming impatient, while the Shanti Kadam activists were gaining ground. They were wooing the villagers by telling them that they'd be given jobs and compensation if they left the villages and allowed mines to be set up in the vacated land. They were spreading the vile rumour that if they stayed back the Maoists would kill them. Where coercion didn't help, they were resorting to violence to move the villagers into the camps. The movement was receiving funds from the state; a couple of elementary schools had also been set up in the camps. The villagers were beginning to ask: How was the violence helping them? Why was no development reaching them? How long would they have to endure this suffering? They wanted food and shelter and security. They wanted education for their children. The activities of the Shanti Kadam were demoralizing the adivasi cadres.

There were times when he wondered if all this would lead anywhere. Could the movement ever succeed? To make matters worse, the central government had launched Operation Red Hunt, which till now had, however, been more active in West Bengal and Jharkhand and was yet to make serious inroads into

Bastar; but it was bound to do so soon. He needed to coordinate more closely with Comrade Prasada in the south Dantewada region and the party high command and determine a way to keep them out. With the party's focus on Operation Red Hunt, he'd been practically left alone to deal with the Shanti Kadam. He felt a sense of self-doubt slithering up along his back like a snake. He felt alone with no one to turn to, not even the local villagers who trusted him and he was closest to. Even though he identified fully with the adivasis and had mastered the Gondi language, he still remained alien to their culture; he didn't feel a sense of belonging or of being accepted by them. At frustrating times like these, he felt an aching hunger for the love of a woman.

It wasn't that he hadn't known love. When Gopal was a student in his second year in college, he'd felt attracted to a first-year student called Sheela Chandran, who had also joined the Maoist study circle where he was a member. Their romance blossomed over the years while they were in college. When he was in his final year, he proposed to Sheela, and she readily agreed to marry him. But then circumstances changed.

At this time, the party high command decided that Gopal should go to Chhattisgarh while Sheela was to stay behind and work in the backward districts of the Telangana region. Gopal requested that Sheela be allowed to accompany him, but the party insisted that if they wanted to work for the party, they'd have to part ways. Gopal protested, but he was told that he was behaving like a teenage romantic and not like a committed Maoist. Love and romance were for the birds, he was told, unnecessary distractions at this stage of the movement.

Being a loyal member of the party with revolutionary heroism surging in his veins, Gopal acquiesced to the party diktat and parted with Sheela. But she could not take the decision as stoically—disillusioned with the party, she resigned. Some months later, Gopal received news that she'd married a computer engineer in Hyderabad. Bitter and sad though he was, Gopal yet resolved to dedicate his life to the Maoist cause. The party high command had surely erred then, he thought in retrospect, and they'd lost a committed worker in Sheela. Otherwise, she could very well have been working with him here in Bastar, shoulder to shoulder.

Gopal closed his eyes. What was he thinking? How did he get distracted and allow Sheela to enter his mind? This was no time to live in the past; a revolutionary has to live in the present. Some years back, he'd sold a Maoist dream to these innocent adivasis. They were looking to him now to show them the path out of their wretchedness and poverty. Moesa and many others in the cadre venerated him as a god. For their sake, for Moesa's sake, he had to go on. There could be no turning back. Now there could be only one mission in his life: to die a martyr to the cause of a glorious revolution; to be revered by posterity as a great revolutionary, just as he remembered Mao and Charu Majumdar.

He needed to focus on finding ways to tackle the Shanti Kadam and make preparations to keep out the Red Hunt security forces. His immediate action should be to take the necessary measures to fortify the base area in the region under his control: dig more trenches, plant more mines, recruit and train more Maoist cadres, gather more intelligence about Operation Red Hunt's plans in Bastar. For all this, he'd require more funds. Nearly half of the five-crore ransom amount had already been spent on paying for arms and ammunition and grenade launchers and he'd sent a crore to Comrade Prasada to make preparations to tackle Operation Red Hunt. He was going to keep some and he'd distribute the rest among the adivasis to win their loyalty. He hoped that after the kidnapping, other miners and thekedars and the steel and aluminium plant owners in the region would continue to send their monthly protection amounts, but it couldn't be determind for how long they'd continue—for it was most likely that the government would provide them enhanced security cover. In any case he now needed to find newer ways to raise resources on a more sustainable basis; something that would give the villagers a livelihood so that they wouldn't drift to the Shanti Kadam camps. He'd learned that one of the Maoist groups had taken to poppy cultivation. He'd also heard that another group of comrades in Jharkhand had raided a bank and looted its lockers. There was a time when he wouldn't have considered these avenues; they maligned and discredited the movement. But things had changed now. Desperate times called for desperate measures.

He needed to quickly establish closer ties with the high command and request them to convene a high-level meeting, where he hoped to accomplish many things. On the last occasion they'd met, leadership had been a vexed issue; the discussions had proved inconclusive and they began quarrelling. He needed to try and wrest control of the mantle; he alone knew the reality on the ground; the rest were mere ideologues. With the support of other Maoist wings, he could organize concerted retaliatory measures against Operation Red Hunt and Shanti Kadam before the patience of the adivasi people ran out. He needed to make quick progress with his dream of starting a school for the adivasi children for the villages under his command. There was so much to be done and time was running out like water from a leaking pipe.

There was a gentle knock on the bamboo door of his hut. He opened the door to find an adolescent adivasi girl standing outside. 'Come in,' said Gopal. He looked out and shut it close soon after she'd entered. The girl was ready when he turned around, bare-bodied except for the twin garland of colourful beads and cowries around her neck and budding breasts.

16

IMPAKT (WITH A CAPITAL 'K' for Kumar) Communications Private Limited was located on the sixth floor of Pankaj Towers, one of the busiest office-cum-shopping complexes in Nehru Place. The area had undergone a major transformation in the five years since Aroon had rented his office in the Towers. What was once a shabby cinema hall was now a fashionable, eight-storey, bustling mall with a cinema multiplex and fancy eateries and a three-level basement parking lot swarming with security guards to ward off terrorist attacks. All the glob and goo and gunk that emanated from the building flowed into clogged age-old drains, either overflowing on to the crowded roads or sluggishly reaching the Yamuna to add to to the river's slick and slime.

Wearing a dark blue tie loose around his collar and shirtsleeves rolled up to his elbows, Aroon stood at one end of the longish ImpaKt Communications boardroom, making a presentation using a laptop and an LCD projector. His face looked fresh with his neat French beard and well-gelled hair.

Mike, the creative head and star of ImpaKt, sat to his left with his gold-streaked hair pulled tightly into a ponytail. Next to Mike sat Aparna, the art director and ace smoke-ring maker, with whom Mike shared a relationship that went beyond the office premises. Opposite them were George D'Souza, the head of client servicing, who had long sideburns, and his deputy Uma Sehgal, a young, smart woman wearing round-framed spectacles, who also doubled up as an event manager for the firm. The surprise of the pack was Menaka, sitting at the far end in a pair of black lycra slacks and a printed top. This was her first meeting in the smoky precincts of the boardroom, and she was clearly not in her element, realizing that this was not her domain and that she'd need to allow Aroon to call the shots.

'Guys,' Aroon was saying, 'in the email I sent you, I said that this would be an "extraordinary" meeting. You'll soon realize why. ImpaKt Communications has reached a turning point, a point from where we either drop out or grow geometrically. In the five years of ImpaKt, we've worked with all kinds of products and services, from motorbikes to pens, from computers to courier companies, from hotels to soft drinks and surrogate liquor. Today, I feel confident that ImpaKt can take on a new challenge.

'Now, consider this. Brands are losing their relevance. With unlimited choice, old brands are losing their loyalty. Customers need something new every day to excite their imagination. So, where do we go? We need a new product, a new commodity, something that can be differentiated from the crowd.'

Here Aroon paused, looked around and smiled before continuing, 'And that commodity, folks, can only be a personality, not an object or a service. Let me come to the point. We've been offered an *absolutely* novel contract. It involves the marketing of one man, a man who, if we succeed, would have the world worshipping him as a god.' Aroon bent over the laptop and, with the click of the mouse, projected the image of Sri Shivaramakrishna on to the screen behind him.

'Look carefully, guys. Does he look like someone who can change the destiny of ImpaKt? Is there anything extraordinary about him? Not really. This man started life as the son of a poor temple priest in a village. So, what makes him so special for ImpaKt? Here are some more images.' Aroon went click-click-clickety-click on the laptop to show a succession of images of the swami in varied moods and poses. Finally, there were several images of the swami assuming the shashank pose followed by a picture of Sri Kripananda in his saffron kurta–pyjama.

'Our brief is to make an extraordinary personage out of this ordinary, hairy swami,' said Aroon. 'The American in kurta–pajama you saw in the end is Sri Kripananda, our wealthy benefactor-financier.'

'Right. I want to hear ideas from each of you on how we can turn this swami into one of the most recognizable personalities in the world. Give full rein to your imagination.

'One last thing. We must thank Menaka for acquiring this project. She'll also serve as our bridge to Swamiji.' Everyone turned around to face Menaka, who responded with a radiant smile, baring sparkling white teeth.

'Any questions? None? Then who'll begin? Mike? Aparna?' said Aroon, moving back to his chair to make room for the next speaker.

One by one, the creative stars in the boardroom brainstormed on how to effect a change in the swami's image. 'He needs a complete makeover, man,' drawled Aparna, her words flowing out languidly like her smoke rings. 'At the end of the day, he'll have to appeal to the youth. Look at the hair on his chest and back, man. And so much in his armpits. It's a veritable forest of hair. It'll *have* to go.'

'We need visibility,' said Uma. 'The swami's image should be plastered all over—on banners, on buses, on kiosks, on balloons.'

'We need something contemporary, man,' said Mike. 'How about flashing images on T-shirts used in night runs? It'd make him an icon for all.'

More ideas were hurled about like children playing frisbee. There were suggestions for bizarre campaigns on television and radio, and events involving Bollywood stars.

'I like many of the ideas, guys,' said Aroon after he'd lent his ear to all of them. 'I love the idea of using illuminated T-shirts. But we first need a strategy.'

'We need a symbol,' remarked George.

'That's right,' agreed Uma. 'We definitely need a symbol the young can identify with.'

'Like a dove?' suggested Menaka.

'Too common,' said Mike. 'Something that'll attract everyone. Both the young and the old.'

'Wait. I think I know an imagery we can use,' said Aroon excitedly. 'Remember the image I showed you of the swami in the shashank pose, sitting crouched like a hare? We could use a white hare as the icon.'

'That'll be neat,' said Mike.

Since it had come from the boss, the others too warmed up to the idea of using the white hare as an icon.

Change was on its way.

17

ASEEM WAITED FOR SWATI outside India Coffee House where they'd agreed to meet before visiting the slum colony. He was a good fifteen minutes early; this was one appointment he didn't want to be late for. The thought of accompanying Swati to the slum was enervating. He thought of her and her large dark brown eyes, her long hair cascading down her back—soft and shining and black. The image occupied his mind happily till she arrived a couple of minutes before the appointed time. She was wearing a delicately patterned salwar–kameez and flashed him a sparkling smile. 'Been waiting long? Shall we go?'

'No . . . I mean . . . I've just come,' said Aseem, stumbling over his words from the excitement of seeing her.

'The slum is walking distance from here,' said Swati.

'Show the way,' said Aseem.

Swati led Aseem through the crowded marketplace and then turned abruptly into a small lane round a small corner shop selling cheap lingerie and cosmetics. The lane ended on a wide open road streaming with traffic. After waiting for a bit to allow the traffic to ease, they ran across the road, stopping at the broken pavement on the far side.

'Well, here we are,' said Swati, recovering her breath.

'Where's the school? And what is this they're building? Is it a boundary wall for the school?' asked Aseem, pointing to a high wall a few masons were constructing just beyond the pavement.

'Well . . . it's a wall all right, but not of the school,' said Swati wryly. 'The municipal department is building it to hide the ugliness and poverty of the slum. It's part of their drive to beautify the city, if you please. Looking at the sordid conditions of the poor is an eyesore for the rich.' Before Aseem could respond, she'd moved ahead quickly. She looked back and said, 'Come, let's go.'

Swati walked Aseem through a gap in the wall which led to a clearing covered with brick-and-stone rubble and discarded plastic bags and then on to a narrow pathway bisected by a cleft in the ground that was an excuse for a drain. There were kuchcha jhuggi-jhopris cheek by jowl on either side of the drain with roofings of aluminium, asbestos or canvas sheets. Old bicycle tyres and stray items that might be of use in the future were strewn across some of the rooftops.

The path narrowed till it reached a point where the only way to negotiate it was by walking with feet placed on either side of a drain like someone with a hot potato stuck in the arse. Noxious smells emanating from the open drain mingled with the smell of food being cooked on fires of dry twigs and on kerosene stoves. The smooth brown bottom of a young boy sitting alongside the drain blocked their path. The boy was humming a Bollywood tune and throwing pebbles into the drain. Aseem pinched his nostrils tightly shut to keep out the stench.

'What're you doing here?' Swati reprimanded the defecating boy. 'Why aren't you at school?'

'Nothing, aunty . . . I'll just go,' said the boy sheepishly, though he didn't seem embarrassed at being caught with his pants down.

They moved on. Low-hung black electrical wires and television cables linked the dwelling units, hanging perilously. The slum dwellers greeted Swati warmly with folded hands, casting curious glances at Aseem. As they walked on, they found their path jammed by a serpentine queue of young girls and women carrying jerry cans and buckets, gossiping and quarrelling, waiting their turn at a solitary municipal tap.

Swati and Aseem cut through the queue to reach the school after walking for another fifty metres or so. The school was an elongated structure made of exposed brick walls and a canvas roof supported on bamboo poles fastened by ropes held down by heavy rocks at the corners. Two stray, mangy dogs guarded the entrance, a canvas flap that served as the door. Aseem could hear the children squealing inside.

Swati and Aseem had to bend forward to enter the school premises. A halogen lamp dangling precariously from a wire was the solitary source of light inside. There were about twenty children inside: a few sitting cross-legged on jute sacks with black slates and pieces of chalk, others throwing paper darts at each other, and a couple leafing through picture books, mostly from Swati's childhood collection. As soon as they saw Swati and Aseem, they hastily gathered themselves and stood up stiffly, chiming in sing-song unison, 'Good evening, aunty; good evening, uncle.'

The children were of varying ages, from five to twelve years, and sat in two groups: the girls in front, the boys at the back. Aseem went to the back to sit with the group of boys. 'Sit here, uncle,' said a boy, making space to accommodate him. 'Here, uncle,' said another. Aseem sat next to a small boy with a snivelling nose.

Swati soon began her class, teaching the children mathematics. Swati's method of teaching was informal; the older children or those who knew more taught the younger ones. They formed groups and taught each other; while Swati went from group to group explaining the more difficult concepts. A while later, she gave them a small talk on how they must keep their surroundings clean. Some of the children paid scant attention to her teaching of mathematics and lecture on hygiene. They were more keen to learn English so that they could grow up and work in smart offices, but Swati had been adamant that they first learn Hindi and other subjects in Hindi.

Some time later an adult couple joined the class. Both of them sat on their haunches near the entrance to the tent. The man, Ram, was about twenty-five years old—he was swarthy and had thick wavy hair and a neat moustache. Ram drove a cycle rickshaw but aspired to work in an office. His wife, Parvati, was short and small-built and cleaned utensils in a middle-class locality nearby. Swati smiled and gestured for them to come in.

The class lasted for more than an hour. Once the children trooped out, a few more adults walked in. They wanted Swati's help with various forms that they needed to fill in for ration cards, job applications, driving licences. Aseem offered to help.

They left the slum late in the evening.

'So, what do you think?' asked Swati. 'Would you like to work here?'

'Yes, I'd love to. It seems so much more satisfying than my job,' said Aseem, walking to the main road. 'Can I give you a drop to your flat?'

'It is the opposite way for you, isn't it?' remarked Swati. 'It's not too dark. I'll easily get an auto to the Metro station. It's not a problem.'

'No problem for me either.'

'Maybe another time. I'm quite used to it,' Swati said with a smile.

Aseem waited till she found an auto and then got on to his bike, feeling disappointed that Swati had declined his offer to drop her home. Perhaps he should take it slowly and not ride his luck too far. He'd wait for the next time. Breathing in the polluted air of the city as he breezed down the road was almost a welcome relief from the smells in the slum. Preoccupied, thinking of Swati, he missed his turn and had to take a circuitous route home.

'You're late,' Ritika said, when Aseem entered the flat. 'I was getting worrried.'

'You shouldn't worry, Ma,' said Aseem, giving his mother a hug and a peck on the top of her head.

'You should've at least called. What took you so long?'

'I was visiting a slum, Ma.'

'Slum?' asked Ritika with a frown.

'I'd gone there with someone.'

'Who?'

'What is this? An inquisition? I was with Swati. I met her at Menaka-aunty's party. I'll probably be going to the slums to teach in the evenings.'

'Teach in a slum?'

'Voluntary work, Ma. I need to do something to get my mind off MCG.'

'Aren't you happy there?'

'C'mon, Ma! Of course I am. This will just be for a change,' said Aseem, and quickly changed the topic. 'What's there to eat? I'm starving.'

18

ASEEM HAD BEEN TEACHING English in the slum for a couple of months now and the students loved him. He was happy and contented. He'd become used to the smells of the slum; he no longer recoiled from the stench. On the days Swati came to the school when he was there, she'd happily take a ride back to her barsati on his motorbike. On other days, he'd go with Swati to watch a film or play, or take her out for dinner to her favourite dhaba.

That he'd had no formal training in teaching English didn't seem to matter. His English classes were always spilling over: there'd be students crowding the entrance flap of the school, pushing aside the stray dogs that stood guard. The classes were overcrowded not only with children, but also with many youth, who'd sacrificed *Superboss*, the new reality show on television, in favour of Aseem's classes.

Aseem liked the adulation and affection he received in the slum—the slum women plied him with homemade halwa; the men greeted him affectionately. The stray dogs would see him off to his bike, which he parked near the main road, barking and racing the bike for some distance till they couldn't keep pace with it.

It was early morning in the month of October; the weather in Delhi was pleasant. In an attempt to trim her derriere and get Rambo to shed some weight, Menaka was walking her pet near her house. She was finding it difficult to restrain him on the leather leash. He strained at it and almost got her running as he went about sniffing at the wild shrubs growing on the roadside. Rambo was about to raise his hind leg over a bit of turd, when Menaka tried to pull him away. But the dog stood firm as a rock, and she had to allow him to mark his territory. Irritated with Rambo's uncivilized behaviour, Menaka turned to go back to the house. Walking was perhaps not the best idea; it'd be better to use a treadmill. She'd seen an ad recently for a treadmill specially designed for dogs. Yes, that's what she'd do: have Rambo work out alongside her in the confines of her bedroom.

Her thoughts were disturbed by a call from Ritika on her cellphone just as she'd reached her doorstep. 'I'm concerned about Aseem,' Ritika said. 'He's been coming home late in the evenings and seems lost in a world of his own.'

'It must be his work,' said Menaka.

'I wouldn't be worried if he was getting late because of his work,' complained Ritika. 'It's because he's teaching in a slum. I just don't understand what he's up to.'

'It's a girl,' said Menaka intuitively.

'But he said . . .'

'I can bet there's some girl around,' persisted Menaka.

'Wait a bit. Maybe you're right. He did mention that he'd been to the slums with Swati.'

'What? *That* Gaajar's daughter?' Menaka exclaimed. 'What a fool he is to go romancing with a girl like that and that too in the slums. What's come over that boy!'

'I don't know what you're talking about. But I'm worried all right.'

'Don't worry, Ritu. Now that I know, I'll take care of it. Just relax and leave this to me.'

19

ASEEM AND SWATI WERE taking a stroll in the well-maintained lawns around India Gate with its full-grown trees: the purple fruit-bearing raj-jamun, the spreading neem, the colourful pilkham. It was a November evening, and while there was a perceptible nip in the air, the cold Delhi winter was yet to set in. While Aseem was comfortable in a full-sleeved T-shirt, Swati wore a light shawl drawn around her shoulders. The lawns were laid with water channels and were cordoned off by a low iron fencing all around. Arterial roads intersected the lawns spreading outwards to the main circular road round the stately, arched structure of India Gate bathed in yellow lights. For many of Delhi's dwellers the gardens offered an escape from the claustrophobic lives they led in their small tenements. There were children taking boat rides in the water channels; families and romancing couples strolling in the lawns; balloon sellers and ice-cream vendors lined the roads doing brisk business.

'I love the expanse of green,' said Aseem.

'Yes, but look at this,' said Swati, stopping under a pilkham tree and pointing to its trunk which had names scratched on its bark. 'Many of these trees are dying because they've been wounded, or because of vehicular exhaust or because their branches have been chopped off to make way for electrical cables. But no one seems to care.'

'That's part of urban life, I suppose,' said Aseem.

'Hmmm,' Swati said, pensively.

Aseem looked at her. She didn't appear to be her usual cheerful self and looked preoccupied. 'Is something troubling you?' he asked her.

'It's nothing.'

'There *must* be something. Tell me.'

'Well, if you want to know . . . there's a new municipal department order to clear out the slum,' said Swati after a while.

'And what's to come up in its place?'

'There's talk of a shopping mall with a three-level basement parking lot.'

'That's ridiculous,' Aseem almost shouted. 'And where are the slum dwellers supposed to go?'

'Search me,' said Swati. 'It doesn't seem to bother the government.'

'Can't they protest?' asked Aseem. 'Go to court or something?'

'I don't know,' said Swati, shrugging her shoulders. 'The politicians may try to do something. Elections are round the corner, so they want their votes. My mother is organizing a protest march.'

'So there's hope.'

'I don't think so. Protests, courts, hunger strikes, dharnas—they don't work. The system is rotten.'

'The least they can do is give the people alternatives and settle them elsewhere.'

'But why should they be asked to vacate in the first place? They are not here out of choice,' said Swati agitatedly. 'They are here for jobs, for survival, to feed their families. Don't they have a fundamental right to livelihood? Is this or is this not a free country, where the least every citizen can find is shelter?'

'But, surely, slums are no answer.'

'Well you can't forcibly evict slum dwellers and shift them to alternative sites,' said Swati sharply.

'Even if one does that, many of them would return to their original homes after selling off their new land,' remarked Aseem.

'I won't say that that's not true. It's happened. But what does one do?' said Swati. 'For this reason, the courts today are not even in favour of providing alternative sites. They say that only the slumlords are benefited because they buy the sites and create illegal estates. They regard slum dwellers as encroachers—they say that providing them alternative sites is like rewarding a pickpocket. Of course, I don't buy this argument. We can't gloss over the reality that in the capital city of fifteen million, four million people live in slums; and there are seven hundred thousand dwelling units in over a thousand jhuggi-jhopri clusters.'

'I didn't know there were so many slum dwellers in Delhi. It'd take a lifetime to resettle all of them,' said Aseem.

'Exactly,' said Swati. 'The task is enormous, costly, and no one's really interested.'

'So, if removing the slums is not an anwer, what are the slum dwellers to do?'

'I don't know.' Swati paused and then said, 'The day's not far when they'll pick up arms and rebel.'

'You really think so?'

'Yes, I think they'll revolt one day,' said Swati, speaking in a softer but deliberate tone. 'Not yet, perhaps, but some time in the future. Do they have a choice?'

Aseem didn't reply. After walking for a while, he said, 'Shall we sit down?'

They sat down on the grass, listening to the breeze rustling through the shady boughs. An orange sun radiating a mystical glow descended languidly behind the trees as time slipped carelessly by. Aseem reached out for Swati's hand, slowly, tentatively. She did not take her hand away.

Aseem's life fell into a pattern: sales rounds for MCG, weekly visits to his grandfather Girdhari, and spending every other evening with Swati. He could think of nothing else. He wanted to be with her always and invented excuses to meet her. On days they didn't have to go to the slum, he invited her to plays and exhibitions or took her out for dinner. She lent him books on Marx, Lenin and Mao, plays by Brecht, poems by Pablo Neruda. He read eagerly what she gave him so that he could spend time with her discussing them when they met again.

Aseem allowed Swati to invade his mind. He too began to romanticize about a world where all property was owned by the community and each person was given his or her due. But more than this, he found himself falling in love with Swati. He found everything about her attractive: her unaffected charm, the loveliness of her face, her intelligence, her commitment to her cause.

Swati felt the warmth of his affection. She saw her image in the depths of his dark brown eyes. She sensed the passion of his undeclared love. She liked spending time with him; she liked his openness and sensitivity and childlike innocence. She was attracted to his handsome face and aquiline nose and his tall, broad physique. She felt a stirring inside her, but she was afraid of getting too close to him. She was unsure if Aseem would be able to walk along with her on the road she'd chosen for herself.

20

MENAKA SAT ACROSS ISHITA on the first floor of Punjabi by Nature looking relaxed and comfortable. The restaurant had a kitsch look about it with a display kitchen and large glass mirrors.

'You haven't really turned vegetarian, have you?' enquired Menaka, reclining on a leather sofa to suck at a bone of the masala bataer.

'I have . . . completely,' said Ishita. 'But I don't miss it. I really don't. I feel healthier and have even lost two kilograms.'

'Wow! Good for you! I don't think I could give up non-veg. I don't have your will power,' said Menaka, putting the quail bone down on her plate. Assuming her most charming tone, she continued, 'Darling, there's something I'd like you to do for me.'

'Sure. What's that?'

'First, promise me that you'll do it.'

'Promise,' said Ishita, laughing. 'What is it?'

'I want you to spy on Aseem.'

'What?'

'Well . . . you don't have to do it yourself,' said Menaka. 'But you could ask someone else . . . your driver perhaps . . . to do it, you know.'

'I don't understand. Why don't you say what *exactly* it is you want me to do.'

'What I just said. I've a deep suspicion that he's involved with a girl.'

'What's wrong with that?'

'The girl is that commie Divya's daughter Swati,' said Menaka. 'She'll lead him astray. She's such a *bitch*.'

'How do you know?'

'I just know, don't ask how . . . All you have to do is ask your driver to follow Aseem a few evenings. A good point to locate him will be at my father's MeRi Plaza.'

'I can't possibly.'

'Of course, you can. Aseem needs to be rescued from that girl. Once I know it's her, I'll plan on something.'

'It seems so mean.'

'Please,' said Menaka. 'Remember, you promised.'

'All right,' said Ishita, after deliberating for a moment.

'Thank you, dear,' said Menaka, smiling. 'You're such a sweetheart.'

A few days later, after their work in the slum was complete, Swati invited Aseem to her flat. She led him up two flights of a narrow, kota-stone staircase. She stopped at the door of her flat, took out the keys from her purse and opened the latch. Stepping in, she switched on the lights and beckoned Aseem to come in. Aseem wiped his feet vigorously on a doormat just outside the door and shuffled into a largish hall, a few steps behind her.

Dropping her bag on a chair and draping her chunni on its back, she walked across the hall into the kitchen. Aseem continued to stand in the hall and look around. The flat was sparse but elegantly furnished. The walls were bare except for framed prints of two Chinese woodcuts. Most of the seating was on the floor; there were colourful cushions and rugs strewn about and two low, jute-strung chairs. There was a teak table in the centre on which lay some pamphlets and a few metal artefacts. Further down the hall was a round dining table. The hall opened on to a terrace at the far end; on one side was a bedroom and alongside it was the kitchen.

Aseem sat down on one of the jute chairs from where he could get a good view of Swati in the kitchen. After a while, he got up and picked up the pamphlets lying on the centre table and flipped through them. The pamphlets contained revolutionary Maoist literature. He was still looking at them when Swati came from the kitchen carrying two mugs of hot coffee.

'Thanks,' Aseem said, quickly putting back the printed material in its original location and taking a mug from Swati.

'Would you like to hear some music?' Swati asked.

'Sure,' said Aseem.

Swati placed her mug on the centre table; moving to a corner, she put on some Carnatic music on a CD player. Making herself comfortable on the rug, she asked, 'You don't mind the music, do you?'

'I like it,' said Aseem.

Swati took out a packet of cigarettes from her bag and lit one.

'I didn't know you smoked,' said Aseem.

'Once in a while,' Swati said, proferring the cigarette packet. 'You want one?'

'No thanks,' said Aseem, smiling at her as she blew out smoke.

'Would you like to eat something?' asked Swati.

'Relax, I'm fine,' said Aseem. He pointed to the pamphlet on the table. 'So, you're a Maoist, is it?'

'Yes . . . in a way,' said Swati, shrugging her shoulders. 'Anything wrong in being one?'

'That's not what I meant.'

'The way things are in this country, a revolution as advocated by Mao seems to be the only answer.'

'Are you really sure? It doesn't seem to have worked elsewhere.'

'It did in China.'

'India is different. And haven't the Chinese started opening up and following the capitalist path of development?'

'The Maoists in Nepal were able to achieve something.'

'Yes, but they too have finally joined the democratic process, haven't they? If you feel so strongly about it, why don't you enter politics and join the mainstream National Communist Party like your mother?'

'You can't be serious. The party's no different from other political parties, hankering after power, chasing big industrialists, forcibly evicting poor farmers from their lands to build factories. How can you call them communists? I'm surprised you even suggested it.'

'Okay, okay,' said Aseem, putting up his hands. 'Forget I said it.'

'It's all right. I'm convinced we can't bring about a revolution through the kind of democracy that we have in this country.'

'It's sad if what you're saying is true.'

'It *is* true.'

Two weeks later, on a cold December morning, Menaka received a call from Ishita.

'You were right,' Ishita said. 'I had my driver tail your nephew. Aseem's spending practically every evening with Swati, often staying in her flat till late into the night.'

'I knew it. *The bitch.* Thank you so much, darling,' said Menaka. 'It confirms my worst fears. They *are* having an affair. No doubt about it. Can you ask your driver to continue to keep an eye on him? I have a plan.'

A few days later, Menaka called up Gitanjali and shared her plan.

'Why would you want to do that?' Gitanjali asked, sounding perplexed. 'I'm told Aseem is going great guns at MCG. He is the star salesperson, you know. Giving him unachievably high targets would completely ruin his career.'

'That girl is unnecessarily distracting Aseem. He has to be brought back on track somehow.'

'I don't normally interfere in the MCG business, you know.'

'I know, darling. But this *is* important. I wouldn't ask you otherwise. Believe me, it's for Aseem's good. And it won't harm MCG either.'

21

IMPAKT WAS HAVING A SPECIAL meeting on the Shivaramakrishna project in their company boardroom in Pankaj Complex on a foggy January morning, a week into the new year. Additional chairs had been squeezed in to accommodate their key clients, Sri Kripananda and Ishita. Menaka was also present. The ImpaKt team had prepared an audiovisual presentation of their proposal on the new image of the swami and how they planned to market him.

Mike, the creative head, was the first to begin. Running his hand through his long hair, he remarked that the name Shivaramakrishna was not evocative enough, and suggested Sri Sri Satyananda Narayanaji or simply Sri Sri Narayanaji as a replacement.

'We've taken the cue from his humble origins in Narayanpur. Of course, we hope that the squared "Sri" will yield benefits in geometrical proportion,' said Aroon, with a wink.

Aparna took the floor next. She'd worked on a digital image of the swami. Gone was the coarse and rough-hewn hairy, hoary look. His hair was flowing and shiny to give it a special elegance. His beard had been shortened and shaped neatly. In the images the swami wore flowing white robes that showed glimpses of a well-built and clean-shaven chest. 'We should requisition the services of Mohit Dhaul for designing his attire. He's the best fashion designer in the city,' continued Aparna. 'I also suggest that we use a new material—ahimsa silk—for his clothing. This will be our USP.'

'We've done some research,' explained Aroon. 'Ahimsa silk doesn't involve the slaughter of any living being. It uses a process that allows the moth to fly away before the cocoons are boiled for reeling out the silken threads. This "non-violent" material could itself become a statement of Swamiji's new image when he speaks the language of peace and love.'

'This is a marvellous idea,' said Sri Kripananda, nodding his head vigorously in agreement.

Aparna, meanwhile, had lit a cigarette and was slowly releasing smoke rings. She then showed a truly contemporary and easy-to-replicate graphic logo of the white hare that could be used to spread the swami's message. To enhance his visual appeal and marketability, the services of two nimble-bodied yoga practitioners would be requisitioned to demonstrate the special exercises alongside the swami.

'Not only that,' added Aroon, 'we hope we can persuade the swami to develop a unique brand of exercises.'

'Besides the branding and visual appeal, we'll need to work on his language and intonation,' said Mike. 'We've done some research on this as well. The best person to do the job for us would be the esteemed professor of linguistics, Professor Nicholas Paul. He's a trifle pricey, but I suppose that doesn't matter. And the best person to work on his diction would be Ms Sabina Contractor. I believe she's a magician when it comes to speech—she's trained beauty queens to help them win international crowns.'

'That'd be great,' said Ishita, endorsing the idea.

Uma was the last to have her say. She'd worked out the media plan to the last detail. Several hours on the leading spiritual channel Vishwas would be booked to air the swami's discourses every day, while the news channel Kal Ka Aaj had agreed to set aside prime slots for the swami to demonstrate his brand of yoga exercises along with the two models. Then there'd be interviews on television, a host of media events, the launch of a website, www.narayanaji.com, and promotional VCDs. Finally, to clinch it, there'd be a cross-promotion of brands: while Sri Sri Narayanaji would endorse the fruit drink Pee Kay, trashing the multinational cola drinks for containing pesticides, all advertisements of Pee Kay in turn would show the swami refreshing himself with the fruit drink and conveying the messsage, 'Pee Kay peeyo-pilao aur fresh ho jao!'

'So, what do you think?' said Aroon, stroking his French beard with self-satisfied smugness and pride as the audiovisual presentations finally came to an end. The trio of Sri Kripananda, Yogesh and Ishita were beaming. They approved the plan without a single change.

Aseem's amazing success story at MCG seemed to have backfired on him. Of late, he'd begun to find that his targets had become impossibly huge. 'You can do it,' is all his boss would say with a rueful grin. Even Girdhari couldn't help him out any longer, and for the first time Aseem began to feel real pressure at work. He was now struggling to meet his monthly sales budgets. Worried about retaining his job, he began working doubly hard. Sometimes, he'd work so late that he was unable to reach the school on the appointed days. He feared that Swati would think he was losing interest.

It was late in the evening and Aseem was still on duty making sales calls. He stood outside Verma General Store in a crowded shopping area near MeRi Plaza, waiting for an opportunity to speak with the stockily built owner, Vermaji, who was attending to a twelve-year-old podgy-faced boy who'd come to buy a packet of noodles. After the young customer left, Vermaji finally turned to Aseem. 'How can I help you, beta?'

'It's been more than two weeks, Vermaji, since you gave me an order,' said Aseem.

'I wish I could help, beta. But your company's packets are still on my shelves. See for yourself,' Vermaji said. 'My main business nowadays comes from small packets, sachets. People have stopped making large purchases. The only thing they want in large sizes are the bargains. Ask your company to switch to smaller packets and you'll have me placing an order every day. Come back after a week and we'll see. Not today, beta.' Vermaji turned his attention to another customer, a plump lady with a heavily made-up face.

Feeling dejected, Aseem decided to call it a day. It was his day off at the school, but he didn't want to go home yet. He called up Swati. She told him that she was going for a meeting and couldn't meet him.

'I've had a bad day,' said Aseem. 'Nothing seems to be working out. Can't I accompany you?'

'Why don't you go home, put your feet up and relax. I'll give you a call when I'm back.'

'Is there a problem if I come along with you?' Aseem persisted.

'You're welcome, Aseem, but it's not something you'll enjoy,' Swati said.

'I'd still like to come.'

'Okay. I'll wait for you.'

Feeling perked up, Aseem hopped on to his motorbike and raced to pick her up from her flat.

The meeting was being held in a large hall near Mandi House to protest against the arrest of Dr Vinay Ahson—a medical doctor and social activist based in Jagdalpur—on the charge that he was helping the Maoists. His arrest had taken place after he'd voiced concerns about police atrocities against the adivasis in Maoist-controlled villages. The proceedings lasted nearly an hour with speeches by human rights workers and social activists. It was decided at the meeting that the protestors would congregate in front of Jantar Mantar the following week and organize a protest march to Parliament the next day.

'So, will you also be marching to Parliament?' asked Aseem as they stepped out of the hall.

'I probably will.'

'I thought you didn't believe in protests,' said Aseem as they walked together to the parking lot.

'That's true. Nothing really comes out of protests. You think the police will release the doctor after the march?' remarked Swati bitterly.

'Then why do you attend such meetings?'

'To express solidarity, I suppose.'

Aseem didn't respond.

'You said you were worried about your job,' said Swati, changing track, as he reached for his helmet hanging on the handlebar of his bike.

'No calamity as yet. But my targets have become really huge and I'm having to work very late. I'm not happy missing the classes at school.'

'Your job is more important. The slum folk can wait.'

Aseem was surprised with Swati's remark but didn't respond. He kick-started the motorcycle and waited for Swati to climb on behind him. When they reached Swati's flat, Aseem brought his bike to a halt and removed the helmet from his head, but kept the engine running.

'You must be hungry. You couldn't have eaten since lunch. Why don't you come up for a bite?' Swati asked after she dismounted. 'I'll rustle up some sandwiches.'

Aseem accepted the invitation gladly. Once they were inside the flat, Swati made a beeline for the kitchen, calling out to him, 'Make yourself comfortable.'

Aseem settled himself on a chair at the dining table, keeping his eyes on her. There were neat overhead storage compartments and a closed cupboard on the kitchen wall and a small fridge in one corner. He saw her take out some slices of bread, a tin of cheese spread, cucumbers and tomatoes from the fridge, and place them on the black marble counter next to a gas stove. He fidgeted for a while on the chair and then got up and walked up to her. 'Need help?'

'Not really,' said Swati, slicing a tomato. 'I'm nearly done. But if you can make some coffee, I'll go and have a quick shower.'

'Sure,' said Aseem. 'Just tell me where things are. I'll finish the sandwiches and make the coffee.'

'The coffee and sugar are up there,' said Swati, pointing to a cupboard overhead. 'The milk is in the fridge.'

'Cool,' said Aseem. 'You go and freshen up. You're looking tired.'

When Swati left, Aseem stood for a while, feeling nervous and shaky. He'd never worked in a kitchen in his life. He'd seen his mother make coffee, so he had an idea of what he had to do. He got hold of a saucepan and half filled it with water and milk from the fridge. Then he lit the gas stove placed the pan on the flame. So far so good.

He stood with his feet apart, arms akimbo, looking down at the diluted milk in the dish. Soon, the white liquid came to a boil; he immediately reached for the knob of the stove, fumbling with it before he turned it off.

He left the kitchen and walked across the dining hall to Swati's bedroom door, which was ajar. She was still in the bathroom.

'Coffee is nearly ready,' he called out. 'Are you coming?'

'Just give me a moment,' hollered Swati from the bathroom.

Aseem waited for a while outside the door, studying her bedroom to see if it could give him clues about her. There was a solitary bed with a printed bedcover neatly tucked in and a small side table with a wooden lamp on it. An open book lay face-down, but he couldn't read the title from where he stood. After a while, he returned to the kitchen. He covered the saucepan with a lid and proceeded to finish the half-done sandwiches. He looked for two mugs on the overhead shelf and took out the coffee, the sugar and two spoons, and waited for Swati.

He didn't have to wait long. Swati was behind him; he smelled her fragrance wafting to him like a drove of butterflies with diaphanous wings. He turned around, her face was clean and glistening after the shower; her hair was open and still wet. She was wearing a loose white top over a skirt. She came close behind him, very close, nearly touching him, and planted a kiss on the back of his neck.

Aseem turned around, and before he knew it he was kissing her on her lips. A passionate madness came over him as he pushed her against the kitchen counter, kissing her on her eyes, her neck, her mouth. She grabbed his hand and placed it on her breast. He fumbled with the buttons of her top, pulling aside her bra, and moved his head down to the nipples of her exposed breasts.

Swati led Aseem to her bedroom. After that, they made love for a long time, passionately, eagerly, hungrily. They were animal-like in their lovemaking, carnal and fierce. Then they lay down side by side for a long time, without exchanging a word, alone in their thoughts; silent and still, except for the sound and movement of their heavy breaths.

22

HISTORY WAS IN THE MAKING; the long-awaited image makeover of Swami Shivaramakrishna to Sri Sri Satyanand Narayanaji was finally happening. Cynthia, the hairstylist, was given the first go. Menaka accompanied the swami on his first visit to Cynthia's beauty saloon for the makeover. One look at the big-built Cynthia fluttering her eyelashes and flaunting her recently acquired twin assets, and the swami wanted to go back to his ashram. It took all of Menaka's charm and persuasive skills to get him to enter the saloon.

Cynthia ran her thick fingers with their manicured, pink-varnished nails through the Swami's beard and hair that grew like an untended hedge. Using digitally morphed images of the swami taken from various angles, she first looked at various options to determine the shape and size of his beard and hair. Once she had the image she wanted, she went zzzz-rrr-clip-zzz-rrr-clip with her scissors. She first worked on the beard, shaping it to an even taper. The swami's hair needed more work: the waves and curls in the hair had to be smoothed out using an extra-strong hair straightener. After she was done, one of Cynthia's assistants took over, clipping the hair in the swami's armpits and on his chest to prepare him for waxing.

When the swami and Menaka were finally leaving, Cynthia made the unkindest cut. 'Dah-ling,' she complained bitterly, holding Menaka back, '*no one*, just no one, dear, would be able to stand that *awful*, oh so awful odour. Do buy him several bottles of cologne.'

Fashion designer par excellence, Mohit Dhaul, who'd held shows in Paris, took over from there. Over the next few weeks, the swami was flitting from the ashram to his studio for measurements and trials and fittings, as Monsieur Dhaul carefully crafted a white flowing outfit for the swami, much like what Caligula had worn. Saffron made way for white to symbolize peace and spirituality.

There was one significant fallout of the Swami's makeover from Sri Shivaramakrishna to Sri Sri Satyanand Narayanaji. The transformation had been so dramatic and compelling that Sri Kripananda found himself unwittingly falling in love with the new cologne-fragranced swami. What was once only Sri Kripananda's devotion to the mind and soul of the swami now extended to the physical self. It was not as though the feeling was not reciprocal: the swami, too, his passions tickled awake by Cynthia's soft touches, had fallen for the graceful ways of Sri Kripananda.

Menaka was quick to notice the new fondess. 'I'm not such a prude, you know,' she remarked to Ishita. 'But shouldn't they conceal their affections?' The pious couple was accordingly alerted and their amorousness confined to the swami's private air-conditioned chambers under the watchful eyes of the new-age swami's old-age guru.

Menaka sat on a soft-cushioned, revolving office chair in a separate cabin in the new extension ImpaKt had recently hired in the wake of the Narayanaji project. An as yet unused digital notebook adorned her desk. She too had had a makeover of sorts. She wore a new, Cynthia-special, layered hairdo and a well-fitting black skirt and coat, having shed inches from her waist and buttocks thanks to her workouts on the treadmill with Rambo for company.

A gilt-edged portrait of the recently incarnated Sri Sri Narayanaji in his new avatar looked down benignly from the wall behind her. A good beginning had been made with the Narayanaji project, but now there was little for her to do but wait for the others—the language experts and the event managers—to do their part. Impatient and unused to sitting for long periods in small spaces, she was like an unsettled moth. She decided to flit across to Aroon's cabin in the main ImpaKt office.

Just then Ishita dropped in, bursting with the scurrilous tales her driver had brought back after his spying adventures. She began popping out the details to Menaka like overripe peas in a pod even before she'd sat down, 'You know, your nephew's begun to even spend nights at that woman's barsati. My poor driver Inder was parked outside her flat the whole night. Discreetly, of course. The young man made an appearance only at nine in the morning.'

'The *bloody* bitch!' exclaimed Menaka in anger. 'Aseem is *such* a fool. I should've known it from the way she was making eyes at him at the party. Have you seen her? She's so plain-looking and dark like coal.'

'No,' said Ishita, shaking her head disdainfully. 'But I can imagine. Thank God, at least now you know what she's been up to.'

'You bet I do,' said Menaka, taking out a crisp five-hundred-rupee note from her purse and offering it to her friendly undercover agent. 'Do give this as a tip to your driver.'

'Don't be silly. This is not needed. Inder's been taken care of already,' said Ishita, pushing the note away.

After Ishita left, Menaka strode down the corridor to Aroon's cabin. Without waiting for him to look up, she remarked, 'Haven't we forgotten Aseem? Isn't it time you roped him into the campaign?'

'Sure, dear, we could certainly use his services,' said Aroon. 'I've always been keen. But how do we convince him to join ImpaKt?'

'I've a plan,' Menaka said. 'I think I can arrange to get him to quit MCG.'

'Quit MCG? A plan?' said Aroon. 'Great! You shouldn't have got him the MCG job in the first place. He would've got so frustrated trying to find one that he would've agreed to join ImpaKt by now.'

'So, it's entirely my fault, is it?'

'I didn't say that, dear.'

'Oh, let it be,' said Menaka, frowning. 'You just figure out how you're going to persuade Aseem to come on board ImpaKt.'

Aseem was delirious with desire. Swati's image haunted him in his waking hours; it appeared in his dreams. Even on the days she was not with him in the slum, he could feel her presence and fragrance everywhere, in the lone chair she'd sat on the previous evening, in the jute rugs on the school floor, in the clothes of the schoolchildren. Her soft, silky hair and kohl-lined eyes always came back to him; he couldn't sleep or eat or drink without thinking of her; he couldn't breathe. She had pervaded his senses, his being; he longed to be with her constantly—his love for her was all-consuming. When he was not meeting his sales targets, his love for her ensured that despondency didn't set in.

It kept him going, giving him sustenance, pushing him to keep trying harder.

Menaka called Gitanjali late at night. 'Sorry dear, it's about Aseem again.' She told Gitanjali what she wanted done this time—a transfer out of the city.

'But why're you doing this to Aseem?' asked Gitanjali. 'He's already having a tough time at MCG.'

'Don't ask, dear. I've good reasons,' said Menaka. 'But they're too complicated to explain.'

Menaka had worked it all out in her mind like a business strategist. Once Aseem received his transfer orders, he'd have only two options: one, that he accept the transfer, and two, that he resign from MCG. It was a win–win situation. In the first case, a posting outside would send Aseem far away from Swati's clutches. In the second, she hoped that between herself and Aroon they'd manage to convince Aseem to join ImpaKt.

A few days days later, when Aseem reported for work he was rudely confronted with a set of transfer papers to Chandigarh. It was the last thing he'd expected. There had been no hint whatsoever of a transfer. His life had just about begun settling on an even keel: he was happy with Swati; he was enjoying the adulation he received when teaching English at the slum school; he was somehow even managing to achieve the stiff sales targets. Even if heavens were to fall, he didn't want to leave Delhi.

He didn't know what to do. He'd got the MCG job with great difficulty; he was uncertain about being able to manage another one in Delhi easily. He was unable to think clearly. He desperately wanted to talk to someone. He called up Swati only to be told that she was busy at work and would be staying late in office. Disappointed, he slipped into a state of gloom.

Aseem received a surprise call from Aroon at lunchtime the same day. 'I just called to enquire how things were going,' Aroon said. 'It's been a long time since we saw you. Why don't you come home this evening?'

'Anything special?'

'Nothing at all, but, yes, if you want to know, I have a proposal for you.'

'A proposal? What are you saying, Uncle? I'm in no mood to marry now.'

'Of course not! It's not a marriage proposal, son,' said Aroon. 'It's something else. I think you'll like it. Why don't you come over if you aren't doing anything special?'

Aseem thought for a bit. The transfer order in the morning had left him despondent. There was no harm in hearing out what Aroon had to offer. In any case, he wasn't inclined to go to the slum that evening.

'Are you there, Aseem? What're you thinking?' Aroon asked again.

'Yes, Uncle Aroon,' said Aseem. 'I'll come by.'

Later that evening, Aseem was standing outside the door of the Kumar household, his briefcase and helmet in hand, pressing the musical chime. Menaka, looking her ravishing best in black jeans and a tight-fitting, hand-embroidered white top opened door. A yelping Rambo greeted Aseem with a bounding leap.

'Hi Aseem,' greeted Menaka, giving him a kiss on the cheek. 'You seem to have completely forgotten us.'

'Of course not,' said Aseem walking into the living room, where Aroon was waiting for him with outstretched arms. They hugged him warmly.

'Good to see you, boy,' said Aroon. 'How about some cold beer?'

'Cool,' said Aseem, settling down in a sofa.

Chilled beer and frothy, friendly banter with Aroon made Aseem feel more relaxed, while Menaka left for the kitchen.

'So, how's our star faring at big MCG?' asked Aroon.

Aseem put on a wry expression on his face by way of a reply.

'Not going too well, son? You don't look happy,' commented Aroon.

'The targets have been tough lately,' Aseem said. 'I was managing somehow. But now they're transferring me to Chandigarh.'

'Chandigarh? What on earth for?' exclaimed Menaka walking in with a plate of kebabs and setting it on the centre table.

'Don't ask me,' said Aseem, shrugging his shoulders.

'You don't have to go if you don't want to, you know,' said Aroon.

'I don't have a choice, do I?'

'Of course, you do. You've forgotten. I told you I've a proposal for you.'

'Oh, yes, the proposal,' said Aseem, gulping down the dregs of his beer.

'Son, I believe you've been teaching children in jhuggi-jhopris,' said Aroon, getting up to refill Aseem's glass. 'It's remarkable. It makes us feel very proud. Must be very satisfying. You know, son, I too have always wanted to do my bit for society, but I never got the opportunity. I think the time has come now. You know what I want to do? Set up a social advertising cell at ImpaKt that would focus on issues such as educating the poor, spreading AIDS awareness, working for peace.'

'Sounds good,' said Aseem.

'And you know something?' continued Aroon. 'I want you to work in this cell. Maybe run it, if you want.'

'Me? Why me? I'll need to think.'

'What's there to think, son? And if you were to set this up for ImpaKt, I'd be happy to pay you much more than you're making at MCG.'

'But I just don't understand? Why me?'

'I'll be frank, son. I need someone whom I can trust. You're family. And you can continue to stay on in Delhi and also teach the slum children.'

'I still need to give it thought.'

'Come, come, let's have dinner now,' said Menaka, interrupting the conversation. 'I've made your favourite chicken biryani.'

Nothing more was said on the topic as the three of them ate dinner. When Aseem left, Menaka pounced on Aroon. 'Why did you say he could continue teaching in the slum? Don't you know the idea was to also get him away from that Swati woman.'

'C'mon, dear. Quid pro quo.'

'What's that?'

'Forget it.'

It was late when Aseem reached home. A groggy-eyed Avinash opened the door for him and asked, 'Have you had dinner?'

'Yes,' said Aseem brusquely. 'I'd told Ma. Didn't she tell you?'

'She did, but I was checking. Good night.'

'Good night,' said Aseem, going to his room and banging the door shut. For a moment it did strike him that he'd been unnecessarily rude to his father a moment ago, but he didn't allow the thought to dwell in his mind for long. He was upset and angry about his transfer orders, and his father couldn't help him in any way: neither with his transfer nor in getting him another job. Dumping his briefcase on the bed, he immediately called Swati. He needed her advice in double measure: on his transfer orders as also on Aroon's proposal.

'A transfer to Chandigarh? Oh hell!' exclaimed Swati. 'Whatever for?'

'I've no idea,' said Aseem. He then told her about Aroon's proposal for setting up a social advertising cell.

'It'll be sad if you were to leave Delhi. But Chandigarh's not a bad town and it's not so far. You need to take your own decision,' Swati said. 'If you ask me, I couldn't care a damn if it's MCG or ImpaKt. They're both part of the same rotten system. You need a job to keep body and soul together.'

'You can say that,' said Aseem, surprised by her answer. 'You've got a proper job.'

'Who told you that?' said Swati. 'My job is as boring as you can possibly imagine. But I still do it. Aseem . . . take my advice . . . all jobs are alike. Choices are limited. You need to buy time for yourself. What you need to see is how much time you are left with to nurture your soul.'

'I thought you didn't believe in the soul.'

'Aseem, if you exasperate me with such talk, I'll hang up.'

'Sorry.'

'You sleep over it now. We'll speak again tomorrow.'

Meanwhile, Avinash had come to Aseem's room carrying a folder in his hand. He stood outside the door quietly for some time but hearing Aseem speaking over the phone he returned to his bedroom.

Aseem went to the toilet and splashed water on his face, trying to clear his mind. Things were changing so rapidly. Here he was now seriously considering joining ImpaKt. A few months ago, he could never have imagined that it would come to this; it was something he'd violently opposed then.

23

ASEEM LAY SPRAWLED LIKE a prince on a rug in the living room of Swati's flat, surrounded by colourful patchwork cushions in various shapes and patterns. Swati had taken the day off and had invited him over for lunch. Only about a month earlier, when the transfer orders had landed on his desk, he'd been terribly vexed about the turn his life was taking. But there was no way he was going to leave Delhi and be away from Swati. The choice between joining ImpaKt and looking for another job hadn't been difficult. At the back of his mind had been the bitter memory of the grind of job applications, the unending rounds of interviews, the uncertainties of the outcome. Once he'd made the decision to join ImpaKt, he'd felt lighter, like a kite gliding among fleecy clouds in the sky.

Aseem moved his eyes across the bare walls of Swati's living room. He looked up at the white ceiling, wondering what the future had in store for him. For the past couple of weeks, life had been on a roll. Aroon had allowed him to take a break for a couple of weeks before he joined ImpaKt. He'd been spending a lot of time in Swati's flat, joining her whenever she was free, in the evenings, on weekends. He was savouring every moment with her, without any worry about the next day. He felt happy and relaxed in her presence. She was easy to be with: she had no expectations, she asked him no questions and accepted him for what he was.

At the same time, she wouldn't allow him to come too close to her; she'd erected an invisible fence that she wouldn't allow to be pulled down. At first he couldn't comprehend her; she was so different from him. He was an open book with a large typeface and many blank pages; easy to read and to be written on. She was a crowded closet that was locked; she was unwilling to give him the keys to her mind. Once he'd understood this, he had given up trying to get closer. Just being in Swati's presence was bliss for him. He didn't want anything more.

Avinash sat in his office thinking about his son; for some reason he hadn't been able to develop a warm relationship with him. Aseem hardly spent time with him and always spoke to him uncaringly, dismissively. He wondered where he'd gone wrong. He shook his head. There was no point blaming

Menaka. He himself was to blame. At some point of time, while Aseem was growing up, he'd stopped being demonstrative with his affections.

He looked around him. His eyes got riveted to the profile of a young new recruit about half his age, wearing a well-fitting orange churidar–kameez and a yellow chunni, working ardently on her computer. He gazed at her for a while, imagining the contours of her body under her orange ensemble. But he felt no arousal, no sinful stirrings of the flesh. And yet, even as she had her eyes on the monitor, she seemed to become conscious of his stare, for she adjusted her chunni to cover her chest. Avinash noticed this and immediately felt disgusted with himself.

From where he was sitting, Aseem could see Swati standing with her back to him in the kitchen. She was cooking lunch with unusual zest, bent over a pressure pan, a steel ladle in her hand, frying mutton pieces and turning them over and over together with the spices she had measured out in tiny spoons. She normally didn't cook mutton or chicken at home, preferring to order the dishes from a dhaba nearby.

Swati was sweating profusely; her kameez was wet and sticking to her back and she wiped the beads of perspiration on her brow from time to time with the back of her hand. Aseem smelled the tangy, rich aroma of meat curry wafting in from the kitchen on the heavy moist air like a fleet of spice-laden ships from a bygone era, whetting his appetite. Swati lowered the flame and shut the lid on the pressure pan.

'I didn't know you were so fond of cooking,' Aseem called out.

'You don't know many things,' said Swati, turning around with a smile. She came out into the living area and sat on a chair at the dining table, drying her perspiration under the fan. After a short while, she got up and looked down to the road below, through a gap in the window curtains. Aseem followed her eyes; there were ominous masses of grey clouds looming in the darkened sky. For the past few days the weather had been damp and sticky, threatening to bring rain.

'It'll be a relief if it rains,' said Aseem.

'Hmmm,' mumbled Swati absently. Aseem rose from the rug and went across the room to stand behind her at the window.

'It's hot,' said Swati turning around and moving away a little. 'How about some beer? There's some in the fridge.'

'Sure. Would you also like some?' Aseem said, moving to the fridge in the kitchen.

'Yes, please,' Swati said, returning to the window.

He carried the beer bottle and glasses to the dining table and poured out the beer.

'Are you expecting someone?' Aseem asked, handing her a glass.

Before Swati could reply, a whistle from the pressure pan summoned her back to the kitchen. Aseem settled back on the rug.

Avinash rose from his chair, went up to the window, and looked out. He leant over the sill, taking in the helicopter view of the park beneath his office. There were young boys flying kites in the lawns below. His eyes focused on a red kite that belonged to a boy in a yellow shirt.

Avinash could never fly kites. When Aseem was approaching adolescence, he became keen that Aseem learn to fly them. Returning home one evening from work, when Aseem was barely eleven years old, he happened to pass a shop selling kites. On an impulse, he'd bought half a dozen coloured kites and a spool of kite string and brought them home, much to Ritika's surprise. That weekend, he took Aseem to a park near their flat with the kites. For some time father and son stood watching the other boys flying kites. Shedding his diffidence, Avinash approached one of the older boys and cajoled him to teach Aseem the skill to get the kites soaring to the sky. He himself agreed to act as a dutiful assistant, holding the kite over his head, while Aseem waited for a gust of wind and pulled at the kite to get it airborne, as instructed by the older boy. Aseem didn't succeed at first, but he was eager to learn.

'Higher, higher,' the older boy instructed Avinash. 'Hold it high over your head.'

Avinash held the kite as high as he could, standing on his toes, positioning the kite for take-off. The kite finally caught the wind and Aseem quickly tugged and jerked at it, sending it adrift in the sky. Avinash clapped his hands and ran swiftly to stand alongside his son to hold the spool of string between the crook of his thumb and forefinger of both hands and allow the line to roll out freely. After some time the kite was kissing the sky, flying high among the swirling clouds, a tiny speck becoming smaller and smaller.

Avinash looked up at the sky. A green kite flying close to the fourth-floor window of his office came swooping down on the red kite. Moments later, snip-snip-snip, the red kite floated rudderless, its line cut by the sharp-edged shards of glass lining the string of the green kite. The red kite was up for grabs now, and the boys below began their chase, their eyes focused on the vanquished kite, which finally landed near a group of young men lying on their backs under the shade of a tree. One of them picked it up by its trailing bit of string and attempted to fly it while still on his back. The boys who had given chase crowded around the youth, who was holding on to the string of the kite, his eyes pleading. The youth teased them by moving the kite away before handing it to the smallest of the boys. The boy scampered away holding the kite aloft in the wind, while the others chased him.

There was a time when Avinash had envied the freedom of the unemployed youth lying under the cool shade of the trees. But no longer. Having nothing to do in office for the past many days had been driving him crazy. He now yearned to go back to the drudgery and tedium of filling in meaningless data in old registers; it helped to pass the time.

He turned away from the window and returned to his desk.

Seeing that Swati hadn't moved from the window for a long time, Aseem got up from the rug and walked across the hall towards her. 'Are you expecting someone?' he asked again as he came and stood beside Swati.

'Yes,' Swati said, moving her head sideways to face him. 'Gopal.'

'Gopal? You've never mentioned anyone by this name earlier.'

'There are many things I don't talk about,' said Swati, turning back to the window.

'Your prerogative,' said Aseem sounding hurt.

'It's not that. I'd been meaning to tell you about him for some time. That's the reason I invited you over today so that you could meet him.'

'Who's he?'

'A friend . . .'

'Just a friend? What does he do?'

'Okay. I'll tell you if you promise to keep it to yourself.'

'You can trust me.'

'Gopal is a Maoist revolutionary.'

'Maoist! Well, that explains the pamphlets I saw here the other day,' said Aseem, taken aback. 'So, what does he do? Is he also one of those terrorists who go around blowing up trains and shooting people?'

'For heaven's sake, Gopal's not a terrorist. Maoists are *not* terrorists,' Swati said emphatically. 'They're fighting for a cause that they think is just. You're the last person who should be calling them terrorists.'

'Why do you say that?' asked Aseem.

'Because . . .' said Swati and paused.

'Because?'

'Even your father was a Naxalite.'

'What're you saying?'

'Didn't you know?'

'I don't believe it.'

'It's true. I believe for a brief period in the early seventies he'd joined the Naxalite movement.'

'How do *you* know?' asked Aseem.

'My mother told me,' said Swati, deliberately.

Sitting at an empty desk, Avinash closed his eyes. He'd stopped dreaming of becoming part of a great communist revolution when he married Ritika. But even in the days that he dreamed, they were someone else's dreams that he'd borrowed and made his own; they were never wholly his. And when Aseem was born, he started dreaming of his son's future and happiness. His happiest days were when Aseem was growing up. He remembered the joy he felt at seeing Aseem's beaming face, when he walked for the first time, when he spoke out his name, 'Ba . . . Ba, Ba-Ba, Baba.' He remembered the vacations they'd taken to enchanting hill stations and the walks under shady trees with Aseem sitting atop his shoulders, holding his head with tiny hands. He remembered their holiday in Kerala: running through the foam-crested waves on the sandy beaches holding a gleeful Aseem by his hand, while Ritika shouted after them to come back and the sea slowly swallowed the sun. Yes, they were good times; they helped him to forget his unfulfilled dreams.

Suddenly, Avinash's mood changed: he recalled with bitterness the times when Menaka, in increasing measure, had intruded on his blissful moments of fatherhood.

The clock on the wall chimed to announce the 1.00 p.m. lunch break. Some of the office staff took out their lunch boxes and settled around one of the desks; others left the office premises for their preferred eating destinations. Avinash reached for his three-layered steel tiffin carrier placed beside his chair, fished out the morning newspaper lying in his, drawer, and got up from his chair. He took the lift and went down, crossed the main road leading to the park and began walking on the red sandstone verge.

A woman was standing under a jamun tree with the pallu of her sari spread before her like a supplicant, waiting patiently for a gust of wind to bring down the dark wine-coloured fruits. He crossed her and walked to a neem tree further ahead. Placing the tiffin carrier on the grass near the base of the tree, he spread the newspaper and sat down on it. He carefully laid out the three tiffin boxes in front of him and leisurely proceeded to eat his lunch, savouring every morsel. He watched the people ambling in the park, the boys flying kites, young men lying in the shade of trees. After he'd eaten, he packed the empty containers, leaned back against the tree trunk and shut his eyes.

'Strange. My father never told me anything about him being a Naxalite,' Aseem said.

'I'm not making it up,' said Swati.

'I didn't say so. But the Naxalites of the sixties and seventies were wiped out, weren't they?'

'Yes, several of the Naxalites of your father's generation were systematically finished off, especially those in West Bengal. They were either put behind bars or shot dead in police encounters. But now the movement has resurrected, risen like the phoenix from the ashes.'

'More like a deadly mutated virus, I'd say.'

'Don't say that. But, yes, the Naxalites are much stronger now. In certain pockets where they're strong, like some interior areas in Jharkhand or in Chhattisgarh where Gopal operates, they're practically running a parallel administration.'

'Do they need to use so much violence?'

'What do you want them to do? Preach peace and non-violence? What do you expect a hungry man to do? Take things lying down? Accept his karma? Pray for a better life after his rebirth?' Swati was vehement, almost shouting. Then she dropped her voice, 'Arm him and he'll fight and rebel.'

'You sound like a Maoist yourself,' said Aseem. 'How come you're not with them?'

'I have my reasons,' said Swati, going back to the window and drawing the curtains apart. She heard a gentle pitter-patter; it had started to drizzle. All of a sudden, there were intermittent flashes of lightning like white light from a stroboscope. Then, with a thunderous clap, the drops came down faster and bigger, hitting the window panes hard now, and then with their energy dissipated, immediately slid down the smooth sheets of glass. Aseem joined her at the window, watching the rain. The two of them stood there for quite some time, without speaking.

Avinash sat slouched under the tree with his eyes closed even as big black ants from the damp soil came creeping-crawling up to explore his legs. Gentle droplets of rain roused him into wakefulness. Soon, he saw lightning crackling in the sky, accompanied by peals of thunder. He got up quickly and, shaking his legs to clear off the ants, picked up the tiffin box.

Avinash walked slowly back to the office, unmindful of the drops of rain falling on him. Within moments, it started raining harder, and he broke into a gentle jog. He stopped abruptly, as he felt a shooting pain in his chest that moved rapidly to his left shoulder. He sat down on the sidewalk and waited for the pain to subside. Then he trudged back to the office, very, very slowly, fully drenched in the rain.

24

THE DOORBELL RANG IN Swati's flat. Aseem went to the door and opened it. A dark, lanky man with bushy eyebrows stood outside in drenched clothes, with a wet canvas haversack on his back. He had an untidy, week-old stubble and looked bedraggled.

'Swati . . .?' said the man hesitantly.

'Yes, she's inside,' said Aseem.

The man walked past Aseem, his wet jeans and shirt leaving a trail of rainwater on the tiled floor.

'Hi Gopal,' called out Swati, getting up.

Gopal removed the haversack from his back and sank into one of the chairs. Aseem went back to his spot on the rug.

'You're drenched, Gopal,' said Swati. 'Don't sit under the fan. You'll fall ill.'

'Nothing will happen to me. I'm used to walking for days in the rain,' Gopal said, pulling out his wet shirt from his trousers and looking curiously in Aseem's direction.

'Aseem, meet Gopal Subbarao, an old friend from college,' said Swati, introducing the two men. 'Aseem helps with my teaching in the slum school.'

The two men nodded at each other. Swati went into the bedroom and returned with a large bath towel which she handed to Gopal, 'Wipe yourself with this.'

'Thanks. But I'd like a bath,' said Gopal, pressing the towel to his head and then on his soaked clothes.

'Sure,' said Swati, even as Gopal took off his wet shirt, to expose a dirty-looking vest with holes. He rummaged in his haversack for some clothes and went into the bedroom.

Swati turned her attention to Aseem, whose eyebrows were raised, and spoke to him in a hushed voice, 'It's not what you think. Gopal and I are just old comrades from college. There's nothing more than that.'

Gopal came out of the bedroom after his bath, rubbing his head with the towel, smelling of after-shave. He'd removed the stubble from his face but had retained the moustache.

'Feeling much cleaner,' said Gopal, running a hand over his face. 'I found a new razor in the bathroom, so I took the liberty of using it. We've not been able to get provisions for the last few months because it's become almost impossible to visit the weekly haat.'

'The razor was Aseem's,' remarked Swati.

'Oh!' Gopal shrugged his shoulders.

Aseem didn't react. 'And so was the after-shave,' he would've liked to add.

'Aseem, will you fetch some beer for Gopal?' said Swati. 'I'll heat lunch.'

Aseem and Gopal sat with their drinks quietly while Swati worked in the kitchen. It was Gopal who finally broke the silence. Cradling his neck in his hands, he asked, 'So, comrade, what else do you do besides teaching in the slum?'

'As of now . . . nothing,' replied Aseem. 'Till a few days back, I was working as a sales executive for a consumer goods company. I'll soon be joining my uncle who runs an ad and marketing firm.'

'Are you happy doing all this sales and marketing stuff?' asked Gopal with a derisive smirk. 'Funny, isn't it? First you create a demand for a non-existent need and then you sell it for huge profits.'

'Well,' said Aseem, taken aback by the accusation. 'I don't know what you mean. Both advertising and selling have their roles in society. Advertising spreads awareness, selling fulfils a need.'

'Da-da-da-da,' Gopal mimicked Aseem's tone. 'All humbug. Its all a capitalist myth.'

'Gopal, do you never tire?' said Swati, coming out from the kitchen. 'Why don't the two of you help me lay the table?'

Once the table was laid, Swati waited for the two men to fill their plates with rice and mutton curry. Then she served herself and sat down next to Gopal. She kept a watchful eye on his plate, refilling it the moment its contents showed signs of depletion, with the fondness of a doting mother. Gopal enjoyed the meal noisily like a hungry adolescent: chomping at his food, cracking the bones, licking his fingers.

Aseem pecked at his food; he'd lost his appetite. He felt like an intruder. When the meal was over, he went to stand by the window while Gopal and Swati continued to sit around the dining table. 'I'd better be going,' Aseem said. 'The rain's stopped.'

'Going already?' Swati asked. 'Stay. What's the hurry?'

'Stay, comrade,' said Gopal, getting up and walking up to his haversack. He pulled out a soggy pack of cigarettes. 'Bloody hell!'

'Bye Swati,' said Aseem, retrieving his helmet from the rug and going to the door.

'Wait,' said Gopal. 'I'll come down with you. I hope there's a cigarette vendor around.'

'There should be one down the road. I'll come with you,' said Swati.

The three of them descended the staircase and walked to Aseem's motorbike.

'Why don't we meet again?' Gopal suggested to Aseem. 'Not tomorrow, but say day after? I'd like an update on the happenings in this part of the world.'

'Aseem, why don't you come over early morning day after?' Swati said, widening her eyes at him. 'You can meet us at seven at the ridge. We can go for a walk and come back here for breakfast. You can chat with Gopal about his work.'

Aseem hesitated. He found Gopal's presence overpowering; it made him feel ill at ease. But the look in Swati's eyes prevented him from saying no to the invitation. 'All right,' he agreed, starting his motorbike. 'I'll be there at the ridge gate at seven.'

'How do you know Aseem?' Gopal asked, puffing on his cigarette, when Swati and he had returned to the flat. He'd now stretched out on the rug earlier occupied by Aseem and was resting his head on a cushion.

'Met him at a party. As I mentioned, he works with me in the slum,' said Swati. 'But he has no revolutionary leanings.'

'We can always change that, can't we?' remarked Gopal.

'I'm not sure,' said Swati, changing the topic. 'Anyway, what brings you here?'

'Many things. Much of it has to do with countering the Shanti Kadam and taking concerted action against Operation Red Hunt.'

'I believe the security forces have become far more active.'

'Yes, but it's the Shanti Kadam that's made life hell for us in the village. It's pure vendetta. The villagers on our side of the Indravati River have been completely cut off. The Shanti Kadam acts with complete impunity because they have the complete support of the state machinery.'

'In what way?'

'You know it. The government has appointed many of them as SPOs. They're exploiting a loophole in some outdated century-and-half-old Special Police Act which allows their appointment as SPOs. They've armed them fully and are paying them two thousand rupees a month to attack us and anyone seen to be supporting us. The bloody SPOs are now strutting about the villages like peacocks as self-appointed protectors, coercing the villagers to attend Shanti Kadam meetings and support their activities.'

'And those who don't go?' interjected Swati.

'They are automatically taken to be one of us,' continued Gopal. 'Their houses are burnt and looted of all grain and chicken and pigs. Things are really bad. The fleeing villagers are then herded into their camps. The activists are giving a clear message to the villagers: "Move to the camps or face our wrath." This, in fact, is the hidden agenda of the state. And that's what Operation Red Hunt is all about.'

'What hidden agenda?'

'Can't you see it? They want us and the adivasis out of the villages to enable MNC and capitalist miners to move in. Anyone who's not in the Shanti Kadam camps is branded a Maoist. Try to understand. The region is very rich in mineral deposits: iron, limestone, bauxite, diamonds. Some years ago, when I was around the Bailadilla mines, I learnt that they were exporting iron ore to Japan and South Korea at throwaway prices. The government is in league with the miners and have partitioned all the land occupied by the adivasis at throwaway prices. Otherwise, do you think anyone would have bothered? Even otherwise, there is so much illegal mining going on with the connivance of the police.'

'What kind?'

'Oh, any kind. Not far from Satwal village, illegal tin mining has been going on for decades. The operation is financed by the thakurs. The villagers bring the ore and smelt it using hand-turned fans in charcoal furnaces. The thakurs smuggle it out on their motorcycles. The police turn a blind eye because they're paid off.'

'But it's not like you're innocent,' said Swati, looking Gopal straight in the eye. 'I know about the protection money you extort from the miners.'

'We do no such thing,' said Gopal refuting the accusation. 'This is all a creation of the media.'

'Come on,' said Swati. 'You don't have to hide it from me.'

'Well, one has to survive,' said Gopal.

'And wasn't your group involved in the recent kidnapping during which four armed security guards were killed?' persisted Swati.

'We were not involved,' said Gopal, stoutly denying the allegation.

'Forget it,' said Swati, not wanting a confrontation. She changed the topic. 'What are you going to do about the Shanti Kadam?'

'We'll strike back of course.'

'Then more innocent lives will be lost.'

'We're left with no choice. This is war, Swati. In war, innocents are often victims.'

'But dealing with the Shanti Kadam is not going to be easy. As you say, they've the backing of the state.'

'That's the reason I'm here. To organize support so that we can take concerted action,' said Gopal, reaching for his packet of cigarettes and lighting another one. 'This is also something I wanted to talk to you about. Why don't you join us?'

'No way. I'm happy here, teaching the children in the slum.'

'Who are you teaching? They are the ones who'll one day join the same goddamned corrupt system,' said Gopal, his eyes fiery. 'You're only perpetuating the system. Tomorrow they'll attack you.'

'That's no reason not to give the slum children education.'

'Fine, have it your way. But the least you can do is to sensitize them to the revolution. I'll pass on some pamphlets which you can distribute.'

'Most of the slum dwellers will not be able to even read them.'

'See, that's what I mean. All this slum work is not of much use. Come and join us instead. We need someone like you who can understand.'

'I'm happy here.'

'We need help,' Gopal persisted, his tone imploring. 'Start a school for the adivasi children in Satwal village. We don't have a trained teacher. We've already started constructing the school which can accommodate about sixty children.'

'No, Gopal,' said Swati vehemently. 'You know my views. I'm not convinced about your methods. Some of them are barbaric, gruesome. You give guns to children. You loot, you kidnap, you use terror to coerce villagers to follow you. You speak of an ideal, just order, and then proceed to violate basic human rights.'

'The local people are with us. We provide justice,' said Gopal. 'We have our praja courts.'

'Don't I know what goes on in your praja courts? So ruthless and inhuman. I can understand violence when you're fighting a war, but cruelty? No right-thinking human being can condone it.'

'Who's been feeding you all this rubbish?' Gopal asked with a frown, feeling aggrieved.

'I keep myself informed,' said Swati.

Gopal didn't respond immediately. He took a few puffs of his cigarette and sat up to stub it in the ashtray on the centre table.

'Listen, I understand how you feel. But sometimes we're left with no choice. You'd be appalled if I told you what the Shanti Kadam activists and SPOs and security forces resort to.'

'That's still no excuse,' said Swati, shaking her head. She went across the room to pick up a book. She returned to her seat and opened it to a tagged mark. 'I must read out to you something from Brecht:

And yet we know well:
Even hatred of vileness
Distorts a man's features.
Even anger at injustice
Makes hoarse his voice. Ah, we
Who desired to prepare the soil for kindness
Could not ourselves be kind.'

'Hmmm,' said Gopal and rubbed his freshly shaved chin. Then he continued, his voice softer now, pleading. 'Don't get involved, keep clear of our dalams. But come and stay in the village and run the school. We'll give you a nice hut near a pond. Yes, we now have water. We recently dug a pond. We're also trying to generate electricity through solar energy. You'll be happy. The villagers will be delighted.'

'You haven't changed, have you? Ever the dreamer,' said Swati, stretching and yawning in a bid to escape further talk on the topic. 'God, I'm tired. I have another long day tomorrow. What's your programme?'

'Tomorrow morning I have to meet a comrade who works in the Home Ministry and has some details of a report about the government's plans for us,' said Gopal. 'After that I have some work at Palika Bazaar. And then later in the afternoon there's a meeting with some Maoist groups to discuss ways to tackle Red Hunt. I'm hoping we'll be able to make progress with CZAR.'

'CZAR?'

'The Comprehensive Zone of Armed Revolutionaries. Once achieved, the CZAR corridor through the states will be able to drive a divisive line through the country and rouse the masses. But my most immediate goal is to garner support to fight the Shanti Kadam.'

'What about the evening?'

'If there's time, I intend to go to the students' hostel at JNU. One of the students, Vijay, who'd worked with us in Bastar, was recently killed in an "encounter" with the police. There's a strong group of committed students in JNU. We don't want them to get disheartened. I want to kind of pep them up, make them feel inspired by Vijay's martyrdom. There are more who want to join us. The movement is catching on, Swati. Come, become a part of it.'

'Will you be home for dinner?' Swati side-stepped the invitation.

'Yes, I certainly will,' said Gopal. 'Only a fool will miss out on the delicious meals you cook. But I may be late.'

Gopal walked alongside the fountains in Central Park in Connaught Place, looking pensive and downcast. His contact in the Home Ministry had given him some inside information about a major offensive that was being planned against the Maoists in Dantewada under the aegis of Operation Red Hunt. There was a report out which stated that the government intended to identify their exact locations using thermal imagery and a sophisticated global positioning system before launching the operation. They would even be using unmanned aerial devices to gather information on Maoist hideouts and training camps. Some helipads were being built around Raipur and helicopters were being rented from private firms for aerial surveillance and airdropping of security personnel. Camps were also being set up in Kanker district, north of Bastar, where a select group of security forces was being trained in guerrilla tactics. We need to quickly work out an action plan to counter Operation Red Hunt, Gopal thought.

He stopped at the stairway leading down to the Palika Bazaar and spoke over his cellphone, seeking directions. 'So I go down, turn right and go on walking till Shop 54. Is that right?'

A man wearing a sports cap and a checked bush shirt was waiting at the shop, which was an outlet for electronic goods. The man asked Gopal to follow him. The two of them waded their way through the crowd of shoppers, turned a bend and stopped near an open area near a stairwell where an old leper woman sat seeking alms by banging an empty tin mug on the tiled floor.

'How many do you want?' said the man with the sports cap. 'You know the price.'

'At least fifty walkie-talkies,' said Gopal. 'How soon can you supply them?'

'Two weeks,' said the man with the cap. 'Where do you want the delivery?'

'Jagdalpur. Same place.'

'Okay.'

'What about wireless sets? We need at least half a dozen.'

'No problem. I'll let you know. I need full advance for the walkie-talkies.'

'Half now, half later,' said Gopal, taking out a thick envelope from his trouser pocket. 'Haven't we always paid?'

The man smiled, pocketed the envelope and quickly disappeared round the bend. Gopal took a few wrong turns before ultimately finding his way out of the market.

25

AVINASH WALKED ABSENTLY FROM the bus stop towards his flat, dragging his feet, the empty tiffin box in hand. He'd barely gone a few yards past the paan shop near his house when he realized that he hadn't bought the customary packet of candy for his little neighbour. He retraced his steps, feeling for change in his trouser pocket as he walked. Seeing him approach, the shopowner opened the glass jar of wrapped candy and, counting out a few, put them in a paper packet. Avinash smiled at him as he took the packet and handed the change to him.

The girl was sitting at the window as usual when Aseem entered the premises. 'Hello, Uncle,' she said cheerfully.

'Hello, bitiya,' said Avinash smiling, handing the packet of candy to her. 'Have you finished your studies for the day?' The girl responded with a smile as she took the packet.

Avinash slowly climbed the flight of stairs leading to his flat. Ritika was already home and offered him a glass of water as soon as he stepped in. 'Tiring day?' she asked. 'How did you like the lunch?'

Avinash didn't reply to the first of the two questions asked back to back. The dreary emptiness he felt had steeped in him an exhaustion of another kind. How could he explain all this to Ritika? But he didn't hesitate to answer the second, exchanging the cleaned-out tiffin carrier with the proffered glass of water. 'Delicious lunch, I loved the karela.'

Just then, hearing his parents, Aseem came out of his room and greeted his father, 'Hello, Baba.'

'You're home early,' said Avinash, as he walked towards his bedroom.

'Yes, Baba,' said Aseem, following him.

'You didn't go to the slum today?' asked Avinash, going into the bathroom adjoining the bedroom, to wash up.

'No, not today,' said Aseem. Then, after taking a deep breath, he added, 'Baba, I wanted to ask you something.'

'Yes?' Avinash called out from the bathroom.

Standing outside the bathroom door, Aseem hesitated before he finally blurted out, 'Baba, were you ever a Naxalite?'

'Who told you?' called out Avinash from the bathroom after a short pause.

'Swati.'

'Divya's daughter?' asked Avinash, coming back to the bedroom.

Aseem nodded.

'Well, yes,' said Avinash. 'It's true. There was a brief period in college when I got somewhat involved in the movement.'

'Tell me about it.'

'It was a long time back. Why do you want to know?' asked Avinash, sitting on the edge of the double bed in the room.

'Just interested, Baba. There's so much about Maoists in the media of late,' said Aseem, sitting on the lone chair in the bedroom facing his father. 'I wanted to know how it was in your time.'

'What do you want to know?'

'Well . . . what drew you to it?'

Avinash was silent for some time. This was a topic he'd never discussed or ever wanted to discuss with anyone. His murky Naxalite past was something he'd consciously pushed to the deep sewers of his mind and shut out with a heavy iron lid. But he didn't want to disappoint Aseem. He felt happy talking to him. The two of them seldom spoke.

He rose from the bed and walked up to his almirah, which was adjacent to Ritika's housing for her gods. 'What drew me to the movement?' Avinash said finally, shaking his head, talking more to himself now. 'I need to gather my thoughts.'

Opening the almirah door, Avinash pulled out a bottle of dark rum. He carried the bottle to the kitchen and fixed himself a drink before returning to the bedroom.

'So, Baba, what was the Naxalite movement about?' Aseem repeated as soon as his father was back. 'How did you get involved?'

'It was such a long time ago,' said Avinash, settling himself back on the bed and taking a large gulp of his drink, remembering U.C.'s lectures and all the literature he'd read in the college hostel. 'You know the historical background, don't you? Even as late as in the sixties the country was in a semi-feudal, semi-colonial state. The conditions were really oppressive in the rural countryside. It was like in the time of the Czar before the revolution in Russia, or China before Mao. There was food scarcity and famine. The poor and the landless were dying.'

'The situation is not very different even now in many parts of India,' remarked Aseem.

'Let me complete,' continued Avinash taking another large gulp. 'Where was I? . . . Yes . . . so, as I was saying, things were really bad for the poor. There was a feeling among us that the country was ripe for a people's revolution and that the path shown by Chairman Mao was the only way out. Remember also that at that time US imperialism was rearing its head, social-imperialism was ruining the Soviet state. If we wanted to liberate India's poor peasants, we'd need to fight against the guns of Soviet revisionists and the evil designs of US imperialists.'

'Hold it, Baba,' interrupted Aseem. 'How would fighting revisionism and imperialism elsewhere bring about a revolution in India?'

'Everything is interconnected,' said Avinash, losing himself in his thoughts. 'What was I saying?' he asked after a few minutes.

'Something about interconnectedness.'

'Right,' said Avinash. 'Our leaders realized that it was necessary to wage a global counter-offensive. The key objective was to integrate ourselves with the broad masses of workers and peasants in the world and spread Chairman Mao's teachings. Only then could we achieve our objective of annihilating the class enemies.'

'All this is confusing,' said Aseem.

'It's confusing because you're not trying to understand,' said Avinash, sounding agitated. 'Annihilation was to be the starting point of a long-drawn guerrilla war. The battle would be fought by involving exploited peasants by first raising their political consciousness so that they could recognize their oppressors. Once this objective was achieved, their potential would be unleashed, and in place of the poor peasant a new person would emerge, a person who'd be free of all self-interest, to the point of even defying death.'

'You believed all this?' asked Aseem.

'Yes, of course', said Avinash, taking another very large gulp of his drink. He suddenly stood up and started speaking loudly with his eyes on the ceiling, as if in a trance, and his right hand raised high, his fingers forming a fist. 'With this death-defying spirit, the revolutionary would close in on the enemy, snatch his rifle, avenge the martyrs, and thus would emerge the people's army. Only the blood of martyrs could inspire and create new persons out of the fighters.'

'What happened?' asked Ritika, who, hearing Avinash speaking loudly, had rushed to the bedroom door. 'Is everything all right?'

'I'm fine,' said Avinash, sitting down on the edge of the bed.

'It's all right, Ma,' said Aseem, getting up from his chair. 'Baba was talking about his college days. When's dinner?'

'Just a few minutes,' said Ritika, looking at Avinash. 'You take care of him. I've never heard him sound so agitated.'

'Don't worry, Ma. He's okay,' said Aseem.

As soon as Ritika left, Aseem turned to Avinash. 'Is that what you wanted to do? Become a martyr?'

'We wanted to overthrow the regime,' Avinash said, taking a sip of his drink. After a while, he continued, 'Listen, I hope you're not getting involved with the Maoists. Steer clear of them. You must focus on your career.'

'Don't worry, Baba. I'm not involved with them,' said Aseem. 'I just wanted to know more about them. So, tell me, what exactly did you yourself do?'

Avinash fell silent. Till now Aseem's questions had been impersonal. Once he'd got into the spirit of things, it'd been easy to talk about Naxalite ideology. But was there anything to say about himself, when, for once, Aseem was looking at him as some kind of a revolutionary hero? What could he possibly tell his son? That even today he didn't know what his role was, that things were so hush-hush that no one among his comrades really knew what they were doing and why? That they'd just followed the diktats of the high command without looking for logic and reason? That he was a failed revolutionary with not even a small deed to his name, leave alone the scalp of a class enemy? That his involvement had been limited to making posters and pasting them on the university walls and writing slogans in black paint? Or, that the only thing of significance he'd done was to participate in a mess strike in support of the cooks and the helpers who dished out lousy food? Or, that he'd acted as a mere courier boy to carry sealed letters? Or, was he to tell his son about the futile visit to a remote village waiting for instructions that never came?

'What did I do?' Avinash mumbled to himself, taking a large gulp of his drink and wiping his mouth with his hand. 'It was all a long time ago.'

Salvation from his predicament arrived in the form of Ritika saying, 'If you two will end your discussion, I'll lay out out the dinner.'

26

ASEEM WAS AT THE ridge well before the appointed time. He dismounted from his motorbike and waited at the double iron gates, alongside two ruminating cows. A monkey with its tail dangling down was perched on the edge of a giant green billboard over the gate that announced: 'Kamala Nehru Park—Protected Area'. A policeman in khaki uniform with his belt slipped below his tummy stood nearby with a bamboo cane in hand, gossiping with a vendor selling papayas wrapped in crumpled newspaper. The policeman's teeth were blood red owing to the tobacco in his mouth, his jaws in perpetual motion synchronizing with the cows chewing the cud.

Standing among them, Aseem felt uneasy at the thought of another meeting with Gopal, whom he spotted sauntering towards him down Flagstaff Road accompanied by Swati.

'Hi,' said Swati, as she neared Aseem. 'You're here already.'

'It didn't take long,' said Aseem. 'There's little traffic at this hour.'

Swati took the lead to negotiate the swivel gates beside the main entrance. The three of them snaked up a winding metalled road through the ridge that led to Flagstaff Tower, an old circular lookout with an octagon wooden pergola. The area on either side of the road had a verdant and fresh look, the leaves having been washed clean by the rain.

'Comrade, you're quiet,' Gopal said, turning his head towards Aseem. 'I hope it's not anything to do with what I said the other day.'

'It's all right,' said Aseem.

'I like it here,' said Gopal, after walking a bit, looking around at the unspoilt, undulating thick green cover: the wide-spreading gulmohurs, the blue-flowering jacarandas, the drooping-leafed laburnums, the shadowy neems. 'It reminds me so much of the Bastar landscape.'

'I believe it is unspoilt and beautiful,' said Swati.

'Breathtaking! Words can't describe it,' said Gopal. 'You must come and see it one day. You too, Aseem.'

'I wouldn't want to risk it,' said Aseem. 'I've heard that you're engaged in some kind of . . . er . . . civil war there?'

'Who told you? Swati?' Gopal looked surprised.

'Nope. I was checking on the Net last night,' said Aseem.

'We're doing development work—fighting for the rights of the adivasis,' said Gopal. 'Our fight is against those exploiting the adivasi villagers.'

'There's something I wanted to ask. Can't you do your work peacefully? There are so many NGOs doing good work without resorting to violence.'

'Comrade, you're mistaken,' said Gopal. 'It's the other way around. People falsely implicate us as being perpetrators of violence. Our fight has always been against the oppressors. When I was in Andhra Pradesh, we fought the feudal lords. Here we're fighting the thekedars and patels who've started an armed movement called Shanti Kadam with the support of the state governmnent to thwart us. We've no choice but to arm the adivasis so that they can protect themselves from the Shanti Kadam.'

'But you also have guerrilla squads who attack the police and government officials,' said Aseem.

'Only those who commit atrocities. Our squads—we call them dalams—consist of cadres born in the families of poor adivasi peasants. They've been innocent victims of police atrocities and exploitation. Many of them are women who have been raped by the security forces.'

'But I read something else,' said Aseem. 'That you've taken over villages by force and are terrorizing the local adivasis into following your ways.'

'Terrorizing? Who . . . we? That's all a pack of lies, all malicious propaganda spread by the media and the state,' Gopal said, incensed. 'Don't you believe it. All we're doing is providing just governance through sanghams elected by the local adivasis.'

A tribe of monkeys cut across the road at a languorous pace, led by a big, ferocious-looking male monkey with flaming red buttocks. Swati stopped in her tracks. Aseem came and stood close to her, ready to ward off any attack. They waited for the animals to complete their crossing.

'Looking at the butts of these monkeys reminded me of something,' said Aseem, smiling to himself.

'What?' asked Swati.

'It's this quote from Mao I read last night that got stuck in my head,' said Aseem, now laughing. 'A revolution's need for a base area is like an individual's need for buttocks.'

'What's funny in that?' asked Gopal, disdainfully. 'This is the core strategy of any revolution. Don't you remember your history? The Chinese revolution also began like that, by creating a liberated zone in Yenan in the thirties and forties. We're also similarly developing a base area in Bastar.'

'How? By grabbing what's not yours through violence and force?' asked Aseem.

'The land rightfully belongs to the adivasis,' said Gopal. 'They've lived there for centuries.'

'They've no legal claim on it,' argued Aseem.

'Legal, my foot! Who's made the laws? The state. That very state that is the pawn of the landlords and capitalists and miners who are trying to garner all the resources for themselves. That's what the whole fight is about, not only in Bastar, but across the globe: controlling the earth's resources which belong equally to all of us. That's why we say: first crush the state. Once the state is overthrown, we can take back the land and the resources and divide it equitably among peasants and labourers.'

'And how do you do that?'

'By seizing political power, even if it means resorting to violence. Everything is an illusion except state power.'

'Violence cannot be the means to capture power. There are democratic means available,' said Aseem.

'That's rubbish!' interjected Swati, who'd kept quiet until now. 'Votes are bought and sold. What kind of democracy are you talking about? Crooks and gangsters and racketeers inveigle the masses to vote for them, using the power of money or sometimes even the gun. Once in Parliament or the assembly they amass wealth through crooked means. Just study the profile of your so-called people's representatives—your MPs and MLAs—and you'll understand what I'm talking about.'

'This way you can dismiss everything,' said Aseem assertively. 'Everything may not be perfect, but elections are the best route.'

'You're naïve,' said Gopal.

'That's no argument,' said Aseem.

They reached a meandering red gravel path to their side. Gopal took the lead, with Swati and Aseem following him. They turned into the path, bordered by grass on either side. The red earth below their feet was soft and slippery owing to the rain the previous day, and was covered with the small yellow-green fruit of the neem tree. Ahead of them, a group of women and children were walking, feet bare, wet firewood on their unwashed brown heads, playful, giggling.

'Just look at them,' said Gopal. 'What's your government doing for them? Do you know what they will be told? That they've no right over the firewood. That they're depleting the forests. Bah! No one tells that to the timber merchants when they cut down trees to make the fancy furniture and the doors and windows of your condominiums. It's the same story in the forests of Bastar. The Forest Department denies the adivasis their traditional rights to forest produce. They won't allow them to pick fruit, collect firewood, graze cattle—things they've been doing for centuries for their livelihood. We've to change such unjust practices by bringing in new laws that empower the poor. And that can only happen when we seize political power.'

'And that'll never, never happen,' said Aseem. 'C'mon. You guys seem to be living in a fool's paradise. How can you ever imagine that a handful of you can take on the might of the state?'

'We aren't a few,' said Gopal. 'Our cadres are growing. Come and join us.'

'No way,' said Aseem. 'I believe in the democratic path.'

'Mind you, even your patience will run out and you'll come running to join us,' said Gopal. 'Just you wait.'

'Impossible. Your revolution will never happen. It's so ill conceived,' said Aseem. 'See what happened in Peru. Their Shining

Path movement is practically over. They're leaderless and their activities are limited to bank heists.'

'It's all media propaganda. Shining Path will revive. The left movement is strong there. But why do you want to compare, anyway? Our situation is different. You don't know the ground realities,' said Gopal.

'What realities?'

'There are several districts which are under our control, where we run our own administration. We've our sanghams and duly elected gram rajya committees that carry out development work.'

'What kind of development work? Do you build roads?'

'You don't need roads for development,' said Swati. 'There are such big, wide roads in Delhi, but have they reduced the number of the poor and the homeless?'

'She's right,' said Gopal. 'The government wants to build roads in Bastar only to help the miners to move their goods and to send tanks to attack us. No, the adivasis are happy with the kuchcha paths through the forests. They first need the basics—food, shelter, health, education. And that's what we're trying to provide. All the land that we acquire we redistribute to the landless. Your government's done damn all for the adivasis.'

'It can't be true,' said Aseem.

'Come and see for yourself,' said Gopal.

They reached the end of the gravel path and returned to the metalled road near an ancient, dilapidated monument. They stopped near a bench and sat down quietly for a while, listening to the rustle of branches and the twitter of birds and the buzz of insects. A man with a crimson tilak and a cloth bag filled with ripe bananas slung on his shoulder came walking down the road. 'Le, le, aaoohh, aaaoohh,' he called out, holding out the bananas from his bag. The monkeys came trooping down, screeching; the more enterprising ones quickly took the proffered bananas. The man upturned the bag and threw the rest of the fruit at the more diffident of the monkeys.

'You know what this man is doing to the monkeys?' asked Gopal. 'Turning them into beggars. They remind me of the Shanti Kadam. They've got these misguided adivasis to come scampering to the roadside shelters with false promises of money and jobs and shelter.'

A few urchin boys in ragged clothes and with twigs in their hands came running down the road to grab the bananas before the monkeys could reach them. The man with the crimson tilak shooed the urchins away.

'See? Don't you find this ridiculous? You'll feed a monkey but not a hungry child,' remarked Gopal. 'That's why, Comrade, we need to bring about a cultural revolution as they did in China.'

'But even China seems to have forgotten Mao,' said Aseem.

'They're making a terrible mistake,' said Gopal.

After a while, they rose from the bench and walked back to the main entrance past the Flagstaff Tower. The morning sun had climbed above the treetops, dazzling their eyes, as they reached the iron gates where the policeman was continuing to exercise his jaws. The papaya seller had left, but a vegetable vendor had taken his place.

Swati and Gopal accompanied Aseem to his motorbike.

'See you at the flat,' Swati told Aseem, beginning to walk away down the road with Gopal.

'No, I'll go back home now,' said Aseem. 'It's quite late.'

'As you wish,' said Swati. 'I thought you'd come for breakfast.'

'Another time,' said Aseem, kick-starting his bike. 'Bye.'

'Bye,' said Swati.

'Lal salaam,' said Gopal, raising a closed fist to his temple. As Aseem rode away, the policeman streaked the ground red with a stream of betel-leaf juice from his mouth.

27

ASEEM PUT ON A BLACK shirt with a white hare motif on the front, readying himself for Sri Sri Narayanaji's first appearance before business leaders. This was a major event, and if they could pull it off it would be a feather in ImpaKt's cap. It had now been three months since he'd been working with ImpaKt on the Narayanaji project. In fact, this had been the lone assignment he'd been given since he'd joined Aroon's firm—to promote and market the swami.

'You'd said something about a social advertising cell,' Aseem had asked Aroon a few days after he'd joined.

'This is it, son,' Aroon had replied casually. 'Sri Sri Narayanaji will spread the message. This experience will stand you in good stead for other social campaigns.'

There had been no further discussion on the topic and Aseem had found himself fully immersed in the Narayanaji project from day one at ImpaKt. There was a lot to be done: working with the media along with Uma, developing a website, starting a new journal, organizing a database of potential customers, helping to conceive the ad campaigns, finalizing the design for the logo, escorting Sri Sri Narayanaji to language trainers. So busy and involved had he become in the project that he'd rarely found time to go to the slum school or meet Swati during the week. To help Aseem to continue with his teaching assignment, Swati had arranged that he take his English classes on Sunday mornings, after which they'd go out.

While most of the activities related to the Narayanaji project had taken place without a hitch, the English lessons had called for considerable doing. While Professor Nicholas Paul struggled to teach the subtle nuances of English grammar, Sabina Contractor had found the task of cultivating the swami's diction and pronunciation easier said than done. And when Menaka and Sri Kripananda volunteered to pitch in, the speech expert was at the end of her tether. 'Am I to teach him English or some cockney American?' she asked, wringing her hands in despair. It was then that she discovered Aseem's English-teaching skills. Soon, Aseem was practising phonetics with the swami while escorting him to Ms Contractor's fancy apartment in Gurgaon and back every second day. In the end, the swami's pronunciation had been corrected but not his sing-song way of speaking, which nobody seemed to mind: they agreed that it lent his speech a more hallowed appeal.

All in all, the time and effort spent on the Narayanaji project had paid rich dividends—the swami's name had begun to spread. His discourses and exercises were being aired on a spiritual channel, a ten-minute slot was now regularly reserved for him on the Kal Ka Aaj channel, a rabbi singer had been commissioned to cut a new album of ballads in praise of the swami. It was becoming difficult to restrain the crowds that had begun to throng the ashram and the organizers had to resort to levying high fees to limit the number of people wanting to attend the discourses. Hailed as the bridge between generations, the swami was slowly emerging as a youth icon and was being discussed on Twitter and Facebook.

With the overwhelming success of the project, Aroon himself was being hailed as the greatest ad guru in the country. Menaka was now a regular feature on Page 3, flanking the swami at socialite dos and new product launches and what-have-you.

As Aseem put on a black jacket over his black shirt, he received a call from the security guard of his apartment complex to say that a car had come to fetch him. 'I'm going, Ma,' shouted out Aseem as he hurried out of the flat.

Four White Commando Guards specially recruited to provide security to Sri Sri Satyanand Narayanaji, armed with AK-47s and wearing all-white uniforms, were scurrying about like rabbits at the entrance to Hotel Grandeur as a white Mercedes drove in. The guards surrounded the vehicle and pushed back the curious onlookers as Sri Sri Narayanaji with his neat beard and flowing hair disembarked. He was wearing a white, embroidered silk robe. Menaka, the self-appointed official escort of the swami, stepped out behind him looking regal in a black coat and a new gold-tinted hairdo. Aseem in a black jacket alighted from the car behind them along with Aroon and Sri Kripananda. All of them had the hare motif stitched on the chests of their garments.

The swami was greeted by rose petals showered by svelte ladies in designer dresses and escorted through the hotel lobby to the Maharaja Hall, down a long corridor flanked by shops selling curios. Huge presentation screens on either side of a stage at the far end of the hall were projecting images of the swami that dissolved into each other. Incense sticks and oil lamps burning in discreet corners of the hall lent an aura of spiritual splendour.

Sri Sri Narayanaji was led to an embellished throne placed at the centre of the stage facing the business leaders who were seated around tables in groups of six. As the swami entered the hall, the corporate bigwigs descended into a hushed silence and got up from their chairs; some of them seated nearby bent down and touched his feet.

After everyone had settled down, Sri Sri Narayanaji began his discourse with a delicate gesture of his hand mimicking the symbol of the hare. He spoke in a measured, well-rehearsed intonation: 'The world today is very challenging. To survive and succeed, you should be able to respond swiftly and nimbly like the hare. And yet you must remain calm within. You can only do this if you're totally aware of your inner self.'

He continued his discourse for a while, his audience hanging on to every syllable as though they were sacred drops from heaven. 'We'll now proceed with an awareness programme that will awaken your inner core, make you alert like the hare.'

The swami clapped his hands. Soon, two attractive models, one of either gender, came running from the sides like circus artistes, carrying a chair each in front of them. Wearing specially designed white body suits that had illuminated hare motifs on the chests and oval-shaped cuts exposing their bellies, they placed the chairs on either side of the swami and assumed their positions.

Moving his white garment aside to expose a taut, muscular abdomen, Sri Sri Narayanaji took a deep breath before he spoke. 'We'll now do the "Kursikriya". These are self-awareness and fitness exercises you can do every day—in your offices, in the comfort of your homes, even sitting in a car or an aeroplane. They'll help you to calm your nerves, make you come alive.'

Copyrighted under the swami's nom de plume as 'Narayanaji Kursikriya', the name, a combination of 'kursi' (chair) and 'kriya' (exercise or work), had been cleverly conceived by the ImpaKt team. Designed specially for industry captains who suffered from stress, the exercises could be performed without having to stand up.

Sri Sri Narayanaji demonstrated the Kursikriya exercises in close concert with the two models. Some of them had to be performed with grunting noises, some with forceful breaths, some with the movement of arms above the head and making short, puffing noises like a coal engine. In the final exercise routine, the participants had to inhale deeply and then allow an eerie sound to escape their lips. 'Phh-eee . . . phh-eee! This is the sound of the hare,' the swami said. 'It will bring peace and calm to your body and soul.

'Spirituality is like a banana, and business is like its peel. What is happening is that you're holding on to the peel and throwing away the banana. You need to balance your business with spirituality and responsiveness—awareness of yourself and the world around you. You need to develop within you the responsiveness and alertness of the hare.

'Overcome your ego, your desire to win. You'll succeed when you stop wanting to win. Look within and without. Search inside and you will find. Welcome fear with a smile, anger with calmness. Change the hearts and minds of those who perpetrate violence. With love and peace. Shanti! Shanti! Shanti!'

Energized and awed by the discourse, the five-hundred-odd corporate magnates broke into spontaneous applause. The hall reverberated with shouts of 'Sri Sri Narayanaji ki jai! Sri Sri Narayanaji ki jai!' The swami blessed the business leaders with the hare-mimicking wave of his hand and floated away from the hall.

Later, a five-course sumptuous meal was served, after which the tuxedo-clad business gentry surrounded Sri Kripananda and Menaka for appointments and exclusive discourses by the swami for their respective companies. In the meantime, Aseem was rushing the swami and his entourage to a television studio for a recording of a set of Kursikriya exercises.

Sri Sri Satyanand Narayanaji had truly arrived.

28

AT PRECISELY A QUARTER past eleven on a Sunday morning in the month of October, when both Aseem and Swati were taking special classes at the slum school, a roaring bulldozer with its yellow iron hide came rumbling down the crowded jhuggi settlement after breaking through the brick wall separating the slum cluster from the road. Hearing the commotion, Aseem and Swati came out of the canvas-canopied school. The bulldozer was moving relentlessly forward with its monstrous, hungry jaws and giant shark-like teeth. The stockily built driver sat tall in the glass enclosure, wearing a yellow helmet, like an emperor guiding the heavy, serrated clasps to demolish the feeble walls of the dwelling units. Meanwhile, a second bulldozer, which had been standing brazenly nearby, like an unrepentant killer taking a brief respite, also began rolling forward. A middle-aged official with upright hair like a hedgehog's shouted out warnings through a megaphone pressed to his lips, 'Take whatever you have and move to the roads before the bulldozers bring down your jhuggis.'

As their homes crumbled, the slum dwellers hurled abuses and mouthed obscenities but the drivers continued in their mission unmoved. Men wearing yellow helmets and carrying pickaxes and shovels helped to clear away the rubble, making way for the iron monsters.

Police jeeps, white Ambassadors and ambulance vans with blue and red whirling lights were parked a short distance away from the settlement on the roadside. Lined beside them were a number of OB vans with satellite dish antennae that belonged to news-hungry television channels. The media was already in the thick of the demolition proceedings, trying to get 'Breaking News' interviews with those who'd become homeless.

Ten kilometres away, Divya Carot-Reddy of Gaajar fame, was simultaneously getting her eyebrows done and her legs waxed at the parlour in Hotel Grandeur when she received an SMS about the slum demolition. Leaving her right leg hairy and unwaxed under her green skirt, she rushed home to change into a starched red-and-white cotton sari, before going to the demolition site.

By the time Divya reached, a part of the slum had already been razed to the ground; it would not be long before the rest would also go. There were signs of wreckage everywhere amid the muck and slush of the drain: electric cables and wires were strewn about as though in a serpents' graveyard; heaps of rubble of broken homes and broken hearts; a small child sitting forlorn on a green trunk containing his family's meagre belongings. There were scores of officials milling around in their safari suits, accompanied by a khaki-uniformed police contingent in protective gear and carrying bamboo shields. The police officers with their hands poised on their pistol holsters were giving instructions on walkie-talkie sets. There was mayhem as the dwellers ran about salvaging their belongings from the ruin—pots and pans, the window bought at bargain price and now shattered, the plastic sheeting that once formed a roof, a cane chair. They'd come to the capital city of Delhi looking for work from distant states—from Tamil Nadu and Bihar and Orissa—and had settled down in the slum. They were once again homeless: rootless, roofless refugees with nowhere to go.

Ram and Lakshmi, Aseem's most ardent students, stood numbed as the brick walls and tent and bamboo poles of the school, the jute sacks, the blackboard and the books, and along with them their dreams of learning English, were broken and mowed to the ground. Swati, her eyes wide and blazing, looked on at the devastation, her hands clenching and unclenching with fury and indignation. A great churning was going on in her mind and a deep anger welled inside, but she didn't stir, didn't utter a word.

Aseem stood beside her, grinding his teeth. 'How can they do this?' He looked helplessly at Vimal, his dedicated front-bencher, standing alongside his widowed mother Parvati, watching the home they'd built bit by bit against the greatest of odds reduced to rubble. He looked away as his eyes met Vimal's angry gaze.

Divya Carot-Reddy meanwhile had accosted a safari-suited gentleman with a squeaky voice and was arguing vociferously with him. Three other officials had come to lend their voices to the squeaky-voiced official. Finding herself outnumbered and outshouted, Divya left them in a huff and went up to an agitated Parvati who'd joined a group of other hapless women. A hurried exchange of words and instructions, and Divya was able to quickly galvanize about a dozen of them to group together. Then, taking the lead, she, along with the other women, walked across and stood in the path of the bulldozer. As the stocky driver applied his brakes, they began shouting slogans, denouncing the officials and the police, denouncing the demolition order, denouncing everybody. A contingent of over thirty policewomen carrying bamboo shields, who till now had been cooling their heels under the shade of a tree, swung immediately into action with their lathis. Divya and her group of defiant women offered resistance, but they were no match for the well-trained, baton-wielding policewomen.

Soon, the uniformed women were leading a yelling and screaming Divya and her band of protesting women away to a waiting blue police van. Meanwhile, the television camerapersons and journalists, who'd recognized the fashionable lady in red-and-white, rushed to the spot. They elbowed their way through the crowd, pushing forward their microphones and shouting out questions at Divya, holding the cameras high above their heads to get clear shots. Divya gestured wildly and yelled to ensure that the keen journalists and camerapersons caught her in action. Satisfied that she'd been able to draw adequate media attention, she allowed herself to be led into the waiting police van, careful to climb in by placing her waxed left leg first and then drawing in the other leg carefully to ensure it remained unexposed under her sari. Parvati and the other protesting women were pushed into the van behind her. The cameras continued shooting even after the rear door of the van had been shut and it had driven away, following its trail for a long time in an extended shot as it disappeared into the city's grey horizon.

And then suddenly it happened.

A stone, not a very big one, came hurtling across like a rocket from one of the windows of a dwelling. With a loud 'thuck', it hit the side of a policeman's head, just below the helmet. The policeman screamed in pain and went down on his knees holding his head, as blood and oozed out on his hand. Hesaw the blood and howled. Three other policemen gathered around him; one pulled out a big handkerchief from his pocket and held it against the wound. Another shouted for the ambulance. More policemen now joined them. Reporters barged their way through the crowd, drooling at the prospect of more exciting footage. Aseem and Swati also moved ahead and stood at the periphery of the crowd. The wounded policeman pointed to the window from where the stone had been hurled.

Two policemen walked towards the dwelling and cautiously entered it. A while later they dragged out twelve-year-old Vimal by the collar and made him stand in the middle of the crowd.

'Sala, haramzada,' one of the policemen said. 'You think you're very smart? How dare you throw stones at us? We'll show you, behenchod!'

The two cops began working on him with orchestrated movements, raining blows from their bamboo lathis, hitting him mercilessly, brutally, on his back, his legs, his raised arms which protected his head.

Swati and Aseem watched the scene from the periphery, Swati holding on to Aseem's arm tightly. All of a sudden, Aseem wrenched his arm free from her grip and elbowed his way through the crowds towards Vimal, screaming at the assaulting policemen, 'No . . . no . . . no! You can't do that!' As he neared, he reached for the lathi of one of the cops who was clobbering Vimal, and continued to shout, 'That's enough! Don't beat him any more! You'll kill him!'

'Don't come in our way, madarchod,' said the cop. 'Tu bhi mara jayega, bhosadhi ke.'

'No,' screamed Aseem, raging with full-throated hysteria. 'You can't do that! This is barbaric!' He put his body between the raining blows and the boy.

'Move away, gandu,' said the other policeman, giving Aseem a practised blow on his back, throwing him to the ground. Swati and two others helped Aseem to his feet and drew him away, where he stood with flaming red eyes, breathing hard.

'Fucking sons-of-bitches,' Aseem shouted, but no one was listening.

'Move, move away,' yelled a police officer, firing his pistol in the air to disperse the crowd. 'There's no tamasha here.'

Vimal, who was shrieking with pain, was carried away by some of the other inhabitants of what was once a slum.

'Let's go,' said Swati, dragging Aseem away by his elbow. 'It's pointless now.'

29

AROON WAS WATCHING TELEVISION, leaning forward in his chair, switching channels rapidly. He only paused to view the media coverage of the swami's launch at Hotel Grandeur. He gloated over the success of the event as he watched clippings from the launch on one channel, an interview with the swami on another, a full story of the swami's life on the third.

Menaka was sitting beside him, dressed in an all-white ensemble, a pearl necklace and pearl tops in her ears. Rambo lay at her feet, unusually listless. Menaka was not her usual bright self, and even her ruddy complexion had turned white like her dress. The attire had nothing to do with Sri Sri Narayanaji. It was because she was in mourning, which had all got to do with the loss of Rambo's 'doghood'.

It all started the day Sri Kripananda had come visiting the Kumar home along with Ishita to discuss the finer details of the swami's promotional launch. As soon as Sri Kripananda had stepped into the marble-floored veranda of the Kumar mansion, Rambo had jumped on him, drooling with his tongue hanging out, like an adolescent boy in a roomful of Playboy bunnies. Clasping one of Sri Kripananda's legs tightly with his forepaws, Rambo had almost immediately begun to rub his thingummy with great rapidity up and down the man's leg. The excited dog would not let go, even when Sri Kripananda tried to shake him off and Ishita yelled, 'No, Rambo, no!' And by the time Aroon had come out to the veranda hearing Ishita's screams and pulled Rambo away by the scruff of his neck, the roused creature had satisfied himself.

Meanwhile, Ishita had swooned and had had to be administered smelling salts to bring her back to consciousness. Sri Kripananda was outraged and, in spite of Menaka's entreaties, he refused to stay on, and promptly returned to the ashram, doing pranayama all the way to calm himself down. On Aroon's advice, Menaka took Rambo to the vet, who advised that the time had come to neuter Rambo. Realizing that clear-cut action was called for to pacify the chief benefactor of ImpaKt's most ambitious project, Menaka conceded that there was no other recourse. With the launch about to take place, it was agreed that the operation would be carried out after it.

So, this morning, Rambo had been driven to the vet's private chambers for the dreadful deed. Thereafter, Menaka, had tried to make it up to her darling pet by driving him down to the Bow Wow Club to feed him Crunch-a-Munch for starters followed by Bow Chick Chop and Lamb Goulash and finally ending the meal with Pup Cake.

But, Rambo couldn't be pacified, and sat moaning at Menaka's feet. Restless at her self-imposed mourning, Menaka envied

Aroon's interest in the Narayanaji project as he surfed channels. Unused to not playing the prima donna, her interest in the project had waned. Instead, she now worried about what would happen to her if Rambo were to breathe his last. She felt friendless and unloved. She needed someone who would understand her, with whom she could share her feelings.

'Just a sec,' said Menaka, all of a sudden, almost shouting. 'Just stop there!'

'That was something about a slum demolition, dear,' Aroon said. 'Thank God, the elections are over and they've begun to do something about clearing it up.'

'Aroon, for heaven's sake! Do what I tell you,' said Menaka urgently. 'Get back to it now.'

'They would've moved on to something else. This is TV, sweetheart, not a DVD.'

'Get on to another news channel, then. I think I saw Aseem.'

'Why didn't you tell me earlier? Where did you see Aseem?' Aroon, suddenly alert, switched to Kal Ka Aaj, where a husky-voiced anchor was saying good night.

'Quick, quick, try another channel,' urged Menaka, moving forward to the edge of her chair. 'Try ABC News.'

Aroon pressed the remote again, and they saw it. First, there was a screaming Divya Carot-Reddy being led away from the dust-filled, ravaged basti along with the erstwhile women dwellers. Then, a while later, there was another shot of her, being hoisted into the police van, flaying her arms wildly. Immediately following this was a brief shot of Vimal being beaten mercilessly by the cops amidst the rampage and debris.

'That's him,' exclaimed Menaka, as Aseem's face flashed on the screen, trying to ward off lathi blows. Finally, there was a long shot of Swati pulling him away. The entire footage was repeated again and again and again, while a bored news reporter recounted the events. Aroon and Menaka sat shell-shocked.

'What in the blazes was Aseem doing there?' asked Aroon, the first of the two to recover.

'It must be the wretched slum where he goes to teach. I told you it was a bad influence. It's all because of that Divya and her horrible daughter Swati. Poor boy! I kept warning Ritika about them, but she has no influence over him. I'd better tell her straight away and find out how Aseem is.'

Moments later, Menaka was on the phone with Ritika who informed her that Aseem had been badly bruised but had suffered no fractures.

'Why didn't you tell me earlier?' Menaka asked.

'Aseem didn't want me to tell anyone,' said Ritika.

'I'm not just anyone.'

'There's nothing to worry about now. Yes, he's terribly shaken up, but by God's grace he's all right.'

'I'll skin that Swati woman's dark hide. We're coming over right now to look him up.'

30

FOR THE NEXT FEW DAYS, Aseem remained at home, unable to stir out owing to his injuries. He waited for Swati to call or drop in, but there was no sign of her. He tried in vain to contact her: over the cellphone, through SMS and on email. He was desperate to speak with her; he wanted to see her, he wanted to know where she was. But he didn't receive a word from Swati. He became increasingly despondent over the following days, moping around the house, eating little or nothing at all. A miserable Ritika heard him mumble Swati's name in his sleep but could do little to help him.

Menaka suggested that Ritika allow her to take him to her home. 'The change will do him good,' she said. 'Also, we must keep him away from Swati and her negative influence. You never know. She may suddenly turn up. It'll be much safer to shift him to our home.'

But Aseem flatly refused to leave his house. Menaka and Aroon came to visit him every evening instead, and so did his grandfather. They would sit around in the small living room along with Ritika, watching each other's morose faces. Sometimes, Aroon would bring along his bottle of Scotch, and he and Girdhari would drink quietly. They tried to persuade Aseem to come out of his room and sit with them in the living room, but to no avail. When his in-laws were around, Avinash would keep to himself in his own bedroom, drinking rum, distressed about Aseem but feeling totally helpless.

A fortnight after the demolition, Aseem received a letter by post. He easily recognized Swati's characteristic rounded letters on the sealed envelope addressed to him. He opened it eagerly, as soon as Ritika handed it to him. He scanned the letter quickly and then read it again:

Aseem,

This may be hard on you, but I hope you'll understand. I'm leaving; I'm going to join Gopal. I've disagreed with him on many points about the movement in the past, but at the present moment I don't see many options. I've never had any doubt that the system had to be changed. But now I'm convinced it has to be thrown out lock, stock and barrel. One can't remain in it and try to change it at the same time. I've tried. The incident at the slum has opened my eyes. The system is too callous and insensitive and merciless. I cannot continue to stay in Delhi and witness the oppression and cruelty and not be able to do anything about it.

I'll miss you. You have a good heart. I do hope you'll find something meaningful to do. Do not try to follow me or find me. It'll make things more difficult for both of us.

Lal salaam!

Swati

It took a while for Aseem to absorb the implications of the letter. When it did, he slipped into severe depression and remained closeted in his room, stirring out only to eat his meals. While the wounds and bruises had healed well and the grisly memories of the demolition had receded from his mind, his heart ached for Swati. In her absence, his love for her grew even stronger. He pined for her and longed to be with her. Menaka, Aroon and Girdhari's visits to the Bahals became less frequent since Aseem refused to see them.

About six weeks after the slum demolition, an anxious and distraught Ritika spoke to Menaka. 'He seems to have slipped into a deeper depression. He barely eats and will not talk. His wounds have healed, but the incident at the slum seems to have affected him terribly.'

'He should've got over it by now,' remarked Menaka.

'He hasn't. He's just not coming out of it,' said Ritika, sounding helpless.

'Has anything happened meanwhile?'

'Nothing at all. But, yes, there was a letter that came by post for Aseem.'

'Why didn't you tell me about the letter?' scolded Menaka. 'Did you read it?'

'Of course not. Why would I?'

'You should have,' said Menaka, certain in her mind that it must have been Swati who'd written. 'Let me see what I can do. I'll come with Aroon as soon as he's home.'

It was Aroon who took the initiative as soon as they reached Ritika's home. Knocking on Aseem's bedroom door, he spoke loudly, trying to sound as cheerful as he could, 'Hello, old boy, can I have a word with you?'

Aroon received no response, but he persisted. 'C'mon, son. It's been many days since we saw you.'

After some time, Aseem came out from his room, looking unkempt, wearing loose pyjamas and a T-shirt.

'You're not looking too bad,' Aroon said, standing at the door of Aseem's room.

'You must be out of your mind, Aroon,' said Menaka, who'd followed Aroon to the door. 'His face has sunk as if he's seen a ghost. What's happened to you, Aseem dear? Your hair is so scruffy and it looks like you haven't shaved for days. C'mon, get ready. I'll shampoo your hair for you. Then we're taking you out for dinner.'

Reluctantly, as if in a stupor, Aseem allowed Menaka to lead him to the bathroom. Switching on the geyser, she made him stand in front of the washbasin. Before he knew it, Aseem's head was bent over the washbasin, Menaka pressed behind him, running warm water through his hair and rubbing shampoo into it. She shampooed his hair twice and then, facing him, began drying his head vigorously with a towel. She noticed him looking at her cleavage and pressed closer to him as she rubbed his head.

'Leave me,' Aseem said, pulling himself away. 'It's dry enough now.'

'You need to shave,' said Menaka, reaching out for his razor.

Aseem stopped her. 'I'm all right. Leave me alone. I can manage on my own.'

Some time later, Aroon was at Aseem's door, with Ritika behind him. Aseem had changed and shaved, but looked as morose as he had earlier.

'You're looking great,' Aroon said. 'Come, we'll go out for a meal.'

Aseem didn't respond.

'Go, beta,' encouraged Ritika, entering the room and placing a hand on his shoulder. 'You'll feel better. The change will do you good.'

'What're you thinking of, Aseem?' Aroon was saying an hour later, picking up a fried tiger prawn with chopsticks. He was facing Aseem across a table for four in Ginger Moon, the recently opened Chinese restaurant in Khan Market with a contemporary chic décor. 'One has to be practical, son. The jhuggis could not be allowed to remain. They are the seat of most crime in the city. The jhuggiwallas can't take over public land and make it their home.'

'It's not that,' Aseem said quietly.

'What's not what?' interjected Menaka, who was sitting beside him. 'Now you just forget the whole incident. You're all right. It's over.'

Aseem didn't reply; he looked down, picking at the noodles on his plate. How could he explain that his present state of mind had little to do with the incident? All he wanted was to have Swati back in his life.

'Whatever it is,' said Aroon, trying to read Aseem's thoughts. 'Time is a great healer, son. You need to plunge yourself in some kind of work. Why don't you come back to us on the Narayanaji project? Exciting things are happening now.'

'He's right, you know,' said Menaka. 'Swamiji has become a household name. His exercises are being aired on three TV channels.'

'Remember the website you helped to create?' said Aroon.

Aseem nodded his head absently.

'It's getting over a thousand hits a day,' continued Aroon. 'All kinds of people are writing in. Big business houses, political parties, research organizations, university departments—all of them are inviting him for special discourses. And, to cap it all, the chief minister of Chhattisgarh has appointed Sri Sri Narayanaji as the state ambassador. No important project in the state is launched without seeking his blessings. It's amazing, isn't it? Swamiji has become a celebrity.'

'No more thinking now,' added Menaka.

'We could do with your talent on the project, son,' said Aroon. 'We'll pick you up tomorrow on our way to the ashram. And I'm not taking no for an answer.'

Aseem didn't respond. He was still in a daze, looking at Aroon and Menaka with glazed eyes. He closed his eyes.What would

Swati have advised? She would probably have said: What's the difference? This is a job like any other. It is all part of the same rotten system.

31

A HIGH-LEVEL MEETING WAS taking place in the new government building housing the state ministry of home affairs in Raipur, the capital of Chhattisgarh. For security reasons, thick curtains had been drawn across the grille-barricaded glass windows. A long teak table and a dozen leather chairs occupied most of the hall. Newly laid wooden tiles on the floor reeked of the plasticky odour of adhesives mingled with the smell of lavender room freshener specially sprayed by the peon for the occasion.

Presiding over the proceedings was the state's home minister, Samar Jonga, a short, dark Gandhian with a balding pate and a large belly concealed below a khadi kurta. On the wall behind him was a photograph of the Father of the Nation, the apostle of peace and non-violence. On either side of the table sat the home secretary, the director-general of police, the divisional commissioner, the district collector-cum-magistrate of Bastar, and the chief special adviser on security issues in Chhattisgarh, Tejender Sekhon, better known as Tiger, now twirling his handlebar moustache.

The meeting had been convened ostensibly in the wake of an ambush attack on security forces at Dantewada, where the

Maoists had trapped and shot dead seventy-five CRPF men. In reality, the urgent meeting had been prompted by the newly appointed chief minister having had a providential escape during a Maoist attack a fortnight earlier while on his way to inaugurate a new four-lane road in Jagdalpur, thanks to his chauffeur inadvertently taking a wrong turn. On his return to Raipur, the chief minister had immediately summoned the home minister and castigated him about the lack of adequate security. 'It's high time, Jonga-ji, that we did something concrete about the Maoists. It's not my life I care for. It's a question of the security of the entire state. It could've easily been you. You must hold a meeting quickly and come up with a lasting solution.'

'Yes,' Samar Jonga had said, imagining himself as the target of a Maoist attack. 'I'm equally concerned.'

'It's very important for the development of the state, you know, that we tackle this Maoist menace,' the chief minister had reiterated. 'There are important deals we're signing with big companies—multinationals—for mining, for setting up steel and aluminium and power plants. It's a matter of our prestige. We already have deals worth over 200 billion rupees. We are one of the world's major mineral repositories, we have over twenty-five varieties of minerals ready to be exploited: three million tonnes of bauxite deposits; kimberlite rocks containing raw diamond particles; tin slag that has uranium and thorium. But if these Maoist attacks carry on, no one will want to invest in Chhattisgarh any longer.' The chief minister had kept himself well informed of the mining potential in the state and to show his commitment had bought a huge stake in the leading mining company operating in the state.

The home minister, eager to prove himself by finding a lasting solution to the Maoist insurgency, listened intently while the home secretary reeled off a spate of incidents where the Maoists had played havoc. 'Sir, even before the Dantewada massacre there had been a steady escalation of their activities. Over 850 incidents occurred last year itself,' the home secretary was saying. 'According to our records, last year there were 435 fatalties, including 170 civilians. This includes a train hold-up, a jailbreak freeing 425 prisoners, a landmine blast where twenty-four policemen were killed on the spot, a kidnapping at a steel plant where four security guards were shot, and attacks on the peaceful Shanti Kadam campaign members, fifteen of whom were murdered, their throats slit and their heads severed from the bodies. It has indeed been a very gruesome year, sir.'

'You're forgetting the bombing of the school,' reminded the divisional commissioner.

'I was coming to that, sir,' said the home secretary. 'Last year, sir, just before elections, the Maoists had bombed a school and killed three policemen who were guarding electronic voting machines stored in the premises. Two civilians who bore the indelible mark on their fingers were also killed.'

'This cannot go on. It is a direct attack on our democratic polity,' said the minister, fixing his gaze on the DGP. 'We need to do something immediately.'

'Swift police action with clinical precision is the only answer, sir,' said the police chief in a measured tone. 'We have to strengthen Operation Red Hunt. We need more help from the centre.'

'We've suffered heavy losses in Dantewada—seventy-five jawans killed in cold blood. We've become a laughing stock. Are you confident that the operation can work?' asked the minister sceptically.

'To be honest, sir, I must confess we may not be able to implement the operation fully,' the DGP said.

'Why?' the minister asked.

'The Maoists are very organized and resort to guerrilla war tactics, sir. I don't know, but they always seem to get inside information,' said the DGP, looking around the table suspiciously. 'They attack using multiple ambushes, sir, which we are unable to anticipate. Our intelligence agencies have now informed us that they're developing military capabilities and acquiring even more sophisticated equipment. They're already armed with AK-47s, Insas and Kalashnikov rifles, light machine and double-barrelled guns. They also use sophisticated improvised explosive devices with iron pellets, rocket launchers, grenades, Claymore landmines, modern wireless equipment and other electronic gadgets.'

'So?' said the minister. 'Don't you have the necessary equipment to counter them?'

'Not adequate, sir. We don't have proper roads, so we can't use armoured vehicles. Even where we have roads we are unable to detect the mines which they are able to somehow embed in the roads. We need much better minesweeping equipment, sir. Also, sir, we must admit this, many of the local adivasis are supporting and sheltering the Maoists. It's not easy to flush them out.'

'What about the peace initiative? What happened to the Shanti Kadam campaign and the SPOs we appointed?' asked the minister, turning his attention to the home secretary. 'Not all I hear is good. Is it true that the SPOs themselves have unleashed violence in the districts?'

'Sir, they cannot be sitting ducks,' said the home secretary. 'They need to defend themselves. We are promoting them as local resistance groups, sir.'

'No, no, we cannot have this continued violence,' said the minister, a frown appearing on his forehead. 'The media is writing about them and we're losing public sympathy. This way we'll lose votes. We need peace at any cost. We want investment in the state. But this can happen only when all the adivasis are brought into the mainstream. They have to be convinced that development is for their ultimate good. If our efforts are not bearing fruit, we have to have an alternative strategy. We have to change their hearts and minds.'

'You mean, WHAM, sir,' said the smart district collector-cum-magistrate, DC for short, Rama Prasad, peering at the others through rimless spectacles.

'Wham?' asked the minister, looking perplexed.

'What you said exactly, sir. Winning Hearts and Minds. WHAM is the short form, sir,' the DC said with a smile.

'That's what I said,' said the minister. 'Call it what you may. Don't waste my time with terminology. Give me practical ideas.'

'I've one, sir, if I may,' said the DC.

'Yes?' said the minister.

'What about using the pachyderms, sir?' said the DC, looking around to see if he'd made an impression.

'Pachyderms?' enquired the minister.

'Elephants, sir,' explained the DC. 'You know, sir, elephants have been entering our territory from the neighbouring states and creating havoc. We can channellize their energy to contain the Maoist menace.'

'How?' the minister asked with a quizzical frown on his broad forehead.

'You may know, sir, that elephants come in search of the liquor which the adivasis prepare from the mahua flower. They have a keen sense of smell, sir. If we can spray the liquor in the Maoist-infested areas, then the elephants will run over the Maoist-controlled villages, sir,' said the DC.

'No, no, no intoxication,' said the minister. 'We've been thinking of converting Chhattisgarh into a dry state and imposing a ban on the sale of liquor, and here you're thinking of spraying it all over. Are you out of your mind?'

'It was only a suggestion, sir,' said the DC. 'I'm sorry.'

'We have to make the adivasis understand what is good for them,' said the minister. 'We have to convince them to peacefully vacate the forests and allow mining to take place. Mines would give them jobs and decent wages. If we can create a healthy investment climate, we can provide them proper . . . er . . . what is the term? . . . exclusive development.'

'You mean to say, sir . . . inclusive?' suggested the home secretary.

'Yes, yes, we want inclusive development,' said the minister.

'May I say something else, sir?' said the DC, who was more familiar with the ground realities. 'We've been instructed to deny them development funds so that they'll be compelled to leave the villages and join the Shanti Kadam camps.'

'Is that true?' asked the minister.

'Well, sir . . . in a way, yes sir,' said the home secretary. 'Development funds would be siphoned away by the Maoists, sir. But we have many SPOs who are being paid a monthly salary of two thousand rupees. They're helping us to convince the adivasis to leave the forests and join the camps, sir. We provide subsidized rice to the camp dwellers. We've even started primary schools in the camps, sir. A lot of development is happening, sir.'

'No, no. We have to win over the adivasis through inclusive development,' reiterated the minister.

'But many of the adivasis are hand in glove with the Maoists, sir,' said the DGP. 'Inclusive development would only land funds in the hands of the Maoists. That would be disastrous. They've killed so many of our brave police officers and civil servants. They must be eliminated, sir. Just take a look at these photographs, sir.' He displayed gruesome, spine-chilling images of mutilated and disembowelled bodies of cops. 'I cannot say more.'

'This is not good, not good,' said the minister. 'We must bring the adivasis supporting the Maoists to the development arena. They must take part in elections. They must learn that power flows from the ballot box, not from the barrel of a gun. We have to have a peaceful long-term view.'

'We're working on that, sir,' said the home secretary. 'We're giving them cash incentives to join the Shanti Kadam campaign and move to the camps. We're also giving them cash incentives to undergo sterilization so that we'll have fewer of them to contend with. The men are being given three hundred and fifty rupees for every vasectomy, the women three hundred rupees for every tubectomy. The cash incentives will help us to wean away the adivasis from the Maoists, sir.'

'What kind of absurd talk is this?' questioned the minister. 'I want results here and now. Do any of you have any concrete plan? Can we not negotiate some kind of deal with the Maoists?' He looked around but on being greeted with silence turned to Tiger. 'What would you advise us, Tejender-ji?'

Tiger pulled himself up from his reclining pose and gave his moustache an upward twirl before speaking: 'These so-called Maoists are nothing but hardcore terrorists. We cannot negotiate peace with them. Terrorism is their ideology. They believe that the manner of killing should frighten more than the killing itself. They're bandits, extortionists, who hold sway through terror. They're getting the support of the adivasis out of the fear of their guns. There can be no short-term or long-term measures. They are now organizing themselves militarily. The situation calls for a two-pronged strategy: one, development work at the district panchayat level, and two, carefully calibrated military action. The DGP did not say so, but the strength of our police force is woefully inadequate. There are a hundred policemen to hundred thousand civilians. Many of them are occupied, if I may be frank, in providing VIP security. Many more trained security personnel are needed at the taluka and district levels, in the thanas. And I don't mean untrained SPOs.'

'What do you have to say?' asked the minister, shifting his attention to the DGP.

'The SPOs are needed, sir. They serve as informers and are supporting us to reach remote villages. But what Tejender-ji is saying is also true. We need many more men in the police force,' said the DGP. 'But why are we forgetting modern technology? There is intelligence available now: thermal imaging, GPS, satellite imagery. It is possible to exactly pinpoint the Maoist hideouts.'

'Is that so?' said the minister. 'I'm not up-to-date on this. Do you mean that we can reach the villages and use technology to exactly identify who is a Maoist and who is not, and then target them?'

'Not exactly, but we can gather intelligence about their whereabouts,' said Tiger. 'Then, all we need is the political will to deal with them. We need a hundred thousand of the best trained paramilitary forces. We need the latest equipment. Most of all, we need helicopters. With the new available technology we'll be able to target them with surgical precision from the air. They are closeted in the most thickly forested areas where there are no roads. We need to bombard their hideouts from the air and smoke them out.'

'No, no, no,' the minister said. 'No attacks from the air. I can't approve this. There are human rights issues involved. Innocent citizens will be killed. We'll lose international goodwill. More importantly, the adivasis won't vote for us and many more will join the Maoists. We need to get to the root of the problem. Why is it that an increasing number of adivasis are supporting the Maoists and not backing us?'

'We can certainly go deeper into the problem later, sir,' said the DGP. 'But right now we don't have a minute to lose. There's no alternative but military action. Violence has to be responded to with violence. Bullet for bullet.'

'No, no, I don't agree. There *has* to be some other way, we *have* to find a way,' said the minister emphatically, craning his neck to seek inspiration from the Father of the Nation behind him. 'Violence has to be countered with non-violence. We have to win the support of the adivasis. We should try to work on their moral fibre, on their souls. We should aim to change their hearts and minds.'

'Sir, I have an idea,' said the Divisional Commissioner, who hadn't spoken till now. He too was a god-fearing man who abhorred violence. 'Why don't we seek Sri Sri Narayanaji's help? I've been attending his discourses and watching his yoga programmes on TV, sir. All my family members and I are his disciples.'

'Yes, yes, yes,' said the minister, immediately warming to the idea. 'At last someone has spoken sensibly. Why didn't anyone think of this earlier? We should immediately invite him to speak to the adivasis and convince them to become participants in the developmental process. I'm also Sri Sri Narayanaji's disciple. It's such a pity that we're not using him. I'm sure that he can change the hearts of the simple adivasis.'

'You're right, sir,' said the home secretary. 'Sri Sri Narayanaji is the son of our soil; he is our state ambassador. We must talk to him.'

'I'm sure it'll work,' said the divisional commissioner. 'I recently read in the papers that even the Nepali Maoist leader Prachanda has taken to yoga. If he can . . .'

'No, no . . . don't take the names of Nepali Maoists,' interjected the minister. 'But, yes, I'll certainly speak with the chief minister. We must arrange a meeting with Swamiji and work out a plan quickly. Fight violence with non-violence. At last we have a practical, tangible, long-term solution. I like the idea. Let us do it.'

'It is your idea, sir,' said the home secretary. 'What an idea—win the hearts and minds of the adivasis. If I may, sir, we can call it Operation Wham.'

The chief special adviser wanted to say something, but held himself back seeing that no one was paying him attention. Everyone was fawning over the minister who looked pleased as he stroked his tummy over his khadi kurta.

Tiger pushed his chair back and walked out of the meeting room, his moustache ends distinctly droopy. The home secretary followed him a few steps behind. After they'd walked some distance, he caught up with Tiger. 'Don't worry, Tejender-ji,' he said in a hushed tone. 'I'll do all in my power to provide support to Operation Red Hunt. Sometimes, we have to humour our politicians. You come tomorrow to my office and we'll discuss your plans. I'll also invite the DGP. I'm with you completely.'

Tiger reached for his moustache once again, smiled and walked away.

32

THE AIR WAS CRISP and cold when Aseem returned, at eleven in the night from Narayanaji's ashram, exhausted. He entered the flat noiselessly using a duplicate key, picked up the dinner plate that Ritika had prepared and left for him in the kitchen, poured himself a glass of water and went to his bedroom.

He was not hungry. He left the plate on the only chair facing a desk in his room, placed the laptop on his bed and sat cross-legged before it. There was a lot of work still left to be done: at Aroon's behest, he'd opened a Sri Sri Narayanaji fan club on Twitter where he planned to post messages in the swami's name. He also had to work on an article for the *Narayanaji Wellness Journal* which was to be hosted on www.narayanaji.com.

But Aseem's mind was fatigued and he was unable to concentrate. He looked away from the lit computer screen and stared at the blank wall. The plaster was peeling and had left a damp patch owing to a leak in the plumbing. Suddenly, in that darkened patch, a face began to emerge and, as it became more distinct, it was unmistakably Swati's face looking at him. But she was not the same: her black eyes had a faraway look. And then her image disappeared into the patch on the wall, as quickly as it had emerged.

His head began to throb with a piercing pain; he closed his eyes. It had been two months since Swati had left. He'd tried to drown himself in work without thinking about what he was doing and why, trying to forget her. But it had been in vain: her eyes haunted him, following him wherever he went, tormenting him. He couldn't get them out of his mind.

'Beta, you're back?' It was Ritika at his bedroom door wearing a shawl, her greying hair scattered over her shoulders. She looked concerned as she entered the room. 'You haven't even touched your food. It must've gone cold. I'll heat it again.'

Aseem turned his head to look at his mother, but didn't say anything. Ritika quietly picked up the plate and left the room. Back a while later with piping hot rice and dal, she sat down on the bed next to Aseem with the plate, taking a portion in her hand and taking it into his mouth. Aseem gently pushed her hand away. 'I can eat on my own, Ma. You go and sleep now.'

'All right, beta, but make sure you eat everything,' said Ritika, rising from the bed. 'You must go to bed now. You're looking tired. You'll fall ill if you continue this way.' She held his face between her hands, gave him a peck on the top of his head and left.

Back in her room, she quietly opened her closet, shut her eyes and fervently prayed for his well-being.

'Hi, Menaka-ji,' said Sri Kripananda, sounding elated over the phone.

Menaka had been warming her feet on Rambo's back under the breakfast table. 'Hi Sr-ree Kr-rreepananda, how ar-rrre you this mor-rrning?' she said.

'Ananda, ananda, it's all Swamiji's kripa,' said Sri Kripananda. 'I've some good news to give. The chief minister of Chhattisgarh has invited Swamiji to give a discourse to change the hearts and minds of the adivasis who are being led astray by the Maoists.'

'Really? Change the hearts and minds of people did you say? It sounds awesome! Did the chief minister speak with you himself?' asked Menaka excitedly.

'No, his PA did. They've named the event surrounding the discourse Operation Wham. I told him we'd discuss it and get back,' said Sri Kripananda. 'Sri Sri Narayanaji thought that we should discuss it with you and Aroon. What do you think?'

'You should've immediately said yes,' said Menaka. 'Imagine, an invitation from the chief minister himself! I must inform all my friends. I'll speak with Aroon and get back to you.'

'Did you hear that?' Menaka asked Aroon across the breakfast table. 'They want Swamiji to give a discourse to the adivasis and change their hearts and minds. What a lovely idea, isn't it?'

'It'll be a challenge,' said Aroon, sounding sceptical.

'We *must* take it up,' said Menaka, and went back to her restricted breakfast diet of half an apple and grapefruit juice.

A couple of days later, Aroon was addressing the ImpaKt team. 'So you see, while Operation Wham will be quite a challenge, if we can pull it off, we would've brought about a marketing revolution. Overnight, Sri Sri Narayanaji will be hailed as the twenty-first-century messiah and peacemaker. And this time, we'll have the entire government machinery and logistical support at our command. That is the assurance we have from the Chief Minister of Chhattisgarh himself. Now, let's get cracking, guys.'

After a fortnight of painstaking research, Aroon and the ImpaKt team zeroed in on Jagdalpur for Sri Sri Narayanaji's inaugural discourse. It was a natural choice given its proximity to the Maoist-controlled Bastar region. In terms of logistics it was nearly six hours by road from Chhattisgarh's capital, Raipur. There were no direct flights to Jagdalpur. The town had an airstrip, which had been built in the forties by the former Maharaja of Bastar, but it was no longer operational owing to disuse.

Meanwhile, Aseem and the ImpaKt copywriting team, in consultation with Sri Kripananda, were working on the script. They searched the Net and scratched their heads; they burst pimples and blew smoke rings in the air; they thought laterally and horizontally and transversely. It had to be an altogether different script from what they'd been writing for their corporate clients. The more they pondered, the more daunting the task appeared. The question that continued to rankle them was: In what manner could they talk about peace and non-violence to an audience that was inured to violence and killing? It seemed most unlikely that the impoverished, red-ant-eating adivasis could be won over by Kursikriya. But what they unanimously agreed upon was that the spirited services of the models in bodysuits would certainly be required to accomplish the problematic task.

33

A SHORT AND WIRY district official, who introduced himself as 'Mister' Ramesh Babu, greeted Aroon, Aseem and Uma, who was the event manager and deputy head of client servicing at ImpaKt. Looking distinctive in a pink shirt and burgundy-coloured trousers, Mister Babu led the visitors through the small but smart-looking terminal of Raipur airport. As soon they were outside,

Mister Babu took the trolley from a protesting Aroon and rolled it over to the peon who was waiting outside. He then offered to unburden Aroon of the camera slung around his neck, but seeing Aroon's angry glare retreated hastily.

'Please to come,' Mister Babu said, walking briskly towards a waiting Scorpio parked under a clump of trees.

Once they reached the Scorpio, Aroon took Mister Babu aside and said, 'I hope it's safe to travel by road. We've heard all kinds of things about these Maoists.'

'Very much safe here, sir,' said Mister Babu. 'The Maoists are not doing hanky-panky in this part of the district. Even otherwise, sir, they're not attacking tourists. They're only attacking gorment people like us and policemen meddling with them. That is why, sir, we're hiring you tourist taxi and not gorment car.'

Mister Babu introduced the visitors to the ageing driver of the Scorpio. 'Vishnu Dev will drive you to Jagdalpur. He is local and is also acting your guide.'

Vishnu Dev, with a salt-and-pepper moustache and curly white hair, opened the rear door of the Scorpio to load the luggage. Till some years back he'd worked as a tourist guide after he'd attended spoken-English classes in Jagdalpur. Two years ago, finding it difficult to make ends meet, he had put together his savings and combined them with a bank loan to buy the Scorpio.

Driver Vishnu opened the doors for the visitors. Aroon sat in front, nestling the camera in his lap, while Aseem and Uma sat in the rear seat. Mister Babu shut the doors.

'Aren't you coming with us?' asked Aroon.

'No sir,' said Mister Babu, feeling relieved that he'd not been asked to accompany the guests. 'Vishnu will take you. Other officers will meet you at Jagdalpur, sir.'

Mister Babu bid the guests adieu and they were off, Vishnu driving away with a ferocity that belied his age. As they left the township of Raipur and drove into the open and verdant countryside, the sky turned a pristine blue with a few white clouds floating along like wisps of cotton wool. The road was more or less smooth for the first part of the journey and later became uneven, but Vishnu didn't let up on his speed, shaking his head in rhythm with the Bollywood songs playing on the car stereo. There were not too many vehicles on the road, just the odd car, bus or truck, which he overtook with impetuous assurance.

With a cool February breeze blowing as they drove across the open landscape of green fields sparsely dotted with dwellings and dark trees in the distance, Aroon deliberated about the publicity plans for Narayanaji's discourse in his mind. There were many things they'd need to do to make it successful. In the rear seat, Uma embarrassed Aseem by behaving coquettishly, winking at him and placing a hand on his knee. Aseem shifted closer to the window on his side and looked out.

They stopped for tea at a roadside dhaba. An old adivasi woman in a short electric blue sari stood by the dhaba carrying custard apples in a wicker basket. Uma said she wanted to buy some custard apples and Aroon went up to the adivasi woman. She didn't want money, the woman said with a toothy smile, but wished to barter the fruit for food or city goods. As Aroon pondered what he could offer, the dhaba owner struck an amicable deal, pocketing a fair number of currency notes from Aroon and giving the adivasi woman a meagre quantity of rice in return. The elderly adivasi woman parted happily with half the custard apples in her basket and they were soon on their way again.

As they neared their destination, the road became steep and winding, and the landscape more hilly and forested. After a climb of a few kilometres, the serene, green valley of Jagdalpur came into view through a clearing in the forested hillside, spread out in the distance. Looking out of the window of the car, Aseem was captivated by the enchanting valley situated on the sandy banks of the Indravati River. The rooftops of the dwellings of the town merged in the landscape like the colourful dots of a Pissario painting. Surrounded by the dense forest of sal trees, the valley was bathed in the golden light of the sun with the waters of the fast-flowing river glistening like a long, silver fish.

'How incredibly beautiful,' said Uma, looking at the landscape through her round spectacles. 'Can we not stop here for a while?'

At Aroon's request, Vishnu took the car to the side of the road, shut off the engine and pulled up the handbrake. He stepped out of the car and disappeared round a bend in the road to pee, while the others admired the magnificent valley. A bracing breeze brought in the fresh fragrance of the forest and the exhaustion of the long journey immediately vanished. Aroon clicked some photographs of the valley.

'Let's go,' he said after a while, breaking the magical spell. 'Or we'll end up staying here forever.'

I wouldn't mind, Aseem wanted to say, feeling like someone being wrenched away from a glimpse of paradise. The view reminded him of his summer holidays while he was in school: Baba holding him by the hand at the edge of a road on a hillside and pointing to a gleaming snow-capped mountaintop in the distant horizon.

34

AVINASH WAS AT HIS new desk in his office; it really *was* a new desk this time, with no broken legs. In fact, it had no legs at all, just flat pieces of ply the colour of lightwood on either side. They didn't even call it a desk; they had a new name for it: workstation. The workstation was L-shaped, with a red laminated top, and Avinash didn't sit behind it, but faced it, snugly fitted in a revolving chair with an adjustable lever, his bulging stomach between the two limbs of the L.

Two ragged-looking hardbound registers with frayed edges were lying on the tabletop. Placed alongside was a sheaf of crisp printouts fastened by a large clip. There was also a brown spectacle case made of cheap rexine on the side. Avinash had recently bought a pair of spectacles, as he had been finding it increasingly difficult to read properly. He was at the moment, however, not using his reading specs or for that matter going through the registers or attending to the clipped set of papers. His mind was far away, thinking of Aseem, wondering what he was doing.

A few days earlier, Aseem had left for Jagdalpur. Avinash hadn't asked him for any details; Aseem had said that it had something to do with the Narayanaji project. Avinash himself had given up on his own career a long time ago, but he'd always hoped that his son would be able to chart out a more purposeful path for himself. How ironical it was that Aseem, *his* son, had ended up working with Aroon and Menaka to market a sham guru. He couldn't have imagined anything more abhorrent than that. Avinash's breathing quickened, his nostrils flared with helpless indignation at the thought.

Avinash stared blankly at the blue tackboard in front of him. After a while, he swivelled around to face the office. It was completely transformed, looking immaculate and uncluttered. The broken glass on the windows had been replaced, the walls had been freshly painted, the floor had new polished tiles. He missed the look of the old, clumsy space, with its broken furniture and dusty files; he'd grown accustomed to it. Now everything had changed. There were so many new faces. It seemed that he alone was out of place.

He had a new computer geek as his boss, a smart-looking man with shiny, gelled hair called Siddhartha Arjuna, who looked younger than his thirty-five years. Siddhartha had been assigned the task of computerizing the office records and research data. A fortnight earlier, he had assigned Avinash the task of comparing the data and statistics recorded by hand in the piles of registers against the final entries and scans prepared by Avinash's neighbour Neeraj.

'Most of the original is in your own handwriting, Avinash,' Siddhartha had said. 'So it'll be easy. All you have to do is to compare the data carefully. You don't need to exercise your mind or make any changes. But make sure you don't leave any errors.'

Since then, Avinash had been working on the comparisons. It had been many, many years since he'd opened the old registers stored in the rusting steel almirahs. Turning back to face his workstation, he took out his spectacles from its case and carefully adjusted the frame over the bridge of his nose. Then, with weary reluctance, he picked up one of the registers and opened it.

Leafing through the pages, now yellowed with age, he noticed how his handwriting had changed over the years. When he'd been younger, his handwriting had been hasty and blotchy, the letters large and ungainly, written with a cheap ballpoint pen. By and by, it had improved, become a little smaller and more legible. More recently, he'd been consciously focusing on his handwriting and had invested in an expensive pen with a smooth roller point. The entries in the register had now become neat and even, written in a slow, careful hand, crafted with painstaking meticulousness.

Avinash found the work dull and mechanical, but he didn't mind the tedium to much—it was better than having no work at all. He pulled out the bottom drawer of his workstation; it opened smoothly, unlike the jerky drawers of his old desk. He'd taken care to see that the new drawer was well organized and contained only the essentials—a twelve-inch scale, a calculator, a paper cutter, a pair of yellow-limbed scissors, an eraser, a ballpoint pen and a pencil. Picking out the pen and the pair of scissors, he pushed the drawer shut.

The top drawer contained the morning newspaper. Avinash drew it out and took out the 'Appointments' supplement. Scanning through the pages, he encircled a few advertisements and cut them out. He then neatly placed them into the folder labelled 'ASEEM'.

The old peon, Ramdass, walked up to him. 'Saab has called you.'

Putting the folder back into his briefcase, Avinash got up from his seat and went to the glass-enclosed cabin at the end of the passage.

'Good afternoon, Avinash. Do take a seat,' Siddhartha Arjuna said, rising from his chair to shake hands with Avinash and pointing to a chair across his polished table. He was wearing dark grey trousers slung low on his hips.

'How are you, Avinash? All well?' said Siddhartha, smiling below a meticulously trimmed moustache.

'I'm fine,' said Avinash as he sat down.

'You're looking prosperous,' commented Siddhartha with a glance at Avinash's belly. 'How's your family? Are your children settled?'

'I have a son. He's taken up a job recently.'

'Good, that's good. And you have your own house?'

'Yes, I have a flat.'

'That's excellent. I still live in rented accommodation. I'm so happy for you. You seem to have taken care of yourself. What more can one wish for when one is retiring.'

'Retiring? I still have a few years to go.'

'I know, I know. But you know, Avinash, sometimes I think how nice it'd be to retire and do all the things one always wanted to,' said Siddhartha, looking away into the distance. 'If I could retire today, I'd travel, see the world. Go to the US, see Switzerland, visit Venice and Rome. Where's the time now?'

Avinash remained silent.

'Have you ever thought of taking an early retirement, Avinash?' said Siddhartha, turning to face him.

'No, I've never thought of it,' Avinash replied. 'I've yet to clear a substantial part of the loan for my flat. And my son is not yet fully settled in his job. I can't possibly think of it.'

'How much of the loan is left? Five lakh, ten lakh?'

'About five.'

'Oh, is that all? That's not much. That can be taken care of.'

'Yes. But it'd probably take me another three years or so to save that much.'

'No, that's not what I meant,' said Siddhartha, his face suddenly assuming a harder expression. 'Avinash, I'll come to the point and not beat about the bush. You've been with the organization for long, but we think the time has come for you to make way for younger people. You know that the government has divested a major stake, which has been bought over by the Rumanis. I've been with the Rumanis for over five years now. They have an altogether different style of working. We don't think you will fit in the style.'

'I-I don't know what you mean,' stuttered Avinash, taken aback.

'Let me complete,' said Siddhartha, pursing his lips. 'I was telling you about the Rumanis. They are very generous and big-hearted. Employee welfare is their chief concern. If you "volunteer" to retire, we'd give you a very good compensation that would not only take care of your housing loan, but would also leave you with a substantial sum, which you can invest to give you a regular income. You would of course get your usual provident fund and gratuity. What do you think?'

'I don't know.'

'Avinash, I'll be frank. You don't really have a choice here. We want to make things easier for long-serving employees like you. If you volunteer, it'll make the process a lot smoother, you know.'

35

IT WAS NEARING EVENING as the Scorpio carrying the ImpaKt reconnaissance team sped towards Jagdalpur, bisecting sugarcane fields interspersed with jackfruit and wild mango trees. In the distant horizon, were the dense hardwood forests of sal, seja and swaju. Soon, the rippling waters of Dalpat Sagar Lake in Jagdalpur, reflecting the green landscape, came into view. They went round a bend to catch a glimpse of the Chitrakot Falls cascading down in six distinct strands like shimmering sheets of silver with golden streaks reflecting the evening glow in the sky.

'Awesome!' exclaimed Uma, leaning across Aseem to get a clearer view, even as he shrank back in his seat.

'As majestic as the Niagara Falls,' said Aroon, quickly taking some photographs.

'How far are we?' asked Aseem.

'We're almost there,' said Vishnu, turning down the volume of the music to make himself heard. 'You can see the eucalyptus plantations. Jagdalpur is only a few kilometres beyond that.'

'They look so elegant,' said Uma, admiring the slender eucalyptus trees.

'But they draw up all the water. There is water scarcity now in Bastar. Even these cashew plantations were not there earlier,' said the wizened driver, pointing to the spreading grove of cashew trees that now came into view. 'The planters want to make more money through these cash crops, but no one's growing ragi and rice for us to eat.'

'What's he saying?' asked Uma. 'I don't understand.'

'I don't know,' said Aroon. 'There's so much water here, everywhere. Look at the river.'

The road now straightened and they drove past bougainvillea shrubs and gulmohur trees and approached an iron bridge over the gushing waters of the Indravati River. It was getting dark, the sun having moved behind the dense forest in the distance, as they crossed the bridge to reach the town of Jagdalpur. Vishnu turned on the headlamps full beam to negotiate his way. The strong light picked out the people crossing the road at a leisurely pace.

The township was pulsating with life. Vishnu knew the streets like the lines on his palm, and he drove down the winding road like a rally champion, constantly blowing the horn. After a sharp U-turn, the Scorpio braked to a halt outside the three-storey Hotel Three Star.

Next morning at 9.00 a.m. sharp a district official was standing on the polished teak floor of the hotel lobby, chewing betel nut, waiting to greet Aroon and the rest of the ImpaKt team. 'At your service, sir. My name is Shri Nakul.' He told Aroon that he would be the official escort of the ImpaKt team during their stay in Jagdalpur.

'So, Shri Nakul, are we ready to go?' asked Aroon.

'Yes sir,' said Shri Nakul through his betel-stained teeth.

'Where're we going?' Uma wanted to know.

'Sir, DC-saab is waiting for you at the Shanti Kadam camp,' said Shri Nakul.

'Shanti Kadam?' asked Aroon curiously.

'The Shanti Kadam is a voluntary refugee group fighting the Maoists, sir,' explained Shri Nakul. 'DC-saab is inspecting a refugee camp for the adivasis being looked after by the Shanti Kadam. Since it falls on the way, DC-saab asked me to take you there to meet him. After we meet him, we'll go to the Chitrakot Falls. No one who visits Jagdalpur misses a visit to the falls.'

It was half an hour's drive to the refugee camp. After a slow, twisting ride out of the crowded streets of Jagdalpur, the road opened up and there were fewer and fewer signs of habitation.

Soon after they'd left the outskirts of the shanty town, they saw the camp with a large number of tarpaulin tents pitched alongside the road. As they drew nearer, they saw many more tents and a few semi-permanent structures with sloping red-tiled roofs and bamboo walls.

Vishnu swerved the Scorpio to the side of the road and jerked to an abrupt halt. Shri Nakul got down and began to walk across a bald patch of land to the camp, the others behind him. A high barbed-wire fence surrounded the entire camp. At a crude bamboo gate, two adivasi boys, not more than sixteen years old and wearing khaki shorts, stood behind a pile of sandbags carrying .303 guns by their sides. They raised their hands casually in salute as Shri Nakul led the visitors through the gate. Soon another two adolescent boys with guns resting on their shoulders joined them and began walking alongside.

'Hello, what's this?' asked Aroon. 'Why're these guys here? Where are we?'

'They're for your protection, sir,' said Shri Nakul.

'These guys don't look anything like regular security guards,' said Uma.

'They are special police officers, madam—SPOs. The state government has been training the adivasis to protect themselves against Maoist attacks,' said Shri Nakul, spotting the DC walking out from a tin shed. 'Our DC will explain.'

Shri Rama Prasad, the DC, was a smart young man with a thick moustache and was wiping his rimless spectacles with a handkerchief.

'Welcome to the Shanti Kadam camp,' said the DC, showing his white teeth. 'I hope you had a pleasant journey.'

'Yes, thank you,' said Aroon. 'I was just asking Shri Nakul who these armed chaps were.'

'It's a long story,' said the DC. 'They're all displaced villagers who've taken shelter here. They're poor victims of Maoist violence. We've inducted some of them as SPOs and have been providing them training in arms.'

'But can you give civilians arms? Is it legal?' asked Aseem, his interest aroused.

'Absolutely. Its perfectly legal,' said the DC. 'The Special Police Act of 1861 empowers us to arm ordinary citizens for their protection. The Maoists had been instilling fear in the adivasis, not allowing them to work in the mines or to take up government jobs. They don't even allow them to vote.'

Aseem looked around. There were small dwelling units with tattered canvas or bamboo walls covered with tin or tarpaulin sheets. Cutting through the makeshift shelters were open sewer drains. It reminded him of the slums in Delhi. Some of the units were fenced with bamboo in front, behind which some poultry wandered about. A few men were idly standing around or sitting on charpoys drinking tea. They eyed the visitors suspiciously. One of the SPOs waved his gun threateningly at the men to make way for the guests. There were more women than men in the camp, bustling around, doing small chores, carrying water vessels, tending to infants with distended bellies, cleaning utensils with soil. Small children ran around, practically naked except for a thread tied around their waists.

'I don't see older children,' observed Uma. 'Are they at school?'

'Oh yes, we have a school right here,' said the DC. 'We have volunteers coming to teach them. Come, I'll take you there.'

The school was an open-air enclosure where children of all ages were sitting cross-legged on the ground with black slates in their laps. A young man with a saffron smear on his forehead prowled up and down in rubber slippers like a tiger in a cage, speaking in staccato tones, 'Write ten times: "My country is great. She is like our mother."'

Noticing the visitors, the teacher greeted them with a namaskar while continuing to pace up and down.

'We have to instil patriotism among the adivasis,' explained the DC. 'We have to educate them about our great culture and traditions. Every morning they sing 'Vande Mataram'. We are also getting a yoga teacher to come to the camp twice a week. All this is the chief minister's idea. It's not easy to make the adivasis learn or understand anything. They're uncivilized, you know. After all, they live in the forests.'

'How long have they been living in this camp?' asked Aseem.

'About three years,' said the DC without batting an eyelid. 'If they go back to their villages, they'll get killed by the Maoists.'

'What happens to their food?' asked Aseem.

'We have a food-for-work programme,' said the DC, who seemed to have an answer for everything. 'We're also training some of them to take up positions as SPOs, for which they get paid.'

'What about government forces?' asked Aroon.

'There aren't enough security men,' said the DC, and then lowered his voice. 'Truth is, no one wants to be posted here.'

'So, are these people always confined to the camp?' asked Aseem.

'Well, some of the braver people venture out early in the morning to collect mahua flowers,' said Shri Nakul. 'They exchange them for other commodities in the nearby villages.'

'We don't of course encourage their going out,' added the DC. 'They can get attacked by the Maoists. But we can't stop them either. This is not a jail, you know.'

'Okay, can we now discuss the possible venues for Swamiji's discourse?' said Aroon, suddenly remembering why they were all there.

'If you ask me, I think the main maidan would be the best choice,' said the DC. 'But you decide. Shri Nakul will take you there. Once you've seen it, we can discuss further. I'll see you in your hotel in the evening.'

'I don't understand,' said Aseem, as they drove out of the camp. 'How come so many of the adivasis got driven out to the camps?'

'The DC explained, didn't he?' said Aroon. 'They were forced out by the Maoists.'

'That's not the entire truth,' interjected Vishnu. 'The adivasis have been lured with money and false promises. The government has signed land deals with industrialists and MNCs for mining. They tell the adivasis that the miners will give them jobs.'

'Is that true?' asked Aseem, turning to Shri Nakul.

'Don't believe him,' said Shri Nakul. 'The adivasis are fed up with the Maoists. There can be no development till they're rescued.'

'So, they're stuck in camps forever, are they?' asked Aseem.

'Till the war between the Maoists and the government's forces comes to an end. This is the story everywhere,' said Vishnu, shaking his head. 'The hapless adivasis are caught between the devil and the deep sea.'

'But I still don't understand,' said Aroon. 'Why can't they get better security people to tackle the Maoists than these adolescent SPOs?'

'Why should the security forces risk their lives when you've got someone else to do the job?' remarked Vishnu bitterly.

'They're adivasis, sir,' added Shri Nakul insouciantly. 'If a few die, it'll do no one any harm. The problem arises when the Maoists attack us. Last week they planted a landmine and blew up a government jeep. Five government officers died in the blast.'

'You mean that they'll blow up any vehicle?' asked Uma, looking mortified.

'We're almost there, sir,' said Nakul, ignoring the question and pointing to the waterfalls in the distance.

A misty cloud of white spray surrounded the Chitrakot Falls. Torrential sheets of the swift-flowing Indravati at its widest span plunged dramatically down a sharp cliff, its frothy waters smashing in the tumultuous, semicircular lake that had formed below. A few boats reeled and rocked perilously in the swirling waters of the river a little further downstream from the base of the falls carrying brave adventure tourists wearing yellow life jackets. On the other side, where the river was calmer, some others were taking holy dips.

Shri Nakul led the guests over an uneven terrain of smooth stones to an area where the falls dropped down sharply, past a couple of luxury log huts, to a conical canvas tent decorated like a frilly frock. They sat there for some time drinking tea and looking at the white waters falling like unending blasts.

'I think we should be going now,' said Aroon, after he'd taken some snaps. 'We've come here to do a job.'

No one protested. Though distracted momentarily by the spectacular falls, they felt frightened after the conversations about the Maoists and were hugely relieved to be returning to the hotel.

On the return journey from the Chitrakot Falls, as they crossed the Shanti Kadam camp, Vishnu pointed to the Mulba Silk Factory with its angular roof and to a plantation of mulberry trees next to it. 'The trees are being grown to feed silkworms,' the knowledgeable driver explained. 'The farms also grow the local saja and arjuna trees, whose yellow leaves are used to feed the tussar silk caterpillars. But the best silk comes from the caterpillars in the wild. They're like the adivasis who don't want to leave the forests. The wild caterpillars refuse to get confined to the farms and so their cocoons have to be collected from the forest.'

No one in the car was interested as the driver proceeded to unravel the silk from the cocoon of his knowledge about caterpillars. All they prayed for was to reach the safety of the hotel. Their prayers were soon answered, the Scorpio zipping uneventfully down the winding road and into the crowded marketplace in Jagdalpur.

Making slow progress on the narrow, crowded road, it took them a while to get back to Hotel Three Star: besides the normal traffic, there were several wedding processions on the streets.

'So many weddings on the same day,' Aroon remarked.

'It's an auspicious day,' said Vishnu.

A marriage party was underway at the hotel as well. A crowd of people was dancing at the entrance to a raucous band in red coats and white pants, playing Bollywood tunes. Aroon, Uma and Aseem waded their way past them. After a quick wash, they were down in the dining hall for lunch.

'We'll meet in the lobby in an hour,' announced Aroon, as soon as the meal was over. 'I hope you've not forgotten that we have to identify a suitable venue for Swamiji's address.'

36

SHRI RAMA PRASAD HAD been right. Identifying the venue was the easiest of their tasks. Shri Nakul escorted them to a maidan not very far from the hotel, a large bowl-shaped meadow the size of a cricket field. There were groups of boys playing cricket with earnest intent, wielding crudely crafted willows of hardwood, inspired by the local cricketing hero Naren Thumi who'd found a place in the national team. Sticks of bamboo dug into the ground made for the wickets. Since Thumi's selection to the team, the boys had abandoned all other sport—the gilli danda and football—and taken single-mindedly to cricket.

'These grounds are where the people usually gather when a dignitary visits Jagdalpur,' said Shri Nakul, turning his head to spit out a stream of betel-leaf juice.

'The maidan is perfect,' said Aroon, looking down at the grounds, standing behind a crude bamboo fencing alongside the road. He visualized the adivasis sitting placidly on the gentle slopes of the grassy land in the natural amphitheatre. 'I don't think we need to see any other venue.'

'If I may ask, sir,' said Shri Nakul, 'what exactly is this event about? Will there be songs and dancing?'

'Well, not exactly,' said Aroon. 'But let me explain. Have you seen Sri Sri Narayanaji on TV?'

'Who doesn't know about him, sir,' said Shri Nakul. 'The government has made his exercises compulsory in all state-run schools in Chhattisgarh, sir. He's very famous in these parts.'

'That's fantastic! I didn't realize he was so popular. It will make our task that much easier,' said Aroon. 'So, you see, we're planning to have him here in Jagdalpur.'

'Oh really, sir!' exclaimed Shri Nakul. 'Will he demonstrate the exercises in person?'

'Well, yes, but we have a larger mission,' said Uma.

'Yes,' continued Aroon. 'We hope that those adivasis who've been misguided by the Maoists will have a change of heart. We're hoping that Swamiji will be able to show them the path to salvation, the path to moksha,' said Uma.

'Umm . . . umm . . .' said Shri Nakul.

'You were saying something?' said Aroon.

'Nothing, sir,' said Shri Nakul. 'I was just wondering to what extent the adivasis would understand the concept of salvation. For the adivasis, there's no such thing as salvation or moksha from the cycle of birth. They believe in transformation; for them life is a continuum. Kinship for them extends to the inanimate world. All objects, all living beings—birds, animals, stones, humans—get transformed, and life goes on and on. After transformation, they believe that they become even more powerful. There's no such thing as death for them.'

'Is that the reason these adivasis don't fear for their lives?' asked Aroon.

'I don't know, sir,' said Shri Nakul. 'There's one other thing. The adivasis are very excitable. They take to violence at the slightest provocation.'

'That's exactly why we're organizing Swamiji's discourse,' said Uma, 'to teach them how to control their emotions through his special yoga exercises.'

Shri Nakul was pouting.

'Why? You don't think it's a good idea?' asked Aroon. 'It's the home minister's suggestion, you know.'

'No, no, sir. I didn't mean that, sir,' said Shri Nakul quickly. 'Of course, the adivasis will like it. My stupid comment comes from my ignorance, sir. Just let me know what I have to do and I'll make all the necessary bandobast for you.'

One he'd learned that the swami's visit was the home minister's idea, Shri Nakul was now all the more eager to provide assistance.

If he could impress Aroon, perhaps he'd be able to persuade the visitor to put in a good word with the minister to have him transferred out of Jagdalpur. He regarded his present assignment as a 'punishment posting'.

That evening, after they had rested, the ImpaKt team gathered together for a meeting in Aroon's suite, the only one on the first floor of Hotel Three Star, together with Shri Nakul and Shri Rama Prasad. The television was on, showing blurred images of an adivasi dance recital on a local news channel. With one part of their agenda—the finalization of the venue—frozen, they were now discussing the logistics of the event. Aseem was officially appointed the logistics manager, and was to work out the details of the bandobast along with Shri Nakul.

Two plates of masala peanuts and a bottle of whisky were ordered to lend clarity to the proceedings. Bent over a centre table, they studied the Jagdalpur district map and a desk calendar.

'This is where the state guest house is,' said Shri Nakul, placing a finger on the map. 'It's not far from the maidan. The government dignitaries will be staying here.'

Then they got into the finer details: the travel and transportation arrangements, the time and date of the event, the security preparations. Aseem took down copious notes.

'We need to talk to the SP about the security,' said the DC, not sounding very convincing.

'We're hoping to persuade the home minister to be the chief guest,' said Aroon. 'We'll need very good security.'

'Oh, if the minister is coming, you don't need to worry,' said the DC. 'The DGP will arrange pucca security.'

'We'll need a high stage with a good sound system,' said Uma.

'That too will not be a problem,' said Shri Nakul confidently. He got up from his chair and went up to a waste bin in the room to spit out tiny specks of chewed betel leaf.

There was some discussion on the publicity. 'We can do it as in the elections,' suggested the DC, sipping his whisky. 'We'll have autorickshaws with speakers announcing the event in crowded places.'

'We want visibility,' said Uma. 'Cloth banners must be put up across all the roads, the special hare-shaped balloons we've designed must fly from rooftops, posters must be pasted on walls, in toilets, on every available vertical surface.'

'Consider it done,' said Shri Nakul.

'Paint Jagdalpur all over with the message,' said Aroon. 'Every man, woman and child in the town should get to know about the Narayanaji event.'

'And we'll have the event aired on all popular TV channels,' said Uma. 'But how will you get the villagers to reach here?'

'We can arrange buses for them from Gole Market. But they'll have to walk from their villages till there. Some will still need to walk for more than four hours,' said the DC.

'But will they come then?' asked Aroon.

'They'll surely come if we give them an incentive,' said Shri Nakul.

'Why don't we give them shoes? They have to walk so much,' suggested Uma.

'The adivasis don't wear shoes, sir,' said Shri Nakul, accustomed to addressing his seniors of either gender as sir. 'They will exchange them for something or the other.'

'I agree. Cash is better,' said the DC, finishing his drink. 'Not too much. Once we just picked them up from Gole Market with a promise of twenty rupees. It means a lot to them. Election time we give blankets—then more adivasis come, in defiance of the Maoists. Then there are so many living in the camps. You just let us know the numbers you want present and arrange for the funds. We'll take care of the rest.'

'Funds are no problem. You tell me how much you want,' said Aroon. 'We'd like a really huge assembly.'

'You come to my office tomorrow and we can discuss the details,' said the DC, rising from his chair. 'We'll be going now.'

Moments after Shri Nakul and Shri Rama Prasad left, Aroon was gripped by a panic attack: What if the barefoot adivasis did not take kindly to the swami's address? He worried about Shri Nakul's observations on the adivasi beliefs about transformation. What if the discourse didn't make the necessary impact? It was not as though the swami had any special powers; it was the ImpaKt team that had fashioned his image and made him larger than life. But marketing too has its limits. All that they'd achieved would come to naught if Operation Wham failed. That was putting it mildly—in fact, it'd be a disaster.

'Listen guys,' said Aroon, scratching his beard. 'I have a doubt. We seem to have assumed that Swamiji will be able to change the hearts and minds of the adivasis. But have you thought of the eventuality in which the adivasis are *not* moved by his address?'

'There's a huge possibility of that happening,' agreed Uma. 'Obviously, the Maoist influence seems much more than what we'd imagined before we came here. The adivasis are different from the corporates.'

'That's what I'm saying,' said Aroon. 'We need something far more dramatic to happen to make them change.'

'I think you're right. Nothing short of a miracle will make it work,' said Uma.

'That's it! You've got it,' said Aroon. 'We need a miracle.'

'It's not in our hands to perform miracles,' commented Aseem.

'Sure,' said Aroon, 'but we can make a miracle happen.'

'What do you mean?' asked Aseem.

'Like Swamiji producing ash from thin air?' suggested Uma.

'That's old hat,' said Aroon. 'We need a more uncommon miracle.'

'What about a miracle cure?' asked Uma. 'It'd be great if Swamiji could demonstrate a cure in front of the adivasis.'

'Brilliant!' said Aroon, jumping up excitedly from his chair. 'This is it! Let's get him to perform a miraculous cure in front of the audience. Now, what could that be?' He sat down and rubbed his beard while Uma lit a cigarette. 'I got it!' continued Aroon excitedly. 'Remember, I told you that Swamiji had cured himself of a disability in his leg through yoga when he was a young boy? We can now have him cure a lame person on stage.'

'But his own cure would've taken a while, isn't it?' said Uma, blowing smoke out of her mouth. 'It can't be an instant cure, can it?'

'Why not?' said Aroon. 'All we have to do is to get someone to fake a limp and have Swamiji cure the person then and there in front of the adivasis.'

'Wow! What an idea,' said Uma, greatly enthused. 'We can get a young boy to come limping on to the stage, then have Swamiji recite a few mantras, do some mumbo-jumbo, twist his leg this way and that, and lo and behold, the boy is cured.'

'Fantastic!' said Aroon. 'The simplest solutions are always the best.'

'But...' said Aseem hesitatingly, 'that'd be deceiving the adivasis.'

'C'mon, son! Don't we do that every day in the corporate world?' said Aroon, rising from his chair and walking animatedly up and down the room. 'Good, good! There's no time to waste. Uma, it'll be your job to find a boy and train him to act out the limp.'

'Hold it . . . but . . . how can you possibly?' said Aseem, raising his voice. 'This would be blatant cheating.'

'Don't be naïve, Aseem,' Aroon said. 'We have a job to do, and we have to do it in a way that will give the desired results. Our loyalty is to our client, who in this case is Sri Kripananda.'

'But will Sri Kripananda himself approve?' asked Uma.

'We'll convince him, don't worry,' said Aroon. 'He's a practical man.'

'This is terribly, terribly wrong,' said Aseem, seething with anger. 'I cannot be a party to a decision to fool the adivasis.'

'It's not the journey which is important, son, it is the destination,' said Aroon. 'Everything we've done is at stake. If we don't succeed, all will be lost.' He then turned to Uma before continuing. 'You begin the preparations straight away. Identify an adivasi boy, twelve or thirteen years old, and train him to do the limping act. It shouldn't be difficult. Look for someone from a poor family. We can give cash rewards to both the boy and his family.'

'Done,' said Uma.

Aseem was livid. He didn't mind small untruths, white lies, sometimes essential in the corporate world, but performing a miraculous cure in front of innocent adivasis to deceive them was completely unethical. His heartbeat quickened in anger, but he remained silent. Aroon's mind was made up and there was little Aseem could do.

Later, alone in his hotel room, Aseem struggled to come to terms with the predicament that he found himself in. He went to the toilet and stood in front of the washbasin, his hands resting on either side of its rim, looking at his tired face in the mirror. He opened the tap and allowed the water to flow full blast into the basin and watched the small whirlpool that formed at the mouth of the drain. He felt trapped like a piece of flotsam at the bottom of the fast-flowing Chitrakot Falls, powerless, dragged along in an interminable eddy. He wanted to break free, but he saw no escape from the gushing, unending waters that threatened to take over his life.

37

GOPAL SAT IN A small room in an obscure guest house near Gole Market in Jagdalpur, with a sheet of paper spread out in front of him, detailing the action plan for the night to his comrades. With him were Moesa and Kuttu, a young adivasi. Kuttu was the leader of a Maoist dalam like the one Moesa led.

'This is your call, Kuttu,' Gopal said. 'Moesa will be in a van close by waiting for you. She will cover you, in case something goes wrong, and help you to quickly make a getaway. I made a recce in the afternoon. There were only two police guards at the station outside. There may be a few constables inside who'll probably be sleeping when you attack.'

'We're ready,' said Kuttu.

'All the best,' said Gopal. 'Lal salaam.'

'Lal salaam,' said Moesa and Kuttu in unison.

Early next morning, Kuttu along with five of his dalam members, armed with rifles and pistols and knives, moved stealthily in the dark shadows of the bylanes near the district police station in Jagdalpur. The sound of firecrackers that were still being burst to celebrate the scores of weddings held the previous evening drowned the plaintive whines of a stray dog.

The police station was a low pucca structure painted in red and blue, with an open veranda and a high iron gate. There was an iron grille fencing around the boundary of the station, lined with a hedge. Kuttu was the first to spot the police guards. One sat on a wicker chair at the gate, his head nodding to one side as he dozed, the other was standing in the veranda. Putting a finger to his lips, Kuttu signalled to his five comrades to stay close behind him as he moved towards the gate, crouching all the time so he was hidden by the hedge. He took out a sharp knife from a sheath tied to his leg. Holding it behind his back, he moved soundlessly towards the guard, keeping himself camouflaged behind the hedge. He kept an eye on the second guard in the veranda. Slowly, quietly, he took position a few feet behind the guard in the wicker chair at the gate.

The guard in the veranda turned around and went into the police station. Kuttu quickly took the opportunity to cross over the hedge and the iron grille, and then, still crouching, he moved within breathing distance of the guard in the chair. He sat for a moment on his haunches like a frog, his knife held firmly in his right hand, ready for attack. Then, all of a sudden, he leapt forward, covering the mouth of the guard with his left hand

and simultaneously bringing his knife down swiftly like a frog's darting tongue. Before the surprised victim could react, Kuttu had stabbed the guard in the chest, again and again. Steadying the bleeding body in the wicker chair, he wiped the bloodied knife carelessly on his fatigues and put it back in its sheath. He drew out his pistol from the holster in his belt and signalled to the others.

The waiting group of five jumped over the hedge and the fence and quickly ran behind Kuttu to the veranda for the final assault, their rifles on the ready. Kuttu peeped in through a window. The guard who'd been standing in the veranda had joined two other constables to play cards around a small table. Holding his pistol in front of him, Kuttu signalled to his comrades to stay close behind. The door creaked as he opened it.

'Who's there?' shouted one of the constables. But before he could even reach the .303 lying by his side, Kuttu had fired his first shot, which was soon followed by a barrage of rifle shots from his comrades. The first constable fell dead on the table over the spread of cards, the others dropped softly to the floor like sacks of tendu leaves, bleeding profusely. Ignoring the dead cops, they quickly looked for what they'd come to take. Heaped in one corner was a huge pile of khaki police uniforms. They made bundles of the uniforms, and picked up the policemen's rifles and all the ammunition they could lay their hands on. Kuttu took out his walkie-talkie and called out.

Not far away, Moesa, sitting in a van along with her own dalam members in the darkness of the night, heard Kuttu's message. Beaming from ear to ear, she asked the van driver to drive to the police station to collect Kuttu and his band and their booty.

Aseem woke up to the sound of a band playing melancholic songs of parting as the wedding party of the previous evening now left Hotel Three Star. 'Tara-tu-roo, tara-tu-roo' went their assortment of brass and local instruments—the trumpet, the flute, the mridangam and the naangor.

Sitting on the bed in his hotel room, the bedsheet crushed at his feet, Aseem wasn't thinking straight: his mind spun like an erratic top. He leant back on the cushioned bedrest and covered his ears with his hands, desperately trying to shut out the cacophony outside and dispel the strange thoughts churning in his mind. He had to get away from this sham and deceit; he'd had enough of it. All night he'd tossed and turned in bed, trying to figure a way out of the mess he'd landed himself in.

There was no one he could go to for advice, unburden his mind. He thought of Swati. If she'd been around, he could've turned to her for love and counsel. For a brief moment, he allowed himself to relive the tender moments he'd shared with her. But soon he remembered where he was—alone in the hotel room. She wasn't there with him; she'd deserted him. He hadn't been able to earn her respect, win her love. He was an aimless drifter without her determination and sense of purpose.

He removed his hands from his ears, deliberately allowing the jarring sounds of the wedding band to reach him, to suppress thoughts of her. He felt abandoned, like an orphaned child, and an overpowering weariness surged in his being. He brought his arms around his knees, hugging his loneliness.

Avinash walked out slowly from Arjuna's cabin in a state of shock. He went back to his desk, his head reeling. He locked his fingers behind his head and rested it against the palms of his crossed hands. It had never crossed his mind that a time would come when he'd be asked to leave the organization on a VRS, or, to put it plainly, that he'd be thrown out. How foolish of him: he should've known it was inevitable.

His thoughts turned to Ritika. She was always composed and uncomplaining. She'd made herself strong like hardened steel; she could take all vicissitudes in her stride. Maybe he didn't know her well enough; maybe she hid her true emotions from him. He'd let her down; he hadn't provided enough for her and Aseem. One word kept reverberating in his mind: regret, regret, regret. Looking back at his past would not help. He could not change what had happened; he must look ahead. He sat deep in thought for a while. After some time an idea crossed his mind and he knew exactly what he had to do.

He placed his hands on the desk and picked himself up, straightening his slouch and pushing in his belly. He reached into the cupboard above his desk and took out a moth-eaten folder marked 'AB—Personal'. He opened the folder and, picking up a pen, started making some calculations.

All of a sudden, he winced as he felt a twinge of pain in his chest. He took a few deep breaths, waiting for the pain to subside. Breathing slowly now, he felt a calmness descend over him, a resoluteness of purpose. Putting the folder in his briefcase, he walked out of the office with determined strides to his bank nearby. Then he took a bus to the main street to buy stamp paper.

Aseem forced himself to get up from the bed; he had to confront the present reality. The first thought that crossed his mind was to remain behind at Jagdalpur and expose ImpaKt and the swami. But he soon gave up on the idea, not feeling energized enough to do it; it was now more important for him to take stock of his own life. He must remain positive, but at the same time he needed to take some hard decisions. Undoubtedly, he must quit ImpaKt—that he must surely do. And then he'd need to find something else to do. What that was he didn't know and couldn't care now; it could be anything at all.

He went to the toilet to wash his face and brush his teeth. Returning to the room, he changed into a pair of jeans and a shirt, put on his shoes and packed his belongings in his haversack. He looked at his watch—it was nearing nine. They'd planned to meet for breakfast at nine-thirty, after which they were to go to the DC's office to meet Shri Rama Prasad at eleven.

Slipping the straps of the haversack on to his shoulders, he walked out of the hotel room, carrying the brass keys in his hand. He went down the coir-carpeted corridor, past Aroon's suite and Uma's room, hoping he wouldn't bump into them. He deposited his room key at the small bow-shaped reception counter.

A young woman at the counter wearing a thick coat of lipstick smiled at him. 'Good morning, sir. Going for a picnic? Would you like us to arrange a taxi for you?'

'No thanks,' said Aseem, wanting to leave as quickly as possible.

'Will you be back in the evening?'

'Yes, evening,' said Aseem, and hurried out of Hotel Three Star.

Aseem half walked, half ran, as if he was escaping from prison, his heart thumping; he slowed down only after he'd gone some distance. The walk helped him to regain a sense of composure—

his heart settled down to a calmer rhythm. After some time, he reached the bank of the Indravati and began strolling aimlessly along it, not knowing where his feet were taking him.

A group of adivasi men and women were walking along the riverside in single file as they were accustomed to while traversing narrow trails in the forest. The men had poles slung horizontally on their shoulders that balanced bundles tied in colourful cloth at either end; the women carried wicker baskets or pots made of terracotta or aluminium on their heads. They exuded a sense of ease and abandon, chatting with each other, lending warmth to the air. As they passed Aseem, they looked at him curiously—he turned his head away to look at the river. The current was swift, creating fast-shifting patterns of reflecting light in the blue-green water. White-tipped shimmering wavelets rippled rapidly, carrying twigs and leaves and floating debris of human habitation. On the other side of the river, farmers tended to their plots of land, goading reluctant bullocks to help furrow the earth with large ploughs.

A passenger-less cycle rickshaw, pulled by a man wearing a checked lungi drawn up to the knees and a dirty vest, came close to Aseem. Slowing down to keep pace with him, the rickshaw puller called out, 'Going to town, saab?'

'Where can you take me?' asked Aseem.

'Gole Market Railway Station Bus Stop Bastar Palace Museum National Park,' said the rickshaw puller, reeling off the more likely destinations in one breath. 'Wherever you want.'

Aseem looked at the wiry frame of the rickshaw puller and continued to walk without responding.

'Where do you have to go?' asked the rickshaw puller, pedalling alongside Aseem.

I wish I knew, Aseem wanted to say, but he remained quiet.

'Do sit down. I'll charge you half the rate,' said the persistent rickshaw puller. 'You'll be my first passenger of the day.'

'No, I'll walk,' said Aseem and watched the rickshaw puller pedal away. He continued to amble along the riverside. He crossed many people walking in the opposite direction, carrying bundles of various kinds; a few with heavier loads were on cycle rickshaws, but most were on foot. A yellow-and-black autorickshaw with flapping canvas sheets on either side of the passenger seat slowed down near him.

'Gole Market?' asked the genial-faced driver.

'Where are all these people going?' Aseem questioned him.

'The weekly market,' said the auto driver. 'It's the day for the haat. Would you like to go there? It's on the outskirts and will take at least an hour.'

'Fine,' said Aseem. 'Take me there.'

After riding for some time, they reached a sprawling, single-storey edifice with a limestone façade beyond an open stretch of patchy green surrounded by stone walls on all sides.

'Bastar Palace,' said the auto-driver-turned-tourist-guide, slowing down. Aseem took a closer look at the building. It had a portico in front with a succession of arches lined in blue paint. 'If you've come to Jagdalpur for the first time,' continued the driver, 'you must visit the palace. It was the seat of power for nearly three centuries. I can stop here for you if you want to take a closer look.'

'No, no,' said Aseem. 'Carry on. Take me to the market.'

As the autorickshaw phut-phutted its way to the haat, Aseem could see more and more people milling around, having travelled long distances from Jagdalpur and nearby villages; many of them had walked as much as thirty to forty kilometres from the forested areas of Bastar.

Aseem alighted from the autorickshaw when it neared the haat, strapped the haversack to his back and paid off the driver. There were men and women from various trades in colourful garments—weavers, silversmiths and potters, small farmers and itinerant traders—selling or bartering all kinds of products from jewellery and boar's tusks to vegetables and salt and turmeric. A few adivasi SPOs, with their .303s strapped to their backs, swaggered about the marketplace. Unmindful of them, the sellers sat with languid ease in rows on their haunches with their alluring wares nestling in wicker baskets or spread out on colourful mats. There were herbs and barks and roots with magical powers, red ant chutney and yam, heaps of millet and unpolished broken rice (known locally as nooka), animals and carts made of bell metal using the lost-wax process. A middle-aged woman with tattooed upper arms sat with a basket of colourful beads and long-toothed combs made of bamboo. A potter couple, with two half-naked children clinging to them, was selling terracotta figurines of a woman with a funnel-shaped pot on the head. Sculptures made from metal scrap competed for attention with lipsticks and handkerchiefs, panties and bras. There were women selling fruits of indigenous trees—the tamarind and amla and amaltas—and various products of the mahua tree.

Who does not know the mahua tree in this part of the land, with its fleshy elliptical leaves, thought Aseem. Its broad leaves when dry were sown together to make cups and plates, while its fleshy seeds were used to extract oil for cooking, for making soap, and as manure. Even its dead wood was utilized as firewood and for construction. The local folk used its small whitish flowers not only to dress up their hair but also as food. However, what they found most relaxing was the country liquor made from fermented mahua flowers. Indeed, the most common wares on display were the rows and rows of the intoxicating mahua liquor stored in pots; for variety there was beer from the salfi tree and taadi liquor made from fermented rice. The adivasi women sitting behind them served endless drinks in leaf cups or in the hollowed-out stems of the twin-bowled bottle gourd.

In a noisier area, with dust and feathers floating in the air, a crowd of men were making wild bets on their favourite cocks spoiling for a fight with sharp knives tied on their toes. Aseem walked through the haat fascinated, watching the local folk milling about, quaffing their drinks, lulled by the luxuriant atmosphere and the rich fare. He almost forgot that he'd left Aroon and the ImpaKt team, that he had nowhere to go. He wished he could get lost here somewhere, among the Bastar folk, drinking the refreshing mahua.

After some time, he left the hustle and bustle of the haat and went back to the main road. The same autorickshaw driver who'd brought him to the haat was still parked there, smoking a bidi. Aseem went up to him. 'Take me back.'

'Back where?' asked the driver. 'Gole Market?'

'Fine,' said Aseem, dumping his haversack on the seat. 'Gole Market.'

38

HAVING FINISHED BREAKFAST WITH Uma in the dining hall of Hotel Three Star, Aroon wiped the remnants of toast from his lips with a paper napkin and looked at his watch. 'It's high time Aseem came down for breakfast, man. Uma, will you please go and wake up the lazybones?'

'I'll buzz his room,' said Uma, pushing her chair back to leave the table.

She was back very quickly. 'He's not in his room. I checked with the girl at the reception and she said that he left around nine in the morning with his haversack. He told her he'd be back in the evening.'

'That's weird,' said Aroon. 'I guess he's gone for a stroll. He couldn't have forgotten our date with the DC. Working out the logistics is Aseem's job.'

'He better be back soon,' said Uma.

'Don't worry. He'll come.' Aroon said. 'We should be getting ready to leave in half an hour. Let's hope Aseem is back by then.'

Aseem walked around Gole Market wondering why he'd asked the auto driver to bring him here. Criss-crossing overhead was a confusing jumble of electricity and television cable wires with a row of pigeons perched on them. Crows were circling over the terraces of the dilapidated buildings of what was once a regal township. Prominent billboards invited students to join computer classes and coaching institutes for professional examinations and spoken English. A narrow open drain ran alongside the road with rotting yellow leaves floating in it. A pile of garbage covered with a mess of polythene bags invited attention with its sharp stench. An emaciated cow with shrunken udders inspected the rubbish, while a stray dog barked incessantly at its legs to move it away.

Suddenly, Jagdalpur had lost its charm; it was like any other shanty town. Aseem felt like a stranger in an alien land. He thought of Delhi and his parents. There was no place to go but home. He went up to a man selling guavas and oranges on a wooden handcart and bought a few guavas. 'Which way is the bus stop?' he asked the fruit vendor as he bit into a guava.

'Quite close. You can easily reach it in five minutes,' said the vendor pointing in the direction of the bus stop.

A grey-uniformed man, his hair parted at the centre, was sitting behind a small semicircular window with iron bars at the bus stop. 'When does the bus for Raipur leave?' Aseem asked him through the window.

The man at the window informed Aseem that he'd missed the only two buses for Raipur in the morning. 'The next one will only leave at one-thirty in the afternoon, once the bus returns from Raipur. You can come back at one.'

Aseem looked at his watch. Nearly an hour and a half to go. He was in no frame of mind to explore any more of the town. He saw a barber shop with a proud display of 'Hair and Kaire Beauty Saloon' on its glass frontage with 'Welcome' painted in a stylized script on its door. He'd had a haircut a fortnight ago; nevertheless, it was a good place to while away some time. He pushed open the door gingerly and went in.

Wearing a khadi kurta and pyjama, the barber was sitting on a narrow, cushioned sofa, one leg crossed over the other, smoking a bidi. On the wall opposite was a row of three washbasins and mirrors, and three empty chairs. Alongside the mirrors were glass shelves with bottles of powders and creams and lotions. Seeing Aseem, the barber chucked the still-smouldering bidi out on to the road without stubbing it out and invited Aseem to occupy a chair next to the window. Aseem put down the haversack on the sofa and occupied the chair.

'Cut or shave?' the barber asked.

'Both,' said Aseem.

The barber wrapped a white sheet around Aseem, securing the ends at the back of his neck. He then took out a couple of film magazines and pointed to the images of a few Bollywood heroes. 'You can choose any style you want.'

'Whatever you think will suit me. You decide.'

The barber smiled. Holding a wide-toothed red comb in one hand and a pair of scissors in the other, he started cutting Aseem's hair with consummate ease.

Menaka was at the Kanine Kare Parlour, supervising Rambo's shampoo and haircut. 'I want the hair all even so that it looks neat,' she instructed the lady at the parlour. 'I want it perfect. My darling Rambo is getting married, you know.'

After visits to vets and dog counsellors, Rambo's troubles had been diagnosed as having been caused by loneliness and deprivation of female companionship of the canine kind. Through searches on the Net, Menaka had zeroed in on a grey-coloured cocker spaniel bitch called Smoky, owned by a rich widow. While Smoky's pedigree was beyond doubt, Menaka was not happy with the colour of Smoky's coat. But seeing Rambo's passionate enthusiasm for the bitch, Menaka had relented, especially after the widow had agreed to streak Smoky's crown with copper colour. A wedding date had been fixed in astrological consultation with Sri Sri Narayanaji who even managed to create horoscopes of the canine couple. And for the past fortnight Menaka had been awfully, awfully busy—making the necessary preparations, fixing a suitable venue, finalizing the decorations and menu, working with Mohit Dhaul for a smart designer dress for Rambo for the wedding, designing gilt-edged invitation cards, making a list of invitees who owned pedigree pets.

'You don't look like a local,' the barber said after he'd worked on Aseem's hair for some time.

'No, I'm not from Jagdalpur,' said Aseem. 'I'm going back this afternoon.'

'Tourist? Where do you belong?' asked the barber, snip-snipping his scissors even when he was not cutting Aseem's hair.

'Delhi,' replied Aseem.

'I've never been to Delhi,' said the barber wistfully. 'I want to go there one day.'

'What'll you do there? It is dirty and terribly crowded,' said Aseem. 'You're better off here.'

'Delhi is the capital city. There are so many places to see. I also want to have Sri Sri Narayanaji's darshan,' said the barber, pushing Aseem's head down to reach the nape of his neck. 'Have you met him? You must've seen him on TV.'

'I've heard of him.'

'There's a buzz that Narayanaji Maharaja himself is going to grace Jagdalpur.'

'Is that so?'

'A government official told me this morning. Swamiji belongs to Narayanpur. That's where I come from, too,' said the barber, removing the sheet covering Aseem and holding a mirror behind his head. 'Is it all right?'

'Fine,' said Aseem, barely looking at his reflection.

'They say that the night Sri Sri Narayanaji was born there was a sign in the sky, a shooting star flying across,' said the barber, powdering Aseem's neck and brushing away flecks of hair from it.

'Do you believe the story?'

'I'm not saying this. This is what the people say,' said the barber, tucking in a towel in Aseem's shirt and beginning to lather his face. 'Whatever it is, saab, he has made Narayanpur famous.'

'Do you watch his programmes?'

'I watch all his programmes on TV. Our cable operator has recorded his programmes and telecasts them periodically, such is Swamiji's popularity.'

Just then, through the glass frontage, Aseem saw a short-haired, young woman in black jeans and a beige-coloured kurta, wearing long silver earrings and carrying a black leather bag, stride past the barber shop. Even in that fleeting glimpse of her profile, something about her arrested his attention. Aseem closed his eyes and went over the woman's image in his mind's eye. How could he possibly have not recognized her? Of course, it was her—Swati. But Swati with short hair? Or, was he imagining her again? No, it was definitely her, the earrings the woman wore were exactly the type Swati used to wear. He couldn't be wrong.

Aseem pulled aside the towel and rushed out of the barber's shop, one cheek still coated with foamy lather.

'What happened? Did I give you a nick?' the barber called out. 'Arre bhai! At least pay me for the haircut!'

But Aseem had sped away.

'Swati!' he shouted, panting, as he caught up with her.

'Aseem? What're you doing here?' Swati said, surprised.

'I can't believe it's you, Swati,' said Aseem, recovering his breath. 'I thought I'd never see you again. You look so different.'

'I'm the same.' Swati smiled. 'How've you been? What's that on your face?'

'Oh!' he said, wiping away the lather on his cheek with his hand. 'I was getting a shave in that saloon down there.'

'How come you're here in Jagdalpur?'

'It's a long story. What about you? Do you stay here?'

'No, I came here to buy a few things. I live in a village quite some distance from Jagdalpur.'

'What do you do there?'

'I'm managing a small school for the adivasis.'

'Does Gopal live in the same village?'

'Yes, he's also there.'

'Can I come with you to the village?' asked Aseem, drawing closer to her and holding her hand gently. 'I miss you terribly, Swati. I don't want to be away from you.'

'I wish I could take you, Aseem,' said Swati, easing her hand away. 'But our paths are different. You carry on with what you came to Jagdalpur for.'

'What I came here for is no longer important.'

'Why are you in Jagdalpur?'

'Does it matter? I came with Aroon to help organize an event for ImpaKt.'

'Of course, I forgot that you'd joined ImpaKt.'

'I was with them till this morning, but I'm not going back.'

'Why, what happened?'

'I was working on the Narayanaji project. The Chhattisgarh government has invited the swami to deliver a discourse to change the hearts and minds of the adivasis and bring them to the path of peace. But I've discovered it's all a sham. I walked out on them this morning.'

'Why?'

'They want to hoodwink ordinary people by staging a false miracle.'

'Good for you. This Narayanaji business was always a whole lot of rubbish. What was your role in it?'

'I was to help plan all the arrangements and logistics to stage the event.'

'Work out the logistics of the meeting, is it?' asked Swati, getting more interested.

'Yes,' replied Aseem. 'They're planning to enlist the support of the Shanti Kadam to organize the event on a massive scale.'

An idea flashed across Swati's mind; she asked Aseem pointedly, 'So, you have all the details of the event, the time, the schedule?'

'Yes. But as far as I'm concerned . . .'

'Just a sec, Aseem. Can you wait here a moment?' interrupted Swati, taking out a cellphone from her bag. 'There's a call I have to make.'

I can wait till eternity for you, Aseem wanted to say. He trailed Swati with his eyes as she turned into a bylane and walked a few yards till she was out of earshot.

'Gopal,' Swati said softly into the cellphone. 'Aseem is here.'

'Who?' asked Gopal from the other end.

'Aseem. Remember the friend of mine whom you met in my flat and we went together to the ridge? He's here in Jagdalpur.'

'Of course, I remember him. What brings him here?'

'That's what I want to speak to you about. He's here to help work out all the logistics of the Narayanaji event.'

'Narayanaji, is it? How did Aseem get involved with him?'

'That's a long story. For the moment what's important is that he has all the logistical details.'

'So?'

'He has walked out of the project and wants to be with us. We could get him to share the details.'

'I don't believe this. He could be working as a police plant. He didn't sound too supportive of our cause when I met him.'

'I know. But he's disillusioned. He wants to join us.'

'I wouldn't trust him.'

'I know Aseem well. He wouldn't deceive me.'

'You've still got a soft corner for him.'

'That's not it. The information he has could be vital for us. Otherwise I wouldn't have suggested that we take him along.'

'All right, if you say so,' Gopal acquiesced. 'But don't bring him with you. If something goes wrong, you may not know what to do. Moesa is here with me. I'll ask her to escort him to the village.'

'Fine, whatever you say.'

'Where's he now?'

'He's waiting near the bus stop. He spotted me from a barber shop. It's the only saloon near the bus stop.'

'Okay. Tell him to wait there for an hour or so. I'll ask Moesa to pick him up,' said Gopal, ending the call.

Swati went back to Aseem and told him that he'd be escorted by someone called Moesa from their village. Aseem was elated.

'Bye,' said Swati and began to walk away.

'But where're you going now?' asked Aseem. 'Don't leave.'

'I've somewhere else to go. Moesa is a short adivasi woman with buckteeth. You'll have no difficulty in recognizing her. Wait at the barber shop for her. I'll meet you in the village.'

'I won't move from there,' said Aseem, exulting at the prospect of reuniting with Swati.

'Great!' said Swati. 'Buy yourself a mosquito repellent cream. And be careful about stepping on snakes on the way.'

39

ASEEM FOLLOWED MOESA, WHO had a cloth bag slung on her shoulders. They trudged on the mud trail, the soles of their feet crunching-crushing the dried yellow leaves on the forest floor. Two adivasis walked behind him in single file, one male and the other female. After some time, Moesa stopped on one side of the forest path. Clearing a cover of dried leaves to reveal a shallow pit, she pulled out an AK-47 and two .303s from it. Aseem looked at the weapons but didn't say anything. Moesa handed the .303s to her dalam members and strapped the AK-47 to her back. She turned to lead the way again.

Moesa stopped after a while at a spot where the path widened and was covered with a thick carpet of dry leaves. 'We'll go from the side,' she told Aseem, extending an arm behind to block him from walking straight ahead.

'Why, what's here?' asked Aseem, looking around.

'You want to see?' she asked, shovelling away some leaves with her feet and pointing to the ground below.

Aseem came up beside her and peered down. Bending down to brush away more leaves, Moesa exposed an elaborate structure of split cross-beams of bamboo covered with jute bags, below which was a six-foot deep trench. The dry leaves had cleverly camouflaged the structure. Aseem recalled reading media reports about Maoists ambushing security forces by trapping them in trenches. He had seen one now.

'Shall we go?' said Moesa, walking alongside the covered trench, scraping the hedges on the side of the path. Aseem followed her cautiously.

The sal forest became deeper and denser, the rays of the sun barely penetrating the thick foliage; only a few tiny specks of golden light glinted on the leaves. But soon in the distance they could see a clearing in the dense vegetation, where bright sunlight shone on a patch of rocky, uneven ground.

As they approached the clearing, Aseem saw a number of miniature tomb-like structures and in one corner a small shrine. Moving closer, he noticed upright stone slabs covered with paintings of yellow tigers, grey elephants and warriors carrying bows and arrows. There were a few made of wood as well, now decaying and eaten by worms and vermin. The structures were embellished with wooden posts and faded banderoles in many colours fluttering in the breeze.

'Is this a cemetery?' Aseem asked.

'No. You won't find bodies buried here. But, yes, they're built in memory of our ancestors,' explained Moesa, walking across to the shrine at the edge of the open land.

'What's here?' asked Aseem.

'Persa Pen,' said Moesa. 'Our great god.'

Aseem followed Moesa to the oblong shed of the shrine to Persa Pen. Open on the sides, it had a forked wooden post holding a covered earthen pot. The floor was washed with cow dung and had a large stone slab and adjoining it a wooden platform containing red Sati stones representing legendary ancestors with small saucer-shaped oil lamps or bans. Moesa and her comrades bowed their heads and stood for a while with their hands folded.

She then turned around and walked back briskly to the forest path and waited for Aseem to join her.

'Have you always lived here?' asked Aseem as he caught up with her.

'Yes, since my childhood. You ask too many questions,' said Moesa abruptly. 'Let's go. This area is not safe.'

'Just one more question, and then I'll stop asking. When did you become a Maoist? Were your parents also Maoists?'

'My parents weren't involved with the movement. Even now they aren't. My father has a small patch of land in our village. But I became a Maovadi when I was fourteen.'

'So young? How come?'

'You really want to know?'

'Yes, I want to hear your story.'

'It's not a story. It actually happened,' said Moesa, suddenly stopping and turning around to face Aseem. Her expression had changed into a ghastly grimace and her eyes were bloodshot. 'I was helping my father sow seeds in the farm when some security forces rounded us up and took us to the thana, accusing us of being Maovadis. My father pleaded with them that we had nothing to do with the Maovadis, but they wouldn't listen. They beat him and dragged him along with many others from our village.

'I was also taken to the thana and put behind bars with some other girls. At night, three of the behenchods came stinking of liquor and raped me and every girl or woman in the jail. Not just that night, but every night for a week. Kutte, saale!'

'Oh hell!' exclaimed Aseem, appalled. 'How did you manage to get out?'

'Gopal-dada,' said Moesa. 'He and his dalam rescued us. A few days later, I told my parents that I was joining Gopal-dada's army. My parents gave me their blessings.'

Aseem listened in silence, not knowing how to react.

As they walked on, they came to what looked like a hamlet, but there were no signs of habitation. All they could see was burnt grass and bushes and charred stumps of trees. Blackened cooking utensils and earthen pots lay around uselessly.

'Now what happened here?' Aseem asked. 'Forest fire?'

'Shanti Kadam. Madarchods! They burn our villages,' Moesa said angrily. 'They're in league with the state to get us to vacate our land.'

Moesa now kept a fast pace like a soldier marching in a parade. After a while, she bent down to pick up a dry twig. 'Follow me closely,' she said, seeing Aseem falling behind. She waited for him to make up the distance to her and once he was near her, she used the twig in her hand to point out the tip of a mine. 'Be careful. It's to keep out the police and the Shanti Kadam.'

Aseem looked around at the forest. The base of many of the trees were covered with moss and lichen, vines and orchids; some had creepers snaking all the way up their trunks. Aseem shuddered. Given a choice, this forest was the last place on earth he'd like to get lost in, with its deadly mines and wild and creepy animals. There were no specific landmarks from which he could find the bearings on his own—the dry leaves covered the footprints, leaving no visible trail marks. He felt like Hansel in the fairy tale.

Further ahead, he was relieved to see some signs of habitation: a few scattered huts with sepia-coloured thatch roofs. Moesa led the way towards a larger hut with an attached animal pen constructed of tree branches tied together with twine. Some corncobs were hanging on wooden rafters at the entrance. Aseem was surprised to see a motorcycle parked near the pen.

'Prakrit,' Moesa called out. 'Are you home?'

An adivasi man came out of the hut after a few minutes with a little girl in his arms. 'Lal salaam, nana.'

'Lal salaam, Prakrit,' said Moesa. 'How's the little one?'

'Misses her yaya,' said Prakrit.

'Time is a great healer. You'll have to become her yaya,' said Moesa. Seeing Prakrit staring at Aseem, she explained, 'Aseem. Friend of Comrade Swati.'

'Welcome. You people must be tired,' said Prakrit. 'Come and rest for a while. I'll make you tea.'

'No, we want to reach Satwal before it gets dark,' said Moesa. 'Gopal-dada and Swati will be waiting for us.'

'I'll get you water,' said Prakrit, placing the little girl gently in Moesa's arms. He entered his hut and returned with water for them in a bottle-gourd stem. He handed the stem to Aseem and he took his daughter back from Moesa. Aseem looked at the stem and gave it to Moesa, who threw back her head and poured water from it into her open mouth. Then she handed the stem to Aseem.

'Lal salaam,' said Moesa. 'We'll go now.'

'Lal salaam,' said Prakrit, raising a fist to his head and smiling at Aseem.

'Lal salaam,' said Aseem, surprising himself by returning the salute.

They carried on for some more time, walking up a winding incline. Aseem strained to climb—he was tired and his bones were beginning to ache. He was relieved to see Moesa stop. He went to a side and leaned his weight on the trunk of a tree, listening to the sighing trees that seemed to sympathize with his weariness.

'Sal,' Moesa called out, looking up the incline.

'Saaja,' Aseem heard a shrill voice calling back from a short distance up and then a sharp whistle.

'Who's that?' Aseem asked.

'One of our guards,' Moesa said. 'We can go now. The way is clear.'

Moesa opened out her red bandana and began to wave it in the air from side to side. Moments later, a moving blur of red responded in the distance. They reached the top of the hillock where the guard on duty, who had been waving the red flag, was standing with a pair of binoculars.

The guard, a young woman in fatigues and a cap, with an AK-47 on her shoulders, greeted them with a salute, 'Lal salaam. Gopal-dada is waiting for you.'

'We'll go and meet him,' said Moesa. 'Lal salaam.'

The young guard resumed her duty while Moesa led Aseem to the other side of the hillock, which opened out to a wide, undulating expanse of land, sparsely covered with hedges. Aseem looked around. At first he didn't notice, but looking closely he spotted guards on red alert crouched behind practically every hedge. There were a few others in fatigues patrolling with guns strapped to their backs. He realized his heart had began to thump.

Continuing to wave her red bandana high over her short, five-foot frame, Moesa led Aseem across the open stretch, where Gopal was waiting for them along with several other uniformed adivasi comrades. He met Aseem with open arms and hugged him, thumping his back a couple of times. He then relieved Aseem of his haversack, swinging it on to his own shoulder. 'I'll take this.'

'Thanks.'

'Come. Meet our other comrades.'

Soon, the half a dozen adivasi guerrillas standing around Gopal had formed a line in front of Aseem. One by one, they introduced themselves. Aseem reached out and shook hands with them. The adivasis, unused to shaking hands, kept their hands loose and limp and it was Aseem who had to grip them tightly.

'Let's go now,' said Gopal, taking the lead, while Moesa and the other guerrillas stayed behind, sitting on their haunches and lighting bidis. 'I know you must be tired, but we still have some distance to cover.'

'I didn't realize it would be such a long walk.'

'It's always like that the first time. But soon you get used to it, and then you can walk for miles and miles.'

Aseem studied Gopal. He was warm and welcoming and looked different from the time they'd met at Swati's. His scraggy beard was back and he wore fatigues and a beige cap with a red star stitched on to it. Along with the haversack he was now carrying, he had an AK-47 strapped to his back.

They reached a vertical stone slab that had been shaped into a pyramid at the top. It had a few etchings of warriors and some writing was engraved at its base. Aseem stopped to look at it, 'Can we halt here for some time? I'm exhausted.'

'Sure, for a bit,' said Gopal, sitting down on a rock nearby. 'But we'll have to move soon. It gets dark all of a sudden here.'

'I'm curious about these slabs,' Aseem said, sitting next to Gopal. 'Moesa said they were constructed in remembrance of ancestors.'

'Yes, that's true. You'll find such memorials everywhere. What you crossed with Moesa was a war memorial for those who died fighting the British during the Bhumkal Rebellion of 1910. As you may know, the word "bhumkal" means earthquake. In fact, the Bastar region has a history of rebellion.'

'Oh! I didn't know.'

'The 1910 rebellion was the culmination of a long struggle by the adivasis against alien rule and its attempt to remould the adivasi culture. In the early 1900s the British had started reserving the forests, snatching the livelihoods of the adivasis. The affected people looted bazaars, burnt police stations and the houses of traders, and robbed them of grain.'

'I wouldn't have thought that the British would have ventured into such an inhospitable terrain.'

'Why wouldn't they? The region's so rich in natural resources. Even before the British came, the Marathas had tried to establish their dominance,' said Gopal, getting up. 'Let's go. It'll soon become dark.'

'And before the British?' asked Aseem, wanting to get a sense of the history of the place.

'Oh, there were several dynasties—the Nalas, the Vatakas, the Chalukyas, the Kakatiyas—who all came enchanted by the beauty. More importantly, they came to exploit the wealth of the region. But whoever came was subsumed by the local culture and way of life. The state of Bastar was, in fact, established by the Kakatiya king Pratap Rudra's brother Annam Deo, who left Warangal and founded his own kingdom here in the fifteenth century. Till the Kakatiyas ruled, the region remained peaceful. But the later rulers started exploiting the adivasis and conniving with the British—that's what led to the 1910 adivasi revolt. In many ways the adivasis feel that they were better off when they were unconnected to the outside world.'

'What happened after the British left?' asked Aseem. 'Surely there would've been some development after Independence.'

'What development? What Independence?' Gopal looked back wryly at Aseem. 'Nothing's changed after the colonials left. In fact, the Indian government ratified the British policy and took over the tribal lands, rendering the adivasis homeless. Your government is now the new colonizer who has continued to commercially exploit the forests in the name of development. The situation has in fact worsened because the government is now taking away the lands and giving it to multinationals for mining. Today, comrade, exactly a century after the Bhumkal Rebellion, Bastar is again the ground for battle between the exploiters and the exploited.'

They stopped talking as they reached a zig-zag path descending to a pond shimmering in the fading light.

Gopal stopped and shouted out, 'Eekpandi!'

'Nelli,' said the voice from a distance below.

Aseem understood now that this exchange must be some secret code among the Maoists. Soon, an armed young man in fatigues emerged from behind a bush and saluted Gopal smartly. 'Lal salaam,' Gopal called out in response and then turned to Aseem. 'Come, we're almost there.'

Crossing the guard, Gopal and Aseem rapidly walked towards the pond. A boy, not more than eleven or twelve years old, wearing a vest and shorts, was sitting atop a jutting rock at the edge of the pond, holding a fishing rod. Another boy stood near him, aiming a handmade catapult at a bird sitting on the branch of a tree. Then, noticing a wild rabbit, he darted away, chasing the animal into the forest.

Gopal and Aseem traversed a narrow path around the pond. A pair of egrets was sitting on the embankment of the pond. The male with its plume down the nape of its slender neck took to flight with a push of its yellow feet, quickly followed by its mate. On the other side of the pond, a man was pumping a treadmill with his foot. 'The pond supplies water to the fields,' explained Gopal. 'Once the water reaches the channels we've dug for irrigation, it goes down easily because of the downward slope.'

'We built it, you know,' he said proudly. 'It took us many months. Earlier, we had to walk miles to the stream for water. And even that was unfit to drink.'

'Why so?'

'Mines. Greedy capitalists mining metals. What do you expect? They allow the untreated effluents to get discharged into the streams. I'll show you a stream one day. The water in it is red, like wine. But if you drink it you die.'

Leaving the pond behind, they went up a steep gradient where the path opened out as soon as they reached the top from where an entire village came into full view.

'Welcome to Satwal,' Gopal said, looking down at the village.

Aseem panned his eyes across the hamlet of scattered mud huts with thatched roofs. The land was undulating and fell into a kind of ditch on one side. The huts were constructed on the higher points of the land between the fields; there was a row of them at the edge of the ditch.

Gopal led Aseem through the village. There were more poultry on the path than people. A few girls and a small boy carrying firewood on their heads passed them by, unconcerned. They crossed two adivasi men standing on the side holding axes on their shoulders. Aseem looked into their eyes: would he see terror in them?

'Lal salaam, dada,' the men greeted Gopal in unison.

'Lal salaam,' said Gopal.

A few farmers were still ploughing bullocks on their small plots of land on either side of the path in the lengthening shadows of the evening. The path took a gentle turn up an incline leading to a mud-plastered structure with a sloping roof made of grass. Here Gopal stopped and slipped Aseem's haversack off his back and dropped it on the ground. 'This is our guest house. You'll stay here.'

Aseem took a good look at the dwelling. The outer walls had been decorated with folk motifs and etchings drawn with limestone chalk and vegetable dye. A bamboo fencing surrounded it on all sides and a couple of tamarind and amaltas trees grew inside the enclosure. There was a raised mud platform outside the open entrance of the hut. An earthen pot, with a steel tumbler on its lid, was placed in one corner of the veranda on a stand made of tree branches nailed together.

'You can drink this water. It's filtered,' Gopal said. 'We've boiled it and strained it through cloth made of kosa silk. There's nothing finer than that.' Gopal picked up the tumbler and handed it to Aseem, removing the clay cover so that he could help himself to the water inside the pot. Aseem drank all the water in one go and then, refilling the tumbler, drank some more, splashing the rest on his face and over his head.

He looked inside the hut: it was clean and had been freshly lined with cow dung. It was a large room contained by mud walls. There was a charpoy covered with a woven bamboo mat, and two wooden stools.

'Do you like it?' Gopal enquired. 'Will you be comfortable?'

'It's fine.'

'Come, I'll show you around,' said Gopal, leading him outside the hut, where there was a small vegetable garden. 'We've grown brinjals, bitter gourd, onions, okra, pumpkins. You name it, we grow it here.' Aseem didn't respond to Gopal's green-fingered boast and looked instead in another direction. Following Aseem's gaze, Gopal pointed to a slate-roofed construction. 'Do you see that structure? That's the school which Swati runs now. You'll meet her later in the evening.'

Aseem's heartbeat quickened upon hearing Swati's name.

'What's happening in the evening?' Aseem asked instead.

'There's a special welcome for you, comrade,' Gopal replied. 'I shan't say more. You rest now. I'll come back after about an hour.'

Aseem removed his shoes in the veranda and washed his feet with water from the pot. Then he went inside and sat on the cot, resting his head against the wall. The fresh smell of clay and cow dung filled his senses. He closed his eyes. It had been a long day. Just as he was drifting into slumber, he heard a knocking sound outside. He opened his eyes to see the boy they'd crossed fishing at the pond standing on the veranda holding a wicker plate.

'Gopal-dada sent this,' the boy said with a shy smile, leaving the plate at the threshold of the hut. Then he abruptly turned around and ran away. Aseem got up to examine the plate. Laid neatly on a leaf plate was a rolled tendu leaf, a custard apple and two small roasted fish.

40

BACK IN HIS HOTEL suite in the evening at Jagdalpur after discussing the bandobast in Shri Rama Prasad's office, Aroon was furiously pacing up and down like a caged tiger. 'Sala, who does he think he is, disappearing unannounced to a place where even the mobile network will not reach.'

'Calm down, calm down,' Uma tried to pacify him. 'He's a grown-up man. He'll come back. Maybe he's found a girlfriend.'

'How outrageous you are, Uma, to think like that!' exclaimed Aroon. 'You must be out of your mind. Here I'm worried that something terrible may have happened, that he might've met with an accident, or worse, got attacked by the Maoists, and all you do is joke about him finding a girlfriend in this godforsaken land.'

The doorbell of the hotel room rang and Uma got up to open the door. Shri Nakul was standing outside chewing betel nut. He looked crestfallen.

'What happened?' Aroon asked. 'Why don't you come inside?'

'No luck, sir,' Shri Nakul said, entering the room and taking out his handkerchief to wipe an imaginary bead of sweat from his chin. 'We've checked every nook and corner. Aseem is not to be found anywhere. No one seems to know where he went after he left the hotel.'

'You're all bloody useless,' Aroon said. 'You should all be shot.'

'If I may suggest, sir,' Shri Nakul said, 'we should lodge an FIR.'

'You mean we report the matter to the cops,' said Uma, looking worried.

'We have no choice,' said Aroon. 'We'll just have to tell them the truth: tell them that Aseem has disappeared.'

'And then what?' Uma persisted.

'Then the police jolly well find him, somehow,' said Aroon.

'You seem to have a lot of faith in the cops,' Uma said.

'No, I don't. But is there anything else we can do? We'll need to pay them some bribe, I suppose, to make them move their asses,' said Aroon, before turning to Shri Nakul. 'Let's go. Take us to the goddamned thana.'

A posse of policemen in khaki were milling around a police jeep outside Jagdalpur District Police Station. The roofs were sloping and covered with grey undulating asbestos sheets. Four policemen armed with .303 rifles stood on guard at the main entrance.

Aroon accompanied by Uma and Shri Nakul was stopped by one of the police guards at the gate. Shri Nakul, trying to look official in his grey safari suit, protested, 'We've come from the DC's office.'

'I have my instructions. Only one person can be allowed at a time,' said the police guard. 'DC or no DC.'

'Strange.' Shri Nakul looked perplexed. 'When did the thana start imposing such tight security? I've never seen so many policemen around here. Let me check.' He went inside and was back within a few minutes, waving a pass. 'Both of you can come in now. Something must have happened. They have a new security drill.'

Aseem and Uma accompanied Shri Nakul into the station. The police inspector, a middle-aged man with a sparse moustache, was sitting on a revolving chair behind a large baize-covered desk, holding his head. The desk was bare save for a pen stand, two wooden trays and a call bell. A black plastic label, fixed to the lapel of his khaki shirt, read: Bhim Singh. He didn't look up when the trio trooped in, waving them to sit on the straight-backed wooden chairs in front of his desk. Shri Nakul stood, while Aseem and Uma sat down.

'Tell me,' said Inspector Bhim Singh.

'We want to file an FIR,' said Aroon.

'What about?'

'A missing boy.'

'Missing boy, uh?' the inspector said and nodded his head. 'I know, I know. Must be ten or twelve years old, isn't it? We've been getting similar complaints recently of young boys being kidnapped and being used for other . . . er . . . activities.'

'I don't understand,' Aroon said.

'The flesh trade,' the inspector clarified. 'Very difficult to catch the culprits. They have a strong nexus with big people in Raipur.'

'The missing boy is nearly twenty-three years old,' Aroon said.

'Oh! Then there's absolutely nothing to worry about,' said Inspector Bhim Singh. 'He'll return. He's old enough to take care of himself.'

'We'd still like to file an FIR,' Uma said.

'All right, but the FIR cannot find the boy,' said the inspector pontifically.

'Look, we've come from the DC's office,' said Aroon.

'DC's office, uh? I see . . . let me see what I can do,' said the inspector, at once becoming more cooperative, and taking out a register and a sheet of paper from his drawer. 'Why didn't you say so earlier? I've been preoccupied. You may write your complaint here.'

'We'll surely file this complaint, but can you not meanwhile send out a search party?' said Uma.

'Search party, madam? I've no staff left.'

'No staff?' asked Aroon, looking up from the register in which he was entering the complaint.

'Didn't you know? Four of my constables were shot dead by Maoists in this very room last night.'

'Shot dead?' exclaimed Shri Nakul.

'In cold blood. They took away all the arms and ammunition and also the annual consignment of police uniforms for the entire district.'

'How ghastly!' said Uma even as Aroon completed the FIR and handed the register to Inspector Bhim.

'Do you have a photograph of this missing person—Aseem?' asked the inspector, reading the FIR.

'No, but we can arrange for one in a couple of days,' said Aroon.

'We'll need that,' said Inspector Bhim Singh, standing up. 'Pay my respects to the DC. If you can, please request him to put in a word to SP-saab to help get me a transfer out of this hell-hole.'

41

GOPAL WENT TO THE guest hut in the evening carrying a battery-powered torch. Though the AK-47 was still slung across his back, he'd changed into a regular shirt and was no longer wearing his cap. Peeping into the hut, he found Aseem sitting on the cot. 'Did you manage to get some rest, comrade?' Gopal asked.

'Somewhat,' said Aseem.

'Ready for the evening?'

'Give me a moment,' said Aseem, getting to his feet.

'Take your time,' said Gopal, smiling. 'We cannot begin the evening without you. You're the guest of honour.'

'Is that so?' said Aseem, taking out a fresh T-shirt from his haversack.

A while later, the two of them were walking down an inclined path through the village. They came to a dwelling similar to the guest hut, with a bamboo fencing.

'This is Swati's hut,' said Gopal. 'I mean, Swati stays in it. No one owns property here. The school she runs is also very close by. It's behind those huts, so you cannot see it from here. You can visit it tomorrow.'

They walked on, listening to the whirring murmur of insects and the cheep-cheep of birds as they marked their branches to settle for the night. The light was fading behind the dark sal forest and the solitary evening star had already made its appearance.

They reached a clearing where the local villagers had begun to gather. The ground seemed to have been cleared by cutting down trees; there were stumps all around. Adolescent boys and girls laughed and chatted. The boys wore vests or half-sleeved shirts and lungis folded up to their knees. They wore strings of cowrie around their necks and some of them had tattoos on their faces and kohl lining their eyes. The girls were dressed in knee-length saris and blouses, and traditional ornaments. Some girls had left their hair open; others had their hair braided and tied into buns decorated with flowers and wooden combs. Seeing Gopal and Aseem, the youngsters hurriedly broke up, looking askance at Aseem. Then Aseem spotted Swati, sitting at the far end on a takht covered with a brightly coloured mat.

She was dressed in the traditional short sari just covering the knees and a necklace of multicoloured beads and her usual long silver earrings. She smiled as she saw the two of them walking towards her. As he sat down next to her on the takht, Aseem felt self-conscious and yet ecstatic. He had not felt such joy in a long time.

Gopal joined the group of youngsters and returned in a few moments accompanied by a bespectacled young woman with a round face and a stubby nose, wearing a traditional dress. 'This is Bina,' Gopal said, introducing her to Aseem. 'Bina is a doctor and has joined us recently to set up a primary health centre.'

'Before that she was working in an ashram in a nearby village,' Swati added. 'Bina's coming here has been such a boon for the villagers. Almost every second person here suffers from some ailment or the other—malnutrition, TB, anaemia, malaria.'

Between Swati and Bina, they told Aseem about the circumstances that led Bina to join the Maoists. What Aseem came to understand was that the ashram where Bina had been was run by a genial soul called Manish Halke who'd been for nearly a decade to empower the adivasis staying in the villages around Bastar. More recently, he'd taken the onus of rehabilitating those of them who wanted to return to their villages from the Shanti Kadam camps. Hearing stories of the plight of the adivasis and the atrocities committed against them by the security forces and the Shanti Kadam activists, Manish Halke began to file formal FIRs against them. There were horrifying stories—an adivasi whose arms had been chopped off; a young girl who'd been raped in front of her grandfather's eyes; an adolescent boy who'd been tied to a pole, stabbed and dragged on the ground till he'd died bleeding; of innocent adivasi villagers who had been killed on the pretext of being suspected Maoists or their informers. One fine day, miffed at Manish's relentless filing of complaints, the government mowed down the ashram, calling Manish a Maovadi. An enraged Bina had had enough by them, and decided to join the Maoist movement.

'Manish-dada is in no way a Maoist,' Bina said. 'He's a simple man who lives his life by Gandhian principles. But even he has now begun to think differently. I'm worried what the cops will do to him.'

'You people have become very serious,' Gopal said, settling on a wicker chair next to the takht. 'We're starting now. They'll begin with a traditional greeting dance followed by a dance-drama. Swati and Bina have jointly written the script. The adivasis need to clearly understand who's on their side.'

The villagers sat down in a horseshoe formation around them, leaving a clearing in the centre. It had become dark—a half-moon slowly made its ascent in the horizon above the dark trees. The lights came on. Some of the adivasi children started clapping.

'Solar lamps,' Gopal explained, pointing to a set of solar panels on a natural hillock a distance away but visible in the moonlight. 'We generate our own power. These lamps can run for more than eight hours.'

The proceedings began with a gentle beating of drums. A middle-aged, bare-chested adivasi wearing a white lungi sat cross-legged on a bamboo mat beating soft notes on a longish drum shaped like an egg flattened at its ends, which rested against his knee. A younger man beat a saucer-shaped wooden drum with a pair of bamboo sticks. Soon, a group of six female dancers in short saris, wearing garlands of stone and cowries, and silver anklets on their legs, came out in to the centre. Aseem was surprised to see a couple of the older dancers bare-bodied above their waists. All of them had strings of white-green mahua flowers shining like peridot and yellow amaltas flowers pinned to their hair. A male drummer joined them, beating the two-sided naangor, hanging from a strap around his neck.

The dancers moved to the beat of the drums, forming a circle and dancing in slow, rhythmic movements, raising one foot and then the other, their anklets clinking when their feet met. Using complex footwork, they swayed and gyrated, moving inwards and back in an anticlockwise direction. As the tempo of the beat quickened, the dancers began to clap and sing a soft lilting song:

'Rela re ro ya, re ro re la,
Jhun jhun jhun jhun jhun,
Jumbak, jumbak, jumbak baala

Jumbak, jumbak, jum,
Rela re ro ya, re ro re la.'

'What's rela?' Aseem asked Swati.

'Rela is the fruit of the amaltas tree,' explained Swati. 'There are several growing near your hut. They bear lovely light yellow flowers—some of the dancers are wearing them on their hair. The amaltas tree symbolizes harmony and exquisiteness. Every adivasi song begins and ends with rela.'

The drumbeats slowed down and the dancers went away as quickly as they had come. A young woman now entered the central arena and in a high-pitched voice gave a short lecture-song in the Gondi language:

'This forest is ours ho, this forest is ours ho,
This land is ours ho, this river is ours ho,
This path is ours ho, this forest is ours ho . . .'

Then she gave a background to the pantomime act to follow. As she stepped away, a group of bare-chested male actor-dancers entered the arena. They wore different feathered head-dresses to distinguish the various characters: the patel was a jackal, the thekedar a wild buffalo and the security forces were bears, while the warriors wore the traditional head-dress of the bison. A battle ensued in dance form, where the 'evil' forces, the patel, the thekedar and the cop, were shown to initially have the upper hand, but after some time the 'good' warriors armed with spears and arrows emerged victorious. Soon, another troupe took the place of the first one: this time the lead 'villians' were a mine owner wearing fancy goggles and a couple of Shanti Kadam activists, while the victims were poor adivasis being driven out of their lands. But soon the tables turned—the adivasis revolted and slew the mine owner and the Shanti Kadam activists. Gopal led the people to clap and cheer the actor-dancers when the performance ended.

While the beating of drums continued, the villagers got up and congregated around four women who started serving the traditional mahua drink and taadi in twisted leavened cups from large earthen pots. A little distance away, dinner was being prepared. There was a thick gruel of coarse millet in a metal cauldron placed on a hearth of big stones. Nearby, above a roaring flame of firewood and suspended from a bamboo pole, a wild pig was being roasted, which had been hunted by the adivasi villagers especially for the evening. A smiling Moesa, looking very different in a traditional dress without the fatigues or the AK-47 but still wearing the red bandana, came towards Aseem and offered him the mahua drink. Aseem hesitantly accepted the cup and took a sip. The bitter-sweet liquor burned his throat and seared his gullet, all the way to his stomach.

'Have some more,' Gopal urged him. 'You'll like it.'

Aseem drank more of the strong-smelling drink. Soon, he took another refill, and yet another.

'C'mon all of you,' said Gopal, addressing the villagers in a commanding tone. 'Why aren't you dancing? Come on, get up and come over here. You must get our guest to join in the dance.'

A group of young adivasis began to dance. Moesa too joined in. Looking at her gyrating rhythmically, Aseem found it difficult to imagine that she was a gun-toting, trained guerrilla fighter. After a while, Moesa pulled Bina, Swati and Aseem to the centre and, before he knew it, Aseem was drunk on the mahua and dancing crazily along with the adivasis.

The piercing cry of a peacock woke Aseem from his slumber. He got up from the cot with a start, and found that he'd been subjected to a ruthless attack by mosquitoes. There were red bite marks on his arms and legs. Mosquitoes were everywhere, circling and buzzing and swarming all around him. For a moment he wondered where he was, and then looking around at the mud hut it all came back. He was unable to remember fully the events of the previous evening; he tried collecting the shards of memory like a scavenger. He recalled the mahua drink and the dance, and Swati giving him something to eat, and then Gopal escorting him back. He had a hangover and his head felt heavy as he waved madly at the mosquitoes with both hands.

In a short while, Aseem stepped out on to the veranda. The orange rays of the morning sun had begun to penetrate the thick foliage of trees. Aseem heard the incessant cuckooing of the brainfever bird and the gentle murmur of a winding river negotiating its way through the narrow valleys between the hillocks. Inhaling the smells of the forest, he looked around, soothing his eyes with the abundance of green.

In the distance, he saw a tall figure like a dark shadow against the dappled light of the sun. It looked like Gopal; the adivasis were much shorter. He seemed to be coming from the direction of Swati's hut. A nasty apprehension crossed Aseem's mind. Had Gopal spent the night in Swati's hut? The thought was painful and he cursed himself for the horrible suspicion. Maybe he was unnecessarily imagining the worst; even if it had been Gopal, he could've gone to her hut in the morning for some work. In any case, what right did Aseem have over Swati? The onus was on him to win her back.

He breathed deeply, trying to change the direction of his thoughts. His belly felt heavy and he looked around to see where he could go for a crap. There was no one around, so he walked across the vegetable garden and down a narrow path to the edge of the sal forest. Pulling down his jeans, he sat down on his haunches, picking up a dry branch to ward off any animal that may come by. A few birds landed near him on the ground—a warbler and a couple of wagtails looking for their breakfast of worms—even as he kept a vigilant eye for snakes that may come slithering through the grass.

Cleaning himself with dried yellow leaves, he went back to his hut and splashed water on his face. He needed to do something about the mosquitoes. He entered the hut apprehensively, but they'd left, chasing the morning light. He went to the cot and lay down, cradling his head in his arms, cursing himself for having had so much to drink that he'd lost his senses and couldn't enjoy the precious moments with Swati the previous evening. Soon he'd drifted into sleep thinking of her.

A shrill whistle woke him up. Hearing noises outside, he came out of the hut and saw a contingent of barefoot adivasis wearing fatigues and caps, marching in double file down the narrow path in front of his hut. He left the veranda and started following them from a distance, but soon they'd broken into a run and disappeared down a slope. He returned to his hut.

Sometime later, Aseem heard a knock outside. A smiling Swati was standing in the veranda, wearing blue jeans and a yellow kurti and the same earrings that she'd worn the previous evening. He went out to meet her, beaming from ear to ear.

'Slept well?' Swati asked

'Like a log. Even while the mosquitoes were feasting on me,' Aseem said, showing the red mosquito bites on his arm.

'I told you to carry a mosquito repellent, didn't I?'

'I did that, but was too knocked out to put it.'

'You were funny last night.'

'Did I make a fool of myself?'

'Not really. Would you like some breakfast?'

'I'm not hungry,' said Aseem, tapping his stomach. 'I'm still feeling stuffed from whatever we ate last night. I've no recollection of what I ate or did though.'

'You enjoyed yourself. I'm worried about the mosquito bites. If you feel any shivering or fever coming on, go and see Bina. And remember to apply the repellent cream tonight.'

'I certainly will.'

'I'm going to the school now,' said Swati, turning around to leave the hut. 'If you like you can come there at about eleven. That's when I take a break from teaching and the children go out to play.'

42

GOPAL WAS IN HIS hut, listening to BBC News. He thought of Swati. He hoped she'd been able to spend time with Aseem and extract the logistical details of the Narayanaji event. She seemed very confident when he'd gone to meet her in the morning. Was that the only reason he went to see her so early in the morning? Could he not have waited till he met her later in the day? There was something about her that he found captivating, that had been drawing him to her, making him want to see her more and more. He could not place a finger on it: What was it? Was it her face, her mannerisms, the way she moved her hands when she spoke, her disconcerting smile, her quiet confidence? The way she argued her point vehemently? Was he falling in love with her? He was alarmed at the thought: he'd never seen her like that earlier. What was wrong with him? He could not afford to allow himself the luxury of romance. No, there was no time for another Comrade Sheela Chandran in his life.

He compelled himself to come back to reality. Once he had the information from Swati about Narayanaji's programme, he'd need to rush to Jagdalpur to work out the arrangements and do the groundwork for the assault, which he'd named Operation Khatam. The prime objective would be the dual assassination of the home minister and Narayanaji. The consensus among the party's high command had been that ordinary people were falling prey to Narayanaji's discourses being aired continuously on television channels. The swami was posing to be a major nuisance and a threat to the revolutionary movement. He'd not taken the swami seriously till now, but his recent call for support to the Shanti Kadam seemed to be giving the movement a high moral ground. The stock of the Shanti Kadam activists was rising; their morale was running high. With the security forces brazenly killing Maoist cadres in encounters after the attacks on their police station and the Dantewada ambush, the dalam members were now looking for an opportunity to take revenge. Narayanaji and the home minister were the perfect symbols to be attacked to quell the Shanti Kadam's activities. The assassination would act as a reminder to the vacillating villagers sitting on the bamboo fence that they'd better watch out if they were thinking of crossing over to the other side.

Yes, he thought, if they could successfully carry out the dual assassination of the home minister and Narayanaji, it would be a great symbolic victory. More importantly, they'd be able to finish off many Shanti Kadam activists and supporters who'd be present at the venue in large numbers. This assault had to be the final, decisive victory over them, the final nail in their coffin. The adivasi comrades had suffered atrocities at the hands of the Shanti Kadam and the police for far too long.

Suddenly, an overpowering rage gripped him. It was now or never, it was do or die. It was an opportunity of a lifetime. The Shanti Kadam had to be made to learn that joining forces with the state could only be at their peril. If he succeeded, he would be able to command the respect of many of his comrades—it would put him back in the running for the party supremo's job. Sure, Comrade Prasada had stolen the thunder from him after the successful ambush in Chintar village in Dantewada on the eighty-strong security team. But surely the high command in the party knew that it was he—Gopal—who'd planted the story by bribing the mukhbir in Jagdalpur to lead the security convoy into Comrade Prasada's trap. It had then been easy for Prasada's dalam: blow up a mined truck, make the security forces run for cover into the V-shaped gorge lined with pressure mines and then attack them from three sides. Sure, Prasada deserved kudos for the successful ambush, but he was no strategist—he was a mere commander. And it was not out of mere ambition that he wanted the top position. He alone had the vision and pragmatism and the experience on the ground that could bring all Maoist cadres under one umbrella and take on the massive state offensive in the shape of Operation Red Hunt. But first the Shanti Kadam had to be tackled. They were running out of time.

Gopal reached out for a volume of papers bound in a ring binder and flipped through it, studying carefully the detailed maps with diagrammatic representations of their strategic plans for Operation Khatam. After he'd examined the papers, his attention shifted to his side where posters lay rolled in a corner alongside stacks of pamphlets and newsletters that they distributed for free every month. Perhaps, if—and it was a huge if—Swati could inveigle Aseem into working for us, Gopal thought, he could develop a campaign that met our requirements. We definitely need a more professional set-up that can spread our message to the masses and build public support.

Gopal left his hut and walked towards an adjoining structure with stone walls and a proper door made of bamboo cross-beams secured by thick coir ropes. The door was padlocked with a metal chain and a heavy brass lock. Gopal unlocked the door and stood in the doorway, making a mental note of all there was inside. On one side was a tall stack of khaki police uniforms. On the other side was all kinds of war equipment, grenades and IEDs, Russian AK-series and .303 rifles, light machine guns and SLRs, Chinese pistols, huge quantities of bullets and ammunition. Yes, it was all there. Satisfied, he took one last look and then padlocked the door again.

Freshly shaved and smelling of after-shave lotion, Aseem left his hut to go to Swati's school. He encountered two girls carrying wicker baskets gathering mahua flowers that had fallen from the high trees touched by the warmth of the morning sun. He smiled at them; they giggled and ran away. He walked further, crossing the health centre, a large thatched-roof structure with clay walls. A white board with a red cross on it and 'Health Centre' clumsily painted below was hanging lopsidedly from a rusty hook. He spent some time studying the dozens of patients waiting their turn outside, standing or sitting or leaning against the wall under the shade of the thatched eaves: a young mother cradling a wailing infant, an adolescent boy with a diseased leg swollen to the size of an elephant's, a girl shivering with malaria, a middle-aged woman bent over with osteoporosis, an old man with a persistent raucous cough.

Aseem reached the school fifteen minutes before eleven. He stood outside and peeped inside the classroom. Swati had modelled it after the school in the slum. The structure was different though: a thick bamboo pole in the centre propped up the sloping tiled roof with overhanging thatched eaves to create a large hall of sorts. About twenty children of various ages were sitting together on the mud floor on bamboo mats around some books.

Swati saw Aseem at the door and went out to meet him, smiling warmly. 'You're early.'

'I'm sorry if I disturbed you,' said Aseem.

'Not at all. It's perfectly all right. Come in and sit down,' invited Swati. 'I was boring the children with the saga of the brave warrior Gund Dhur who led the Bhumkal Rebellion of 1910 against the British. Can you believe there's no recorded history of the region; most of it is oral.'

Aseem followed Swati into the classroom and stood in one corner, looking at the children, who stared back at him with blank expressions.

'Aren't they too young to be given history lessons?' asked Aseem. Seeing Swati frown, he quickly added, 'Sorry, I shouldn't be interfering.'

'Maybe you're right,' said Swati. 'In fact, even the parents—whom I also teach—are not interested in their history. All that they're keen about is learning arithmetic. They say they get duped by the thekedars and at the haat because they can't count.'

'What do the children like?'

'Oh, they love stories. In the morning, I'd narrated the story of the monkey and the two cats and how the monkey had cheated the two of them of their roti. The adivasis are naïve and innocent, so I tell them such stories so that they become wiser,' said Swati animatedly. 'Just give me a moment and I'll call for a break now so that the children can go out and play.'

The children were happy to run out. Aseem looked around the now empty classroom—its mud walls had colourful drawings of tigers and wild pigs, of wild boars and snakes, of flowers and birds, of fighters in fatigues carrying guns.

'Very colourful,' said Aseem.

'All done by the children,' said Swati proudly. 'Let's go out.'

The two of them left the school enclosure to watch the children play the games that she'd taught them: of cops and robbers but where the Maoist cadres were the cops and the miners were the robbers; of cruel thekedars exploiting tendu leaf pickers who then revolted and killed their oppressors.

After some time, Swati invited Aseem to her hut for tea. Aseem felt strange as he followed Swati into the hut, nearly stumbling on its threshold. She went straight to a corner table on which there was a hot plate running on solar power. Aseem was reminded of how she'd head for the kitchen the moment she stepped into her flat in Delhi. He looked around: apart from the folk drawings on the walls, Swati had decorated her hut with woven wall-hangings and wood and metal carvings done by local artisans. There were also a few drawings that looked like they'd been done by the children in the school. The colourful hut was quite a contrast from her city flat with its bare walls.

'Can I help?' asked Aseem.

'Relax. Why don't you sit down?' Swati said, pointing to the bed, which, unlike the one in his hut, had a soft cushioning below the bedspread. 'I'll just take a minute.'

Swati filled a small aluminium vessel with water and placed it on the hot plate and then added sugar and tea granules. When the tea was ready she poured it into two earthen mugs and went across to Aseem. 'I'm afraid you'll have to drink black tea,' she said apologetically, handing the mug to him and sitting down beside him on the bed. 'The adivasis don't milk their cows or buffaloes or goats. They believe that the milk should be kept for the calves. But they don't have problems eating meat, be it mutton or beef or pork. For some strange reason, they don't allow women to eat eggs. We've been trying to persuade them, but they just won't listen.'

'They have their own logic, I suppose,' said Aseem.

For some time, the two of them sat silently, sipping their tea.

'So, do you like this place?' asked Swati, breaking the silence.

'It's very different here,' said Aseem. 'The people are very warm. I found it awkard looking at the women without a covering on their upper bodies. But after some time I got used to it.'

'Yes, the adivasi thinking and culture is quite different from those who live in the city,' said Swati. 'It's not because of poverty that the women don't cover their breasts. Traditionally, the men didn't want their wives to wear colourful garments because it would made them look more attractive and then they'd go astray.'

'Really?' said Aseem. 'I'd never have imagined.'

'It's true. But they're changing. We've been also trying to bring about some change in their thinking.'

'Is that good?'

'What do you mean?'

'Well . . . to interfere with their thinking and culture.'

'We're very progressive in our views,' said Swati abruptly.

'You misunderstood. I didn't mean it that way. Tell me, does Gopal manage everything in the village?'

'No, of course not. There's a different style of governance here. There is a sangham consisting of elected members who govern each village. They report to an area committee and then there are divisions and then of course there is the national party. A committee of elders hold praja courts to settle differences.'

'Praja courts?'

'People's courts,' clarified Swati. 'Incidentally, there's one being held in the afternoon today. You can attend it if you like, I guess.'

'Will you be going?'

'I wasn't intending to. I've been to one earlier. It's an experience. But I could accompany you if you're really keen. I'll have to ask Gopal, though, if he'll allow you.'

'I'd definitely like to go.'

'You'd better be mentally prepared. It is not the kind you may imagine and could come as a shock to you,' warned Swati, sipping her tea.

'I'll be fine. You check with Gopal.'

'Sure. I'll get back to you on this,' said Swati and then paused for a while before continuing. 'Now, tell me more about this Narayanaji of yours. I believe he's become quite a sensation.'

'Joining the project was a monstrous blunder on my part. I don't know why I agreed. I don't really want to talk about it,' said Aseem ruefully, rising from the bed to keep his empty mug on the table beside the hot plate.

'It's good to speak about things and get them out of the system.'

'Maybe. But I don't want to talk about the Narayanaji project. That's the reason I didn't go back to Delhi.'

'You don't have to go back to Jagdalpur or Delhi. You can stay here as long as you like.'

'Let's see. I feel like a stranger here.'

'You'll be all right. Just try to relax,' said Swati, drawing closer to him. 'Speaking about the Narayanaji project, when exactly is that sham guru of yours scheduled to hold the discourse in Jagdalpur?'

'In a week from now, on the day of the village haat later this month. On the twenty-seventh.'

'Hmmm. And what's the plan? Who all will be present?' asked Swati, resting her hand casually on his knee.

Bit by bit, Aseem gave Swati all the details he knew of the Jagdalpur discourse—who'd be attending and when, the schedule and sequence of the events, and so on. He spoke freely, and for some time Aseem felt as if he was back with Swati in her flat, as though nothing had changed. Swati listened attentively, making a mental note of the facts. Then, gently squeezing Aseem's thigh, she got up. 'I have to go back to the children now, Aseem. I'll check with Gopal about your attending the praja court. We'll meet for lunch. You come to my hut around one. You'll be hungry by then.'

Aseem reached Swati's hut at the appointed time. Swati had arranged for two plates from the community kitchen. Each plate consisted of millet rotis sweetened by mixing dried mahua flowers in the dough, an okra dish and a dark-looking chutney.

'What's this?' asked Aseem looking at the chutney.

'Try it and then I'll tell you,' said Swati.

'Not bad. Somewhat sourish,' said Aseem, as he took a dab of it with the roti. 'What's it?'

'Red ant chutney,' said Swati, smiling.

'What?'

'The adivasis relish this. They call the ants "chapda"—they're really not red, more like the big ants you see around in the garden or in potted plants. They pour water into the ant holes or place an overripe fruit at the opening to draw out the ants. Once they're out, they collect them in leaves and carry them home. To cook them, they grind them on a stone slab, fry the paste lightly, add salt and chillies and, voila, the chutney is ready.'

'Fascinating,' said Aseem, venturing to eat some more of the chutney.

'Gopal has said that you can attend the second session of the praja court,' Swati told Aseem when they'd finished eating. 'You relax for some time in your hut. I'll come and pick you up when it's time.'

Aseem was asleep when Swati came to his hut late in the afternoon. 'Asee-eem! Ready?' she called out from the veranda.

Aseem came out rubbing his eyes. 'Just give me a moment.'

Swati informed him of the basic rules of the praja court and how the village elders pronounced judgement after giving the accused an opportunity to explain their side of the story. 'Fair trial, speedy justice. No waste of time, no long-drawn-out court hearings.'

'Instant justice like instant coffee, is it?' Aseem was half mocking in his tone as he went into the hut.

'It's no joke,' said Swati, following him. 'See it for yourself.'

Aseem began preparing to leave. Swati kept sitting. 'There's time yet. We'll go after a while.'

Some time later, the sound of a succession of shots fired from an automatic rifle rent the air, sending birds screeching to the sky. A jackal howled.

'What was that?' asked Aseem.

'Justice,' said Swati, with a wry expression. 'Let's go. It's time for us to attend the praja court.'

43

SWATI WALKED ASEEM TO the same open patch of green where they'd watched the adivasis perform the previous night. There was a gathering of over two hundred and fifty adivasi villagers sitting in two semicircles as they'd done the previous evening, but this afternoon the atmosphere was palpably tense and charged. Most of the villagers were armed with some kind of weapon or the other: guns and rifles, bamboo sticks, bows and arrows, sickles and scythes and spears, and mortar made from galvanized iron pipes. As they neared the group, Aseem saw a young state security officer in khaki uniform being dragged away by two armed Maoists in fatigues. The man had been shot in the temple and the body left a trail of blood.

Swati passed them unflinchingly, and made her way though the gathering. Aseem followed close behind, numbed at the sight of the dead body. On the same takht where he had sat a day earlier were seated three village elders, the final arbiters of justice. Gopal sat on the side in a wicker chair, and beckoned the other two to join him, calling for two plastic chairs for them.

'You can start now,' said the village elder sitting in the centre with a thick bamboo stick and a week-old white stubble.

Two armed guards pushed the accused, a middle-aged man with sunken eyes and hollowed-out cheeks, into the open arena. The man begged for mercy with folded hands and fell at the feet of the elders.

'Stand up like a man,' said the village elder holding the bamboo stick.

'Forgive me,' pleaded the accused, standing up with his hands folded in front of his face. 'I lost my senses and do not know why I did it. I'll accept whatever punishment you give me.'

The accused had stolen a bag of salt and two chickens from his neighbour's hut the previous night while everyone was preoccupied in merry-making.

'You know what the punishment is,' said the elder, gesturing to a couple of members of Moesa's dalam. 'Let's not waste time.'

The accused was trussed up with coir ropes and hung upside down on a long bamboo pole. Then two dalam members holding their rifles from the wrong end and about a couple of villagers with bamboo sticks started raining blows on his back and legs and the soles of his bare feet. The suspended man whimpered, but the dalam members were merciless. Up went the sticks and rifle butts and down they came, up and down, thrashing the poor man relentlessly.

Up and down went the soft hands of the lady masseur on Menaka's back, moving down to the cleft of her buttocks and then back to the nape of her neck between her shoulders. She went through the motions again, gently, allowing Menaka to experience the soothing massage.

'Ummm,' Menaka moaned.

The masseur turned to her side and spooned out a chocolate-and-almond oil mixture, which had been warmed on heated stones, on to her hands.

'Why've you stopped?' asked Menaka.

'Just for a moment,' the masseur said, as she now drizzled the warmed chocolate cream on to Menaka's back and then began to slowly rub it in. 'This not only revitalizes the skin, madam, but also replaces lost nutrients.' She took some more of the creamy mixture and applied it on Menaka's legs, moving her hands down each leg, slowly, and then up again. Then the masseur started pressing her fingers on specific points. Menaka winced a bit, but soon started enjoying the sensation.

'These are the energy points, madam,' the masseur said. 'The pressure allows the body's natural energies to flow freely.' But Menaka was no longer listening; she was filled with ecstasy and well-being and delight all at the same time.

The chocolate massage had been entirely Menaka's idea, but it had been Ishita who had first thought of opening a spa at the swami's ashram. At Ishita's behest and under Sri Kripananda's supervision, a special building called the Narayanaji Wellness Spa had been designed and built on the ashram premises. It had a special semicircular dome and white marble walls and arched entrances on all sides. There were different zones for saunas and water and thermal pools, and relaxation zones; each zone had a distinctive colour and décor to reflect the individual treatments. Ishita and Sri Kripananda had wanted the spa to offer only Ayurvedic therapies, but Menaka had insisted that they needed to project a more global orientation. So, Swedish massages and East Asian aromatic therapies with floral herbs and chocolate massages with special cocoa flown in from Africa had been introduced.

The persistent ringing of her cellphone brought the moaning Menaka back to reality. Still lying on her stomach, she put the instrument to her ear. It was Aroon at the other end. 'Hello, where were you?'

'In the ashram. But where are you? Weren't you supposed to return yesterday?'

'Yes, but something has come up. Listen carefully. I need Aseem's photograph quickly. Can you get hold of one?' Aroon was speaking with some urgency.

'Why do you need it?'

'I don't have time to explain. Will you please courier the photo right away? It's urgent.'

'I can't send it now,' said Menaka, lifting her head to look back at her chocolate-smeared body. 'But what's happened?'

'Nothing has happened, but please do what I said.'

'Is Aseem fine? Where is he?'

'Aseem is all right. Everything's fine.'

'Are you hiding something? When are you returning?'

'I don't have time to answer your questions right now.I can't return before Swamiji's discourse. You'll have to accompany him here to Jagdalpur.'

'No, no, I can't come. I'll send him with Ishita and Sri Kripananda. I have to make arrangements for Rambo's wedding which can only happen after the discourse at Jagdalpur. By the way, when is it?'

'When is what?'

'The discourse.'

'On the twenty-seventh of this month. I have to rush now.'

'Then Rambo can get married only next month,' said Menaka ruefully. 'I'll consult Swamiji for an auspicious date for the wedding.'

'Remember to send Aseem's photograph.'

'Fine. Give my love to Aseem,' said Menaka, and went back to the epicurean world of cocoa.

When the beating was over, the accused was untied and allowed to stagger away. Gopal turned to look at a stunned and shocked Aseem and an expressionless Swati sitting on the plastic chairs. 'We have to maintain strict discipline here,' Gopal said by way of explanation. 'Stealing is something we abhor and cannot allow. Even if the theft is of a petty amount.'

'But this is so barbaric!' Aseem exclaimed, looking outraged.

'It'll be difficult for you to understand at first,' said Gopal. 'The adivasis prefer to go through this kind of punishment rather than jail. They're so used to living in the open that they find the very idea of confinement even for a night torturous. They'd rather die than go to jail. Can you imagine the plight of so many of our comrades languishing in jails for petty crimes and awaiting trial? Many of them try to commit suicide. The women comrades have it worse. They're molested and raped. Which is better? Jail or a bit of thrashing?'

Aseem didn't reply and turned to Swati for a reaction. Her face remained devoid of all expression.

44

WHILE THE TWENTY-SEVENTH of the month happened to coincide with the weekly haat that was held on the outskirts of

Jagdalpur, the day of Sri Sri Narayanaji's discourse was chosen for many other reasons as well. The date was most auspicious owing to the arrangement of the stars, Sri Sri Narayanaji had said, because it happened to be the day when the moon would be on the ascendant, which was necessary since the hare which was born of the moon was their symbol. Moreover, in numerological terms, the numbers two and seven added up to nine, which was perfectly divisible by the number three, and the place where the date was decided was Hotel Three Star. But the swami had added an ominous warning: 'Remember, the moon cannot dispel the darkness of the black night completely. You'll need to be careful and not allow evil thoughts or violent forces to come anywhere close.' No one had paid heed to his words then and the date had been happily fixed.

The streets of Jagdalpur wore a festive look with colourful buntings and banners hanging on every lane: 'Experience a transformation of your heart and mind!' 'Don't miss the opportunity of a lifetime!' The slogans were written in bold red letters in the centre with the hare symbol at one end and Sri Sri Narayanaji's image at the other. Orange-coloured hare-shaped gas balloons were flying from rooftops. Posters were plastered on all walls and in every corner and cranny of Jagdalpur on shop windows and shutters, outside public urinals and on railway platforms, at bus stops and on buses, even below the 'Welcome' sign outside Hair and Kaire Beauty Parlour. Young boys and girls distributed pamphlets announcing the details of the discourse at every traffic light and to every passenger in trains and buses. From dawn to dusk hired autorickshaws roamed the streets with loudspeakers announcing the discourse. All local television shows carried thirty-second spot ads while 31 FM,

Jagdalpur's favourite radio station, broadcast announcements of the event every ten minutes. Even the Shanti Kadam camp on the road to the Chitrakot Falls hadn't been spared; on top of the bamboo poles of every dwelling unit fluttered white triangular flags, which had Sri Sri Narayanaji's image on one side and the hare motif on the other.

Sri Sri Narayanaji had become truly ubiquitous.

Shri Nakul had proved his resourcefulness by finding a twelve-year-old local adivasi boy who would enact the miracle. Once it was announced that parents would be rewarded handsomely, there was no dearth of candidates and Uma had a difficult time choosing from among the young hopefuls. The selected boy, chosen because he had the spindliest of legs, had been renamed Chamatkar.

Uma immediately got busy with the task of training Chamatkar to act out the miracle. She put in solid hours of practice with the boy every day: first the perceptible limp in his left leg and a simultaneous raising of his right slender hip, and then the collapsing of his right knee. Every time the same limp, the same leg, the same hip, to make sure that nothing would go wrong. So perfectly did Chamatkar master the act that at the end of each session Uma had to remind him how to walk normally.

Gopal unveiled his strategy on the ground, graphically explaining his moves to Moesa and Kuttu and other key dalam members by drawing lines in the earth with a dry twig to indicate the bowl-shaped maidan. From time to time, he referred to a ring-bound volume lying by his side containing the diagrammatic representation of their strategic moves. 'Moesa is to attack from the main entrance gate while Kuttu will cover the rear,' explained Gopal. He'd also planned some distractions to divert the attention of the security forces. Altogether there'd be close to a hundred and fifty armed dalam members, who by his calculations would be sufficient to take on the security guards in the maidan, provided they could catch them unawares. Gopal had taken it upon himself to carry out the assassinations.

Aroon sat with the ImpaKt team, reviewing their plans on a laptop placed in front of him. Sri Sri Narayanaji would now be the centre of attention—owing to security reasons the home minster had decided to duck the event. It was then decided that the swami would not travel by car but use the helicopter the home minister would've used, landing on the helipad that had been constructed for the minister at one end of the maidan. The helicopter entry was perfect. What more could a marketing man ask for than to have a godman descend from the sky?

Shri Nakul and the other officials had been asked to ensure that the local folk turned out in huge numbers, including those living in nearby villages and in the Shanti Kadam camps. All those attending the discourse would be given a cloth bag containing a kilogram of millet and a choice of branded footwear as incentive. The latter had been Aroon's ingenious idea, which he'd been able to successfully sell to the leading shoe-manufacturing brands—Reebok and Nike, Adidas and Bata—quoting case lessons in marketing. They had all warmed to the idea with the fond hope that they'd succeed in generating a demand for luxury footwear among the barefoot adivasis. Nike had taken the first step and signed up the local cricketing hero, Naren Thumi, to endorse their brand, and ads were already being aired on television with Thumi doing yoga wearing a pair of Nike shoes.

Late in the night, on the eve of the discourse, the Police Commissioner, who had flown in especially from the capital city of Raipur, was at the Jagdalpur police headquarters reviewing the security arrangements and giving last-minute instructions for Operation Wham. He was relieved about the decision to not allow the state home minister to be present at the event. Now they had only the swami's security to worry about. Sitting around the commissioner were the inspector-general of police, the deputy superintendent, two assistant superintendents and the superintendent of police, who would also be in charge of the security at the venue. The commander of Sri Sri Narayanaji's White Commando Guards responsible for his security was also present as a special invitee.

'Nothing, I repeat, nothing should go wrong,' the Police Commissioner reiterated. 'Sri Sri Narayanaji is our State Ambassador. There can be no lapse in security.'

45

ASEEM SAT AT THE edge of the pond next to a young adivasi boy, a fishing rod in his hand. A gentle breeze was blowing from the sal forest, creating ripples along the surface of the water. He'd been captivated by the natural beauty of the landscape, but the recollection of the bloody trail of the dead body and the brutal thrashing of the man hanging upside down sent tremors down his body. The lathi blows he'd suffered on the day of the slum demolition were nothing in comparison. He was unable to comprehend the Maoists. How could they live in these tranquil surroundings and yet adopt violence as a way of life?

He felt uneasy and strange being in Satwal village, although the villagers had become accustomed to his presence and greeted him with the lal salaam. Sometimes, he'd go to the health centre to help out an overworked Bina or spend time with Swati in her school, taking a few classes in mathematics. English, she'd told him, could wait.

He was unable to fathom Swati; his relationship with her had made little progress since his arrival. At times, she appeared to be warm and friendly, but at other times she kept him guessing. He knew that he'd soon need to start thinking for himself, come to terms with his life. He thought of his parents and wondered what Aroon would have told them about his disappearance. He longed to be back with them and regretted being unable to call them because of lack of connectivity; he wished he could speak to his mother and tell her that he was alive and well. Gopal had promised to arrange for him to be escorted back to Jagdalpur the following week and he looked forward to it eagerly.

Ritika smiled to herself as she made the preparations for her puja, recalling with tenderness the moment when Avinash had put his arm around her the previous night, drawing her close to him.

Later, he'd turned around and snored, while she'd snuggled up to him and slept peacefully.

She arranged the small plate with the agarbatti and lit the diya and the incense stick for the arti, which she performed in front of the open cupboard door of her shelf of gods, her left hand holding her right elbow. She didn't ask the gods for anything this morning; she thanked them for answering her prayers to bring peace and tranquillity to her family.

For the last few days, Avinash had been unusually cheerful and calm. When she'd ventured to ask if there was any special reason, he'd merely smiled and mumbled about his being given a new desk. A couple of days earlier he'd taken the day off, and after she'd returned from school he'd taken her to a multiplex in a newly opened glitzy mall, where after watching a film they'd gone to a cafe for coffee and hamburgers.

Ritika finished her prayers with thoughts of her son. Menaka had told her that he was stuck in Jagdalpur but that he was doing a great job with the Narayanaji project. Ritika prayed that Aseem remain happy and contented with whatever he was doing.

Aseem felt a gentle tug on his fishing line, which disturbed his thoughts; the moment he realized it, the tautness had gone. Noticing the lapse, the boy sitting beside him expressed his frustration by picking up a flat stone and throwing it into the water, the stone skimming the surface a couple of times before sinking. Even before the stone could reach the bottom of the pond, Aseem heard a loud sound like that of a bomb blast across the rolling hills, followed by a succession of gunshots. The sounds died down, but only briefly, and soon he heard more shots, and many more, all coming from the same direction, piercing the quietness of the landscape.

Aseem handed the fishing line to the boy and got up. He walked in the direction of the sound even as shots continued to be fired intermittently. Slowly, cautiously, he went up a gentle slope till he reached a clump of short trees. Beyond it were wild bushes with tiny yellow flowers. He crouched behind a bush, looking down through the gaps between the branches. He saw a wide open field where scores of young men and women, most of them dressed in fatigues and carrying guns and rifles, were undergoing training in rifle shooting.

Even from the distance he could make out the figure of Gopal standing alone at one end, watching what would have been about sixty adivasis being trained in rifle shooting by Moesa. About twenty of them were lying on the ground on their bellies, their left elbows holding rifles in their upturned palms, the rifle butt resting on their left shoulder, their right finger on the trigger, taking careful aim. The remaining forty-odd adivasis were lined up behind the twenty on the ground, waiting their turn. There were almost an equal number of adivasi women and men, if they could be described as such, for many of them who held the rifles were barely fourteen years old. Moesa was bent over a girl with bobbed hair, adjusting the rifle against the young shooter's shoulder and her small right hand on the trigger. At the far end, near the edge of the sal forest, were targets painted in bright red, yellow and black. Aseem waited quietly, watching the target practice and hearing the guns go off.

After some time, Gopal blew a whistle and everybody got into a formation of threes height-wise—the shortest in front, the tallest at the rear. Then they began doing various kinds of exercises—leapfrogs, long jumps, sit-ups, jumping headlong through old rubber tires dangling from a rope. Once the exercises ended, Gopal made them jog down to one end of the open ground where a series of bamboo hurdles had been posted at three-yard intervals. The cadres now performed some more exercises on the hurdles: jumping over them, crawling under them, running around them. There was strict discipline, every guerrilla member doing each exercise at the intermittent calls of Gopal's whistle, 'Phee . . . phee . . . phee.' Aseem watched the exercises for some time and then returned to his hut.

After an hour, Gopal signalled the end of the exercise session with a long whistle. He looked pleased. Tomorrow was D-day, and he wanted the dalam members to get as much practice and exercise as possible. With Moesa taking up the rear, he now marched the contingent back to the village in single file like an army of red ants, around the embankment of the pond and down the path cutting across the huts. He led them straight to the padlocked structure near his own hut, and threw open the bamboo door.

Some of them were seeing the police uniforms lying stacked there for the first time. One by one, the cadres trooped in excitedly, choosing the closest fit by placing the khaki uniforms against their chests. Since there were many women cadres, they found the uniforms long and baggy. Moesa showed them how they could double roll the trouser bottoms from the inside to shorten their length. The long sleeves of the shirts were to be similarly rolled up. Gopal then distributed the ammunition among the cadres.

An hour later, the dalam members, looking smart in their newly acquired police uniforms, gathered for a final meeting over a special lunch of boiled chicken, millet rotis, rice and vegetables, spiced with red ant chutney to fire their bellies. It was going to be a long march to the edge of the forest where they were to camp for the night. From there they would leave at the break of dawn for the Jagdalpur central maidan for the final assault.

'Gopal, wait,' shouted out Swati, catching up with Gopal and the dalam members as she saw them crossing the school. 'I'd like to come with you.'

'What will you do there?' questioned Gopal. 'It'll be very dangerous for you. You stay here. I can't allow you to go.'

Swati turned around disappointed. As she walked back to her school, an idea crossed her mind.

Gopal, Moesa and the dalam members were up early the next morning. After some hot black tea prepared on a fire of dead branches together with dry rotis they'd carried in their backpacks, they were ready to leave carrying their guns and wearing the police boots. Some of them, clearly unused to the heavy footwear, chose to sling the boots around their necks by the shoestrings and go barefoot. After walking for some hours, with very brief halts, they reached the main road where a truck was parked with a pile of logs beside it. The driver and his helper lowered the wooden hold at the rear end of the truck held by metal chains on the sides. One by one, the cadres climbed on to the truck, first handing over their rifles to those who were already inside and then hoisting themselves with the aid of the chains on the side.

Once most of them had got in, logs of wood were placed in the truck to conceal the cadres. The wooden hold was then raised and secured tightly. Gopal, clean-shaven and wearing khaki pants from the police uniform and a checked bush shirt, sat in front with the driver, his prized pistol snug in a holster and the khaki shirt safely ensconced in his backpack placed near his feet. The truck roared away, belching out a cloud of grey diesel smoke.

The truck was stopped at a police checkpost by a languorous and bleary-eyed armed constable.

'Relax. Keep sitting,' said the truck driver, unruffled. 'I'll deal with it.'

Keeping the engine running, the driver climbed down from the truck and casually went up to the constable. Soon, he was shaking hands with the cop and talking to him animatedly. When he returned, Gopal enquired what had transpired. 'Nothing much,' said the driver with a wink. 'This is routine for us. We pay them a fixed rate every week for carrying illegally cut wood, but the behenchods still stop us for more bribe.'

There was no hitch after that, as they went down the winding road, past the shimmering Chitrakot Falls in the distance and then the Shanti Kadam camps and the silk factory. As they neared the crowded marketplace they had to slow down as hordes of people headed for the maidan, walking or overflowing in cycle rickshaws.

Gopal asked the driver to stop once they reached a point on the main road overlooking the maidan. This was where Kuttu was to meet them along with his contingent. The driver and the helper alighted and helped a couple of the cadres to climb down over the logs. Then, the cadres who had got down slowly lowered the wooden hold, allowing a few of the logs to roll down first, before the rest of the contingent could get down. In the distance they saw another truck come to a halt. Soon Kuttu and his dalam, also in police uniforms, could be seen marching down the road.

Operation Khatam had begun.

46

SWATI WAS AT ASEEM'S hut before daybreak, carrying a large battery-operated torch. Sans any make-up except a thin line of kohl below her eyes, she was dressed in faded jeans, a long-sleeved kurti and thick-soled shoes. She wore no jewellery, not even her usual silver earrings. Carrying a small haversack, she walked straight into the hut without bothering to knock. Aseem was already up, tying his shoelaces. He began to put all his belongings into his haversack.

'You don't have to take everything,' Swati suggested. 'Just carry a few essentials.'

A hazy waning moon lent a cloudy, indigo darkness to the sky, as Swati led Aseem down the familiar path to the pond through the village habitation, her torch beam lighting their way. Some crickets glimmered around the bushes. The two of them trudged along, shuffling over dry undergrowth, round the pond and up the winding incline to the open land, where they were greeted with the faint orange rays of the rising sun. Swati slowed down here, treading slowly and carefully, in a zigzag path to avoid landmines. Once they'd crossed the open patch, her gait became more brisk and confident. With the sun now making a fuller appearance to light the path through the morning mist, she shut off her torch and put it in the haversack on her back.

After an hour, they reached a largish hut. Aseem recognized it immediately by its animal pen and the motorcycle parked outside. Swati untied the bamboo gate fastened with twines. A cock crowed to announce their arrival, while a slothful pig raised its forelegs on the bamboo fence to peer at the early morning visitors through his slit eyes.

'Lal salaam, Prakrit-da,' shouted Swati.

Already roused awake by the cock and now hearing Swati calling out to him, Prakrit emerged from of the hut in a tight-fitting vest and lungi. 'Lal salaam. Where're you both off to so early?'

'Jagdalpur,' said Swati.

'Oh! I know,' said Prakrit. 'That swami's discourse. You shouldn't be going there, you know.'

'Aseem's going with me.'

'You're both risking your lives. You'd better be careful.'

'We will,' said Swati and pointed to the motorbike. 'Prakrit-da, I was wondering if we could borrow your bike.'

'Is it something you need to ask, comrade?' said Prakrit. 'It belongs to all of us. But there's not much fuel. You may need to get some filled on the way back.'

The atmosphere was festive outside the main gate of the central maidan of Jagdalpur. There were vendors selling eatables: fruit chaat, alu-tikki and freshly cut fruit on wooden carts. A few enterprising people were carrying wicker baskets with religious beads and relics they claimed had magical powers. But what drew most attention was a gorgeous-looking young woman wearing glass bangles up to her elbows serving specially brewed mahua from an earthen pot in plastic cups. She seemed to have particularly charmed the young SPOs on duty at the main gate, who buzzed around her like honeybees, happily imbibing the mahua liquor. What none of them knew was that she was a Maoist in disguise.

Across the road, a long canvas tent had been propped up on bamboo poles with four eye-catching stalls of the leading shoe manufacturers with large billboards advertising their brands and banners: 'Free Sample', 'Step Inside', 'We Care for Your Feet'. Each stall had huge colourful photographs of their respective brand ambassadors and local sporting heroes of the likes of Naren Thumi. Specially recruited guards in black uniform tried to fend off the crowds. 'Step back . . . step back,' they shouted. 'Later . . . come later . . . after the event is over.' The free samples of footwear would only be distributed after they'd attended Sri Sri Narayanaji's discourse and cleansed their souls.

There was a full contingent of armed security personnel at the main gate, supported by scores of SPOs of the Shanti Kadam proudly carrying .303 guns. Inspector Bhim Singh, who'd been given the responsibility of manning the security at the entrance, stood near the main gate. With a black walkie-talkie in his hand, he watched, with considerable annoyance, the adivasi woman selling the mahua drink to the young SPOs. He heard the voice of the deputy superintendent of police on the walkie-talkie calling from inside the maidan, 'DSP calling, DSP calling. Over.'

'Inspector Bhim reporting, saab. Over,' said the inspector, standing at attention.

'All well? Over.'

'Peaceful, saab. No trouble, saab. Over.'

'Be vigilant, Inspector. We've heard that there could be a Maoist attack. Over.'

Inspector Bhim Singh became alert immediately, placing his hand on his pistol holster. If they knew about an impending Maoist attack, why the hell hadn't they sent in at least one more police contingent? These SPOs were no good, no commitment, no proper training, and now they were getting inebriated. There was no way he could stop them; he had no powers over them. Yet, he'd have to do the best he could, and if the day passed off without any security lapse maybe his request for a transfer out of Jagdalpur to a more peaceful location would be entertained.

Aseem stopped the bike on the side of the road at the edge of the bowl-shaped maidan. He got off the bike after Swati had dismounted and hiked it on its stand. Both of them walked up to the bamboo fence and stood at a vantage point from where they could get a helicopter view of the maidan. Aseem found it almost unrecognizable from the time he'd first seen it along with Aroon. There were no children wielding the sal willow today; in their place was a veritable sea of humanity of all ages and sizes, in a multitude of colours and clothing. Hare-shaped balloons and cloth banners and printed posters of Sri Sri Narayanaji were everywhere.

A short distance away two brightly painted trucks were parked on the side of the road with flaps on their rear wheels that said in Hindi: 'You there with evil eyes, may your face turn black!' People were still streaming in from the outskirts of the town on their way to the maidan. Two young boys, their arms around each other's shoulders, walked by singing an old Bollywood melody in perfect harmony, 'Shaka-laka, shaka-laka, laka-laka, laka-laka, boom, boom.'

Aseem heard a whirring sound in the sky and looked up to see a helicopter make its descent on a helipad just behind the rear gate of the maidan. After a little while, he saw Sri Sri Satyanand Narayanaji, with a neatly trimmed beard and flowing hair, step out to the beat of adivasi drums, and being led to a high platform that had been constructed with a white canopy at the far side, up the natural gradient of the maidan. Soon, the swami was seated at the centre of the dais on a resplendent throne sparkling with jewels, wearing a glittering white robe and a double necklace of big shiny pearls. Giving him company were two khadi-clad politicians—the local MP and MLA—and two senior bureaucrats wearing white safari suits specially ordered for the occasion. They tried to look busy and important, surveying the milling crowd. On either side of the dais were giant-sized screens showing dissolving images of the dais and its occupants from four camera angles.

There were police and security forces everywhere, outside at the main gate, inside the premises and mostly near the main dais. Four White Commandos carrying AK-47s guarded the swami zealously, their black pupils darting from side to side, on the alert for anything suspicious. As additional security, the front of the dais had been blocked with a bamboo barricade and red flowerpots. Armed policemen guarded the area around the dais while the SPOs patrolled down a red-carpeted aisle extending from the main gate to the dais. There were a few rows of red rexine-covered chairs on the other side of the barricade on which sat the VIPs and special invitees. The masses of local adivasis sat cross-legged behind them, cramped on mats and durries, knee touching knee. There were others who shuffled restlessly at the back or had taken vantage positions up the natural slope on the sides. Some waved pamphlets to fan themselves and shoo away the uninvited horde of insects that had come to add a buzz to the gathering.

'Shall we also go down to watch?' Aseem asked Swati, leaning forward on the bamboo fence.

'No,' Swati said firmly, placing a restraining hand on his and pointing to the giant screens showing images of the swami and the blaring speakers hung on tall bamboo poles. 'We can see and hear very well from here.'

As Aseem turned his head to look at the screens, he heard the sound of heavy boots on the road. Moesa, in a police uniform, an AK-47 strapped to her back, was leading an all-female contingent marching in double file down the winding road to the maidan. Clean-shaven and looking smart in an inspeçor's uniform, with his hand on the pistol holster, Gopal followed them with an all-male contingent.

Aroon, in a shimmering white sherwani, stood behind the side screens on one side of the dais along with two models in bodysuits and four adivasi drummers. He didn't want anything to go wrong now—he'd planned everything carefully to the last detail. Uma stood on the other side with an arm around Chamatkar, the adivasi boy, giving him a piece of chocolate to calm his nerves.

There was a roll of drums—Operation Wham had begun. The home secretary, who was invited to give the welcome address, extolled Sri Sri Narayanaji's virtues in glowing terms. The MLA then held forth, speaking about peace and development in the region, about the multinational companies that had lined up to invest in the state only if there was cessation of violence. He continued speaking for a long time, till the MP, annoyed that his junior was hogging the limelight, signalled to him to wind up and return to his seat.

It was now the turn of the MP. The terrorist acts of the Maoists had pushed the Bastar region behind by decades, he passionately declared, it was time for the citizens to rethink. Showering fulsome praise on the Shanti Kadam, he thanked them for their support and sacrifice, drawing loud claps from the Shanti Kadam activists sitting in the middle.

Sri Sri Satyanand Narayanaji was finally asked to take the floor. The swami rose majestically to chants of 'Sri Sri Narayanaji ki jai', which filled the valley with a little help from carefully controlled computerized acoustics. He began by mimicking the gesture of the hare and an invocation to the moon. Two models in immaculate bodysuits glided to the dais and assumed the now familiar hare pose. The swami invited the audience to perform the pose; telling the VIPs in front to keep sitting in their chairs. Then, he began the breathing exercises, the models demonstrating them through the heart-shaped cuts in their bodysuits around their navels.

But something seemed to have gone wrong. The supple-limbed models did not appear to be exciting the imagination of the Bastar inhabitants; their belly movements failed to draw the expected response and arouse their spirits. By the time the swami had completed the shashank pose and was ready to deliver his discourse, they'd begun to snigger and yawn and taken to slow-clapping to indicate their ennui.

Asking Kuttu to move his contingent to cover the rear exits as per their carefully conceived plan, Gopal ordered the marching members of Moesa's female contingent to halt some yards away from the maidan. Leaving them there, he walked forward confidently to the entrance gate where Inspector Bhim Singh, spotting the rank on Gopal's shirt, saluted him.

'SP-saab has sent me with an additional contingent as reinforcement,' announced Gopal, returning the salute without batting an eyelid. Looking at the contingent marching behind him, he continued, 'They'll man the gate. I'll go inside the maidan and report.' Inspector Bhim Singh looked relieved—his prayers for additional reinforcements had been answered.

Gopal quickly moved into the maidan, making his way nimbly through the warp and weft of people. He slunk to the side, creeping steadily towards the left of the dais from the flanks behind the screens as unobtrusively as he could, moving like a tiger on the prowl, his hand firmly on the holster. Outside, as planned, Moesa and her other comrades panned out around the entrance gate.

Aroon was quick to notice that the crowd was getting restless. It was time for Chamatkar to make his entrance. The drums rolled out again as Aroon walked in from the wings with a mike in his hand to announce that Swamiji would now bless the needy. Giving a moving account of Chamatkar's 'handicap', he called for the boy to be brought centre stage. Chamatkar made his sad entry, with a mournful expression on his face, limping out to the dais in well-rehearsed movements. Sri Sri Narayanaji rose from his embellished throne and slowly walked forward to the soft beat of adivasi drums from the wings to give his blessings to the spindly legged boy.

Sipping mahua liquor, one of the SPOs blinked his eyes rapidly and turned to his colleague. 'I can swear by Sri Sri Narayanaji that that man there in the police uniform is Beeju from my village. He's most definitely a Maovadi.'

'Who? That man there standing next to the pole?' asked the second SPO.

'Yes, I'm sure, it's definitely him. Quick, let's inform inspector-saab,' said the first SPO.

Stunned to hear about the Maoist in police garb, Inspector Bhim Singh wasted no time to reach for his walkie-talkie. 'Inspector Bhim calling, Inspector Bhim calling. Over.'

'Yes, Inspector Bhim, I can read you. What do you have to say? Over.'

'DSP-saab, there is an emergency, sir. An SPO here says that he recognizes a Maovadi in police uniform here. Over.'

'What are you saying? A Maovadi in our uniform? Are you sure? Over.'

The SPO standing next to the inspector nodded his head vigorously in assent.

'Pucca saab. Over,' said Inspector Bhim Singh, recalling the raid on his police station—they'd then only worried about the policemen killed on duty, not about the stolen uniforms.

'Challenge the impostor. Ask him for his ID. I'm coming out. Over,' came the instruction over the walkie-talkie.

Inspector Bhim Singh took a deep breath before walking up to confront the suspect. His mind was seething with rage, wanting revenge on the Maoists for the cold-blooded murder of his four colleagues. Taking out his pistol from the holster, he stomped over to the stranger wearing the constable's uniform and demanded an identity proof. The adivasi hesitated, looking towards Gopal for a cue.

Gopal crouched behind the raised platform of the dais, taking cover behind Aroon and the drummers in the wings, looking for a clear view of the dais. He noticed that the home minister was not sitting on the dais—only the swami sat in the centre with a few government officals. He focused his eyes on the swami moving forward to bless the sickly looking boy.

One of the White Commando Guards found the movement of a crouched figure in uniform highly suspicious. He quickly panned his AK-47 in that direction, keeping a close watch on the suspect with his trained and watchful eye. Gopal stood up straight with his pistol in his hand, steadying it to take careful aim at the swami. But he was a fraction of a second too late. The White Commando was quicker and let go a volley of rapid-fire bullets from his automatic into the would-be assassin's chest and temple. Gopal crumpled to the ground, blood flowing out of him like the red streams of Bastar, the pistol still clutched tightly in his hand.

Moesa was watching the giant screen showing the adivasi boy limping on the dais towards the swami. Just then, she noticed an inspector walk up to one of her comrades. Sensing trouble, Moesa took the AK-47 strapped to her back in her hand, alert and ready for any swift action she may need to take. At that moment, she heard the flurry of gunshots from the maidan and turned to see the magnified image of the White Commando shooting at Gopal on the giant screen. In a flash, she reached for her backpack and taking out a hand grenade hurled it towards the main gate. The impact of the blast dispersed the armed guards and sent the people around scurrying for cover. Under the screen of smoke from the blast, Moesa swiftly moved in the direction of the inspector and pumped bullets into his chest. Inspector Bhim died instantly.

Then, before the security guards could react, she charged into the maidan like a raging bull, heading straight for the dais, firing from her automatic. 'Rat-a-tat-tat,' went her gun, 'Shaka-laka, boom, boom, rat-a-tat-tat-tat, boom, boom.' Her comrades ran behind her, with their fingers pressed on the trigger of their rifles, shooting at the police guards and the SPOs. Caught unawares, it took some time for the security personnel to react and take their positions to return the fire.

As a ferocious gun battle ensued between the Maoists and the security official, the shocked crowd—those in uniform and those in civilian attire—broke into a stampede. Hordes of men and women and young girls and boys shouted and yelled in panic as stray bullets started hitting the traumatized spectators. 'Yee-ee, Yee-eee,' they screamed and squealed and made a mad rush for the exit points, trampling each other, clambering over the chairs, uprooting the barricades. Those sitting on the slopes of the maidan came glissading down or ran hysterically up the incline to the road.

In the ensuing mêlée and mayhem, the two battling sides in identical uniforms became more and more confused, neither able to identify the face of the enemy, but continuing to fire in the desperate hope that their bullets would get those of the opposing camp.

On the dais, the well-trained quadruplet of White Commandos, unambiguously clear that their sole task was to protect Sri Sri Narayanaji, got him to duck down and move on his hands and knees as swiftly as he could. Forming a human shield around him, they managed to get him out to the makeshift helipad. The politicians and bureaucrats also fell on their hands and knees and followed suit, pushing and shoving each other in a bid to remain closer to the swami for maximum protection. Meanwhile, Aroon and Uma hastily made their escape from the rear gate and ran to the road where their Scorpio was parked.

Moesa reached the dais just as the White Commandos had escorted Sri Sri Narayanaji away. She stood silently for a while near the slain body of the martyred Gopal. Then, wrenching her bloodshot eyes away from him, she ran frenziedly after the fleeing men on the dais, shouting revenge in Gondi interspersed with choice abuses in Hindi, 'Kill! Kill! Bhosadhi ke! Haramzade! Don't let any of them leave this maidan alive! Kill!' Then, noticing Chamatkar clambering up the incline of the maidan, she yelled at him while giving him chase, 'Sala, behenchod, chootiya bana raha tha.'

All this while, Aseem had been standing with Swati at the edge of the maidan behind the bamboo fence, unmoving and stunned, unable to comprehend the terrifying nightmare that he was witnessing below. Almost in the blink of an eye, the maidan had been reduced to a red rubble of dead and dying bodies; many more were dying or being maimed and mutilated in the maddening pandemonium in front of his unbelieving eyes.

In this bloody game of chess, the poor adivasis had become pawns—there was no black or white left now, only a checkmate of gory red and grey.

There was no logic or reason for the killing and madness. Who could explain such senseless bloodshed and violence? Aseem looked towards Swati for an answer. She walked away.

Standing broken and forlorn on the main road, he saw Moesa and some of her dalam members running crazily up the incline in hot pursuit of a young boy, whom he recognized as Chamatkar. Moesa called out to Aseem and Swati to get into the truck, waving her hands. Swati started moving to the truck, but Aseem stood where he was as Moesa caught up with the boy some twenty yards away on the road. Grabbing hold of Chamatkar's collar, she slapped him hard several times on both cheeks. The boy fell down howling, crying for mercy. She began to kick him with her heavy police boots. Three of her dalam members joined her and brought him down, beating him with thrusts of their rifle butts.

'Don't hit him,' shouted a horrified Aseem, running to rescue the boy. Swati turned around and ran back to him, restraining him with a firm grip on his arm.

'Let's go from here,' she screamed at Aseem. 'Come, we'll be safer in the truck.'

Aseem, filled with outrage, wrenched himself free of Swati's hold and went up to Chamatkar. Moesa gave the boy one last kick and led her comrades to the waiting truck. Aseem helped the howling boy stand up, while Swati walked away to the truck without looking back.

Chamaktar stumbled down the road on the opposite side, leaving Aseem alone, his heart pulsating with ache and anguish. His head began to reel and he felt a nauseating, racking pain in his stomach. He threw up. He stood, bent double for a long time, till he collapsed.

Sitting in the Scorpio as it slowly went up the winding road away from the maidan, Aroon suddenly saw Aseem lying on his back by the road, his mouth open. He yelled out to Vishnu to stop the vehicle and rushed towards Aseem. Aseem seemed to be in a dazed, semi-conscious state. Aroon pulled Aseem to his feet with Vishnu's help, and both of them took him slowly to the car.

47

A FEW WEEKS AFTER Aroon had brought Aseem back to Delhi, Ritika heard the doorbell of her flat, and went to open it.

Standing at the door was Menaka, her face glowing with revitalizing therapies at Narayanaji's Wellness Spa and wearing a pink frilly shirt, a long black skirt and black high-heeled shoes.

'It's good you've come now,' said Ritika. 'I needed to go out, but didn't want to leave Aseem alone.'

Brushing past her sister, Menaka walked through the short corridor leading to Ritika's living room and made herself comfortable on a three-seater. 'What's your hurry?' Menaka asked. 'I've just come. At least give me a glass of water before you leave.'

'So, where do you have to go?' asked Menaka, after she'd drunk the water Ritika had brought her.

'To the market to pick up some vegetables,' said Ritika. 'I just realized there are none at home for dinner. I don't know when Avinash will return. He's gone to the park.'

'Where's Aseem?'

'In his room.

'How's he?'

'He's still the same. Again, not eating much. The moment I enter his room, he tells me to leave.'

'Is he still angry?'

'I don't know. He doesn't say a word.'

'Don't worry, you go now and buy vegetables and whatever else you want. I'm here for at least an hour.'

Menaka called out to Aseem the moment Ritika left the flat, walking towards his room, 'Ass-ee-eem, Ass-ee-eem?' Not receiving a response from him, she pushed open the door of his room. 'Can I come in, sweetie?'

Aseem was sitting on the bed with his legs drawn up, wearing a checked bush shirt and shorts, his head buried in a pillow resting on his knees. He didn't look up when Menaka walked in. She sat beside him on the edge of the bed.

'My baby,' she said, stroking his back.

'Let me be,' said Aseem. 'Leave me alone.'

'I'll never leave you,' said Menaka. Seeing no reaction from Aseem, she lifted his face up from the pillow and turned it towards her. 'Don't worry, everything will be all right.'

Avinash unlocked the front door with his key and entered the flat. He looked for Ritika in the kitchen and, not finding her there, he went to Aseem's room. He opened the door slightly and peeped in. Menaka was sitting next to Aseem with her arm around him, his head resting on her chest. Soundlessly, Avinash stepped back and left the flat, gently closing the door behind him.

Holding Aseem's face in her hands, Menaka looked into his eyes but he averted his gaze. Bending forward, Menaka kissed him on the forehead and then on his eyelids, one by one. Aseem tried to shrug her away, but she held his face firmly with both her hands, kissing him on his nose, and then below his lower lip. Aseem turned his face away, his expression a mix of shock and bewilderment.

Menaka bent forward and kissed him on the side of his neck. Aseem edged to his side, turning his back to her. She quickly reached down to her high-heeled shoes and slipped them off. Then, climbing on to the bed on her knees, she hugged him from behind, her breasts pressed to his back. She kissed him on the nape of his neck, caressing his chest and unbuttoning his shirt. She ran her fingers over his bare skin, gently teasing his nipples. Aseem's breathing quickened. All of a sudden, she turned him towards her and pushed him down on the bed, her lips over his face.

'What are you doing?' Aseem said in a low voice, protesting feebly.

'Sh-hh,' Menaka said, keeping him pinned down with one hand clutching at his hair, and covered his mouth with her lips. She moved her lips down to his chest, her pink polished nails trailing down his stomach, caressing him. She moved her mouth down to his navel. His skin trembled, kissed as if by a soft breeze on the rippling Satwal pond. She moved her hand to the noticeably hard bulge in front of his shorts; opening its top button, she pulled it down. Quickly, breathing hard, she unbuttoned her shirt and reached to unhook her bra straps. She held his hand and brought it to her breast. Then, she eased out of her skirt and lay full stretch on him, flesh to flesh, her wet mouth on his, devouring him.

Aseem's mind was numb, bereft of thought; his hungry soul was adrift, his body following its own course, like the gushing waters of the Indravati. For a long, long time he'd not known passion, not known love—he'd been alone, longing for the warmth of human touch. For interminable nights, he'd wept in cold despair. He didn't now resist the overflowing surge that flowed in his veins, allowing the scorching passion to engulf his aroused being.

Menaka's mind was in a whirl. She'd really not planned this. It'd just happened in the heat of the moment. But Aseem had needed this, he had needed her love. She hurriedly got dressed and went to the toilet to reapply her make-up.

Aseem lay on the bed, unmoving. After a while, he got up, pulled up his shorts and buttoned his shirt. He went to the toilet and splashed water on his face. Then he went back to his bed and sat there for a long time, with his legs drawn up to his chest, drained and disoriented.

Menaka made to leave the moment Ritika returned from her shopping. 'I must rush now. I've some work at home.'

'Thanks Menaka,' said Ritika, giving her sister a hug as she left the flat. 'I wish you could have stayed longer.'

'Aseem beta,' Ritika called out from the kitchen, 'dinner will be ready in a few minutes. Tell Baba, and then come and help me lay the table.'

Hearing no response, Ritika called out to him again, 'Beta, did you hear me?'

'Coming, Ma,' Aseem finally responded.

After a while, he was standing at the kitchen door, 'Ma, Baba is not in his room.'

'What do you mean? It's nearly eight-thirty. Did he not return from the park? He's always on time for dinner.'

'I don't know, Ma.'

'This is strange. I'm worried, beta. Can you go to the park and see if he's there?'

'Don't worry, Ma. He must have gone for a longer walk.'

'Please go and look for him,' said Ritika, looking most worried.

Aseem walked out of the flat and down the road. He needed the walk. His mind was still in a state of befuddlement, his life an untidy mess like a pile of smelly, unwashed clothes. A strong breeze was blowing, dispersing the foul smells of the city. He breathed deeply, hoping to bring some clarity to his muddled thoughts.

The park was about a fifteen-minute walk from the flat. It had been many years since he'd visited it. He'd even forgotten what it looked like. It was ages since he'd been here; when he was in school, he'd accompanied Baba one winter morning when he was going to fetch milk.

Lost in his reverie, Aseem nearly forgot why he was out there at night. He started as a stray dog yelped on the roadside. He crossed the road, keeping his eyes alert to see if he could spot his father lumbering back. There weren't too many people on the road. An adolescent boy came riding on a bicycle; he let go off the handle in a daredevil act and began whisting as he passed Aseem. Down the road, the paan shop was still open. He glanced at it: a few rag-tag lumpen boys were hanging out smoking, talking loudly, their conversation interspersed with obscenities. There was a time his father used to smoke, though never inside the house. Skirting the paan shop, he walked further down, under the neon lamplights that cast strange shadows.

Aseem crossed a cement culvert covering a drain to reach the park. The entry to the park was through ingeniously designed, parallel waist-high iron gates that allowed humans and dogs but kept away cattle. A solitary spherical lamp illumined the rectangular park and the branches of a neem tree at its far end. Aseem walked along a redstone pathway skirting the park green. The park was noiseless save for a gentle breeze rustling through the trees. Two pigeons nestling on an overhanging branch of the neem tree flapped their wings, disturbed by the sound of Aseem's approaching footsteps.

Aseem saw a solitary dark figure sitting slumped at one end of a bench under the tree. As he neared, he saw it was his father. 'Baba,' he called out softly. 'Baba.'

There was no reply.

'Baba,' he called out again, coming close, placing his hand on his father's shoulder gently. At his touch, his father fell on his side on the park bench.

Tears streaming down his face, Aseem ran back to his house.

The cremation was fixed for three o'clock in the afternoon at the electric crematorium. Ritika was distressed that the funeral would not be performed in the traditional way on a pyre of wood, but Aseem had been adamant that it had to be an electric crematorium.

Aroon and Girdhari made the arrangements for the funeral: summoning a priest, calling for the hearse, arranging for a bier. Aseem remained beside Ritika, holding her when she became inconsolable. The priest gave the necessary instructions for the preparation of the dead body and listed out the paraphernalia that needed to be procured for the rituals.

The corpse needed a fresh set of clothes. Ritika opened Avinash's cupboard with Aseem close behind her; averting her eyes from the bottle of dark rum, she reached for a white kurta–pyjama set. Lying on top of the stack of kurta–pyjamas were two plastic folders. Handing over the folders to her son, she left the room.

Aseem looked closely at the folders. The top one had a label that read 'AB—Personal' in his father's handwriting. He opened it and flipped through the papers. A letter on Avinash's office stationery caught his attention.

'Dear Mr Bahal,' it began. 'The management is pleased to accept your resignation as per the Voluntary Retirement Scheme.

Under the scheme . . . .' The official epistle went on to give the details of Avinash's termination from service under the voluntary scheme. Aseem was numb with shock. His father had kept all this to himself.

He examined the rest of the folder, turning the pages slowly. There was a set of papers pertaining to the loan for the flat, which seemed to have been paid in a lumpsum very recently. There was another document on stamped paper, titled 'My Last Will and Testament'. Neatly written on it in his father's hand was a short list of investments and the details of the flat, all of which he had willed to Ritika.

Closing the folder with trembling hands, he put it aside and picked up the second folder. It had his name on it: 'ASEEM'. There were no official papers or documents here; all it contained were dozens of newspaper cuttings from the 'Situations Vacant' and 'Appointments' supplements for candidates with Aseem's qualifications and experience. He was astounded—he'd never known the extent to which he'd been in his father's thoughts. Tears streamed uncontrollably from his eyes.

He felt overpowering remorse at never having tried to understand his father and showing so little concern for him when he was alive. He recalled how his father had assumed an altogether different persona while revealing details of his revolutionary past to Aseem. The story had remained incomplete. He wondered now what had happened during his father's youth that had changed him so much; his father's life had remained unfulfilled, almost barren. He wiped his eyes and put the cuttings back into the folder, but sat on the bed for a long time, lost in thought. No, he would not allow this to happen to himself; that was his father's legacy. He rose from the bed, put the folders back into the cupboard and left the room.

Avinash's dead body lay on the floor in the centre of the living room where the furniture had been moved to make space for it. A diya had been lit and incense sticks burnt beside it. Neighbours trickled in to pay their last respects.

The priest called out to Aseem. Following his directions, Aseem covered the white-clothed corpse with a shawl and fastened it to the bier with jute strings with the help of a couple of neighbours. Garlands of marigolds and rose petals were scattered all over it.

Aseem went up to Ritika, who was sitting next to Menaka on the three-seater. Ritika started weeping silently. Seeing him approach, she got up. Aseem put his arms around her tightly, and held her for a long while. 'It's time to go now,' she said, finally, gently removing his arms. Aseem nodded slowly, unable to hold back his tears. Ritika lowered his face with both her hands and kissed him on the top of his head. Aseem touched her feet and turned around.

Menaka, who'd been watching the two of them, got up from the three-seater and followed Aseem. 'I'll come with you,' she said. Aseem showed no sign of having heard Menaka. He walked slowly up to his father's dead body. Aroon had moved up beside him and bent down to help him lift the bier. Aseem, reaching to his side, also bent down at the same time. He nudged Aroon's hand away and grasped the bamboo pole himself. Along with the other three pall-bearers, Aseem gently lifted the bier on his shoulders and walked slowly to the hearse.

Watching the bier go by her window, a little girl in the society complex wept silently.

Acknowledgements

I AM INDEBTED TO several secondary sources—books, articles, websites and other writing on the Internet—for the historical background of the Bastar region, and details of geographical locations and adivasi culture. While I have taken liberties in altering the locations or changing names of movements or operations (though readers more familiar with the region will immediately see parallels), these references helped me to sketch a reasonably plausible picture of the regions described in the state of Chhattisgarh.

The short excerpt on p. 153 is from the poem 'To Posterity' by Bertolt Brecht, translated by Michael Hamburger.

There have been many people who have helped me during the writing of this novel in its various avatars. Shyama Warner read and edited various drafts like a hawk and gave constructive comments. I am thankful to my perceptive publisher Nandita Aggarwal for her faith in my writing and her insightful suggestions. Poulomi Chatterjee of Hachette India sensitively looked through the final draft. Harsh Sethi commented on an initial draft and we regularly had animated discussions while the manuscript was in the making.

Others who offered useful comments on the manuscript or portions of it include Rosamma Thomas, Jolly Kaul, Urvashi Butalia, Ashima Kanwar, Naghma Zafir, Subhas Chakraborty, Deeba Zafir, Aradhana Sharma, Saloni Sharma, Sandhya Gandhi-Vakil and Vimala Ramachandran. I am also grateful to Ruchi Shroff, Satish Jha and Bharath Chandra for their inputs.

Finally, I thank my wife Rekha for her invaluable support in innumerable ways, including reading the manuscript in its raw form and patiently listening when I bounced off ideas. My children Neha and Nikhil were most encouraging and freely gave their suggestions.